Absolution

By

Diana Gerdenits

Order this book online at www.trafford.com
or email orders@trafford.com

Most Trafford titles are also available at major online book retailers.

Note for Librarians: A cataloguing record for this book is available from Library and Archives Canada at www.collectionscanada.ca/amicus/index-e.html

Printed in Victoria, BC, Canada.

ISBN: 978-1-4269-1562-8 (Soft)

Our mission is to efficiently provide the world's finest, most comprehensive book publishing service, enabling every author to experience success. To find out how to publish your book, your way, and have it available worldwide, visit us online at www.trafford.com

Trafford rev. 10/16/2009

www.trafford.com

North America & international
toll-free: 1 888 232 4444 (USA & Canada)
phone: 250 383 6864 ♦ fax: 812 355 4082

Foreward:

I think I should begin this by confessing that I am not a writer by profession. I don't pretend to write books to make money pandering to publishers with formulaic prose. I have not the slightest intent to comfort, nor coddle you, the reader with easily digestible reading that will remind you of dozens of other books of the same genre. Neither do I consider myself an elitist literary artist, above the reproach of critics who seem to enjoy convincing us that what they like must be what we like. I am simply a person, like so many of us, with a story. It is neither fiction nor non-fiction as life is never so simplistic as people would have you believe. Perceptions of reality and the past are as unique as the person telling the story. I am telling this story, names and events have been altered to protect the innocent and not so innocent. In some cases I may have been guilty of embellishment, and in others trust I have lived up the phrase, "truth is stranger than fiction". I hope you enjoy this story, and the unconventional way it is written.

Absolution:

"if those who lead you say to you, 'See, the Kingdom is in the sky,' then the birds of the sky will precede you. If they say to you, 'it is in the sea,' then the fish will precede you. Rather, the Kingdom is inside of you, and it is outside of you. When you come to know yourselves, then you will become known, and you will realize that it is you who are the sons of the living Father. But if you will not know yourselves, you dwell in poverty and it is you who are that poverty."

*** Excerpt from the Coptic Gospel of Thomas.***

Dedication:

Aside from all the characters in this book who have real names and hearts that beat...to whom, as my muses, I am eternally indebted. I am convinced that with you all in my life I am incapable of knowing what boredom is. I want to also thank Ellen Ferguson for her assistance and Pat Ferguson (not related) for his encouragement.

Chapter 1

Bryn had waited two years for this night, well, probably longer. He had every detail planned. I had driven him crazy with my impatience. Now as I stood in front of him, the full weight of it was sinking in to my thick skull. I found myself frantically trying to find an excuse to postpone it. I stood in his ground level entryway somewhere in Surrey, England, with a golden robe on, staring up at him.

"I wish I could postpone this longer…but I can't. It must be tonight and I curse the Gods for making you so young! They revel in making a monster of me." He paused, looking at me. The lighting in the room did make him look like a vampire, I thought. It enhanced his phantom-like profile, his black hair, slicked back to reveal his pale skin and sharp angular features. To me, he was easily the most handsome man I had ever laid eyes upon, even if his appearance at times seemed almost frightening – again I felt that stab of fear.

He stepped back from me towards a door I had never noticed before. It was heavily locked.

"I've never showed you my back yard, have I?"

"No…"

"Well, tonight I want to introduce you to my secret sanctuary – the Cathexisphere."

"The what?"

"This…"

With that, he unlocked the heavily secured door that opened into a dark back yard with what looked like significant stone masonry. As I got closer, I saw a circle within a circle with a raised stone dais in the middle. The outer stone circle must have been 30 feet or so in diameter. On the outside circle of masonry were four columns, pillar-like. Each pillar stood about 5 feet high. There was a channel in the masonry from the bottom of each pillar to the next circle of masonry, finally culminating under the center of the raised dais. The inner circle had about four or five black wrought iron candleholders, and each had a white candlestick in it. There were carvings and engravings everywhere. It was incredible!

I turned back to Bryn who was smiling, obviously enjoying my awe of this structure.

"First we kneel at the dais and share the wine. Then I want you to walk to all four pillars, beginning with North, and I will tell you what to do with each." He pointed to the one on the upper left side of the dais. There was no moon in the sky and the only light source was the abundant stars. We walked to the dais and I saw that he had brought a crystal long stemmed wine glass and had a bottle of red wine. He filled the glass.

"Take off your ring." I looked up at him and, without looking down at my hand, pulled it off and handed it to him. He put it on the ground outside of the dais circle.

"I know this is a significant rite of passage for you. This is far more important because it is a binding ritual as well. The more pure the vessel, the more powerful the sacrament, and thus more binding the ritual, no doubt why they made you so young – bastards!"

He drank from the glass and handed it to me. I took a sip, but I am not very fond of wine. Who is when they are sixteen?

He motioned for me to get up and walk to the North pillar. When I got there, I could hear Bryn in my mind, "Move the wind funnel in the direction of the wind." So, I did. Then I walked to the West pillar.

"Push the button on the base." It was a bit of a challenge to see the small black button, but when I pushed it a little water fountain sprung up. Cool, I thought. I moved on to the South pillar and pushed that button and a torch licked up into flames. When I got to the East pillar I could see that there was a strange looking plant growing on top of it.

Then I heard Bryn ask me to rejoin him at the dais. When I did, he put his hands on my shoulders and suddenly every candle around us lit up brightly and I could see much more around me, including Bryn in full, frightening Technicolor, and there was no longer a smile. I could tell I was beyond formulating any excuses to delay this. Bryn's mouth locked onto mine; his tense, hot body seemed to engulf me entirely, wrapping himself around me like a constrictor. The adrenaline began pumping in my blood so heavily that I felt like I would pass out. His hands, in what seemed a methodical frenzy, searching and rubbing me everywhere—resolute in their drive. His waiting was over, and he had waited so long that he seemed like a ravenous wolf. His driving passion seemed incongruent with his cologne – which was now a scent burning indelibly into my mind.

When I opened my eyes, I was looking up at the black sky, partially eclipsed by Bryn's cold grey eyes, wild yet distant – seemingly possessed. Suddenly, I was aware of the cool stone beneath me, and that his lithe body was grinding me deeper into it. Hard, savage kisses worked their way down my chest to my breasts, hands ripping in frustrated anger at what they couldn't unfasten. Silence all around—Bryn is a monastery. He then peeled out of his suit jacket and shirt, retaining only his Talisman he had concealed in a pocket. He held the Talisman over my chest and said something that sounded like Latin or Hebrew, and then laid that damn Talisman between my breasts, continuing with me as if he had never broken off.

The wind was cool and if not for the warmth of his body on me, I would be cold. Bryn pulled my bent legs apart, causing me to stiffen, wanting to pull them back together. Bryn moved down my torso unperturbed, kissing me until suddenly, as if he had broken some magical barrier within me, I felt my apprehension melt away and my legs went slack.

I didn't really understand the significance of this ritual, why it was so important to him, but I loved him and I wanted him to be my first. With calculated control, he held back both my wrists in one hand over my head and covered my mouth with the other; and penetrated me. Tight, hot pain seared me, but Bryn continued unrelentingly. Tears streamed down my face yet still he watched me undisturbed, swept up in the maelstrom of his long awaited passion. My hands felt like they were in a clamp and his hand over my mouth felt as if it inhibited my ability to breathe. I just stared in disbelief at how this moment was every bit as nasty as I was afraid it would be. Somehow, the pain made it impossible for me detach my conscience from this experience. This was nothing like I had hoped it would be. Bryn's grip on me became tighter and tighter, his intended source becoming deeper and more painful. All the while, he kept me pinned in place and stared directly into my eyes making me feel intensely violated.

Finally, he moved his hand from my mouth and reached for one of my knees to open my thighs more, so he could be completely inside of me. I want to make sounds of pain, but his eyes had me transfixed into silence. He had told me a long time ago that for my part, I was supposed to focus on yielding to the entire process; he never mentioned how difficult that would be. He raised his body and moved my locked wrists, which were now completely numb, to my chest on top of the Talisman.

"Say it Aileen!" He then put both of his hands around my throat, almost cutting the circulation to my brain.

"Ego redimio meus mens, corpus, animus vobis intemporaliter" I croaked with a suffering voice. Instantly the candles all went out and there in the darkness, Bryn moaned, releasing his oxygen-depriving grip on me, and crumpled beside me. It was over.

I knew what to say. Bryn had me learn it a long time beforehand. Bryn was a true believer in rituals. However, I had no idea that I would have sounded so wrecked when I said it. My whole body throbbed in agony: arms, thighs, mouth, neck and most of all, my cunt.

'Ding ding ding ding –ding ding ding ding…' (to the tune of Big Ben's chimes).

I opened my eyes with a start! I recognized the sound of my doorbell.

"Oh! Shit no!" I heard myself say in a strained voice.

"Dear God, tell me that it was just a dream, a bad dream." I was in my bedroom; that was a relief! I was in Canada – that much was clear. I had gone to my bedroom at 4 pm Thursday afternoon September 16, and it was now 8 pm according to my clock. It was so confusing because it was September 17 for me just a minute ago. Wait a minute…Okay, so it was now four in the morning in England, it's the next day. Who was at the door? I was in no condition to see anyone, and I was the only one home tonight, so forget it! I just went back to bed and waited for the day in Canada to match where my head was.

I eventually stumbled out of bed at seven in the morning, which is ridiculous when you realize I had been in bed for something like fifteen hours. But I couldn't lay there anymore and I knew I had to face my dresser mirror. I shuddered at the morning face that greeted me there. I looked like hell. My wrists were bruised. I couldn't believe that it had happened. I looked on my bed sheet and sure enough, I had a bloodstain in a decided place. All I could think about was how to cover it all up. No one could know. I'd wear long sleeves, and take the bus instead of walking through downtown, since I was in no condition to walk, never mind run. Once I was dressed and camouflaged I thought about Bryn in his world right now, as I was in mine. The link lasted only a few hours a day if we're lucky. We had been doing this for a couple of years and I was an expert at going into my room, sometimes for hours, and coming out completely calm so that my mother was utterly unaware – I was lucky she worked.

How the hell Bryn could do this was basically twofold. He was a very talented warlock and secondly he found that Talisman when he was twelve. The Spirit that came with the Talisman became Bryn's teacher. This spirit's name was "No", a strange name for sure. Of course, when

Bryn was twelve I was a toddler. I was a baby for heaven's sakes! When Bryn was thirteen, No found me. In those days, Bryn was just a voice, an imaginary friend many kids have. How Bryn could move me from England to Canada was a trick I learned from my friend Kat, who I had to meet downtown today. However, let's not get ahead of ourselves; this is how I met Kat.

Chapter 2

It was about the same time of year, September, two years ago. I was just beginning ninth grade. The previous summer my mother and my teachers were getting concerned with my behaviour, so they sent me to get a battery of tests. I was unwilling for the most part. I didn't hold much faith in psychology or adults thinking that they could test my brainwaves or give me an I.Q. test to find out why I was such a pain in the ass. I hated schools, I hated the social pressure of conforming and the curriculum was mindless. I got into a lot of fights in school because I was standing my ground as a non-conformist and I found it hard to listen and obey teachers whom I had little or no respect. The test results were not what they were expecting. They probably wanted to be able to call me attention deficit, or some other thing. They explained to my mom how I had checked out as normal to above normal including a high I.Q. Other than my mind bogglingly low blood pressure and abnormal brainwave pattern, basically, there was no physical or chemical reason that I was a problem – what a surprise. I looked like any other teen, but I was different. Much to my mother's chagrin, there was no diagnosable disorder that compromised my ability as a young adult. I had a bad attitude and the doctors were determined to help my mother convert me into an obedient, non-rebellious pre-teen. My mother, tired of the constant trouble I was continually finding myself in, thought that sending me to go to a smaller school in a better neighbourhood would help me salvage my education.

My mother stayed in touch with her friends from when we lived in Burnaby and one of her friends recommended Royal Oak Junior Secondary.

Her daughter, Linda, was my best friend when we were neighbours, and my mother liked the idea of me reacquainting myself with her. It is funny now, looking back. I remember when I went with my mom to her place. I met up with my childhood friend, Linda Swift. I remembered her and her family back when we lived next to each other. My parents moved from Burnaby to Vancouver when I was six. However, Linda had no memory of me. Her mother explained that after we moved, Linda had many blackouts and had lost her memories from the age of four to six. At the time, I didn't think much about it. I just kind of felt sorry for her. Now, looking back, there is one nagging correlation: my imaginary friend. Linda was the only person I talked to about my imaginary friend. When I was young, I didn't think it was abnormal – and only your friend would listen to you anyway.

I tried to jog her memory but it was no use. Her mother told me about how she had home movies of me running through their house, taking my clothes off, and just generally being my goofy self, but that none of it ever jogged Linda's memory.

So on the first day of school I showed up with an old friend by my account and a new friend by Linda's account. Either way, I was the new kid in school. I wore jeans and a t-shirt on my first day, drab and as typical as any teenager of the time.

The school, Royal Oak, was small, with a population of no more than 500. The school was surrounded by a large field area, ill kept and not partitioned off for specific sports. The fields were so muddied that the sparse grass had no solid earth to take root. Similar neglect and lack of care was evident throughout the school grounds. The structure of the school itself was your typical, garden-variety three story, institutional building, with a one story breezeway. It was obviously built in the 1950s to deal with the baby boomers, and was never meant to be in operation this long. The misery of the complex and its surrounding fields spread its ill influence to all the young people who loitered, waiting for the bell to ring.

Linda directed me around the school, pointing out people: students, teachers, and lunch staff. She made in-depth critiques of all who passed us, essentially pointing out either people that I should avoid, because of the way they dressed or horrid rumours about them. Whether any of these rumours were true or not she didn't know nor did she appear to care. Upon finalizing her lecture of the outside of the school, she directed me inside the building to the important facilities, like bathrooms and cafeteria. She then showed me into a tiny classroom-size library, which would only make sense in so squalid a school, wherein a modest collection of books and only two rectangular study tables inferred a repository of scribed learning. There were only two occupants within this room; they were both students as there was no librarian.

So this would be where the socially bankrupt would hang out. I admired the two girls sitting at the table they were not bookends. One girl required no description from my friend: it was obvious she was the school brain. The "Brain" was of Asiatic origin. She wore glasses, orange polyester knit boy's vest, and men's jeans. Her hair was an oily blunt cut clump, the kind you achieve using a gripped hand and any semi-sharp knife. Her shoulder length ebony mass was held back in an elastic band. She was deep inside a medical text of one form or another.

The other girl however was quite unlike any I had ever encountered. She had a peculiar look, not just her clothes, but also her actual looks. You could tell she was tall, over 5 foot 6 inches at least, dressed completely in black. She wore a black polyester tunic, with bat-winged sleeves, and tight black velvet pants. For a belt she used a golden chain not less than an inch wide per link, wrapped around a waist, which was no more than 22 inches around! Her skin was very pale with an olive tint. Her long black-brown hair went bluntly straight down her back till it met with her tiny waist. Her figure was rather wasp-like, meaning that although her waist was that small, she had average hips and chest, without the aid of a corset. Her long pointed fingers were wrapped around an Egyptian history book in which she was presently very entranced. Her profile reminded me of that Egyptian bust of queen Nefretete.

I turned to Linda expecting an explanation, "That's Jennifer... She's a witch! Don't ever talk to her!" My friend whispered to me then attempted to pull me out of the room.

Just then, Jennifer put her book down and looked up as though she overheard us. She looked at me, and a creepy smile spread across her face, the smile breaking the very Nefretete profile and exposing a more youthful face. I think she might have said "hi" or something, or was it in my head? I didn't know for immediately my friend whisked me away.

I would see Jennifer from time to time, in the hallways and cafeteria, and she was in some of my classes. Occasionally she would attempt to communicate with me. Initially, I was polite but brief, so as to not to offend anyone. But such as fate would have it, soon afterwards we became friends. I suppose that it was destined to be, since I had an incurable case of curiosity. Deep down inside I just wanted to know what made her tick. She seemed far too interesting a person not to get to know. Within a month we would be spending our lunchtime together.

Unfortunately for me, within a month I became an outcast just like her because of my association with a 'witch'. All my acquaintances I made when I started school stopped talking to me. Some threatened that it wouldn't be long before people started wanting to have fights with me and so on.

I didn't take the threats seriously. At five feet, ten inches tall, muscular and an experienced scrapper for the last three years – I was all about fury. I had transferred to this school from Windermere, a much tougher school in East Vancouver. Windermere was infamous for its problems with drugs, weapons and gangs. In truth, I was a shit disturber in my old school. I did and said whatever I wanted and was quite prepared to deliver consequences to anyone who dared to threaten me. The fighting was the main reason my mother transferred me. I always had my ghost watching over me and it somehow made me feel pretty fearless.

As time went on Jennifer became more and more comfortable around me and opened up more. Her stories became increasingly strange. Now, for the most, part Jennifer's parents had round the clock surveillance on her. They drove her to and from school every day; she rarely took the bus or walked. She had Royal Conservatory piano lessons at home, attended a youth teen church program on Sundays at her parents command, and had extra-curricular activities as she played flute in the school band. So we mostly just spend recess and lunch time together. However, eventually she asked her father, when he came to pick her up, if I could come over for a visit and possibly stay for dinner. Her father sized me up, hesitated for a moment and then agreed to drive me to their place and said that the decision for staying for dinner would be up to his wife.

We drove up Moscrop Road to a house that seemed ridiculously large; it encompassed almost all of the property such that there was no space for a lawn or back yard garden.

The car parked under the house and we climbed the staircase to the main floor of the three-storey house. Along the staircase was a painted portrait of a woman in a shiny ivory gown (reminiscent of the late 40's, early 50').

"That's a portrait of my mother." Jennifer saw me looking at the portrait.

"She was quite beautiful wouldn't you say?"

"Wow! When was the portrait done?"

"I don't know, my mother won't tell me, as it would expose her age."

I topped the staircase and I was immediately staring at a statuesque woman with thick, short dark hair, white skin, dark eyes and glasses. She was wearing a navy blue leisure suit. She eyed me for a moment.

"Jennifer, is this a friend you brought home from school?" Jennifer put her homework bag on the floor by where she hung her coat and walked around me.

"Yes mother, this is Aileen. You remember me talking to you about her? I invited her over and was hoping that she could stay for dinner."

"Ah yes, Aileen… Well, I am Mrs. Wilson. Yes, you must have dinner with us; we are having Jennifer's favourite, chicken and rice. You must call your parents of course and let them know that you are here and ask them if it is okay to have dinner here."

"Sounds great" I said, observing Jennifer behind her mother making the facial expressions that made it clear she was not in fact fond of chicken and rice. I was also surprised that Jennifer called her mother, well, mother. It seemed so formal and detached.

We put our homework bags to the side, set the table as per her mother's directions and then retired to the living room where Jennifer played for a while prior to dinner.

"You like music, Aileen?"

"Sure."

"Any particular genre?"

"Oh, I don't know, I like rock, you know like CCR and Nazareth. I also like some pop, you know, like Blondie; how about you?"

"Well, I like a great many types of music. I suppose it would be easier to say that the only music I am not fond of is Country. I also enjoy composing my own music. What do you think of this? I call it Percius." She began to play a very beautiful melody that reminded me a bit like belly dancing music.

"You composed that yourself? It's way awesome man."

"Dinner time." Jennifer's mother called from the dining room carrying the roast chicken onto the table.

So we all sat down in the huge, Spartan dining room and dished up our food. Of course I was ravenously hungry and just wanted to dive into my dinner. Dinning room etiquette wasn't a priority in my house when you have to fight two brothers and a father for food.

"It is so rare that we have a guest for dinner. Aileen would you do us the honour of giving thanks?"

I looked up from my plate to Mrs. Wilson's eyes. She seemed to be smiling or smirking I couldn't figure out which but either way I had no idea how to give thanks or pray, which I was pretty sure was what she meant.

"We don't do that at my house, so I am afraid that I don't know how." Good move Aileen I thought; blame it on your parents. Jennifer had warned me that her parents were God fearing Christians and I was worried that if they didn't like me, they wouldn't let me hang out with her.

"Good gracious! Well that is unfortunate, isn't it Dad?"

"Yes dear." The first words to come out of Mr. Wilson's mouth since we got back to Jennifer's house.

"Well Jennifer, I suppose you better say grace so that Aileen can learn." Jennifer smiled a frosty smile, and in a patronizing voice said,

"Thank you Lord for this meal we are about to receive. We give thanks for all our blessings, in Jesus name, Amen."

We all echoed the Amen chant and I dove into my plate lustily.

"So do you play any musical instruments?" Mrs. Wilson asked piercing a piece of chicken delicately and pausing to look up at me with her inquisitive brown eyes, no doubt ághast at my table manners.

"Ah, no… I dance though. Yeah, I am pretty involved in dance. I have been dancing for five years."

"Oh really? Do you take tap dance, ballet, or maybe highland dance?"

"Well no, actually I used to be a majorette in a marching band. But for the last while I have focused on contemporary jazz, Hawaiian, Polynesian, and Tahitian dance."

"Oh, like those dirty solid gold dancers? Dad, did you know that they allow girls so young to dance like that?"

"No dear I didn't." There was a pause in the questioning and I gratefully gulped down food.

"Jennifer tells me your family does not go to church, is that true?"

"No, not very often."

"You do believe in God don't you?"

"My father is atheist and religion is kind of forbidden in my house." Why did I tell the truth, why can't I just tell a white lie and get this lady off my back?

"So you don't believe that God is the Holy Father and Creator?" She said looking obviously upset.

"I was taught about the Big Bang and evolution..."

"Well, then if you believe that your ancestors are monkeys and the world came from an explosion, who created the explosion, and the universe to explode into?" Her voice became shrill and it was clear that I was upsetting her. I had been a happy atheist for these past fourteen years and I knew this was a no win argument. But like I said before, I am a shit disturber.

"Well, I believe that sometimes a pen is just a pen. I try not to give inanimate objects like the sky or the solar system a human consciousness. I think the universe has no divine driver, and if it did, talking to us would be like me caring what an ant thinks or feels." Well it came out of my mouth before I had the opportunity to think better of it. I suppose this was my first and last dinner here – once again the words come out before my brain can stop me for being careless.

"Dad did you hear the filth in that poor lost child's mouth?"

"Yes dear, I did."

"My daughter goes to a teen youth group every Sunday in North Vancouver, Aileen. I would like to invite you to join us this Sunday as it is clear that you are a Godless sinner..." Jennifer never said a word during dinner but the expression on her face was clear as if she were screaming at me, "Are you fucking crazy?" Well, I thought, my boorishness would impress her; obviously I was wrong.

"I will ask my parents if I can go." I said sheepishly.

"Problem with schools these days is they teach all that science and the kids don't get any solid morality in school anymore. Handing our children right into the hands of the Devil, wouldn't you agree, Dad?"

“Absolutely right, dear.” I could have replaced this man with a decorative lamp fixture and attached a skipping record to him and you wouldn’t have known the difference.

After dinner Mrs. Wilson allowed us one hour to visit before she insisted on driving me home. Apparently, it was not okay for me to walk a mile and a half home. We retired to Jennifer’s room which was obviously a refuge to her. She had it all done up like an Egyptian shrine, complete with the Pampas Grass plumes over her bed, Egyptian paintings and drawings that she had done herself, decorated the walls.

“I’m not fond of church nor the whole of Christendom myself, Aileen, however you showed some characteristically idiotic insolence.” She seemed angry and for a second I thought she was really pissed at me. But then she began laughing, well, cackling actually. So I joined in and laughed with her.

“I have never seen my mother so stunned! I hope you don’t talk to your parents that way. But seriously Aileen, I want to ask you a few questions of my own if that is alright with you.”

“Sure, I guess I owe you after that blunder at dinner.”

She paused, looked up at me, and then grinned creepily. She proceeded to tell me about a group she belonged to. This ‘club’ consisted of herself, her boy-friend (I was surprised, all things considered, that she even had a boyfriend), and a girl named Tyra.

Jennifer sat on her bed, leaned back against the wall and stared at me. I was sitting on her desk chair and just returned the blank stare. I was then inundated with a barrage of questions,

“Have you ever had a deja vu?”

“Yeah, I suppose, why?”

“Do you know if something is going to happen before it does?” she pressed.

“I don’t know, maybe once or twice.”

“Have you ever had a close brush with death, but miraculously survived?”

"Actually, as a matter of fact yeah, when I was 7 or 8 years old…"

"Do you know what people are thinking even thought they haven't said a thing?"

"I don't know about that"

"Do you know when people are lying?"

"Sometimes. Why are you asking me all these damn questions?"

"Can you feel other people's joy or sorrow, even if they say nothing?"

"I don't know, I never thought about it."

"Have you ever seen spirits?"

"Sure, Vodka, Tequila, Wine – that's a spirit right?" I said smiling nervously but curious.

"Spirits, ghosts, apparitions. Can you see things that you know no one else can see?"

"Why? I mean no, but why?"

It had occurred to me that she had done this a number of times in the past. So my evening had become a two-fold interrogation, first by her mother, then by her – neither were welcome. After she no doubt analyzed my responses to all these questions she broke off and was silent.

I hated talking about the paranormal because it was not normal conversation of teenagers, but more importantly, it made me think about my rather distressing secret I kept hidden from everyone for as long as I could remember. Long ago I had decided to call him a ghost, for lack of any better description. But he was usually with me. I knew intuitively that something in my life was beyond the realm of acceptably normal. It was also natural to deny, hide, bury, or otherwise overcompensate for this given abnormality. Like a really tall girl who has poor posture from a lifetime of slouching, my staunch Atheism masked an overriding desire to 'normalize' my entire haunted life. It was okay as a child to have an invisible friend, but it was not okay to have one that never went away. The other thing that I knew was not normal was that as I aged so did my ghost. My ghost was all grown up and a man now – I knew from the time I was five that I could no longer talk about my friend who I used to think was Peter Pan. For the most part I was quite convinced I had some form of mental illness. I was lost in my own murky thoughts when Jennifer faced me seemingly annoyed at my ignoring what she was saying. She recognized my nod of comprehension and continued.

"I think you have the making of a good ECAW acolyte; In fact I think I'll make you my personal apprentice."

"hmmmph? Say what? Acolyte of what, if you don't mind? "I must have been lost in my own thoughts longer than I thought.

"I think you have the potential to become a reasonable witch. I'll train you in the Wiccan art." She said flatly.

"A Witch? Wiccan? What on earth, are you talking about? I thought that was all school gossip." I was loud at this point.

"Shhhh! Of course I'm a witch! A good one too, I'm the leader of a Wiccan group calling themselves ECAW! The Enlightened Coven of Ancient Wicca, are you interested or not?"

My mind began whirring very quickly as I took everything in.

"So you are telling me that you are a witch and that you belong to a group of witches and that you want me to join your group?" I asked her in sarcastic disbelief.

"What's the matter Aileen? Scared?"

"Sure, I'll join. Gonna teach me how to turn the math teacher into a frog?"

"He already is one." We both laughed.

The hour was up and Mr. Wilson drove me home. My brothers and father were out, and only my mother was home. I got in the house and talked to my mom for awhile about Jennifer's family and how bizarre they seemed to me. I then went into my room to do some homework.

That following Saturday I was invited to Jennifer's house. This was great as I had all kinds of questions to ask her, that I didn't have time for on my last visit. While we did see each other during the week at school, we just never had enough privacy most days for me to question her about ECAW. So whle I was back in her room admiring her pampass grass over her headboard, I asked Jennifer to explain in more detail what her group specifically did. She explained that ECAW consisted of just three young people that included her as the leader of the group, and that all members had a pseudonym, as was the Wiccan custom. Jennifer's was Kotic Katmandhu, or simply Kat for short. Her boyfriend was Rodan, and Tyra was Darius. Jennifer or Kat created this group to study all paranormal theories and all known religions, so that through synthesis, theological truths could be revealed. She told me that she was convinced this was the strongest method for developing bona fide skills in Wicca craft.

Everyone had their own religions that they would study and bring key issues of that religion to the attention of the group. Kat explained that they would take notes and compare and contrast the various religions of man through time. It sounded like quite an undertaking, but I could see that much of the revelations from this would be very rewarding. Darius had all the typical ones like numerology, astrology, palm reading, and to a lesser degree tarot card reading but she was also responsible for Aztec/Mayan mythology. Kat pursued Egyptian mythology, Greek/Roman mythology, as well as the blacker arts, Satanism, Necromancy, Demonology, the fundamentals of Herbology and Wiccan art, the quintessential pagan. Rodan was into the Quantum Mechanics Theory and the idea of alternate and adjacent dimensions on top of his Judaism, and Christianity, the ever popular and more mainstream philosophies.

Soon we headed out of her bedroom; I was gunning for my shoes as we were going to go to the doughnut shop. I needed a coffee after that enlightening bit of information. When we were safely out of her parents' earshot range, I had a burning question;

"So Jennifer?"

"When we are in the group or alone, please call me Kat."

"Okay, Kat. Where did you learn all this stuff?" That caused a thin-lipped grin to spread across her face. She zipped up her scarlet red jacket and smoothly pulled her long chestnut brown hair out from inside her coat to cascade magnificently down her back smacking her miniscule waistline.

"Well, a year ago, when I was still living in North Vancouver, there was an import store that sold all manner or artefacts from all over the world, particularly Asia and particularly from Egypt. Well as you can imagine, I fell in love with the store and became quite good friends with the proprietess. She took me in as if I were her own daughter and taught me much. She gave me priceless books and was a constant source for all my needs including ceremonial candles, potions, and knives." She paused for a moment and looked at me to see if I was still listening, which of course I was.

"She taught me the basics of Wicca. I intend to teach you the same. Soon after I learned the basics I was able to summon my own familiar, and I haven't ever looked back."

"A familiar?"

"Yes, Aileen. A familiar is a spirit assistant usually in an animal form. Any good witch has one."

"What? Like a black cat on a witch's broom?" I was laughing.

"Yes, however, my familiar prefers the shape of a crow." She maintained her composure while I laughed which was kind of impressive, considering my mirth almost made me trip over my own two feet.

We rounded the corner of the street and I could see the Nuffy's donut shop sign at the corner of Wellington and Moscrop.

"Aileen, as I have told you before, knowledge of our previous lives gives us insight and an advantage over most mortals in our spiritual evolution. I wish to tell you of the travels that your fellow coven members are currently aware of so that you understand where they are in their development. We want to find out yours soon as well." She said as we marched down the hill to the shop.

"Go ahead then, lay it on me…" I said thinking that this was a good opportunity to strike up a cigarette.

"Well as for myself, I have been informed that I have a very old soul and I know that I operate within the negative energy plane. Now that does not mean I work for the devil, so just check the Christian centric dogma at the doorstep please." Kat smiled and jabbed me in the ribs.

"Come on admit it, you are the daughter of the devil – where's your pitchfork?" I said laughing uproariously, no doubt pissing her off.

"Rodan also has an old soul, though this is his first life spent on this planet. For some reason, he had to do one life here – though we don't know what lesson he has to learn here."

"So let me see if I got this right, Rodan is an alien from another planet?" I busted a gut in a fit of laughter. Kat watched me and stopped walking.

"Are you finished with your impertinence?" Kat spat at me. I realized that she didn't find this funny, which of course, made it even funnier.

"Okay, okay, really I'm fine. I won't laugh anymore…" I broke out laughing again and then my tear stained eyes met hers and I took in a deep breath and shut the hell up.

"Sometimes I can't believe how immature you are…" She protested.

"Come on Kat, what do you expect? I was half expecting you to tell me that Tyra was Napoleon in a past life." I said still failing to control my hysterics.

"Pharaoh or servant the soul has no hierarch. The soul of the servant can be infinitely wiser and transcendental than the soul of Pharaoh. Mortals measure Napoleon on what he achieved when all the advantages were on his side. He was cunning, ruthless, and filled with desire for conquest. You need to learn how to measure him according to the spiritual measures of Wicca. What did he achieve when he was at his lowest? When there was no advantage, when hope and faith left him in his darkest moment?" She paused as if asking me what he did. I had no recollection of the life of Napoleon, and frankly, I was surprised she knew Napoleonic history. I just stared back at her. She continued to wait so finally I told her, "I have no idea of Napoleon's life." She rolled her eyes up to the sky and sighed.

"He committed suicide. He could not overcome his own vanity and pride. Ultimately, he had the soul of a coward. In this life you will meet people of great fame and fortune, you will meet people of meagre means. You will measure them on the merits of where in their developments their souls are, not on where fate, greed, or circumstance has put them, do you understand?"

I nodded absently in comprehension. I didn't know that Napoleon committed suicide, but I was blown away by her perception of the world. I really wanted to know more. Suddenly, even the most bizarre things that came out of her mouth didn't seem nearly as crazy as Christian, don't think –just pray to a 2000 year old crucified Hebrew, philosophy that she hated.

"Our coven does not pray for blessings nor do we refer to misfortune as the work of the devil. We understand that all things are a cycle." She grabbed hold of the shop door handle and peered at me sincerely,

"Divine understanding requires its own price...But you are a little green for that conversation." She opened the door and waited for me to enter then followed behind me.

She ordered tea and a cherry doughnut and I ordered a coffee and a Belgian crème filled doughnut. We didn't talk much, my thoughts wandered to my dark secret. At this point I knew that the ghost I grew up with from the time I was five was not in fact Peter Pan. I knew this because when Peter Pan started to completely loose his boyish looks and look like a man I was nine years old. I remembered one night when that voice, that presence was in my bedroom I asked him, "Are you really Peter Pan, cuz I think you are growing up?" In the dim light of my room I could barely hear him but the voice was so distinct.

"You can call me Peter, but I am not Peter Pan, I am your watcher – I'll always protect you." Then I remember this kind of white, shimmering face smiling at me with the hugest eyes. The face was ghost-like and only seemed to materialize for two seconds. I wanted to believe that it was some relative that was watching and protecting me. But every time I talked to my mother about our family history, it was clear I had absolutely no relatives in England, Scotland, Ireland, New Zealand, or Australia and the voice was definitely one of those kinds of accents. That is probably why I was convinced that I might very well be suffering from some psychiatric problem. But, while that was the easy answer the previous summer I had gone to the hospital. So many specialists had checked me, why couldn't they find it? I wrote I.Q. tests, looked at Rorschach inkblots, talked to psychiatrists, had Electrical encephalograms – you name it. They said I was normal, how could they miss it? Part of me wanted to tell Kat, that if ever I had met someone who may have the answer it was she. However, I was scared that she would reject me from the group for being mentally unfit for Wicca. I had to keep it secret, at least for now.

Chapter 3

I was back at school, another miserable day. I stood outside in the rain, at the end of the breezeway with my cigarette. I was skipping home room as it seemed like a stupid idea to have to sit in a room and stare at people you don't like – in a class that is just about attendance. In this school your class teachers took your attendance anyways, so why 15 minutes of home room? I waited for the last bell to ring, butted out my cigarette, and walked to my class wet.

The morning's first class was English. Kat was in this class with me. The rabble were in an uproar at my befriending Kat and they delighted in annoying us before, during and after class.

"Hey Kovacs, did you and your friend ride on one broom, or do you have your own now?" They enjoyed using my last name, as if for some reason it was an insult in itself.

"Well actually Simon, your father drives me everyday. Ever since I caught him necking with the principal (the principal was male)."

Simon tried to hide his anger and shock at my rebuke. People around us jeered alerting the teacher to the in-class distraction.

"Settle down class..."

"Yer so fuckin' dead Kovacs." Whispered Simon sticking his middle finger up at me.

"Yeah? You and what army? – You fag!" I returned the favour by showing him my finger. But I could see that many of his friends were looking at me and mumbling how they were going to gang up on me after school.

Kat just looked at me and shook her head. Well, she'd be there to support me Right? Wrong! At the end of classes I went out to the gates where about fifty fellow students had convened for some gladiatorial entertainment – but no Kat. Well, I had been in this situation before, and with a big deep breath, put down my homework bag, and went to find out what this school was made of.

After about 30 minutes, I was walking back into the school because one of the teachers stopped the fighting. I was held on one side of the boys' gym teacher and Simon was being held on the other side. My parents were going to freak if they found out I was in yet another fight. My father even threatened to put me in some kind of military school. I didn't know what that actually was, but he made it sound pretty bad. We were heading towards the office when I heard a familiar melody coming from the band room.

I'll be damned; Kat was in the band room the whole time! That melody was her own composition she played when I was at her house. All I could think of was: thanks for the support Kat – obviously she was no fighter.

So the principal heard both stories and surveyed the uneven damage sustained by both parties.

"Aileen, if you wish to continue coming to this school, you will behave according to our rules of conduct. You don't live in the catchment area for this school and therefore we can expel you if you give us sufficient cause."

"I didn't start this fight, Simon did sir."

"That is immaterial. You finished it, didn't you? I don't want to see you in my office again over fights and bullying – do I make myself clear?"

"Yes, sir."

"Good. You may go."

I left the office—pissed off. I didn't ask for a fight and the principal acted like the whole thing was my fault! I was walking along the hallway and I could still hear the piano playing in the band room. Well, at least I could get in a good yell at Kat.

"Where the hell were you?" I was still hot from the fight and I was dishevelled and sweaty, still riding the adrenaline high that one gets when they are in the throes of rage.

Kat's calm demeanour, plinking away at the piano keys, just lit me up.

"Aileen, just because you allow foolish mortals to get the better of you, to goad you on, don't come looking for support from me. I ignore them and I have survived just fine. Why do you care what they think?" She finally moved her gaze from the keyboard to look at me. She tilted her head towards me inquisitively.

"How can you stand being the butt end of their jokes? You may like playing the coward – but I would sooner fight than let them take pot-shots at me in class."

"You will find that in life there will always be an idiot trying to drag you down so that they appear superior. I hope that when you are older you find a more constructive method to deal with these people. I believe that ignoring an idiot is the best. You see, just because you *can* fight, doesn't mean you *should* fight. This is a lesson that Achilles never learned either. I have however had an inspiration while you were out there impressing fellow students with your street rat techniques. I now have your Wiccan name..."

"Yeah? What is it then?"

"Dragon"

"Dragon? Why Dragon?"

"It refers to a woman with a fiery temperament – that is you."

For all my anger and adrenaline, I had to laugh. I liked the name. The more I said it, the more I saw how true it was. She was smart; I had to give her that. It was the most fatal flaw in my character, and every time my Wiccan name was used it was a reminder that I had to check my temper and relax.

Kat decided to shave off some of the workload between Tyra and herself, and informed me that my fields of study were to include elemental science, alchemy, necromancy, Assyrian mythology/history, and Shinto mythology. I thought that was pretty cool, even though at the time I had no idea what the heck most of these were.

Saturday, October 25 was here and Kat was due to visit my place. My bedroom, a typical teenager's bedroom, colourful and cheerful with blue walls and a deep purple rug. My headboard and dresser were all painted in a high gloss candy blue. My queen size bed dominated the rather small room – my sleep room.

I welcomed sleep, when it came to me. If you sat at the edge of my bed very quietly and listened, you could faintly hear the hum of something – something not quite natural. It was in some unexplainable way soothing. I was free to walk and escape my room whenever I wanted. But realistically, I was expected to spend at least eight hours a night in that room – alone? I always felt I was being watched or monitored. I would often dress for school under my blankets or in the bathroom. I had a beautifully large bedroom window and my mirror was on the opposite side of the room so that the light would reflect all over the room. The last place any parent would look for something altogether sinister. My ghost or shadow had been with me for so long it had become a fact of being me. Since I was convinced that this apparition was a product of my neurochemistry, I never thought much about the fact that the strongest encounters happened to usually be in my bedroom. Well, until Kat came to visit me.

"So this is where you live?" Kat said as she entered my room.

"Yeah, I painted the room and my furniture myself."

"I like the colour..." She paused seeming to be listening for something. She walked and looked around my walls quietly for about a solid two minutes.

"There is magic here. Something..I..." She broke off, tilting her head as if waiting for some explanation.

"There is?" I said genuinely surprised, and a little freaked.

"Quite." Again, she paused looking around my room. "Intriguing..." She then shot an accusing glance back at me and lifted an eyebrow.

"What? No explanation? Have you been casting spells Aileen?"

"Well, I have been practicing" I lied hoping that we could get to the point of her visit. She paused for a moment with a very serious expression surveying me in silence and after what seemed like minutes finally broke off her stare, smiled and dug into her napsack. She then drew out her magic book and another much like hers. It was a black leather bound book with a small golden symbol on it.

"This is your very own book of shadows, use it well. You will begin by transcribing into your book the name of our coven and your name with us. Then you will copy our language and code of ethics. Following that, all symbology that we use in the coven, you will draw with the description next to it." She opened the book to expose the blank beige coloured parchment within.

"That is going to take me a bit of time." I said looking at her while she grinned back at me.

"Not one spell shall be put into this book until you have completed all the transcriptions – it's the Wiccan way." She then closed the book and handed it to me.

"You had better take the time to use your best hand writing, you pay in spades down the road with griffinage." She added. I knew she meant that I had to write neatly, something I was not good at.

"I don't expect that you will have the transcriptions done by Samhaen. You will bring my tome to Samhaen, do not forget it."

"You can depend on me."

"One more thing, Dragon..."

"Sure, what?"

"No more magic until you have been properly trained."

"I promise." I didn't know what the hell she was talking about, but obviously something about my room bothered her.

Well, I figured out why we had to write out all this stuff in this book, it forces you to memorize it. With the ECAW jargon, it was fairly straightforward.

According to their philosophy, many people have some level of psychic power. However, there are a few people with enough to spellcast and they are called Hodens. They distinguish between people who use this power benignly and people who use it for essentially evil, destructive purposes – they are referred to as Aserhodens. That defines the difference between someone like Mahatma Gandhi versus Rasputin. Organized groups of people who actively seek out to eradicate Hodens are referred to as Adivar –which has been historically controlled and led by Aserhodens. ECAW had its own language; it was possible to write letters and even talk to each other with absolutely no chance of anyone understanding. With the exception of the odd word, it was rarely employed that I saw. I also discovered that ECAW had their own philosophy in terms of how they perceived the organization of the universe.

The ECAW concept of the universe believes that the spirit is indestructible and that it flows from body to body over the millennia. Every soul is like a fragment of some larger thing, much like a tapestry. These Wiccans believe that there is polarity to the energy sources that they draw upon. A spirit that is a fragment of a negative poled tapestry cannot draw power from a positive force and vice versa. I suppose the best analogy I can think of is that we all have different radio frequencies. We can only tune in on those frequencies, but some are more powerful than others. They made no excuses that their concepts of Wicca deviated from the more mainstream concepts; however, they were passionately committed to this perception and it did seem to make some amount of sense. Hence there was no real distinction of black or white witches.

Although I had not transcribed all of the information into my book of shadows, Kat taught me how to tune into my energy, to focus it, and of course the most difficult trick in Wicca – clearing the mind. So challenging is this that it is said that as a person ages, they are less likely to be good at Wicca. As we age, our minds fill with all manner of woes and troubles that inhibit our ability to clear our minds and focus the spiritual energies. I was also granted access to the multitude of collected texts they possessed.

Meditation, clearing of the mind and focusing your own inner energy to move even the smallest candle flame in a room with no wind are all part of the energy focusing practice that I was expected to learn to master. Kat wanted everyone in ECAW to be able to stop at a heartbeat and be able to draw upon his or her energy and focus it at a specified target. Mind clearing was seemingly impossible enough, never mind attempting to get good enough at it to do it at the drop of a hat – I dreaded it.

History, philosophy, and theology rounded out my reading list. Some of it was quite interesting; some of it could put a sane person into a deep coma. I would literally read two pages and fall into a deep sleep. But as most of this material was considered mandatory knowledge, I had to fight insomnia and get through them.

ECAW philosophy regarding life and the journey of our souls is simply this: we all have souls that are at various levels of age and development. We come back for successive lives to fulfill certain mortal developments to aid us in our part of the bigger picture in the spirit world. Basically, mortal life is the elementary, high school and University education of our souls so that we can do our real life's work in the greater fabric of the spirit plane. There appeared to be no direct worship of any God or Goddess. Instead it seemed to be an intense focus on how to manipulate the vibrational energies that exist in the world to do whatever you wanted. A theoretical quest to uncover a new physics was exciting to me – if it worked. So even though Hallowe'en was coming up this weekend and I was not too impressive with my skills to date, I was an eager student. I was also keen to see if all this mumbo-jumbo was actually real. Kat and I decided to have lunch off the school grounds and headed towards Kingsway Street for a restaurant.

"I had a vision." Kat said calmly, putting cream and sugar into her tea.

"Ya? What? A dream or something? " I was surveying the crowd, didn't want anyone listening in.

"I saw you and myself," she paused. "We were friends, just as we are now. It was destiny that brought you to me Dragon."

"What do you mean, Kat?"

"Don't you remember back in oh, about 1472, we were friends, you and I? You were the Miller's daughter named Daphne, and I was that lowly orphaned shepherdess Kia." She regarded my face while she spoke her words, trying to get a fix on my reaction, no doubt. I noted the obvious play on names: Kat/Kia, Dragon/Daphne. Altogether unimaginative and uninspired, I thought.

"Care to jog my memory for me? I mean after all, I'm your apprentice, I'm learning from you." I said. What did it matter what she said now? Who would I tell? After all, her friendship was at the expense of other friends.

She continued, "Even then I was training you in Wiccan arts. Herbology was your favourite thing to learn then. You were beautiful, you had unusually light coloured hair and were the envy of all women in the village, and that was probably why you died."

"Well now you have my curiosity piqued. How did I die?"

"Well…" she said recovering from what appeared to be deep thought. "One day you and I were enjoying each other's company in the fields when one of your envy-filled village girls was sent to get us to try to heal an ailing woman in the village. When we got there, we realized that she was in very bad shape, and that very little of what we could do would save her. There were women all around the bed praying. We tried all of our herbal remedies, but to no avail. She died hours later." She broke off and took a long deep breath before continuing. I stared at her in silence, waiting to hear the finish.

"We were accused of using the devil's art. We were tried as witches, and sentenced to burn, as it was believed it was the only way to kill witches."

For a long time neither of us spoke. We just stared at each other.

"It was no coincidence that we became friends. The first thing you must learn, Dragon, is that there is no such thing as 'coincidence'. It's a word invented by mortals, because the paranormal scares them so."

"In what part of the world did this happen, Kat?" I asked, trying to tie a time and place for later evaluation.

"Approximately Wales, as we know it now." She replied very quickly as though this was indeed the God's honest truth. The idea of being burned at the stake in 15th century Wales wasn't too much of a stretch as in those days they would kill for any reason, but witches? Was there already such a presence of Christianity in Wales in the 1470s for such a concept? I made a mental note to research this.

The following Monday, I skipped class and went to the Vancouver public library on Robson and Burrard street and conducted my own exhaustive review. Apparently, it was not only possible; it was going on fairly regularly during the late 15th Century. In fact Joan of Arc was burned as a witch over thirty years prior. I also discovered that fourteen years after our alleged death in 1486 two Catholic men wrote the *Malleus Maleficarum*, a book which basically spelled out what was a witch, how to detect, torture, and destroy witches – it notably stated that men could also be witches. During this time most of the women killed were those that practiced the old pagan use of herbs and medicine. Did Kat really do this research or did she just fluke out? The majority of the ECAW material Kat had access to actually pre-dated the dark ages. Kat studied the Old Testament, and Egyptian history. How could a thirteen year old know about the dark ages in Wales?

Kat was very excited as Samhaen was fast approaching, Hallowe'en for the non-practicing. For ECAW it was the most important festivity for the year. Kat showed me how she made cat-tail bread. She also showed me a horrid drink known as Klaw, a fermented apple drink which is sweetened with blackstrap molasses in a pumpkin. The only way to make it even remotely palatable is to drown the concoction with dark rum. So the goal seemed to get moderately drunk, with that Klaw possibly a little drugged, and join in and fuse our energies. As per requirement we donned our robes for the event and drove out into the country where Rodan lived, in Langley. I had met Tyra briefly at the church in North Vancouver when Kat's family dragged me there, but this was my first introduction to Rodan. When we got to Rodan's house Kat introduced us. He was tall, slim with black wavy hair, blue eyes and fair skin with freckles. He was about three or four years older than me. He seemed very polite and mannerly. I would have never been able to picture a partner for Kat, but this guy seemed perfect. Once there, all kinds of strange music was playing and we socialized for a few hours and sipped sparingly on the Klaw. We then convened outside in the gathering darkness and discussed the objectives and goals of ECAW in the upcoming season.

It must have been getting close to midnight when we put down our drinks and joined hands in a circle. This was my first ceremony with the group and I was willing to give it a serious try. Everything that Kat had taught me, and my small amount of actual practice, was going to be tested tonight. This would also be the night that I would find out for sure if all this ECAW stuff was actually crap, so I was excited. The way this ritual worked was that you couldn't join in your voice until you could sense the energy from at least one side of yourself. It forced me to concentrate, since I had to sense the energy from one person, as it moved through me in one direction, mixing with my own and then hopefully merging with the person on the other side – it had to be a circle to work. The experience was supposed to increase your inner power. Clearing your mind was hard enough to learn in the quiet of your own space; here we had to do it in the company of each other. The Klaw actually helped.

So into the circle we joined and my one hand held Tyra's and the other Kat's. My voice was the last to join. I joined my voice into the fray and soon all voices were in harmony, there in the dark. I could sense things from everyone. It was as if I could read any strong emotions from everyone, and I felt exposed. I was standing there focused yet amazed that this shit actually seemed to be working, when suddenly I became aware that my thoughts were drifting back to my ghost. While I was trying to think of something else, I happened on the thoughts of Rodan. I turned towards him without opening my eyes. I could sense desire, as though he was letting me know that he was attracted to me. I was shocked and flattered. I had no desire to take Kat's boyfriend away, and while he was attractive, this was neither the time nor the place to make sudden or rash confessions. What was stranger still to me was the duplicity as I could sense he still had very strong feelings for Kat. I pushed the thoughts from my mind, as I was scared that Kat would read my thoughts or even worse, his thoughts. I tried to feel what Kat was thinking or what emotion I could read from her, but nothing came to me. She was far away, and a novice like me would never be able to unravel it.

I don't know how long we were in the circle but it felt like half an hour. Kat dropped her voice from the circle first and then the rest of us fell out. When it was done I just stood there staring at the ground in shock. We all laughed at Kat at school, but this group was really doing something, and it was working. Our minds joined for a period of time and I could sense a real energy between us. I couldn't wait for the next ritual. I slowly looked up and noticed that everyone else had left me. I was alone. I slowly turned around and made my way back to Rodan's house to get my coat and things before heading to the car. Before I left for the car from Rodan's house, he put his hand on my shoulder, turned me around and kissed me on the lips. He looked at me without a smile or a word and let me go. My first kiss from a guy and it had to be my friend's boyfriend. I felt horrible. I felt like I had betrayed my best friend.

I was about to jump into the car when Tyra and Kat came out of the bush and walked over to me. They were deep in conversation.

"No, it was definitely something – I know what I sensed, Darius…" Kat said eyeing me as she rounded the last slope towards the car.

"Probably just your retarded familiar, Kat!" Darius spat back. Which caused Kat to spin around in what looked like anger, facing Tyra.

"Darius! I know the difference, OKAY? It wasn't Thromm. Whatever it was, it was huge!" With that Kat turned around and smiled at me and put her hand on my shoulder, "Not bad for a neophyte! You did well."

"What are you guys talking about?" I interjected. Tyra's eyes rolled up and Kat smiled,

"Nothing, just two witches bitching." Tyra and Kat proceeded to laugh and get into the car.

All I could think of was, thank God, Kat didn't seem to know. I was worried about what Rodan would do at our next meeting. I would have to take him to the side and talk with him.

Kat seemed to be quite busy and mysterious for the following month and it wasn't until December that again Kat was able to sit with me and take some time to train me in more Wicca. After our ceremony on Samhaen I was chomping at the bit to learn new things and so I was anxious when we finally did meet.

"So you proved that you can focus your energy and join the group. Do you think you are ready for the next step?" Kat said with a smile on her face. We were sitting in her bedroom and she was surveying her record collection.

"Absolutely! What's the next step?" I pointed to a record that I hadn't heard yet from her collection. She smiled, peeled off the cover, and put it on her small record player.

"Do you think you are ready for hypermeditatation, you know, the dreaded Tyrrean Trance?" She moved the needle into position and adjusted the volume.

"What do I have to do?" I asked.

"Well, Dragon. Tyrrean trance is much more difficult than what we did on Samhaen. During that ceremony you had the help of everyone. With Tyrrean Trance you are on your own. You need to refine your

Wiccan skills and warding is paramount. Trance pulls your spirit from your mortal coil and while it is an incredibly useful skill it does have its inherent dangers. This realm where your spirit is free to roam unfettered is a crowded world. There are spirits that would jump at the opportunity in the mortal world and your vacant body is an open invitation." She broke off for a moment. However, I trust you will not seriously pursue Trance until you are certain you can more expertly cast a circle of protection around yourself. Warding your soul is paramount." She broke off again.

"It is unlikely that you would be able to do this little trick for some time. It requires great skill and a fair amount of energy. However, it is a good thing to practice. Meanwhile, you will have to familarize yourself with all the Gnostic texts as well. She reached into her bag and pulled out a fairly thick book. This is some of the translations and discussion of the group of texts known as the Nag Hammadhi, have fun.

She spent the remainder of her visit teaching me the finer points of sealing a room, circles of protection and, of course, the art of the Tyrrean Trance. I listened greedily, excited to try it all. But her news that the circle of protection and room seals were only as powerful as the caster depressed me. I knew I was pathetically weak at this point, relative to her anyway.

I knew that there was a ritualized order of operation associated with any Wicca. Kat had warned me repeatedly of the dangers of omitting any part of a sound development in the Craft. I could have taken more time practicing seals, and wards. So why did I practice the Tyrrean Trance without any regard? Why was I taking such a foolish risk? Was it because I didn't really believe that there was any way that a spirit could infiltrate my body? Was it because I always secretly felt safe and protected because of my ghost? Or was I just a typical stupid teenager that just didn't listen to any good advice? I just don't know. Whatever the rationale, I was determined to become proficient at Tyrrean Trance. For whatever reason, I had to know if it was possible to get out there. Every night I practiced. Besides, Kat said it would be very difficult for me to do it successfully anyways.

I suppose I should have at least poured salt around my bed, but I didn't. I used the mantra-like words to clear my mind and slowly lay down and continued to mantra until my heart and breathing were as slow as I could get them. Clearing my mind enough for me to focus on my remarkably small amount of inner energy and push it out. The energy feels like it is coming from the solar plexus and the middle of the forehead. The 'thread' that I became aware of was lifting and I finally could feel a 'pull'. Suddenly, I was aware that I was looking down at myself. I had just started acclimating to looking down at my body, when I realized I was not alone. By the closet stood a dark shadowy man in a trench coat and hat, smoke rising from his indistinguishable face. Everything Kat had warned me about was coalescing in my mind and the fear was causing me to want to jump back into my body... However, something was blocking me from doing that. I was freaking out, panicking; I could feel myself backing away when he drew the cigarette away from his face.

"Aileen, don't be afraid, we have been waiting for you... Please take my hand; I want to introduce you to someone." The voice was cold and breathy, like tangible wind.

"Who are you? What are you? Are you the devil?" I couldn't tell if I was talking or thinking since my vocal chords were still lying on the bed. He just smiled and took another drag of his cigarette, and his chest rocked in some sort of silent chuckle.

"My dear child there is no devil. Leave that notion there in your mortal world." He pointed in the direction of my unconscious body.

"You can call me Mr. No" he said. To this day, I don't know if he meant Know or No. Due to lack of choice, I took his white hand and by the time I noticed how cold it was, I was blinded for a split second and then suddenly aware of being in another room, who knows where! Looking around, I then followed Mr. No's raised hand who was pointing in an intended direction. There was a still man on a bed and a strange rock was glistening in the dawn, and an odd hum was coming from it. A familiar hum, a sound which rang a bell deep inside my consciousness. The apparition, or Mr. No, moved from me dissolving into the shadows, and as he did my whole body started feeling heavier and heavier. While I was admiring the fact that I felt like a solid mortal again, I saw the man sit up. He hadn't been sleeping, no. He was meditating and he was coming out of it. His eyes opened and locked onto mine. A smile spread across his face, and in that instant another bell rang again as my body and mind stood in absolute recognition awakening every fibre of my being!

Chapter 4

"Peter..." I gasped, drawing the name out, and stepping back. His smile seemed to broaden.

"I always said you could call me Peter, but I want you to know my real name now." He gestured with his hands that I come closer. I didn't.

"My real name is Bryn." He stopped smiling and cocked an eyebrow at me.

"Bryn..." I said the name aloud, but even as I said it I was beginning to realize just who he was.

"You're that musician? No wait a minute, that can't be, your alive. This makes no sense." I was shaking my head. I had heard Kat and others talk about some of the newer bands, while I had never heard Bryn's music, the band was widely talked about at school.

"Aileen..." He said reaching out for my hand. I just nodded and stared frightened in the corner of this room, which appeared to be a large bedroom -- amazed and confused. His voice, his face – he was real. If I'm not mad, and he's not a ghost what the hell was going on?

"Please come closer Aileen, you can't be frightened. Remember, I was the one who would sing the pinochle song to you when you were scared, like the one time when you were lost, remember?" My mind reeled back to when I was an eight year old lost somewhere in a crowd after a dance performance my mom took me to. There was a massive crowd, and after I left the park, I went up and down all kinds of streets, becoming more and more lost. I was crying so hard that my ghost came to me and began singing a silly song,

"The worms crawl in, the worms crawl out, the snails play pinochle upon your snout..." The silliness of the song helped me stop crying and then he told me to ask the first person on the street to take me back to the park. I found my mom frantically searching the park for me. My life was full of these moments of him, always there. I snapped out of it and looked at him in utter amazement. Part of me wanted to hug him, but instead I took three difficult steps towards him.

"I could never really figure out where you exactly were, but you figured out how to find me. You are truly a clever girl. We have bridged the distance between England and Canada – and now that I have you, I shall never let you go." He held out his hand again and this time I felt compelled to give him my hand. He touched my hand, and something else was there, a kind of energy that I was probably too young to fully appreciate. I was fourteen years old. There was an immediate sense of my father, teacher, and lover, for he was all these things to me. He looked into my eyes, kissed my forehead and pulled one of my curly strands of hair away from my face.

"How old are you now Aileen?" It was a simple enough question. He had seen me for almost all of my life and I was surprised he was unsure of my exact age. His hand was still holding mine and the sensation between us was tangible. It was a comfortable habit to lie about my age, but I was struck with the sudden embarrassment of my youth and a need to be taken seriously, and so...

"I'm turning eighteen, I lied."

His face responded and I could tell that he believed me.

"Well, we have time and I am a patient man. I have found you and now we have a lifetime to get acquainted." He got up from his bed and stood, seemingly to size himself up next to me, I noted he was about six feet tall, and very thin. I told him I was in school now and living in Vancouver, I told him about my friend Kat and how she taught me hypermeditation. He seemed enraptured at my every word and I was very happy to have the absolute attention of him. His eyes were aglow, giddy as a schoolboy, full of excitement and joy. It was hard not to return the smile. I felt like I had been reuinited with a long lost relative. After awhile he let go of my hand and sat back on his bed, that piece of rock in one hand.

"Do you remember how I told you that one day I would tell you everything? I think I did one better today. You know you are in England right now?" He said with a grin, obviously very proud of himself.

"England? " I said walking over to the window and squinted at the increasing daylight. Well one thing for sure, it didn't look like East Vancouver. He kept his distance from me, and seemed to just focus on looking at me. After a lifetime of him following me, I suppose I was used to him watching me.

"Bryn? What do you mean by being a patient man?" I asked turning away from the window and back to him. I think my directness surprised him, of course it wasn't assertiveness as much as it was sheer naïve ignorance.

"I don't want you to think that I am going to pressure you into doing things you are not emotionally ready for now that we can come together this way." He said this quietly and I sensed a degree of shyness and apprehension which was comforting.

"You are obviously mortal, a warlock. How is it that you can have such power, such skill?" I slowly sank to the floor with my back against the wall. He paused, watching me and then finally raising the rock in his hand, he said,

"I possess this Talisman, last surviving remnant of the staff of Viracocha, the antecedent race. It was forged by the very hands of Shemhazai before he was cursed; the staff which was handed down to Moses who was no more Hebrew than was he Egyptian. I have the Talisman and now that I have you, I am complete." His eyes really did kind of glow, I was sure it wasn't just a trick of the light.

Like a delayed reaction, the adrenaline had subsided enough that I was able to realize that this wasn't fun and games. Bryn wasn't a ghost or a bad case of schizophrenia– this was a guy with a whole pile of power and magic and I knew whatever was going on was way over my head. The gravity of the mess that I had inadvertently gotten myself into was slowly sinking into my pea-brain. I must have given him quite a look because he instantly reacted to my body language, got up and walked over to where I was by the window and put his hand on my shoulder,

"Hey, I said no rush. We are just friends –have we not been forever?" He gave a reassuring smile as I looked up into those huge eyes.

"Why me?" I said in a whisper. He furrowed his eyebrows and stole my hand into his.

"Am I the only one that can feel that?" He said locking his stare at me with intense sincerity.

Oh I felt that! Surges of energy, warm and overwhelming the longer we touched, like an electrical current. The irresistible pull between us was like feeling whole, a completion. I don't know how to describe that feeling, but it overwhelmed me so entirely, I felt touched by something divine.

"Who was that "No" guy?" I needed to change the subject and regretfully remove my hand from that intense, narcotic-like touch. It was too intense. He looked at his empty hand and paused as if he hadn't heard me at first.

"Oh... No? Well, he was a watcher. He is my assistant…" He put his face in my hair and whispered into my ear,

"How I have longed for that touch." I felt the warmth of his breath against my ear, his silky voice and then, instantly, I was back in my room, in my body, in Canada – away from him. That 'touch' while incredible was frightening. It was a little more than I was prepared to handle. The way he said it was disturbing, very disturbing. He had succeeded in scaring the hell out of me!

I woke up on Sunday morning scared to death. I felt torn. On the one hand I should be so happy to finally know how it was possible for me to have this apparition in my life all these years. I wasn't crazy after all right? But on the other hand, now he knew where I was and how to get me without me leaving my bedroom. I was in way over my head that was for sure. Maybe Kat could give me some advice, after all, she knew this magic stuff way more than I did.

There was a London Drugs by our school. I made sure to go there and pick up a copy of this Bands latest release. There on the cover was a picture of him. If only I had seen this album cover before Tyrrean Trance. I would have instantly recognized that face, those eyes, and that voice. I suppose the only thing that would have changed would be that I would have known it wasn't a relative, or the dead. I suppose I still would never have guessed that he would find me in Trance. Who the hell was Bryn? Why would some rock and roll guy from England, want to haunt a kid in Vancouver?

The next day I bounced into school to tell Kat I had successfully completed a Tyrrean Trance. I had decided to spill the beans about my past and my dark secret. I knew it was time to get some advice from her.

"So, I've been practicing my Tyrrean trance." I said trying hard to remain in control of my excitement.

"Good. How has it been going?" Kat was looking particularly distracted and she seemed almost irritated by my jocularity. Lately something was definitely up with Kat, she seemed so occupied.

"A total success!" I tried to ignore her coolness.

"Fabulous. Go anywhere?"

"Would you believe England?"

"What did you see there?"

"A man."

Indeed? Well, out with it woman, I can tell you are bursting at the seams to tell me something." She cast her gaze at me, finally acknowledging her full engagement in the conversation.

"I did everything you said, well, except for the ward and I was pulled to the house of a rock musician.

"Woah! You didn't bother to ward yourself?" She put her lunch bag back into her homework bag and scowled at me.

"Why bother? My warding would be good for nothing."

"So you expect me to believe that while you cannot ward yourself remotely adequately, you can travel to a rock musician's home, in England?" She seemed agitated.

"Look I am sorry I was an idiot and forgot to ward myself..."

"No, you didn't forget. You just didn't bother." She shook her head. "Your spirit was drawn to a mortal rock star? Rock stars are by their very nature self obsessed, most of which are far too cerebrally underdeveloped to have any knowledge or even skill in the Craft. Also, to be a successful musician you need the media to constantly hound you. This flies in the face of any worthy Wiccan." We were in the basement of the back end of the school sitting along the stairwell, a new quiet location for our lunches. I was about to defend myself, to let it all out, but Kat interjected.

"Dragon, look, I know you want to move on to spell casting. I will train you on some good stuff soon. I have to deal with some other issues concerning Rodan right now but when I get a chance, you are first on my list. Please don't make up or exaggerate stories hoping that I will be fooled into thinking you are more ready than you are."

I just shook my head. No point in continuing this conversation I thought. Besides, her mentioning Rodan made me suddenly aware that she may know about last Samhaen.

"How is he? What's the matter?"

"Rodan wants our rituals to move onto the next level, and he knows we are not ready yet. Furthermore, I am disturbed that he is requesting this immediately after the induction of a new member. I fear we need more male membership." Something about the way she looked at me made me realize she knew but was far too polite to bring it up.

"What is the next level?" I didn't realize that there were levels in Wicca rituals."

"All spiritual observances require a certain level of self-control. For instance the Roman Catholic monks have many such self-imposed restrictions; celibacy, flagellation, silence, some even have dietary and social restrictions. The Muslims and just about any other religion have these accepted religiously impugned measures. Wicca is no different. I suppose that the only difference is not in the self-imposed restrictions but in the ceremonial or ritual indulgences that are unique to our ancient rites. There are blood rites, sexual rites, group and individual rites all of varying power, all feared and maligned by the more mainstream philosophies. Remember that mainstream faiths are very useful to the established aristocracy or governments because these imposed restrictions offer a kind of mass control, particularly the invalidation of women's power. Because Wicca encourages the development of and empowerment of the individual it is not surprising that the governing establishment would seek out to destroy it. However, I digress. There are group rites and individual rites. There are blood rites and sexual rites. Of course the most powerful rites would be the group blood rites, like the ones the Aztec's were infamous for. However, group sexual rites are powerful. Solitary rites without any form of sacrament are the least powerful and of course as a Wiccan, I hardly see the purpose of it. We are not ready for blood or sexual rites as far as I can see."

"How big does a group have to be in order to be classed a group rite?" I was wondering how big our group had to be in order to be of any use.

"A group rite can be as little as two people – it's still infinitely better than one."

I was pretty sure I knew what Rodan was up to now. I was fairly confident looking at Kat that she knew too. So there I was staring at my friend, completely innocently, and yet my first big strike against me was made. I could tell looking at her she distrusted me. Why did Rodan do this? Was it his way of getting rid of me? Was there a reason he wanted me gone? I was getting angry; I had to make an excuse and go off the school grounds and have a smoke. So much for my big confession to Kat.

True to my theory whenever I attempted the Tyrrean trance, I was inevitably pulled into Bryns' world in England. It became a common occurrence, I would slip into my bedroom, lay down and in moments I was in Bryn's house. We would often go to his audio room downstairs packed thick with all manner of electronic equipment. There he could conjure the most amazing sounds. Often he would sing. I would just walk around the room and listen to the music absorbed in the synthesizer sounds, as they seemed to transcend into a language all on their own, like non-verbal communication. Bryn believed that with the advancement of the synthesizer technology one day it would be possible to control people just simply through sounds. He was interested in pursuing the research of how music and media could control the masses. He said he had already done some preliminary work that was surprisingly successful. Why he would want to control people and what his ultimate plans were, I had no idea. He would occasionally talk about the future; his vision was apocalyptic and scary. He was passionate about his music and very determined to achieve his objectives in frighteningly short timelines. By all accounts he was obsessive. He would talk about how young minds are like vacant fertile soil, waiting to be sown with ideas and philosophies.

We initially met fairly often, at least a couple of times a week, whenever his crazy schedule would allow for it. We talked for hours about his family, his childhood, and about music. I didn't mind, as I was quite curious about him. I knew some things, but it was nice to have the gaps filled in. Hearing him talk about his school life and his first job was comforting; it helped make this 'relationship' more normal.

It wasn't just our age; Bryn and I were different in just about every conceivable way. When he met people he was very shy, and didn't talk much. He didn't appear to like people and was somewhat of a xenophobe, which I found unusual for a musician. I was more of a people person. I was talkative, and had no problem embarrassing myself by being loud. We liked different foods. Well, Bryn didn't really like food. Like any teenager, I suppose, I am a bit of a slob Bryn, by contrast, was a manicured perfectionist. In spite of our differences and beyond any logic, I noticed that I was developing a crush on him.

So there I was on a day like any other, six in the morning, well if you care about Greenwich Mean Time, in a large house near London, the rain falling heavily down, casting a gleam on everything outside. Bryn was lying on the floor of his livingroom with just his housecoat on and there I was in my jeans and shirt on the couch, staring down at him. I was admiring the hair that peeked through his housecoat. Neither my dad nor my brother's have chest hair, so it was somewhat fascinating.

"Come here…" The sound of his voice broke the silence and caused me to stop staring at his chest and look him in the eyes. He patted the floor next to him, causing me to become uneasy. I slowly got up and walked over to where he was laying.

"No, come lay here beside me." He rubbed the floor more impatiently and glanced up at me smiling. I did as he asked and lay down beside him. My eyes met his, and he then reached out a hand to pull me towards him. When I was right next to him he let go.

"That's better." He ran his hand through my hair, pulling strands away from my face and then touched my cheek.

"I look at you and I see why the descendants of Elohim were betrayed by their desire. It is my turn." He then put his hand behind my head and slowly pulled me towards his face for a kiss; a long, deep, lingering kiss. This kiss was nothing like my first one with Rodan, this one was wet and I could feel the stubble from his face. I was definitely not ready for this. He paused, as if sensing my reaction, then pushed my head away from his. He stared at me wordlessly for a moment searching my eyes.

"Aileen, you liar—you are not 18! How old are you? – tell me now!" His tone was stern and his voice more commanding than I had every remembered. His expression was clearly flaring up with anger. I rolled away towards the couch but I could tell his eyes were still on me, burning holes into my back. Without facing him, I confessed.

"I turn fifteen in April." When I did turn to face him Bryn seemed to physically flinch. He immediately got up and walked over to the hallway and looked down at the floor and then at me again. He was shaking his head; he looked up to the ceiling saying something in a foreign language but I caught the name Enoch in it. Then he turned to look at me. His kind, warm expression had completely changed. He glared at me with furrowed eyebrows, his expression cold.

"Don't ever *lie* to me again! You understand? I have to be able to *trust* you; don't *force* me to be *unpleasant*." There were words that he emphasized, they stuck out like swords in my heart. Wow, was he angry! So I learned he had a temper. My age obviously upset him – a lot. There was nothing I could do to make myself older and it was too late to take back the lie. Staring at his cold face, hearing the way he turned his last comment into a command, it was obvious he wanted something from me but not while I was fourteen. I can't describe how naked I felt realizing what that *something* was. Paralyzed in fear and shame, I just stared back at him...analyzing every word. Wondering why he cursed and who Enoch was. Finally, I broke the uncomfortable silence.

"I'm sorry; I promise I won't lie to you again. Please don't be mad at me. I guess I just lie about my age so often, it was force of habit." I walked over to where he was to give him a reassuring hug, a move that took an incredible amount of courage. When I did, he took both of my arms and removed them from either side of him.

"Don't touch me, child. This changes the timetable and everything. It is time for you to go home." He was still holding my arms and it kind of hurt.

"Bryn, please don't..." Well, that is as far as I got and then I was looking up at the ceiling of my room. The livingroom outside of London was gone. I was mad that he called me a child but I was more overwrought with sadness that I had let him down, so with no other choice, I cried.

Chapter 5

School dragged on at a snail's pace. The oppressive school had a colourful roster of teachers. My English teacher, Mr. Bordeaux, would frequently get sidetracked from the lesson of the day by two of his favourite subjects: his glory days as a fireman, of which he would relay rather graphically tragic tales; his other favourite subject, which also had little or nothing to do with English, was a rather large chested girl in class. He would harass her with verbal sexual innuendoes, flaunting this harassment in front of us all.

My math teacher was a Scottish gentleman who was a good instructor with three interesting attributes. He was always the first one out of the school. Everyday he beat even the slyest slackers, like me. He had an annoying habit of doing a formal roll call with the boys called Master and the girls called Miss. This normally would not be remarkable, but unfortunately one boy in my class had the last name Bates and endured unbridled laughter every roll call. The last unique feature of Mr. Fraser was his malodorous air. I'm talking very serious body odour. I came to class with aerosol sprays, and Mr. Fraser seemingly never got the hint. Other people in class, girls in particular, brought out their perfumes and colognes to use as a kind of smelling salt, no doubt to keep them from yakking onto the floor. It was difficult to concentrate on algebra when you were trying so hard to breathe.

Another character was the Foods and Nutrition teacher. Mrs. Eccles was no more than 5 feet and 2 inches, over 50, she wore the black horn-rimmed glasses popular in the 1950's and she was slim, well actually, *very* slim. Now teen-age girls had enough trouble with feeling awkward and unattractive, but in this school we had the nutrition expert who was anorexic.

There were many such colourful 'teachers' at this school which definitely leant themselves to questioning just how far down on the shit list you had to be with the teachers' union to get a position in this school. But into our classes we were dutifully herded, and instructed in whatever manner the instructor felt accomplished the task. I just tried to focus on the fact that Bryn liked it when I went to classes. Bryn was like my father now. Don't drink coffee, no smoking, no drugs or alcohol –be a good girl Aileen. Whatever… It kind of irked me how I would do just about anything to keep him happy.

"Kat?"

"What?" Kat was digging through her bag looking for her familiar lunch that her mother tirelessly packed for her everyday.

"Who was Enoch? What is Enoch?" I asked stuffing my headcheese sandwich into my face, hoping that Kat wouldn't notice the type of sandwich I had because I love headcheese but everyone thinks I am a freak for liking it. She found her lunch, scowled at her chicken sandwich, and opened the plastic wrap.

"Isn't that from the Bible? Yes, I am pretty sure, Old Testament. More Rodan's area than mine – you should ask him, I bet he would love to help you." She raised an eyebrow at me and then popped a corner of her angle sliced sandwich into her mouth.

"Well that figures. I'll call him. What have you been up to lately? Have you and Rodan come to some kind of agreement?"

"Yes Dragon, I believe we have resolved our problems amicably and I am hopeful for the future."

"Great. I was worried about you two, I am glad you both figured it out." She smiled back at me.

"Don't you worry about us, we are fine. I am glad you are part of the group and I consider you an asset. I think you have potential."

I was very encouraged by her words and so thankful that Rodan hadn't completely screwed up everything between Kat and myself.

That night I got home and gave Rodan a call.

"Rodan, What can you tell me about Enoch and the descendants of Elohim?"

"Dragon. It is a pleasure to hear from you. I would love to tell you whatever you need to know. Enoch is the seventh generation from Adam and Eve. So he is an ancient figure in biblical terms. We are talking around the time of the flood, so he is pre-deluvian. Why?"

"The descendants of Elohim were betrayed by their desire? Desire for what?"

"Hmmm…I'm not sure I follow you. The descendants of Elohim, you must mean the sons of God, that's a controversial reference to Fallen Angels, watchers, the Nephilim. There are writings that are not part of the Bible's accepted cannon; you are talking about the Apocrypha and the Psuedepigrapha. But in an obscure section in Genesis where they go through the genealogy of Enoch and talk about how some 'sons of the true god" take on the daughters of men as wives and have children with them, these children are 'mighty' or like half-gods'. There is some controversy as to whether these 'son's of God' were angels or the direct lineage of Enoch. But regardless of whether you buy into the biblical version or the Book of Enoch, it is hotly debated amongst theologians that some divinely empowered men with lifespans close to millennia desired these beautiful, mortal women and it led them to defy God's laws and they begot children with them. These children, or Nephilim, were evil aberrations in the eyes of God, this was the main impetus for God bringing the flood. The creation of these children brought about the end of times for that age. Why are you curious about such an obscure part of the old testament?"

"Just doing my homework, you know –brushing up on biblical characters." I was trying to sound nonchalant but I was completely confused. So Bryn was trying to tell me he wanted me. But wasn't he also saying that having me was a sin? Maybe I was reading too much into it. Maybe he was a typical rock star and thought he was so much better than me that it was like a god being with a mere mortal. That lit my fuse.

"Thanks Rodan, I really appreciate your help."

"Not so fast, when do I see you again? Why don't we meet for lunch this Saturday and I would be happy to discuss any other biblical research you are doing." His voice was smooth and polite. He had an easy manner to him that was calming and reassuring and I found myself saying things I didn't want to.

"Sure, you gonna come pick me up?"

"Absolutely. I will come get you on Saturday at 11 am. I look forward to seeing you." He hung up the phone before I could change my mind or rethink what I was doing. I said yes while in the throes of thinking that being with Rodan would for sure piss off Bryn and I knew that he kept a tight enough surveillance on me, that he would know...oh yes, he would know. How dare he think himself so much better than me?

Saturday I sat in the livingroom in a skirt, with my hair done. Smooth walking and talking Rodan showed up fifteen minutes late and I ran down to his car, hoping that at any moment Bryn would make his usual call – that haunted voice in my ear. He opened the passenger door and then got in himself.

"You look very nice today, Dragon. How about Chinese?"

"Sure, I have never eaten a Chinese before; are they tasty?"

"Ha ha, very funny." We drove to a nearby restaurant and talked a bit about the Old Testament. I still wasn't exactly sure what Bryn meant by his comment but at least I discovered that his assistant, whom he called a watcher, was some kind of fallen angel. I just couldn't decide if that meant No was an angel, or a demon, or none of the above. After all, he did tell me to leave my Christian concepts here in the material plane. Rodan patiently answered my questions but then asked me about me. He smiled a lot and I could tell he was quite attracted to me. I found it a bit amusing that I had been pretty much ignored by guys and now I had two to contend with.

"Kat told me you and she talked? What have you two decided on?"

"Oh, we broke up. Did she not tell you?"

"Holy crap, no. Why did you two break up?"

"I think you know the answer to that?" He casually reached across the table and took up my hand in his and kissed my fingers. I just didn't know what to do or say, I was stunned.

"I like you a lot Rodan, but I don't think that I can do this." I may have been in the mood to piss off Bryn, but I didn't want to get involved with Rodan. My heart really wasn't into it. Somehow I felt I was spoken for. Bryn and I never had acted like a couple or discussed it, but Rodan's touch felt like a violation. Besides, even if Kat wasn't with Rodan anymore, it just felt wrong. I couldn't believe that I was the reason they broke up!

"You just need to relax, close your eyes, and enjoy the ride. You're just nervous." Well, I was nervous alright. I ate uncomfortably, went for a walk and then I made excuses so that he would take me home. Before I left the car though he planted a big kiss on my lips and I felt this unimaginable betrayal. I couldn't get over the feeling. I didn't even feel the kiss just the huge burden of disloyalty. Bryn's words were like knives in my heart, "I have to be able to trust you…" I walked into the house, feeling dirty. I had a bath. Of course you can predict what happened. I was enjoying my bubble bath my eyes closed and just about to relax when I heard his voice calling me.

"You're naked. I hope your friend is gone." I materialized on Bryn's bed, still wet from my bath. He was lying next to me.

"I was having a bath –alone."

"Look, I'm sorry I got so mad. There is a tremendous amount of pressure on me and you shocked me when you told me your age. I still can't believe it. I will not let our future obligations interfere with your life now. Do you forgive me?" He had rolled onto his side and with one hand on his head he was looking at me, his other hand playing with my wet hair; I think he touched my hair to avoid touching me. Or maybe, being the obsessive perfectionist he was, my tousled locks begged organizing.

"Of course." I reached my hand up to his, to liberate it from its task of mobilizing my hair away from my face. I folded my hand into his and moved it down to chest level.

"What are these timelines you are all worked up about anyways Bryn?"

"Just the things I want to accomplish and as you know, timing is critical."

"For what?"

"For now it is irrelevant, when the time comes, I will ensure you are prepared."

"Let me guess, I am too young right now to understand?" I shot back sarcastically, which won me a scowl from Bryn.

"You said it, not me. But I do have an important request, I need to ask you to do something for me."

"Anything Bryn, just ask."

"Promise you will save yourself for us."

"You mean…"

"Yes, I do."

Whoa, that was heavy. I had never seriously considered… well, the act itself before. Even when I did, I had more a guy my own age in mind. My stomach began to churn as I realized I had inadvertently agreed to something, with someone that scared the shit out of me. The mere subject caused me to become overwhelmed in shyness and embarrassment. I put on the bravest face I knew.

"How long would you mean for us to wait?"

"Hopefully, not until you are eighteen. Is that reasonable for you?" I exhaled and realized that I had been holding my breath.

"Yeah, I can do that. That's like four years away, it's no problem for me; what about you?"

"Actually, three and a half for you, half a century for me." He smiled and I could tell that he wasn't angry at me anymore. He sent me back to my bath and I was glad that he wasn't angry about the kiss. At what point does a ghostly manifestation decide that it is your lover? Who besides me would ever ask such a question? I was attracted to him, but I was scared of him as well. Wasn't I just a kid to him? There was another thought that crept into my head. The criminal interpretation. I don't know about UK laws, but in Canada, seduction of a minor was a crime and I knew I wasn't at the legal age of consent. I didn't know how old Bryn was, but he was easily ten years older than me, when I thought back to my childhood.

Rodan never called me out for another date. I confess at the time I didn't care, but in hindsight. I suspect one Mr. Bryn being somehow directly responsible.

I tried to not let my mind wonder onto painful thoughts and questions like, is Bryn a pedophile or did he scare Rodan? I enjoyed the times we were together. He talked to me about practicing the Craft. He would occasionally reward me with a story of his life and it helped me gain insight into the man. However, as our visits increased, I became aware of a growing frustration of our emotional closeness coupled with a complete lack of physical closeness; he must have been going mental! My mother always told me that men are by their nature weaker than women at resisting their carnal drives. This made me wonder how he controlled himself all this time we spent together. As time wore on and he continued to retain a parental distance from me, I jealously suspected that he had some English woman that was keeping him physically happy, perhaps a couple of them. But I also knew that no one could quench his deeper emotional thirst like I could. If there were such a person, he wouldn't always come looking for me.

From the time of our first contact in December to nearing the end of the school year in May, his continued self control made me angry because I was certain that he thought of me as a mere child being so many years his junior. My 'jealousy' eventually came out.

"You had better go home; I worry about your marks in school when you spend so much time here with me." Bryn was searching through his refrigerator for a can of pop.

I was lying on his large leather couch in the living room, which had a clear view of the kitchen. I sat up and crossed my legs. "Yeah, I am sure you have a big day ahead of you. So when you are not with a ghost, whom do you spend your time with?" I said in a bitter tone. He popped open the can and took a swig of Pepsi, gauging my body language.

"Aileen, you can't let yourself get distracted from your life in Canada. I have found you. You are going to go on and get on with your life. You are only what? Fourteen?"

"I am fifteen now!" I interjected.

"Fifteen is it? But we must wait; our time will come – take comfort in that." He sat in his wingback chair and eyed me with a fatherly glare and in his second swig probably downed half the can of pop. I crawled over to where his feet were and looked up into his eyes. He could see the mischief in mine, putting down his pop and smiling down at me. I pounced up on him, intending to pull him off the chair and onto the floor where I would wrestle him under me and pin his arms to either side of his head. I was only partially successful. As I pounced, a rather spectacular pounce I must say, he moved aside and snaked around to grab me by my waist. As if reading my thoughts, he instead wrestled me into the same prone position. I wriggled around like a slippery fish, got almost out of his grasp, tickled his sides, which caused him to cackle loudly and release his hold. I in turn sat on his pelvis and was about to move when I noticed a hard bulge under me. I paused and grinned back at him a little shyly, and stole a quick kiss from his lips before he threw me off of him.

"Enough! Go home. You try my patience so." He said jumping up from the floor and adjusting himself with a blushing face.

It was my second kiss on the lips from him, and I had to steal it. I wanted more, and I was so stubborn I thought I could convince him to give me at least a goodbye kiss.

"I won't go anywhere until you give me a kiss, a real kiss. Why do you treat me like a child?" I asked, folding my arms. He looked at me and I could feel his mind deep in my head. He was scanning my thoughts an altogether not entirely painless process. This was the first time I was aware that he was actually in my head, scanning my thoughts. How many times had he done this before?

"Do you think this is easy for me?" He moved to his chair and locked his eyes on mine. "Another lifetime, and yet again, I am sickened by my desire." He said in an almost whisper. I saw his temper beginning to surface again. It was the first time I ever felt I had gone too far, that I had ever truly felt shame for my careless words and boldness. All those years in school, where I didn't give a damn, and now I saw and understood how painful my impertinence could be. His eyes fixed on mine, he was probably still in my head, reading my thoughts like a book. He opened his arms and grabbed my shoulders, and looked down at me.

"A new incarnation, a new millennia, I am again haunted by guilt and shame. I will not to touch you, not till we are ready. I would never hurt you my angel, but never doubt how I feel about you." The intensity of his words echoed into my heart, like so many things about Bryn. As was so often the case, I looked up at him-- wide eyed like a little girl, naïve, innocent and quite awestruck with wonder. I feared him, I loved him, and he was my world – the only one I cared about.

"I Lo--",

"Shhhh!" Bryn interjected before I could say anything. He put his index finger over my lips, touching them, taking all desire to talk away from me, then he literally shooed me away. He talked about other lives and incarnations. If the emotions weren't so intense at the time, I would have asked questions. But I lost all sense of what he was really saying.

Chapter 6

Mornings in Vancouver, during the fall, winter and the spring really just equate to: grey skies, fog, rain, puddles, and an entire city full of people enduring Seasonal Affective Disorder. Like everyone else, the weather was beating me down. During the morning hustle, I was running in the rain to catch the eastbound express bus to South Burnaby. I snaked through the slow moving herds of people to get to the stop – I made it. Reaching into my pocket, I pulled out some change while showing my Fare-card so I didn't have to pay adult fare. I smiled to the bus driver and, of course, got no smile back. I slid my Walkman out of my pocket and pulled my headphones over my wet hair. By three songs I would be at my stop and I might not be late this time. As I walked towards the school I watched the water descend into puddles on the side of the road as the traffic sped by, wheeling chaotically in their frantic rush to get to work on time. I joined a couple of other teens as they gave the finger to the white Toyota Celica as it sped away after carelessly soaking us with muddy puddle water. I was cold, wet, dirty, and about to go to Royal Oak Jr. Secondary –fucking yeah.

Now May was about to be finished, my birthday passed and the good news was that the end of the rainy season was soon at hand, and as well, the end of the school year. Just before lunch Kat had Science and I had Math. Complete with the smell and the usual laugh at Master Bates, my math class went as per normal; the same could not be said for Kat in her class. During lunch she relayed what had happened during her class.

"Well Dragon, I think Darci Smith should be having a very interesting weekend indeed," she said, seating herself easily into a very narrow chair in a corner of a quiet classroom where she and I decided to have our lunch.

I looked down at her while I pulled my lunch out of my backpack. "Darci? Why would you think she would have an interesting weekend, I thought you didn't like her." I sat down and proceeded with inhaling my liverwurst sandwich.

"Today in class I brought one of my pictures which I have been working on. You know the picture of my familiar Thromm?"

"Which one was that Kat?"

"The one with him as a great winged beast at the dark gates; you know, the one done in pencil?"

"Oh yes, I think I remember that one."

"Anyway, I was finishing it – placing symbols on it and trying to imbue negative psychic energy into it. I was marvelling on how well I thought it had turned out when I could hear the Adivar teasing me from behind. Finally, Darci interrupted my peace and began to ask questions about the picture, laughing all along of course. Well, I couldn't resist the opportunity when she asked if she could have it. So I added to the picture a direction to the negative energy I had built within the page." There was pride in her expression, and I could tell she was looking for moral support. Did I mention I was a shit disturber?

"How did you direct it to her?" I asked genuinely curious.

"Simple. I scribed a curse to her on the back which read: To Darci Smith, a person whom I would like to show the things which may come." Kat grinned quietly; seemingly unfazed by the adolescent controversy she was creating in her class.

"You're telling me you just calmly and quietly turned over the paper and wrote that, and she never even thought that was odd?"

"Well, she read it, turned to her idiot Adivar friends snickering, and no doubt thought no more upon it. Of course, I think she will have an unpleasant next few days if I know Thromm."

"Kat, you realize you just purposely provoked that by bringing your material right into the classroom. Don't bullshit me; you did that on purpose because you wanted a guinea pig to test your spell craft." In her own way, Kat was cruel and vindictive, but unlike my approach where I take matters into my own hands, she would manipulate situations or rely on a spell to get even.

"And what if I did? It's not like she doesn't deserve to be my guinea pig."

"Well, I suppose you know what you are doing, right?" We talked a little more of what kind of things that could result from the curse. Kat was expecting things like nightmares, visions, and bad luck. Two more classes after lunch and that marked the end of our Thursday. Friday came and went, and though Darci Smith was not in school, no one took note as some of those Adivar girls drank heavily and did soft drugs from time to time and a missed day was fairly common. When Darci didn't show up for Monday or Tuesday however, people, even Adivar, began to notice.

Half way through Wednesday a somewhat transformed Darci wandered into class. She was without her usual heavy component of makeup, her hair dishevelled, and her face—pale, gaunt, and drawn. Immediately her closest friends surrounded her and asked all kinds of questions. Although we were not privy to the original statements of Darci herself, we certainly heard the version that spread like wildfire throughout the school. Apparently she had a few days of absolute, well, hell. She relayed to her friends, one of which told us that Darci had endured an extraordinary weekend. She had come home on that Thursday afternoon, and hung her newly begotten picture on her bedroom mirror, the best place to put a Wiccan invocation for maximum effect, worst place if you are the intended victim. That night she said she had seen the devil in the mirror, Thromm, no doubt. Her boyfriend, who had knowledge of the occult, told her that he would not have anything to do with her until she got rid of the picture, fearing his own safety. Darci thought her boyfriend was paranoid and cowardly and told him he was over-reacting.

However, for the rest of the weekend, she had apparently dreadful bad luck and misfortune, loosing friends, injuring herself and some damage of her personal items. As well, she reported that all weekend she had unrelenting insomnia, shakiness in her hands, an unsettling fear, and an inability to relax in any way. Finally, heeding her boyfriend's wise words, she threw the picture away. She did not burn it, the way it should have been handled; instead she just tossed it in the garbage. However, this seems to have broken the spell, and she slept on Tuesday night, though fitfully.

I expected Kat to dread this news. I expected Kat to feel exposed, that her abilities and the 'rumours' of her being a witch as being no longer rumours, requiring Adivar to punish her. But instead of her feeling scared in any way, she gloated. She was obviously very proud of herself. The fact that more happened to Darci than she had intended didn't seem to bother her at all. I must also confess that this caused me to reconsider my own opinion of her ability. She obviously could cause some things to happen in an unexplained manner as just one look at Darci that day told volumes. I thought about two things: that either Kat's alignment or association with Thromm had a serious thread of overt cruelty. By alignment I mean that the poling of negative energy to spell craft might be the cause of this tendency towards the cruelty. I knew that she was in regular congress with this familiar. This familiar was most likely a negatively poled spirit, who knew what kind of spirit it was? I had serious concerns over Kat being potentially dangerous as much as in danger.

The reaction of the students also surprised and seemed to warn me. I was expecting a real avalanche of harassment and potential danger for Kat. But instead it seemed as though most of the student body really feared her. Aside from the odd comment or sneer, they just stayed clear – gave her a wide berth. It was really kind of spooky.

However, the Adivar were not without their usual accouterments of tricks. For whatever reason, they seemed to take their hostility out on me! I wasn't even in that class, but I got the brunt of the abuse. They hurled insults at me and told me I was a freak for hanging out with Kat. At this point I was getting upset at the school population and I blamed Kat for this situation. Probably more importantly, at this point Kat actually succeeded in scaring me. I felt that I had learned all I could from Kat, as Bryn was obviously teaching me now and his skills far outshone Kat's. As Kat appeared to have little regard for the bullshit she had put me in, I decided it would be in my best interest to cave in and stop hanging out with Kat at least in school. Her ability to do stuff through Thromm's spirit ended it for me. I knew what Bryn could do and that was bad enough.

I waited until we had our next ECAW meeting to tell Kat I didn't want to hang around with her anymore at school.

"Kat, as you know that shit you pulled at school has put me in a pretty bad situation and I just think that since school is almost over, I need to keep a low profile. I don't need the abuse."

"For the sake of a few Adivar you are going to cast aside your teacher?"

"Well actually lately, you haven't been any help for me on that front. But some of the stuff that has been going on lately kind of has me freaked. Thromm really freaks me out. I am worried about what is happening to you, I think Thromm is changing you."

"So now that you have the ECAW knowledge you think you can just bail out and that I shall just watch and wave good-bye?"

"You know what Kat? I am not saying that I will bail from ECAW. But you put us into this situation and so I am TELLING you that I am bailing from you at that fucking school."

"Take heed Dragon. I took thee under my wing, I have shared sacred knowledge and I shall extract vengeance if you back down from your vows to the group and to me." She said in a quiet, guttural voice that actually was kind of amusing – if it wasn't for the fact that I kept thinking about Thromm.

"Kat, I don't want to start a war with you. I am just tired of putting up with the bullshit at school."

"The Adivar are children."

I realized that she would not understand. She was accustomed to continual abuse by peers and she could shut them out utterly, as opposed to me who had a limit. In anger and frustration, I left her there at Central Park thinking I had dealt with the whole stupid business.

I woke up the next day to find my favourite ring broken. Yup, the band was split. How the hell did that happen? Well, to tell you the truth, one word: witchcraft. Kat obviously thought that my ring must be my source for focusing energy, which is common in witchcraft. Certain metals, crystals, as well as places, can be charged with energy. The idea of a wizard with a magic sceptre isn't so far off from reality. I actually had no enchanted items. Behind Kat's back I had been so busy with Bryn, and he removed any fear I had for my spirit or my mortal coil that I never thought to ward or protect myself or provide for myself any enchantments. I needed nothing; I had Bryn. I was mad because I was careless and hadn't yet sealed my room, however, as Kat said before, if I had sealed my room, it would not have been strong enough to keep Kat's power out anyways. But I knew she magically entered my room and broke my ring and that pissed me off. Kat had started a little war.

Sure enough, I went to school and there was Kat, grinning from ear to ear. She was trying to make it known to me that she was wholly responsible for my ring's destruction. I wanted to kick her minuscule butt, but I thought I would give her a taste of her own medicine instead. So that very night after school I set about to attempt the same spell. I was at a disadvantage from the start for two main reasons. One, I didn't have her experience, and two, I had not armed myself with any energy focusing amulets. I focused my energy from the same place I got the energy to meet Bryn and directed that energy to Kat's place and went about attempting to infiltrate her heavily sealed room. Busily looking for any item of value of hers from outside of her warded room, I located her onyx necklace. I attempted to the point of headache to destroy it, but could not. It was either protected or the power in it was too great. I needed another option ... so in desperation, I did the only thing I had power enough to do – I hid it.

I don't think that she noticed it missing for a while because she never approached me nor did anything peculiar for quite some time. I was confident this would not last for too long. I saw her at school on Monday, and she didn't look too happy. I sneered back at her, hoping she got the point to stop harassing me. Of course, I foolishly forgot that she had a trump card.

Early June isn't when you would normally see evening fog in Vancouver, this June evening was an exception. So, as per my habit, I was in bed at around 11pm. Soon my lights were off and I was relaxing, happy that the school year was soon over, and contemplating when I would see Bryn again as it had been awhile since I had last seen him. My dresser was across my room and as I was getting ready to fall into the world of dreams I thought I would go to my dresser and brush my hair before bed. I looked at my reflection that showed the opposite wall, with the window revealing the blackened world outside on the second floor.

I tried to see if I could find the moon or any other celestial body in the fog, thinking of how proud I was of my achievement with Kat's necklace when from above I caught from the corner of my eye two piercing, glowing red eyes. I felt a cold clamping in my neck, when I tried to scream. Frozen, I saw slight movement and caught the fading moonlight glisten on what looked like a v-shaped mouth with razor-sharp mercurial fangs. I don't remember if I fainted, or just sat in silent shock for a long time staring at the window. But the eyes blinked, moved, and then vanished -- absolutely terrifying! I kept asking myself why it hadn't come inside the room since I had no wards or seals – very unsettling. I tried to tell myself that I imagined it, that it was a nightmare. But I knew like everyone knows when something horrible happens whether you imagined it or not. I wanted out of this nasty exchange, I wanted out of Wiccan dabbling, I feared for both of us. I couldn't beat her at her game, but then I remembered my game.

The following day I approached Kat.

"If you do one more magical thing to me, if you send Thromm to me one more time, you better make sure you remove my ability to walk cuz I swear I will kick your fucking ass!" I roared. I didn't wait for response; instead I walked away the anger in me almost beyond my control.

I suppose the fear of another visit from Thromm probably compelled me as much as my affection for Bryn, when I found myself that very night looking for him.

"Bryn, if you can hear me, I really miss you." I said under my breath, feeling the power of the request resonate all through me. I could feel myself pulling, reaching all the way to England for him. Immediately I was mad at myself for feeling so helpless. But my request was unanswered, and when Bryn was unavailable there was a block that would not allow me to even see his house. I would have to wait for another day, it was the second night in a row when I really needed to be with him – I had never felt so alone.

Summer Soltice was the last ceremony before the summer break up. ECAW as part of our observance to old Wiccan traditions we had to get together. Rodan came and told us he was leaving the group and Kat seemed to know this ahead of time. There was just Tyra, Kat and myself then. The other part of ECAW was who would be leader of the group for the following year. I had no idea that it would involve a physical competition, considering that all of our pursuits seemed to be of a non-physical nature. Kat, being more of a lover type than a fighter, just handed it over to me. I was surprised that her ego was okay with that, particularly after everything we had gone through. Maybe it was the fact that she knew in a dual, I'd win. Her description of Napoleon and cowardice came to my mind. Was Kat a coward? Right now, I would have looked forward to an opportunity to upstage Kat physically. I also thought about Rodan, who seemed to be ignoring me, where was the Don Juan I went on a date with?

The rest of the school year went off without too much friction between Kat and myself. Finally June 18th marked summer holidays, and I, like the rest of the populace of that school, rejoiced. The annuals were out all over the school grounds on that last day of class, young people running from person to person to have their annuals signed. I didn't attend photo day, so only a silhouette was above my name. I didn't go to any of my classes that day, but I was smoking a cigarette on the school grounds, watching the rabble laughing, talking loudly, and signing furiously each other's books. I watched but I was deep in thought. Where was Bryn? It had been months since I last saw him. That Talisman must have a lot of power associated with it. He told me a whole genealogy of the stupid thing and I just couldn't remember it... something about Moses, and some Shemzai person that was cursed? I needed to do some more research. I wonder if Bryn would give me answers or more riddles.

Chapter 7

East Vancouver isn't what one would call the ideal part of this glorious city. In fact it was the area where most of the immigrants lived. My neighbours were Italian, East Indian, Native, German, Ukrainian, Yugoslavian, Irish, and the few 'true' Canadians were usually the single mothers on welfare. There were all kinds of gangs, doing all kinds of crimes and all kinds of drugs. Ah yes, it was home. It is no wonder I spent almost no time in this particular neighbourhood. I usually went to the West end of Vancouver.

Vancouver's West end is the safe area, home to the Gay community and the prostitutes were being 'pushed' out. Providing you had no problems with gays, this was a great, safe part of the inner city. I had no problems with gays, I mean it's not like they ever hit on me. This was the perfect environment to keep me out of trouble and to keep my promise to Bryn. So I spent my time either with Tyra or some of my other friends and hung out on Davie St., Granville St. or Robson St. There were always books, magazines, T-shirts, and of course, records to buy. Just being down there and being part of the environment was probably the coolest part. There were three or four movie theatres all on Granville St. so I was never bored. The summer progressed with me going about my usual unproductive business of adolescence:

ignoring my parents, spending whatever money I had on clothes, pop, and records, and hanging out with my friends. I generated cash flow from delivering newspapers, doing chores for my dad, and baby-sitting. I was in a blissful state of normalcy…

"Aileen? Where are you? Come to me, I need you now!" If it weren't for the fact that it was very early in the morning and I was brushing my teeth on the second floor of our house at the time, I would have thought the voice came from outside. But those clues plus the fact that I had goose bumps up and down my back told me for sure that the voice was in my head. The voice kept repeating itself, the voice I recognized so well, him. So insanity was coming back. I went into my room, laid down and focused on emptying my mind of all thoughts and surrender consciousness from here in East Vancouver to Surrey, England.

As my focus cleared, I could see him. He was in his living room on his couch. The heavy curtains were closed tight and the lights were dim, and Bryn was wearing a housecoat.

"Where have you been all these months?" I asked with poorly veiled hostility.

Bryn opened his eyes slowly, and the small light danced beautifully in his large blue-grey eyes. They seemed to always change colour.

"I'm running a business, a high profile business. Whenever my schedule allows I seek you out – trust that my luv." He said in a strained patient voice.

"With all the bad press I've been getting lately, I thought I could benefit from your magical embrace." Without moving his eyes from me, he raised his arms.

I walked over to him and I could feel my spirit form rigidity. I could feel the warmth of his body pushing against mine, and his arms across my back. His face nudged against mine and I could feel the rasp of his stubbly chin. Ahhhh…That wonderful feeling of wholeness was back. Bryn's life was a matter for public records, I knew all about the reports from England's press. After all, I went to all the import magazine shops in Vancouver and read all the English gossip papers. There were articles that slammed Bryn for his innovative music, charging that this new music sensation was a charismatic performance to brainwash young people into buying all his music. They also maligned his personality, referencing interviews where he seemed distant and non-communicative, or shockingly sincere, brutally honest, which inevitably causes animosity in the artificial 'GLAM' world. I held him in my almost solid arms and did not tell him that I knew, as it was bad enough all of England and Europe had this gossip. I didn't want him to think it was all over North America too. After a time, he let go and I stepped back finding his big over-stuffed chair to curl up in.

"So what has been keeping you occupied lately Aileen?" He asked shifting his housecoat while sprawling himself out like a cat along the couch. I told him about all the movies I had gone to, the walks around the sea wall by myself and with friends and that I hadn't practiced any magic, well, until this moment.

"Why are you stopping now my sweet? You are so well disciplined. You are to be with me and that means a lifer." A lifer is one who actively practices the Craft for life.

"Bryn." I paused. Magic came so natural to him. He was so comfortable about it. Even Kat wasn't as comfortable as Bryn.

"You know I have a friend named Kat?" I continued.

"Yes?"

"Well, I believe she draws her energy from the negative poles. It is powerful, but I know it bears a terrible cost. I think she realizes the cost, but doesn't care." I then proceeded to tell him of what had happened before the end of school and I told him about Thromm.

"She did WHAT?" Bryn's already large eyes seemed to conquer his face, filling with annoyance.

"Thromm is her familiar. I suppose she thought it would send me a message and scare me. I am sure she didn't mean me any serious harm…"

"Your friend Kat can do this? She broke a ring of yours?

"Yeah."

"Impressive skill for one so young. So your friend has a familiar? Bugger. I will have to take care of this now." He reached for my hands and looked into my eyes and said, "I must set to protecting you! It is my fault; I should have done this sooner. You are my responsibility – I'll 'ave a word with 'er."

"But I…"

"Not another word." He said shushing me. He pulled out his rock from the pocket in his housecoat, grabbed my hand and placed my ring finger on top of it and muttered something in some foreign language. He then got up walked to the kitchen and came back with a fairly large knife in his right hand. He bypassed his big chair and swept up next to me.

"Look into my eyes Aileen." I obeyed and felt a tingle, much like when you get an electrical shock. His eyes kept mine locked with his, and his hand laid on top of mine for a time, maybe 4 or 5 minutes. He then smiled, kissed my nose in a fatherly way. When I looked down and saw his hand on top of mine, he had a gash between his index finger and his thumb. When he pulled his hand away, I saw that I had a gash in the exact same spot on my hand. Our blood had mingled; he then ran upstairs and came back down to where I was, admiring my wound. Somehow he had managed to cut himself and cause the same injury on me in the exact same spot.

"I was going to give this to you anyways." He held up a gold ring with a green stone in it. He put the ring on my ring finger and covered it with his injured hand and then held for a while.

"Aileen, this ring of protection can't cross the spirit world with you; I will mail it to you and please promise to always wear it." I was about to say something to Bryn, something like, "What was that for?" or the reasonable equivalent but I opened my eyes and found myself in my room. Well that confession had ruined my evening with Bryn, causing it to be short-lived. I lifted my injured hand to my face, and saw that there was a little blood and I could definitely sense a power emanating from my hand and coursing its way throughout my body. I got up, walked over to the mirror and looked at my reflection to brush my hair. I could feel I was a little drunk from the sensations moving from my hand to the rest of my body, I began giggling uncontrollably and I completely forgot that Bryn had said something about 'talking' to Kat. Within two weeks I received the ring at the post office and had to sign for it. The ring perfectly fit my ring finger. I couldn't believe I was wearing a ring he got for me.

Chapter 8

A Kat goes to the Okanagan

I couldn't wait to get away from Vancouver, my parents, that horrid school and Dragon. As much as Vancouver is a city with a wet, temperate environment, Naramata, a small hamlet near Penticton in contrast is a sunny, semi-arid part of British Columbia that truly warms my heart. Dragon certainly had been an energetic addition to the ECAW group although I knew full well that her physical disposition would probably be a recurring problem. Beauty is a liability. Although I knew that she held no affection for Rodan, his quick betrayal made me hate that aspect of Dragon – men were inextricably drawn to her. I dispatched with him of course. I banished him from the group, as I could not work with a Warlock and boyfriend who thought he could play me for a fool. I wasn't upset that Dragon wanted to forgo being around me at school, although I let her believe that. I didn't like how she was able to dethrone the cool-headed heart of Rodan – that truly stung. ECAW is a group concept and I had serious concerns that she would continue to complicate any male inductees. I found myself battling the dilemma of retaining Dragon as she was a boisterous and exuberant addition to the group, or getting rid of her due to her overriding liability.

This summer was turning out to be an excellent distraction from my woes with ECAW. Aphrodite may not have cursed me quite as much as she did Dragon. I am not without my feminine wiles. While at this camp, I have found a new young man to fill my days. In fact, there are a few young men that I thought could have potential as aspiring warlocks in our group. The first young man was named Trent Hammond; a tall, slim, blonde the same age as I and, like myself, a great lover of books. Trent was definitely the one to whom I was becoming attached. Jason Ferguson was the eldest, and the shy quiet one. And finally, a redhead named Lance Pierce. Of course before I would tell any of them anything, I had my bag of questions that I ask anyone I consider joining the group.

I was disappointed with Trent because in areas of Wicca he showed the least potential. It did not make me like him any less, but I knew I would have to assure him that it was a kind of club and not in fact a Wiccan Coven. It was clear to me that the one of the group I could be completely direct with was Lance. He was easier to talk to than even Dragon.

One evening when I was going back to my cabin after spending a fairly romantic sunset with Trent, I happened to see Lance heading down the main road towards Okanagan Lake.

"Lance, wait up…" I yelled running to catch up with him. He just stopped, without turning around as though he knew I was trying to catch up with him.

"Lance, I want to talk to you. Are you heading back to Penticton?" I asked.

"Yes, I am going to the lake to meditate then I will be returning to the city, I'll be back in a couple of days." He smiled.

"Well I wanted to talk to you about this group I was telling you and Trent about."

"What?"

"Actually, it isn't actually a mindless inner circle of friends. It's a little more involved than that, I just don't want to really tell Trent too much as I can tell he wouldn't handle it as well as you." At this Lance smiled some more, his pale blue eyes glowing, his bright red hair returning the glow in the setting Okanagan sun.

"Intrigue. Well you had better tell now." He continued his walk to the lake and expected me to follow him.

"ECAW studies and practices various forms of Wicca." I said, watching Lance's expression intently, hoping I had judged his personality correctly.

"Really. How long have you been at the Craft Kat?" His choice of words surprised me, as usually only Wiccan's refer to it as 'the Craft'.

"Five or six years. Are you still interested?"

"Absolutely. Don't worry about Trent, I won't tell him. Why would you want him in this group when you know how narrow-minded he can be about these things?" He asked in a very genuine tone. I really liked that about Lance.

"I am hoping between you and I that we can turn him around." I replied.

"Well Trent is about as mentally flexible as I am physically, so we would have our work cut out for us. Perhaps he would be willing to change for someone he loves." At the sound of those words I just melted. The tantalizing thought that Trent might actually really have a big crush on me, or even better, fall in love with me sent my heart sailing into the stratosphere. We made it to the lake and it was starting to get dark so, with a farewell, I left Lance to do his thing while I made my way back to my cabin – floating on a cloud.

The following day we were all sitting under the cherry trees by Jason's house eating cherries and drinking beer. I noticed Lance take a deep gulp of his beer and peer at Trent with a decidedly evil grin and a wink towards me.

"The local church here truly does have a remarkable collection of leatherbound antique books. I bet they are worth a fortune; eh Trent?" Trent returned Lance's smile and also took a sip of beer, a much smaller sip of beer.

"No doubt about it; why?"

"Just wondered what would happen if one day the minister showed up and found them all missing?"

"They would round up the usual suspects and Trent would be chief among the invited guests..." Jason interjected returning Lance's grin with a raised eyebrow which one could instantly tell was a fatherly way of telling Lance to stop egging Trent on. It was obvious that Lance was in rare spirits and wasn't about to be brow beaten by the reasoning and rational pragmatism of Mr. Ferguson.

"They could round me up, but they would need proof before they could hang me, eh Lance?" Trent said, smiling broadly at me and inviting my opinion on yet another crazy act of hooliganism being forged in my midst.

"ECAW is not above acquiring knowledge from dubious tactics and sources." I replied as I didn't much care for the shenanigans, but truly wouldn't mind acquisition of such wonderful books.

"What could be nobler than risking great odds to win the affection of a fair maiden?" Lance raised his beer bottle towards me, downing what was left in it, and winked at Trent.

"Well, in that case, I will not need help from either of you, as I am quite capable of stealing into the church myself." Trent had barely finished his sentence when Lance burst out in laughter and with eyes moist and shining said,

"Quite so, quite so. To Trent, our hero for all our crazy exploits!" This caused Trent to puff out his chest and bang one fist on it, likening himself to a gorilla. Simultaneously, Jason shook his head and frowned at Lance – utterly aware of the fact that Lance was in his own way showing off his superior intellect to me.

That very night Trent stole into the church and with a large bag in hand proceeded to bring out as many books as he could carry. He then expertly snuck away to hide his ill-gotten booty. But that wasn't enough trickery for our dear friend. He also put all the song books in the men's bathroom, stacking them up by the urinal. Without Jasons' knowledge,

Trent hid his sack of stolen property in the garage of Jason's house, and begged me to maintain silence of exactly what he had done.

The next day as predicted the clamour began. Jason came to gather us all and then informed us that the minister's assistant found the songbooks next to the men's urinals in the washroom. Some were damp, as the urinals are old and leaked. Ten songbooks were far too wet and malodorous to be returned to the church pews.

"The minister is beside himself in anger. He never mentioned the books though. Where are they Trent?" Asked Jason sincerely.

"Don't worry Jase, I got 'em someplace they will never look."

"Well for your sake I hope so; you were the first name the minister mentioned." He said he was going to ask certain key people what they knew and you were among the first. I suggest you work on your alibi." Turning his head from Trent, Jason smiled at me and walked away, in the direction of his house.

"See ya tomorrow at the lake Jason!" Trent called to him as he walked away.

The following day was Saturday. Lance was back up in Naramata and we had all agreed to meet at the lake for some much needed cooling off in the shade and swimming.

"Where is Jason? It's 2:00 pm. He doesn't sleep in this much on the weekends." Lance said to Trent signalling for him to get out of the water.

"You worried?" Asked Trent, pausing from his playing with me. We were tossing a Frisbee back and forth while in the water. Lance paused before speaking.

"Yeah, I have this feeling that something is up. Let's go to his place and see." Lance turned off his ghetto blaster and put a bookmark in the book he was reading to signal his haste. I didn't know what to make of it but Trent seemed to respond instantly to the gravity in Lance's voice and, retrieving the Frisbee, headed for his towel on the shore. He looked back at me and motioned with his head to follow him.

We headed up the hill to the road and then meandered our way to Jason's house. We barely got a view of it when we saw a police car pulled up in the driveway. Lance instantly turned to Trent,

"We better make sure no one found your books. Where did you hide them?" Lance asked.

Trent's eyes widened and then he bit his lower lip as if to stifle a swear word.

"Where are they?" Lance repeated annoyed. Something in Lance's tone made me wonder if he somehow knew the answer to his question.

"I hid them in Jason's garage..."

"You did WHAT?" Lance stared at Trent in disbelief, he shook his head then ran both hands along either side of his forehead pushing his bangs back as if warding off a bad headache.

"Did you know this Kat?" He looked at me with an intensity and scrutiny that made me feel like I was a kid with the hand in the cookie jar. I just stared at him not knowing what to say.

"Oh, Christ Kat, why didn't you tell Trent to find a different spot –Jason is going to fry for this, his dad is the head councillor of Naramata!" Lance continued to rub his temples.

I had actually gone in stealth the previous night and had taken five of the books that I really wanted for the ECAW collection. But there was no way I was going to tell Lance and Trent that now.

"If I was Jason, I would rat you out!" Lance spat at Trent. Trent just sneered at Lance.

"Jason is a true friend, he will find a way to get out of this – he is the Teflon man, shit doesn't stick to him. He would never rat me out!" Trent spat back to Lance.

The two guys split company on that hill and I did not follow either. Feeling so worried about Jason, I had to see him. I made my way to his front door, bypassing the police cruiser.

I knocked at the door and Mrs. Ferguson answered.

"Hi Mrs. Ferguson is Jason home?" I asked doing my best to appear utterly unaware of the police car.

"Jennifer, Jason is in a meeting. Could you come by tomorrow?" She said as eloquently as she could. I saw through the opening of the door that there was a policeman talking to Jason's dad and Jason was sitting next to his father.

"Is Jason okay?" I asked, as it was obvious that I was looking at the policeman sitting by Jason and his dad.

"We hope so." His mother replied before shutting the door.

Sunday the day of church, and we all went. I have to of course, as it is a mandatory part of this camp – Bible camp. The entire Ferguson family was there, and I waited for any expression from Jason. However, I got no indication of anything during the service. I had to wait to jump him after church.

"What did the cops want?" I caught him as he exited the church quietly and headed towards the road.

"Meet me at the park in ten minutes. Bring everyone." Jason then walked over to his dad to talk to him for a moment. I dutifully dug up the guys and we all headed over to the park – more of a kid's playground. Not long after we got there Jason sauntered across the field in his nice grey suit towards us.

"Are you okay man?" Trent broke the silence. Jason cast an irritated look at Trent.

"My father stumbled upon the stolen books which were hidden in our garage. He immediately contacted the minister, who then called the police. The police questioned me and of course my father provided me with a solid alibi. I was home all evening both nights in question and so was incapable of being linked in the theft. The minister then told police that it was likely one of my friends, namely a Mr. Trent Hammond. The police then approached me again looking for a witness or confession from myself to incriminate you." He glared at Trent again.

"However, I assured them that if it was any of my friends they certainly would not leave stolen merchandise around my house where it would be sure to be found, and the blame placed squarely on me." They seemed convinced that it had to be another hooligan, likely some young person who didn't like me. They then asked me to name some local young people who may want to get me into trouble." Trent looked at Lance and grinned.

"Told ya, Jason is the Teflon man! You the shit Jason!"

"Trent. The next time you get suckered into going off half cocked by that instigator Lance, I am going to see that you get hanged!" Jason looked at Trent menacingly, he then punched him in the shoulder and laughed out loud.

"Christ Trent you are a fucking shit head – you know that? I was so scared when my dad and the police came to me that I nearly shat my pants! I thought for sure this time I wasn't going to be able to slither us out of it." Jason continued laughing but amidst the light heartedness and hilarity of Trent, Jason and I, Lance wasn't joining in. Lance looking rattled, sitting on the picnic table, oblivious to the frivolities. As I watched him, I also stopped laughing and tried to read his thoughts. It was clear he realized that his fun at pushing Trent into stupid games would inevitably one day cost his dearest friend Jason his freedom or at least his reputation. It was the first time I could really tell that Lance deeply cared about anyone. His bond to Jason was infinitely deeper than the one with Trent. I wonder how long this game between the three of them had been going on.

So my summer progressed. Trent was fearless and loved to show off, Lance was smart and aloof often demonstrating exasperation at having to communicate with people of normal intelligence, and Jason, sensible, pleasant and able to relay stories that imparted magic to this part of the world. For my part, I thoroughly enjoyed being the token female. I dreaded the impending day when this would end. There was one other nagging complication that troubled my otherwise bliss. How would these guys react to Dragon? I didn't really want Trent to meet her. But maybe, just maybe I could distract her with Jason. Sensible, polite Jason –Dragon would love him.

It was our last day together; somehow Vancouver and the return to school were looming on the horizon like clouds threatening my peace. Trent and I had this whole day together, and I was determined to spend it with him alone. "Damn," I found myself sighing to myself, "I'm falling pretty hard for this wonderfully fun loving and carefree spirit." Trent was such a refreshing change from the intense and serious Rodan. It's was a sunny day and we walked, hand in hand to the small convenience store in the village, as there was only one cure for such hot summer days — Popsicles. I decided to wait outside and enjoy the sun while Trent went in to get us some sodas, popsicles and cigarettes for himself.

I was not going to be indoors at all today. I would be back to Vancouver soon enough with its miserable rain and grey clouds. How different the weather is, five hours drive from this paradise. The thought of having to return to that horrible school and boring myself through yet another year, being away from Trent instantly depressed me. I forced myself to not dwell upon tomorrow and instead revel in today. The intensity of the heat was wonderful and as Trent entered the store I wandered into the full sun across the street next to the adjacent orchard. Suddenly, a black crow flew right at me,-swooping down low as I jumped back and ducked to avoid it. Well, a visit from my minion, Thromm was a surprise; I made my way to a grove of apple trees not far from the convenience store to see what he wanted.

"Thromm you mischievous misanthrope, go whence you came, I need you not today." I said with all the lilt and lightness I could when in so good a mood. However, when I made it to where the crow left I heard a rustle of grass and branches behind me. I turned and, was confronted by the manifestation of a man, all in unnatural shadows below a hulking willow tree at the corner of the orchard. I tried to focus, but couldn't make out any face. I felt my heart racing in my chest, as I jumped back, startled. I knew at that instant that this was not Thromm! Suddenly, an invisible hand clenched vice like against my throat, my eyes widening with fear as it tightened, choking off my breath.

"So you are Kat. Good. I will bypass any introduction and make this short; you will find little sport in Aileen as of now. You will assure me that after our little talk; you will cause her no further grief nor visits from your familiar lest you enjoy this kind of suffering. Further, you will not worry Aileen by confiding in our little meeting." My body was incapable of moving, I felt paralyzed.

My mind was thinking quickly, who was this? What was this? What did he mean "little sport?" He obviously knew I sent Thromm to Aileen; this spirit did a good job of imitating him. What kind of demon would have this kind of magic in the material plane? Suddenly, my sense of pride welled up and I thought to myself, 'Who did this bastard think he was, to talk to me in such a way? The nerve...' I stared back defiantly trying desperately to perceive any clue as to who this assailant was. I tried to make out any facial clues. There was nothing to perceive, except that voice...something familiar – the accent!

"Do I make myself clear, Kat?" the voice said as I began to feel faint and I thought to myself that I had better acknowledge what he said before he rendered me unconscious. I nodded my head, and thank the gods, he released his hold. I put my hands to my neck and the shade quickly vanished, dissolving into afternoon sun and heat.

I stood there, stunned. I had nothing to go on, except a voice. But that voice, something about it was familiar, I was pretty damn sure I had heard it before. What if Dragon was not lying? What if that god damn musician was a warlock! How on earth could a fledgling Wiccan like Dragon find a warlock not only with that kind of power, but so unswervingly protective of her already? First, I would have to find out who this musician was. Then I would make Dragon suffer the consequences of keeping secrets from her teacher.

The young men I had met here in the Okanagan all wanted to be part of ECAW, and did not know Dragon. If I could build ECAW in my favour, find the source of this warlock's power and figure out how to attain it, my work would be done. It should be about as easy as apple pie. I knew that when I got back to Royal Oak I would have to mend the rift between Dragon and myself in order to win back her trust. Then, I could squeeze her for information on her protector. I knew one thing, as a rock star he could in no way have as much time as I to study and plan – my advantage. I heard Trent calling for me and I ran out of the orchard. Trent peered around the bushes looking for me; I turned around, forced a smile on my face and ran after him.

Chapter 9

Well the summer, as it always does, came and went and as usual I made many resolutions to be more organized, stay on top of all my subjects and to get better marks. One by one each of these resolutions was broken and cast aside. I detested the gloomy school, which bore a striking similarity to a mental institution. I tired of the instructors, whose daily diatribe bore the same pain-stricken effort and enthusiasm as any individual having a tooth pulled without benefit of Novocain. I couldn't tolerate being around the morose student body of nobodies – content to go on to lead productive lives as welfare recipients, drug addicts, or for the seriously ambitious, –criminals. I found myself getting on the bus in the morning and for some inexplicable reason, not getting off. No, I just kept riding that bus. I would wind up either in Port Coquitlam or sometimes I would turn myself around and go to the West End, escaping the oppression that was weighing me down.

But somewhere else, deep inside, something was getting stronger. Perhaps it was the blood rite between Bryn and I, or maybe I was just growing up. Whatever the reason, I felt an inner awakening getting stronger within me, a voice that was increasingly more my own. I felt a hunger to learn more, to be more—a need to go out into the world and explore. I became aware of my growing frustration that I was not as good at casting spells as Kat. I knew that because her abilities were strong, that it would drain her – it would explain her fragile appearance. 'Divine understanding requires it's own price...' I remembered Kat mentioning during one of our first conversations about Wicca. She later explained to me that the greater the magic cast, the greater the mortal toll. The tale of the haggish old witch would have come from the ancient knowledge that greater power requires sacrifice. She liked using her magic and I knew that it was draining her energies, manifesting it physically. I thought about Bryn, he sure dealt out the magic –surely that Talisman couldn't have been absorbing all of the drain he would be paying. There is this deadly dance between power and mortality being played out in Wicca, and I was just scratching the surface of it.

I wondered how deep into this dance Kat and Bryn were willing to go – how deep I would go... When I did go to school, I'd be sitting in class, half listening to the teachers and half thinking about why the use of magic required a physical mortal toll. I realized I would have to research the roots of all this and discover what makes it work – the physics of the paranormal. I was so involved I barely paid attention to the entire Samhaen ceremony when it blew by in October. I remember the new recruits from the Okanagan were unable to make it. I wasn't going to meet them for another couple of weeks.

After spending a rather exhaustive day in the archives and libraries at the University of British Columbia in their ancient history sections and library for the physics and physical sciences I headed on the bus for home. It was dark by the time the Broadway bus deposited me off at Broadway and Rupert. I had no desire to wait for the bus and decided to just walk up the hill towards home, so I could just digest more of the research I had been reading. I got down the hill to the train tracks when I had to look behind me because I could hear footfalls. I turned around and there was no one. Of course I kept hearing them. Normally, something like this would freak out a person. For me, this is normal --Bryn was around. When I was a girl I used to always look behind me, hoping to see someone there. I was always so sad when I never saw anyone. But I knew I was never alone. He was always there; I just couldn't see him. The really weird thing was when Bryn told me he experienced the exact same thing. I remembered following Peter Pan around lots. I would hide from him and laugh – he too, could sense me.

"Bryn, I am not home. I am still about 40 minutes from home." I said to the air quietly.

"Go sit at the next bus stop and get home sooner." I could hear the whisper in my ear.

"Will you make it worth my while?" I asked, being bellicose as usual.

"You couldn't handle me making it worth your while Aileen. Now get home, I need to see you."

I instantly took that as a challenge.

"Try me."

"Watch this." He said. With that I saw a gathering shadow in front of me take on an almost tangible form and then it spread into bat-wings and appeared to fly to the next bus stop that was on 12th and Rupert. The shade then turned into a solid human form, Bryn. He was standing on the stop beckoning me to join him at the bus stop. I ran like an idiot to the bus stop to catch up to him. I was just so excited to see him in Vancouver, maybe even take the bus with me. I reached the intersection and stood on the opposite side of the highway staring at him as he smiled and waved for me to hurry up and join him. When the lights changed I was running again towards him. As soon as I was even near his side of the intersection, he vanished. I was about to get very upset when I noticed the lights of the bus heading down towards the tracks, I knew I would soon be home and with him anyways. I couldn't believe that he could just appear like he did, could he always? Why hadn't he done it before?

When I got home and in trance I saw his livingroom was dimly lit by white stick candles that encircled the room. Sitting on the overstuffed leather chair sat Bryn looking at me while I formed in front of him, his Talisman clearly visible in his hand as he watched me.

"Why were you out so late?"

"Doing some research. How am I to know when you decide to drop in?" I walked to the couch and sat down aware that his stare was fixed on me. He was in that parental mood I could tell.

"Is it not a new moon?"

"You don't always come on new moons, Bryn."

"When I do it is, November 26 – yes definitely a new moon."

"So I have to be home every new moon?"

"It would make me happier. I worry about you, you know." His smile looked forced.

"Wherever I am, you find me anyways, so what's the big deal?"

"A pretty girl like you shouldn't be walking deserted streets alone at night." He was beginning to sound patronizing and irritated.

"Am I ever really alone?"

"Don't be a smart ass; I can't be around you all the time. One day I may not be around – then what?" I just felt like saying the job of father was already taken, asshole!

"Bryn. You really care don't you?" I knew I sounded sarcastic.

"I'm serious Aileen. Promise me that you will have a little more care over your safety. If anything ever happened to you..." He put his fingers to the small of his nose and closed his eyes in what looked like exhaustion.

"Don't worry, I promise I'll be a good girl." I said trying not to appear condescending, and wondered if I could take this opportunity to steal a big hug. I walked over to where he was sitting and knelt down to put my arms around him. He was wearing jeans and a shirt and, as usual, he smelled fabulous. When I pulled away, slowly, I paused by his neck. I wanted to kiss him right there. I pushed my lips to his neck along his jaw, causing him to push me away as he jumped out of the chair.

"Down girl." He said dismissively.

"Well, then what did you need to see me about? Just to lecture me about going outdoors alone at night?"

"No, in fact, I need to talk to you about this business of the ritual when you reach your 18th year."

"What about it?"

"Do you understand what it is? Do you have any questions?" This line of questioning annoyed me. He had been so resistant to talk about his 'precious' itinerary and then at our last visit had suddenly confided that our 'little agreement' was going to be ritualized. It was the fact that I felt more like a recipient than a participant that bothered me. This made me really think about some of the questions that were plaguing me. Why did we have to do it this way in the first place? I mean why so ceremoniously? Couldn't we just bond the way every other normal couple does?

"It's a bonding ritual, you told me." I said sounding bored.

"Yes, but do you know what that means?"

"That for some reason you are crazy enough, with a world full of women to want to bind with me. Someone you won't kiss but insist on lecturing like a little girl."

"I swear Aileen, your attitude will be the death of my saint like patience." That stung, because I could tell he really wanted to say, 'childish attitude.'

"Bryn, I know this ritual is a serious binding of us together – if you're making sure that I am okay with it, I am – you're a part of me." I tilted my head to one side and dared to return his intense glare which always gave me a pain in the chest.

"When the time comes Aileen, will you be able to give spirit and body to the binding ritual – to me?"

"Yeah, why not? What do you mean?"

"Prove to me tonight you can control your spiritual will, put out all these candles without blowing them out."

"What?" I shot a dirty look at him with a raised eyebrow.

"You heard me, do It!" He then stepped back and pointed to a candle on the far end of his mantle.

"Start with that one." So here was my big moment to impress him with my very pathetic magical powers. He made it sound like my future with him depended on my ability to do it so I bent my mind to succeeding. I cleared my mind and focused on the candlelight as it sucked the air around it to feed on the wax below it. I focused on choking out the oxygen around the delicate wick. Creating a vacuum of space around the wick utterly deprived of oxygen. It took me a little while, but sure enough, that wick faded out and the fire died. Without any prodding by Bryn I went to the next one and then the next one, till all seven candles were out and we were in total darkness. Bryn walked over to me and put his hands on my shoulders I could barely make out his face, but I could tell he was smiling.

"You should give yourself more credit. That was well done. With practice you could put them all out at once." In an instant the seven candles were burning brightly again and the light revealed a grinning Bryn.

"Do I pass the test then?" I refused to act impressed at his abilities, no sense in stroking an already huge ego.

"On the night of the ritual, your whole mind should be engaged in the process. We are one; you must ensure you complete the pact for it to work. I needed to know that you understand the seriousness of this. I know the Craft is like a fun and games thing to you, but this is much more serious than you realize. From that night on you will no longer have the luxury of being a careless, fanciful young girl – not to me."

"You're scaring me."

"I'm sorry love, I don't mean to. We have dire business to attend to, sooner than I hoped. I need you to be ready. I promise to put it off as long as the Talisman will let me."

"Sooner? Like how much sooner?" Just looking at his face I could see the blood rushing to colour his usually white face. He was shaking his head in irritation, I could see he didn't want to talk about it. I waited for him to respond, and when my patience wore out – all of about three seconds.

"Out with it Bryn, tell me…"

"I'm sorry Aileen, I don't think we can wait till your eighteenth birthday. I'm so sorry. There is no doubt that after this ritual there will be no turning back for me." He turned his face from mine, moved away from me rubbing his forehead while he cast his glance downward.

"Clearly you are not ready. What must I do to prepare you?" He said more to himself, I could see tears forming in his eyes. Why this was such a big deal? Somehow this was really bothering him. He certainly didn't feel like burdening me with it. His emotions caused an intense empathetic wave within me. I had to convince him I was ready. I had to be strong for him.

"Does it talk to you? You know, the Talisman?"

"Sort of, I serve it as much as the previous owners did. That is the fate of us."

"What do you mean, 'fate of us'?" He looked back up at me and I could see that his eyes were reddish and moist as if in tears.

"We have an appointment with destiny as the saying goes. It is a shade darker than most others I fear."

"Who was Shemzi or Shemzai or whatever you said who made that Talisman?"

"His name is Shemhazai and we do not serve him. However, it is our destiny to help him and his kind, and I fear that you will hate me before we are done." He then stood in front of me wordlessly and hugged me for a moment, withdrew and puts his hands in my hair.

"Woe to you, Shemhazai. Look upon her, so fair. Yet I will take her with me and you shall never know her." As usual, I had no idea what he was talking about. But there we were, his body was pushed up against me and his arms were around me holding my hair and well, it affected me.

"Bryn, kiss me." I whispered. I was aching for him to kiss me. He paused, staring at me. His hand was right there, he could have touched my chin or better. However, he abruptly let go of my hair and stepped backwards.

"Oh Aileen, I shouldn't, I just can't... You should go now." I saw him back up towards his chair, put his head in his hands and then I was on my bed in Vancouver. I could see he was beginning to lose it. I could tell his nerves of steel, his indomitable self-control was seriously eroding. Standing that close to him, I could feel the heat from his body, the intensity of his desire. Yet he sent me home, Wow! What a weirdo.

Everything living and inanimate is a part of the total sum of energies, both potential and realized; these energies are poled, like magnets having a positive and negative force that maintains them in our space-time dimensions. So, in order for all things to exist in our consciousness, it needs to have the neutral space between the forces of both poles exerted on it. This 'third force' expresses itself as no force at all, but rather the 'push' in between the two 'pulls'. This is the best way that I can think of to describe this energy in all things.

There was a schism developing in me. I was beginning to become increasingly aware of it. Two lives, one of them entirely secret. I had friends, family, school and ECAW. Then there was Bryn. One aspect of my life forced me to grow up in a hurry. Bryn was older and it was an entirely adult relationship and he found my childishness to be something of a sore point so I made an effort to be mature, serious and responsible. I tried to be just an ordinary teenager at home. However, I suppose that being forced to grow up in one side of my life, bled off into my normal life. I managed to read enough to learn that indeed using a lot of magic required a sacrament or offering. That the two were directly linked. That spiritual manna was a tangible thing. So we were like bank accounts and we had a certain amount of power points that we could use. This told me that I was near bankrupt and Bryn obviously had more than he honestly needed. I also learned that the more they used their magic, the more it would 'cost' them and it could result in a physical or mortal cost. Maybe you would go prematurely grey or die early as testified in lots of the ancient texts, like the effect on Moses whenever he was in the presence of God. Kat liked to use her magic and

I was pretty sure that it would cost her physically somehow. But what about Bryn? How much of his magic was modified by that Talisman? I was obviously distracted from my life and studying. Things were slowly coalescing in my mind and I was having a hard time retaining focus on Canadian History and Algebra.

"Whatever have you been up to, my friend? You must improve your attendance if you ever entertain the idea of getting out of this abysmal school" said a familiar, melodious soprano voice.

"I suppose you are right, Kat. I had better drop out of home economics and take two blocks of math." It appeared that the summer break had quelled the rancour of the Adivar and Kat was rather happy and friendly, so I suppose we were back to social terms at school.

"Don't be coy, Dragon, I know you were kicked out of home economics by Ms. Eccles. I heard about the cake you made, or should I say boiling dish of oil." Kat said chuckling loudly. I returned the laughter and then began relaying to her how I got the dry ingredients and my partner got the wet ingredients and that we mixed up the measurements such that we put in one cup of oil and a tablespoon of flour. She seemed to marvel at my utter inability to bake.

"I think I will have to actually study and do work on my weekends to get through this Kat."

"Well I hope you haven't forgotten this Saturday."

"What's happening this Saturday?" I asked genuinely curious, realizing that I really have been lost in my emotional fog for too long.

"This weekend you will meet my new boyfriend and his friends. They are all now to be initiated into ECAW. I can't believe you forgot." Kat looked equally surprised by my forgetfulness.

"Oh! Shit ya. Klaur, Margon and that other guy…what's his name? I will be there. I will pick you up and we will go together, it's at the Planetarium isn't it?" Kat had already told me at length about these guys whom she wanted initiated into ECAW. As the new leader, apparently I had the final say as to if they were allowed in. However, I wasn't as big on wielding the alleged power I had. I was eager to see fresh minds in the group. I was eager to meet Kat's new boyfriend. She had already come up with ECAW names for them and she had told me that Trent was Klaur, Jason was Margon, and even though I couldn't remember the other code name, I knew he was otherwise known as Lance.

"Yes, so get all of your homework done Friday night and do whatever on Sunday, you must be there."

So on the Saturday, having read many chapters of English, Socials and Math, I readied myself, taking my book of shadows, my camera, and cleared my mind from thoughts of when I would see Bryn again to the excitement of meeting guys my own age. I thought about how odd it was that such a strange looking, not to mention eccentric, girl like Kat could make young male friends so easily. The thought occurred to me that she was out looking for it while I was definitely sending out the "get lost" vibes.

I picked up Kat and endured her father's endless attempts to drive us or somehow be with us, as he was fixated on protecting his precious daughter. I then finally grabbed Kat and we were out the door and heading for the bus stop. I wanted to ask her about these guys, if she could trust them, and if we should be totally honest about what we do right off the bat. I tried to convince her that we should wait and ensure they were appropriate for joining our group. But Kat would have none of that. She was quick to remind me that by slapping everything in their face they will respect our sincerity. I couldn't find a good reason to disagree, after all, her crazy tactics worked on me. She then began to drill me as to what I had been up to lately; obviously saw I had been distracted lately. I think part of her considered any attempt to rival her power as a potential threat. I knew she was very good at reading thoughts and I always had to be on my guard to focus on thinking about truly mundane things. I was keenly aware of a real power conflict between us.

"Come on, are we not compatriots within our group? You are the closest Wiccan to me; surely you can confide in me what has been occupying so much of your time. I have missed our talks." She said in a warm voice.

"Nothing you need worry about, Kat. Truly."

"Well, you are lying of course, Dragon; however, tis not the time, nor the place for such a conversation. I will enjoy you relaying what you have been up to for so many months on another occasion. Soon I trust." Something about her formal way of speaking and her soft voice, which was somehow reminiscent of the hissing of a snake, instantly put me on edge.

We arrived at the Planetarium in Kitsilano. A beautiful building that reminded you of an ice cream dessert dish turned upside down. It stood on a field cleared to the ocean not more than a two-minute walk away. As per the custom of ECAW, each one in turn approached me, introducing themselves, and offered to serve ECAW to the fullest of their abilities, as was tradition.

The first who approached me had a large smile on his face and looked the eldest. He had dirty blonde hair, was slim and wore glasses.

"Good evening, Dragon, I am Jason Ferguson. May it please you, they call me Margon. I offer my ability to draw, draft and build what you will."

I was surprised by his formal and friendly nature. I had hoped that this was Kat's new boyfriend and that I had mixed up the names. I could have sworn she called him Klaur or something. But I was sure she would choose someone like this young man as he was as polite and formal as she, and yet had something endearing and kind about him.

"You are welcome to our circle, you bring valuable skills." I shook his hand and returned his contagious smile.

The next one approached. He was almost as tall as the first, just as slim, his hair the same color but without any curl, blue eyes, but no glasses. His demeanour however, was radically different. Upon approaching me, I could sense his sullen, inner defiance. Like a tide I could sense his emotions, I hoped my increasing ability to read thoughts was more to do with my research in the last four or five months than from the ring on my finger and that scar Bryn had left on my hand. Whatever the reason, I could easily read his thoughts. He was a person who was used to being front and center of attention and meeting me this way was a sour, bitter taste in his mouth.

"So, you are Dragon. Kat has told me of you. I should enjoy getting to know you. I offer my leadership and ability with weapons." He said without telling me his name, without offering his hand, and without any warmth at all. I instantly disliked this person, and I had a sinking feeling this was the one that Kat had chosen.

"You bring skills which I feel I already foster, however, welcome." I managed to choke out of my mouth, under direct protest of my conscience.

"Klaur", for I was certain it was he. He then turned and walked back to Kat and took her hand into his; my heart sank.

The last one approached, he looked nothing like the other two. He was heavier set, with blood red hair, pale skin and the iciest blue eyes.

"Margon is the artist, Klaur, as I am certain you have seen, is the bureaucrat, my skills lie in computers and codes. You can call me Lance or if you prefer, Aggarate." He looked at me, and not another word escaped his lips. He made it obvious that he was blocking me so that I could not read his emotions and thoughts—clever, so he is already skilled in the craft too. So there I was, within 20 minutes I had decided we had one sweet, young man, one rebel, and one mystery. In my estimation – a plate full.

I watched as the new recruits met Tyra, and watched as Klaur and Kat shamelessly carried on. I watched perhaps jealously as they smiled, touched, held each other and looked into each other's eyes with that youthful exuberance of puppy love. They were so natural, sweet, wide-eyed and happy. Kat didn't have any fear of her future with Klaur like what filled me when I was with Bryn. In fact, this display bore no similarity at all. Somehow, everything they did seemed wholesome and natural. I was painfully aware of how alien everything they exhibited seemed to me and again I felt a wave of jealousy. I thought about how I yearned to feel Bryn hold me like that and kiss me. I thought about how much I wished I had no fear, like Kat. I was burning from the inside, a tide so high, beyond any hope of navigating –drowning in the flames of this insane need for him. A passion and fear so beyond natural, so twisted that watching Kat was physically painful. .What the hell was wrong with me? I felt possessed. How much longer would Bryn make me wait? Whatever sick animal he was turning me into, I just needed to be completely baptised.

Suddenly my eyes snapped open and I was aware that Agarrate and Margon were admiring me lost in my own thoughts. I smiled and we had some idle chit chat however, I was distracted for the rest of the festivities—my thoughts were full of Bryn, I wished he were here in Vancouver with me. I was grateful that this ring would block Kat from invading my brooding thoughts.

The long weekend came and went and Kat had her tearful goodbye with her friends from the Okanagan. We now had three guys living in the sunny Okanagan and three girls living in cool Vancouver. I had to laugh when I remembered Rodan. This would have been the perfect scenario for him, three males and females for those group, sexual rituals that Rodan wanted. Of course, I wasn't allowed was I? I made a promise to save myself. Well, if Kat never mentioned it I would be happy.

I needed to focus on improving my grades in school. I attempted to catch up with my homework. I worked and studied like a nerd, but I was getting a little annoyed that I had not heard from Bryn in months. It would just be typical that he wouldn't bother with me until my 16th birthday. I focused on my work and on ECAW and not my impending birthday. I was ready to kill him if he tried to wait that long to contact me, but like clockwork, on the night of my birthday, I looked up from my hands, into his face.

"Bryn." I said meekly because part of me wanted to kill him and part of me wanted to just dive into his arms as his face completely mesmerized my heart.

"Quite so. Happy Birthday!" He replied utterly ignoring my mood.

"Where are we?"

"Oh, we are in Sydney, Australia. I have a concert tomorrow night and I thought I would have a quiet evening, just the two of us." He said grabbing my hand and brushing it against his face and seemingly smelling me. I jumped up and sort of back stepped away from him, towards the wall. Reading my cold expression he began judging how he was going to make his next move. We looked like two chess pieces. He took a step back. It was a large room with a living room, sitting room and swung into an L-shape for the bedroom and dinning room.

"Is everything all right, Sweet?" He said in a quiet voice, almost unlike him.

"No, everything is not alright. I haven't seen you for months and I just don't feel too comfortable." I said in a voice attempting to sound assertive. His expression changed as if I had slapped him in the face.

"You are right of course. I apologize. I have been very busy." He moved to the table and sat on one of the chairs and looked at me wordlessly before he began again,

"Some of my more elaborate spells have resulted in a considerable amount of hair loss, and weight loss so I have been going about things in a painfully normal way as I have avoided using the Talisman."

"So using that Talisman does drain you!"

"yes, I'm afraid so."

"But that isn't what is bothering you right now, is it? There is more isn't there?"

"I have done some questionable things. You have to promise not to get upset."

"What? That you have been getting down with every groupie who says, "Cor, you're hot!" I said with a harsh, accusing voice.

"You know Bryn, I can read! We get the British tabloids in Vancouver, I know who, where and when!" I knew I sounded jealous, but it was more an overriding possessiveness. How dare other women, older women, hang out with him while I am stuck at that crappy school. I was mad that he could so cavalierly dismiss me; and then just show up and expect what?

"Most of what they report in the tabloids is all crap!" He retorted.

"No? So you haven't been getting it on with anyone over the last few months?"

He looked tired and spent.

"It was empty, hollow and utterly spiritless; it's all over anyway..." He looked at me and I had a flood of emotions and thoughts. Bryn opened his mind to let me read everything. It was overwhelming at first as most of it was a mixed up flood as I stared at him, tears in my eyes. But I could piece them together, bit by bit until the whole picture became clear. Bryn was selectively using these women; they were making tabloid headlines because these spurned women were reporting them to make money. Why would Bryn use those women? Why would he? He almost seemed to be going through them as if it was his last days on earth. It was a mechanical process, with absolutely no emotion at all. I was shocked that he could be so cold; like a vampire feeding on blood. He had so coldly avoided me and now he let me know that he didn't just have sex with one, no; he had sex with legions of women. It didn't matter whether or not I was emotionally ready for us. In that moment, I felt like a victim of an alternate form of sexual abuse.

"You will never understand how I have suffered. It's one thing to have duties and responsibilities it's another to have a temptation thrown at me, I will not allow my mortal weakness turn me into a monster. I couldn't trust myself to be with you. In this incarnation, I need you. I did what I had to do, so please don't be upset with me." He looked up at me with a stricken expression. Guilt and shame washed over his beautiful face.

"You know they meant nothing to me." He whispered, as he got up off the chair and headed towards the couch where I was sitting. I looked at him as he approached me. I was so deeply hurt I had no words. I just didn't want him to touch me.

He sensed my emotional and mental 'pushing away of him'. His dire look began to change to something akin to fear, although I had never seen fear in him before.

"I was scared of hurting you. I made a colossal mistake and I am willing to spend the rest of my life making it up to you. Tears were running down my face, my whole body was in a cold, numbing shock.

"Bryn, 'us' is weird enough! You compounded my pain by doing this...I…I can't feel my hands. You are not the only one that suffers! You and that Talisman have already succeeded in destroying my childhood, you must know that." I got up and walked over to the windows that overlooked the last gasps of daylight hanging over Sydney harbour trying to understand what I read in Bryn's mind; I knew I was not ready for the level of relationship that I was reproving him for. I secretly longed and feared our upcoming ritual. But this didn't negate the fact that I hated that he could be such a slut. While I was thinking, Bryn sat on the couch that I had just vacated. Wow! Sydney, this town looked as beautiful as Vancouver – maybe even more. Bryn could show me the world…

"Please say you will give me another chance? Please say you will try to find it in your heart to forgive me?"

" You may be a powerful warlock, you may be a famous rock star, you may have been my ghost most of my life but you are a controlling, manipulating bastard and part of me really is hating you right now. But the deeper truth that I have to admit is that I am more upset about you being away from me for so long." Which was a lie, truthfully, I was aware of that numb feeling, it wasn't going away. More than anything, I wanted to feel again.

"The rite will change all of that. After that, everything will be perfect. We will unite and neither you nor I will suffer so." He walked over to where I was and rubbed my back. His touch like magic brought feeling back to me.

"So you seemed to have some criteria for those fodder type women? I could read in your thoughts that you were looking for something specific."

"Yes, you are correct. They need only be the children of Eden."

"Doesn't that cover off just about every human on the earth?"

"Actually Aileen, no. No, it certainly doesn't."

"What other types are there then?"

"Your type"

"What type is that? Wiccans?"

"In a way, you are exactly right."

"Why do you refuse to give me straight answers?"

"I always give you straight answers. I expect you to be better read so that my answers have meaning to you."

I was still burning about his wanton fornication, and I didn't care what the criterion was, my anger sent me miles away, thinking about Kat. She was shamelessly throwing herself at her new boyfriend, much like these women throw themselves at Bryn. Was she to be treated the same way at the hands of Klaur? Should I forgive Bryn? We had no prior agreement that stated that while he waited for me that he had to subject himself to two years of celibacy. But did he have to be such a pig about it?

"Please tell me you forgive me, Aileen." He said as he put his arms on either side of my shoulders, turned me around to face him and buried his face in mine, his kiss causing my legs to buckle. He moved his arms to wrap around me and for a while the overwhelming feeling drowned out all of my senses. His mouth opened and his tongue was introducing itself to mine. My body, heart and soul could forgive Bryn's every transgression it seemed yet my brain laid in absolute horror at my slavish dedication to what was, after all, just a man. I surrendered to that kiss, yet my brain retaliated reminding me that I was possessed.

He raised his face from mine and I caught my breath. Silently staring at each other in what was considered by his militaristic adherence to the rules of conduct of our Wiccan pact an absolute contravention of contact. My first embrace with him and I was higher than any drug could ever have taken me.

We made an agreement to spend more time together, which was rather impressive considering his hectic schedule. But I was happier with that and I hoped he was too. There was no ritual that night, and I worried that this agreement would cause him to loose more hair. It just seemed the more magic he used, the more physically drained he became. But the more time he spent with me resulted in less reports of him mistreating women.

Chapter 10

April came and went, and sure enough I did better at school and I was quickly pulling up my marks to C's and C-'s with the exception of math that I was still struggling with.

The tabloids were quiet on Bryn. What had happened to their favourite musician to pick on? Where was he? They sent their horrid photo boys everywhere to try and get some dirt on him. Bryn and I met once a week or so and just hung out together, played cards or went for car rides into the country. I was sixteen, occasionally his attitude about my age would upset me, other than stealing the odd kiss, I was forbidden property and it made me feel like something dirty.

Meanwhile at home, my father was giving me a hard time. He didn't like my grades and thought I would be better off dropping out of school and going into Hairdressing College. I didn't want to drop out of school and I certainly didn't want a career pandering to feminine vanity. Bryn seemed overjoyed that I wanted to continue my education. I tried to stay focussed on my studies at school to pull up my grades. It's not that I lacked the intelligence to do well in the exams; it was more that my frequent absences from class that ultimately affected my exam results. I hated that school. There were no teachers that inspired me, no clubs or facilities that engaged me, and the student body were more reminiscent of a juvenile detention facility. A part of me wanted to quickly get some kind of career and get over to England, but my overriding ambition and stubborn independence won out, I wanted a degree from a University and I was motivated by Bryn's delight in my ambition.

The hum of ECAW was busying itself now in two towns: Vancouver for us girls and Naramata for the boys. This is pretty much how I saw the guys. Margon the eldest, kept writing frequently and always had drawings, patiently illustrating life from his home in Naramata. He had many literary sources for continuing research on the most ancient of civilized history, and we incorporated much of this knowledge into our permanent records, including some very old leather bound references which he acquired – no questions asked. He appeared by far the most calm, the most steadfast and reasonable. Aside from drawing, hiking forays into the hills surrounding his home and canoeing, he also read a lot and was the most avid fan of Jean Michel Jarre. He rarely used coarse language, was always a gentleman, and never had ill to say of anyone. He was a respecter of persons and I envied his easy personality.

Klaur, the youngest, had to be the focus of attention. He was moody and his sullen expression on his long face with his small, close set eyes made me realize how much his looks reminded me of Sean Penn. he was prone to childish temper tantrums. He seemed to contrast Margon so much; it surprised me that they were friends. He had no patience for the fine arts and preferred instead to spend his time smoking cigarettes, throwing knives, and listening to heavy metal. This was a recipe for trouble with me as I despised having someone who appeared more rebellious and Adivar than me. Klaur's rebellious nature to everyone was a major irreconcilable difference between us. Rebellious, crude, and rarely having anything nice to say or evince of anyone – Trent made it very difficult for me to like him, and I didn't.

Agaratte wasn't sunny and cheerful like Margon, nor was he starved for attention like Klaur either; he was an entirely different animal altogether. He and Margon spent a great deal of time discussing music and creating sounds on computers, as Agaratte was razor sharp with computer technology. He wasn't very talkative, but usually very polite and always mysterious. By mysterious I mean you somehow knew that Agaratte knew more about things than he was willing to let on. Being the brilliant young person that he was has its downside for him though – boredom. Agaratte had periodic bouts of depression that seemed related to frustration at not being able to make better use of that massive grey matter he had in abundance between his ears. He would forgo sleep for days at a time, researching the minutest portions of our larger projects. He could create entire programs and databases on his computer in a couple of sleepless days. He read entire works of scientists, encyclopaedias, The Bible, Koran, Torah, Assyrian vs. Egyptian timelines etc. Industrial and Gothic music played while he worked. This culminated in Agaratte's already dark disposition growing darker. Agaratte seemed to thrive on dark, negative energies. This is when he was most productive.

I may have not been crazy about Klaur but I really enjoyed having the young blood in the group, it was a welcome distraction. Of course, eventually into every life cayenne is added into the chocolate sauce.

"Oh Dragon! What am I going to do? Klaur and his family are moving to Australia for one year. His father excepted a teaching exchange." Said a very distressed Kat as she pulled out her chicken sandwich from her lunch bag; we were in the same sad little classroom we always had lunch in. I laughed as I realized this poor soul would be enduring chicken sandwiches for the rest of her life living with her parents. So the timing of my internal humour was probably ill.

"Rejoice and find someone new!" I said as I laughed. That earned me a big scowl and stern set eyes till I felt obligated to interject some empathetic and compassionate words as she was looking for a friend who understood. Yeah, like I could fake my excitement at loosing Klaur.

"Australia eh? I've been there, well, sort of. Nice place. I hope they live close to the coast, I hear inland sucks." I said attempting to sound caring.

"You don't get it! He'll be gone." Tears started to stream down her face, she reached into her homework bag to locate a tissue to wipe her tears. Meanwhile, I put my book down and tried to think of what to say, I had little personal experience to work with in sympathizing a friend for a situation I was grateful for.

"Kat, I know it is hard to have long distances between the ones we love. But remember, you survived when he lived in the Okanagan and you were here in Vancouver. Make sure he writes to you regularly and make the odd phone call. I am sure that the year will go by fast and you will be with him again; one year is nothing, trust me on that. Everything will be okay." I stopped and took her hand into mine and looked straight into her eyes,

"If you two feel as strongly for each other as you believe, then he will have to come back for you. It's just that simple."

"How can you be so sure?" She asked snuffling a bit and letting go of one hand so she could grab her sandwich.

"Experience Kat. Besides, who could he find anywhere on the globe that could compare to you? You are truly one of a kind." But as I said this to ease her feelings I had hoped that Klaur would never return. He had been more of a nemesis to me than a friend, always contradicting me and trying to lead ECAW. I was glad to see him go. We continued to eat our lunch in silence, only occasionally glancing at the door to see the odd student give us a long sideways glance. It was interesting to see Kat's reaction to Klaur's leaving. She clearly did not trust him and she feared for the permanence of her relationship with him. What was it about 'normal' relationships that made one feel that they were 'hanging on a thread'? Again, I was aware of how alien my feelings for Bryn were. What was it in my relationship that rendered such unquestioning security?

"You can see him, can't you? You see him regularly, don't you?" Kat asked accusingly. I kept looking at my Liverwurst sandwich, lest my eyes give me away. I was acutely aware of the fact that I had been deep in thought without attempting to block any of it. I knew what she was talking about, but it was the first time she had directly asked me about whom I had been spending my time. Then I remembered the ring, I looked down and realized my ring was still by the bathtub at home. Kat was reading my thoughts no doubt. I realized that part of the gig was up and I would have to confess somewhat to get her off my back. A smile crept across my face, the big give away.

"How real are you when you get there?" She asked genuinely interested.

"Almost totally solid, but not quite." I said somewhat excited at revealing my secret to her since the first time it ever happened almost two years ago.

"You are kidding me. How?" She appeared surprised.

"He does it really; I can't do it on my own. He has some kind of sto..." I stopped midsentence remembering what she did to my ring the last time she was a little peeved at me, I wasn't about to have her break my only link to Bryn. I continued trying to use all of my Wiccan strength to block her.

"I don't really know how he can do it." I finished trying my best to look nonchalant.

"Are you pulling my leg? He must be quite a warlock to be able to focus that much energy. Who is he?"

"You wouldn't know him." I said.

"Indeed." She said rather dubiously. Her expression put me on edge.

"He is dangerous, Dragon. You should stay away from him."

"I am not crazy about Klaur and I trust Thromm even less; besides, you don't even know him!" I shot back defensively, surprised that she, of all people, she would question my judgement. I looked down at my vacant finger void of its newest gift from Bryn.

"I noticed that ring when we were at the Planetarium. It's really nice, where did you get it?" She asked watching me.

"Oh, my mom bought it for me." I said smiling, hoping that she could in no way read my thoughts to know whether or not I was lying.

"Well, Dragon, I don't think there is much I need to know about your new familiar, I can only imagine what ghastly things he probably has already done to you. I suppose you and I have one thing in common, we dislike each other's affiliations. But I think you should find a boy you can enjoy in the physical realm." She laughed. I suppose what she said hurt my feelings, and it made me realize one lingering bit of business yet to do. I continued to block my mind and wondered why Bryn still had a 'hands off' rule. At my age, weren't we supposed to experiment and play around? He said he was going to postpone as long as possible, but why? Did he think after everything he had put me through that I wasn't ready? He had to know that the damage was already done. What could he possibly do to affect me more from what has thus far transpired? I knew he was waiting for something, I wanted to ask him, but the whole subject made me nervous when I was with him.

Chapter 11

Kat says Good-bye to Klaur

Dragon didn't fool me for a bit. That ring was what was making her impossible to read. It was just stupid luck she hadn't been wearing it when we had lunch together. I must say, I was surprised by the emotions that she unwittingly let me be privy to. She was hiding great secrets, this I knew. Her words were wasted on me as I could read her feelings and expressions. A good Wiccan doesn't just rely on magic. This musician was obviously a warlock and did have something that he drew his power from, and she wasn't going to tell me what it was. This was her secret, she was protecting that bastard and lying to me for him – I couldn't believe it! How could she trust him more than me? This artefact appeared in Dragon's mind to be small enough for him to carry. I would have to do some research to determine what this device was. Without even wanting to, Dragon was invaluable for information.

I decided that the year that Klaur was away would be a good time for me to do some research and focus on getting that artefact. I was doing far better than Dragon in school and could afford the time. On the weekend, I cast my spells and brought my servant, Thromm to me. I commanded him to seek out this artefact and whom the owner is. I set him to follow Dragon to her warlock, and to report how the artefact was used, and who the owner was so that I could narrow my research. Soon I would know who Dragon's protector was.

With the unfortunate time for Klaur's departure soon at hand, I needed to devise a way to see him off. My parents did not approve of my association with anyone, particularly males, so it was little surprise that they disliked my friendship with Klaur. Klaur called me and informed me that he was going to come to Vancouver ahead of his family to visit me prior to going to Australia; I was overjoyed and asked my mother if he could stay with us. I was stunned when she agreed.

"I would prefer the young man stay with us so I can meet him and know what kind of young people you are associating with while I am at work." My mother said. Upon Klaur's arrival, my parents were surprisingly civil. They insisted that he sleep in the basement, as the stairs to the main floor were directly by my parent's room. However, this was no big deal. We still managed to go for walks to the park together for privacy.

"You will wait for me won't you Kat?" Klaur asked as he sat on the swing. I sat on the swing next to him.

"You know I will. We must promise to write to each other regularly."

"Just a little over a year and I will be back in your arms, maybe my family will move to Vancouver and we won't have to live in different towns." He was obviously trying to comfort both of us. There was no rain today but the park was wet anyways and the air was cold. I reached my cold white hand over to his not so white hand and instantly was gratified by the warmth.

"We must somehow work out a way that when you get back that we can be together – and end our distance challenged relationship. Besides, I may have figured something out before then…" I said. I was picturing myself with the mysterious artefact, bringing Klaur to me the way Dragon's warlock drags her to England. Klaur had no idea what I was thinking, but he just smiled and bent over to kiss me. We continued the kiss, mingling for some time, when I could hear my father's voice – quite shrill.

"Jennifer! Get home right now!" Well, I was busted and I knew that my overly protective parents were going to have a meltdown and it wasn't going to be pleasant.

It was incredibly embarrassing to watch Klaur pack his bags and head out of my house amidst grossly oppressive Christian slanders of his conduct. I gritted my teeth and apologized to him repeatedly, but it was clear he was making a bee-line for the door to get the hell out.

"I am not surprised by your behaviour, Jennifer—fornicator is common enough for your kind!" My mother said to me after the door closed and Klaur was gone.

"I never told you this, but the reason why your dad and I spend so much time taking you to church and trying to teach you solid Christian morality is because we know that by nature you have none!" My mother continued in an annoyed and angry tone.

"What does that mean?" I asked flatly.

"Well, it's about time we told you. You were adopted. Yes, your natural mother was a whore! She was of Arabic descent and you are the love child of her careless affiliation with an English ex-military man. You aren't even white!" She said in the most demeaning tone she could muster – really hoping to drive me to tears.

"You know what Mrs. Smith, I already knew that!" I replied, refusing to give her the satisfaction.

"What do you mean you already know – go to your room!" With that I went to my room and as I passed her, she slapped the back of my head. Of course I wasn't lying. I did in fact know that I was adopted; through my magical meditations, I had uncovered the fact that I had a mother, brothers and sisters. In fact, I knew more than my mother did. This ex-military man was married and had an affair with my biological mother. Upon learning of her pregnancy, he paid her to keep it secret and immediately give it up upon birth, to save his marriage and his reputation.

Knowing this didn't reduce the fact that I hated Mrs. Smith's thinking I was less than her because I was half Arabic. No doubt, she considered any race of people that was mostly not Christian as being less than she is. Christianity had to be about the dumbest religion around since UFO cults. I sat in my room for hours contemplating calling Thromm to rid me of this mother, fully prepared to pay the psychic costs associated with such a spell -- but then ultimately decided she wasn't worth it, and for right now she was my meal ticket – Fucking white fundamentalist bitch!

Chapter 12

Around the end of June, Klaur's family left for Australia. I was overjoyed and hoped that during his absence Kat would have time to fall hopelessly in love with Margon. She went to Naramata on occasion and I enjoyed knowing that she was staying at Margon's place when there. I hoped that their friendship would blossom into something larger. But at our meetings it seemed as though everyone thought I should have a mate. I was the eldest female in the group and often there was laughter at the fact that I had no seeming desire to date anyone. I quite honestly didn't notice males, let's face it, I was messed up. I was emotionally preoccupied with Bryn.

As the months progressed with Klaur's absence, Kat surprised me yet again, as her affections and attentions appeared directed more to the dark, mysterious Agaratte and not to bright, sunny Margon. By the end of the school year, Kat was receiving a steady stream of letters and phone calls from Agaratte. For the first few months she complained of never getting enough mail from Klaur, but later seemed unperturbed by his very infrequent contacts with her. So Kat found a consort with Agaratte and soon she stopped troubling me with her lamentations over Klaur.

"It's your turn." I said to the lazy loaf on the overstuffed chair, who hadn't bothered to get out of his pajamas yet – it was lunchtime. Instead, Bryn looked up at the plastic contraption, eyeballing the marbles and the few remaining straws holding the mass of marbles against gravity.

"Are you sure you took your turn? You wouldn't cheat while I was in the loo." He grinned boyishly.

"Cross my heart, now go for it" I pushed. Bryn sized up the straws, realizing that the laws of physics were stacked against him no matter which straw he chose.

"I don't like the odds sweet, but I shall pull a red straw for love." He then put his fingers on a straw and elegantly stole it away, and within half a second the victorious sounds of 20 or 25 marbles issued down the body of the contraption and spewed into his receptacle.

"Yeah!" Victorious squeals and giggling erupted from me until I saw him lunge at me – he wanted to wrestle.

"Let's see you get out of this one then." He said laughing. Bryn reached for my arms in an attempt to hold me down, but I snaked away and tried to tickle him. The mere attempt at tickling him sent him screaming in laughter, and redoubling his effort to hold me down. Somehow I managed to wriggle my way out from under him and went screaming out of the livingroom and running to his bedroom, into the master bathroom, which I knew I could lock. I made it to the bathroom, locked myself in, waited and listened but there was no sound, Bryn seemed to vanish. I waited another five minutes and then I carefully unlocked the door. The door swung wide and an evil smiling Bryn grabbed me and threw me to the bed. He jumped on top and held down my arms, laughing in triumph.

"Gotcha now! I knew your sense of curiosity and impatience would be your undoing."

"You're not going to tickle me are you? Please, I'll do whatever you want, just don't tickle me." I pleaded laughing; I was so sure he was going to torture me in tickles.

"No, I'll do worse then that my pet." He let go of my hands and kissed my neck, and then down my chest. I was overwhelmed by the sensations, he hadn't shaved and his stubble rasped against the fabric of my shirt. He was just about to touch my breast when he stopped cold and jumped off of me.

"No! Not yet." He said quietly with a frown. I sat up and stared at him confused.

"When?"

"Soon, be patient, timing is everything."

"This is mental." I said shaking my head with incredulity.

"Go." He snapped.

"What?" I asked my laughter completely gone now.

"Go." He left the room and I was in my bedroom again. BANG! Just like that. Every time I had built up any self-confidence or thought we had an understanding or comfort in the relationship, he crushed it. Was this a sick game to keep things exciting or was he trying to drive me crazy? I was beginning to suspect that we would never be intimate. A learned coldness was germinating amidst a heart so shattered, bleeding, broken and yet besieged in the sickest form of possession.

During the early part of the summer, I received a postcard from one of the acquaintances I made while in Royal Oak Junior Secondary, named Natalia. She had gone to Calgary for a holiday and was hoping to stay in touch with some people now that it was summer. She wanted to meet me when she got back from holidays and go to a movie. There was a new movie out called 'Poltergeist' and she wrote that if I was interested I should call her at the number she wrote down and we could plan a day to go. So after about two weeks, we went out for dinner and the movie 'Poltergeist'. Natalia was a little surprised to see me wearing nice black slacks with black boots and a ruffled blouse under a black leather trenchcoat. I had over 100 dollars on me, so I thought nothing of buying the pizza for both of us. She seemed surprised at my generosity. I think she was also genuinely surprised that, outside of school, I actually made an effort to do my hair and make-up.

We talked about how glad we both were that we were out of the hole known as Royal Oak and then we discussed what were going to do in September. She was going to go to the richer side of town in Vancouver and go to a high school there called Prince of Wales, while I was not too concerned about what new school to go to. After the dinner and the movie, it was late and we were talking, getting acquainted. I had a great time; we seemed to have so much to talk about – and I actually liked being around someone who had nothing to do with Wicca.

I didn't want the night to end. To prolong the time better we agreed that I would walk her home. She lived just over the bridge from downtown, and we could continue the conversation, enjoying the beautiful evening.

"So Aileen, don't get upset with this question but why would a seemingly normal person like you hang out with a freak like Jennifer?"

"School is dull and she isn't. I mean, Kat is a lot of fun and actually a surprisingly interesting person."

"I'm sure of that. But you really took a lot of crap from that school for being her friend. Like personally, I wouldn't openly associate with the town leper."

"Yeah, I guess I did. But you know what? I think she taught me that whatever a group of brainless adolescents think is really not that important. It took me awhile, but I began to care less and less about whether or not I was popular."

"Well, she must have been worth it. What is she really like? You know, out of school? Did you find her magic broom? Does she own her own cauldron?"

"I don't know, pretty much like she is at school. Actually, she is more fun, because she doesn't have the pressure of a bunch of idiot teens judging her and looking down their noses at her." Natialia's jokes were funny, but in a cruel way which made me feel bad.

"No. What I mean is, does she still do the weird witchy stuff? Like talking funny and making hex signs in the air?" I had to laugh. I never personally saw her do this at school, but she must have done it the year before I got there which would have given her the apt reputation she was now currently enjoying. My laugh was infectious and soon we were both laughing and impersonating Kat doing the classic witch scene from Wizard of Oz. After we walked for a time talking about our families and the joys of being immigrants to this great country she drifted back to the subject of Kat, obviously, a subject that intrigued her.

"So are the rumours true? Is she a witch? She sure acts like one."

"I don't know. I don't think I have ever met a real witch to know if she is one or not?"

"Well, she told me once that she really was. I was wondering whether she really believed that."

"When did she tell you that?" I was surprised that she and Kat would even get into any sort of discussion of the sort.

"Well, she and I have a mutual friend, Samantha. I got in on the conversation one time while we were all having lunch." Well, since Kat was foolish enough to spread her secrets to all who wished to hear, I felt no compunction to lie for her.

"Well Natalia. That is what she tells me too. So I suppose if one believes they are a witch, they may as well be one."

We got to the middle of the Granville Street Bridge, stopped and looked over into the black water of False Creek and the glowing lights down below of the newly built False Creek Condominiums without talking to each other. I suppose we were both thinking the same thing: Where will we be when we have careers? What kind of women will we grow up to be? It was clear from our conversations that night that we both have a strong sense of independence and loved the idea of having a place of our own.

"I would just love to have my own place right there with a cat." Natalia said.

"No man, no kids, no hassles." She added. We both kept looking down at those twinkling lights and the odd boat moored to the docks. I had to admit I agreed with her. I could feel those bitter seeds of inner pain evaporate as I looked at the buildings, thinking about being completely free

"Freedom." I said in a quiet distant voice that is, by all accounts, not like me. People make new friends everyday. That day I knew I was going to be in Natalia's life for the rest of her life. Don't know why, don't really care. There was just something about us together we were kindred spirits. Natalia's parents escaped Czechoslovakia via Austria when she was a year old. A family that narrowly averted growing up in a communist country and instead lived in the suburb of Langely before moving to Kitsilano. She, like my family were old fashioned and strict. Our families had taught us the benefits of hard work and Natalia was an excellent student. She had an elf-like quality to her looks. High cheekbones, wide face, long dark brown hair with red highlights, dark skin with freckles on her nose and cheeks, standing 5'5 inches tall, tiny feet and heavy chested. She was shy, quiet, and had a cutting talent for sarcasm. In many respects, she was a female equivalent to Agaratte.

We spent a lot of time together. We went to movies, any kind of ethnic restaurant, and did all kinds of shopping together. Best of all, she let me do her hair, makeup and occasionally dress her up. The summer seemed to fly by between her, my endless efforts to maintain employment and cashflow, and the occasional awkward, often frustrating visit with Bryn.

"What were you and Jennifer up to all yesterday?" I was stuffing the last remnants of my Ping Pong ice-cream into my face when Natalia jabbed me with her elbow inquisitively.

"Just hanging out."

"Yeah. You're part of her whole witchy thing, aren't you?"

"Natalia, why don't you jump into the frigid water and cool off?" We were on the beach at English Bay, better known to us as 'Gay Bay'.

"Well, if I am going to be your friend and we are going to hang out. You can't exclude me from shit. So you are going to have to tell Jennifer that I want to join." That caused me to arch and eyebrow and look at her. I sat there looking at her smiling expression; it caused me to return the smile. Why the hell not? I thought, if Kat can find new recruits, why can't I?

"You want to join a witch's coven?"

"I knew it! I knew you were in on it. Yes, I want to join. I'm tired of Jennifer having something between you and her and I am excluded." I don't think I fully understood the implied jealousy in that statement. But I did realize however that she probably didn't think that this group was serious.

"You do realize this is no teen club. It is serious. We don't party. It's mostly a lot of work."

"Yeah sure, whatever. Have you ever known me to shirk hard work?" That was a deliberate hack on my academic performance compared to hers. I decided to let her win that argument without a fight, mostly because she was right.

I reintroduced her to Kat. Kat and I confided in her about ECAW and she was indoctrinated. She was initiated and her name then became known as Lactavia. Our number in the roster had now become seven.

Royal Oak Junior Secondary School shut down, with our tenth grade year being the last graduates. I transferred to a school back in Vancouver. Since I had acquired a job in the summer at a hairdressing salon as an assistant, I decided that my school should be close to my work. There was this huge school next to Vancouver's largest cemetery. I thought that it would be the most appropriate school for a creepy kid like me, so I was the new student at John Oliver High School. This was an excellent school with highly professional teachers and a building that was designed to house the bodies of learning for time out of mind. The gymnasium, theatrical stage, shop rooms, and classrooms were all adequately large and well maintained. It was like a breath of fresh air. Even the cemetery was a nice place to go for lunch, but so were the neighbouring restaurants. I was ready to roll up my sleeves and grapple with grade 11. I enjoyed my job, even though it required that I pander to feminine vanity. Kat went to a North Vancouver school, and Natalia went to Snob central, Prince of Wales.

On a Thursday night, September 16th I had to heed the call from a familiar voice.

"Hey there. Wow. You look great! What's the occasion?" I asked upon seeing Bryn by the door of his house, all dressed up.

"Put on that and let's go. Tonight's our night." He said calmly whilst pointing in the direction of his overstuffed chair where was draped a beautiful robe in gold. I looked at the robe quickly and then looked him straight in the eye in either disbelief or distress.

"What?" "What do you mean?" I asked my eyes becoming as huge as his. He just glared at me and grinned saying,

"Exactly, now quickly—timing is everything." He glanced at his watch and then back at me. That look sent a chill down my spine. I grudgingly grabbed the robe, stripped and right there, put the robe on. I was pretty sure I knew what day it was. I kicked my pile of discarded clothes to the corner, under a chair and looked back up at him wordlessly. Bryn put his hand on my shoulder and looked me in the eyes,

"You know what to do?" Well, that confirmed what we were up to right there.

"I think so..." I paused, looking up at his serious expression, noting a lump of pain in my chest before I continued,

"Yes, I know."

Chapter 13

Samhaen for Kat without Klaur

My meeting with Dragon downtown was proving to be enlightening. We were once again at her favourite restaurant and amid the afternoon chaos of the crowd and the introductory pleasantries between Dragon and me. I could see she obviously could block me easily. Reading her mind was not possible. Her magic ring was on her finger and I was sure I knew who imbued it with blocking power. However, reading her body language was an easy enough matter. There was no longer any doubt in my mind that there was something more to this relationship with her warlock than strictly platonic. Just watching her was revealing. Could she not tell there were huge marks on her neck? There was bruising on her wrist. I caught that when she reached for the sugar for her coffee. She looked very tired; I had never seen her look so spent. She looked like a Thai bordello slave girl. This was clearly a case of abuse, and it appeared severe. What manner of creature could do this and retain such physical evidence if she was in spirit form? Perhaps he had come here in person to do this to her? Why would he risk legal prosecution and the enormous press scandal on this fledgling witch? If assault of a minor was his vice would he have to go to this length to find a victim?

Most musicians were magnets for female attention. No. There had to be a specific reason for his choice, but what? I didn't know what, and Dragon wasn't about to tell me.

"You look like you've had one hell of a night?" I eyed her carefully trying not to betray anything. She looked up from the table and when her eyes met mine she quickly looked beyond my face to the table behind me – avoiding eye contact.

"My little brother and I had a bit of a scrap last night. He got me pretty good." I just laughed out loud. That was the lamest excuse I had ever heard. She was a miserable liar; that was for certain.

"Is your brother in the habit of giving you such excellent hickies?" She reflexively put her hands to her neck and attempted vainly to cover them. She then put her head down looking into her coffee cup.

"No..."

"So how did he do it, Dragon? Did he come visit you here or did you go to him? Who the hell is he? You have been plucked; of that there can be no doubt. As your friend and mentor why can you not confide in me? I alone could help you if you are in any danger."

"Yeah, like he would ever come see me? You know Kat, for all you know; I got lucky with any guy."

"Too true, all men desire you. The problem is, Dragon: I know there are no men in your life, save one."

"Could have been a one night stand?"

"If I didn't know you, it would be the only rational explanation. But you and I both know what really happened. Don't we?"

"Kat, I don't even know what really happened. If I was in any danger, you weren't there to save me. It's too late now. I want to talk about something else. What about Margon, let's talk about Margon and you." She was agitated; she almost looked ready to cry. I was going to press more but she was so clearly upset, I thought better of it. That poor thing, what the hell had he done to her?

Reading through the lines it was obvious that he had the power to take her and do his deed so completely that she was heavily anointed in the material plane. No mortal, not even one trained in the black arts, could wield such magic without substantial physical damage. He had flaunted his ability to me. Was he challenging me or frightening me? Somehow, he was able to use that power and not wither away. The only thing that I can think of that would allow this impossible feat of physics and magic would be a power source... But what? The literature is full of alleged objects that can amplify magic; the list too numerous for me to sequentially exhaust. No, I needed a more direct approach. I bided my time until the weekend and amidst the fading twilight I set to channelling my power to read the thoughts of my faithful servant Thromm.

"Thromm, find this warlock. Find what object he possesses. Look for any object he is holding or wearing – we must know! I don't know where he is or when he is in your world. You must watch my friend Dragon. Watch for when he comes to take Dragon and follow them. And Thromm, this time don't fail me." I pushed my directions into the realm in which my servant lives. Thromm departed and I had a sense that he was immediately setting out for Dragon's home. By morning I awoke to a crow tapping on my window. When I got up to open the window the crow disappeared but the clearest image was sent to my mind. It was a dark room, heavily curtained. In it there was a small night table with a drawer half open. Thromm could get no closer but assured me that there was a huge energy source within it. He had followed Aileen's spirit to some brick built home that very night. The image Thromm sent me showed Dragon embracing a man with translucent skin. When their faces parted I was dumb-struck to recognize a musician I knew well. So Bryn was the warlock! Of all the women on the earth for him to fall for Aileen, a fledgling fool. This service of Thromm's confirmed the existence of Bryn's power source and where it is. Not bad for a night's work. Connecting with Thromm was not among my favourite things to do, but how could I complain when so tantalizing an object lay one brilliant scheme away? This prize, regardless of what it was, could arguably make me the most powerful mage, if not the richest! How convenient that it was so small too. Fitting easily in a small drawer.

Throughout the ages items of great power and books of magic have been fought over, the winner being the more clever or devious. There is no shame in ruthlessly pursuing arcane knowledge; no one can really claim ownership over it. Dragon told me she had no idea as to Bryn's power. Was she really that dumb to think I would believe her? I had to laugh. The thought of taking Bryn's little toy away and breaking his connection to Aileen, or even more juicy, destroying his musical empire filled me with euphoria.

Throughout all of my research into items of unnatural power there are great tales told about many objects of power. For example, The Arc of the Covenant, thought to hold awesome power, was currently understood to be in the secured hands of an ancient sect in Acheron, Ethiopia. The joke being that the Arc that is vigorously being protected in the temple in the Holiest of holies is in fact a fraud. The real Arc is buried below the actual temple, under the foundations. Like myself, I am aware of a few Wiccans that know of its true location. You need only be able to truly move your spirit through Tyrrean Trance to see the power source and where it emanates from. But Tyrrean Trance is a vastly lost art, one I was fortunate to learn by a considerate, maternal witch. The Arc of the covenant is an object of such fundamental and fanatical significance that keeping it buried for all time is the only rational thing to do. Why divulge where this object is when it would ultimately be used against you? Frankly, if I could destroy it, I would. For now, I am happy knowing that getting to it would require destruction of an ancient and significant temple. I am comforted to know that it will never happen. But Bryn doesn't have the Arc.

There are stories in ancient writings about Egyptian, Aztec and Hebrew artefacts that are all allegedly powerful. Most of them I don't even believe are all they are cracked up to be. Whatever it is that Bryn possesses, it is a great magical tool. I was determined on one point: he wouldn't have it for long. I completely believe that there are no coincidences in life. Dragon was supposed to enter my life at this point; she was supposed to lead me to this artefact. I was so close to it now; I knew I had to keep her as close to me as I could, to ensure I knew exactly what it was and how to get it.

Dragon. We had spent so much time together and yet still I had no real sense of her. Never had I known a girl so passionless. In matters of the heart, it seemed no man ever seemed to interest her. Whenever I was with her in the past, I could read her thoughts, and when I could read her, even her relationship with that warlock, Bryn appeared utterly platonic. Obviously, this had changed. Did Dragon's feelings change? Dragon always appeared so in control and carefree. But what I saw last Friday wasn't anything I recognized. Who was she really? Why did I have the sense that I never really knew her? For the first time I could feel a real fear in her? What if this warlock was abusing her and she was too terrified to expose him? The bruising on her wrist would seem to indicate involuntary participation on Dragon's part. I had to try to protect her; I was the only one she knew that was powerful and crafty enough to help her. I had to set things right.

When I wasn't busy with issues of the artefact, I focused my attention on Klaur in Australia. We wrote to each other; I mostly to him, of course. We talked about us moving in together when he got back to Canada. After my mother's hateful words, I was determined to be rid of her in my life once and for all. I told him that I was through with living with my mother and that I was planning to leave and move to the Okanagan with him. I asked him if he would move in with me. I also told him about some of my tactics I had planned to help finance our relocation. I had a plan of working my father into leaving with me.

I was worried about Dragon and tried as much as possible to make time to see her and make sure she was okay. However, whenever I spoke to her about my plans for Klaur and me she would 'preach' about staying at home. Did she not understand the frustration my mother caused me? Did she not care how much I loved Klaur and needed to be with him? It was clear that she was very distracted and had become a very unsympathetic friend. She would blather on about how I should stay at school and put up with my mother and that if Klaur truly loved me, he would be patient and take things slowly. How could I possibly expect Dragon to understand matters of the heart? I don't think she had one. Besides, whatever she was up to certainly didn't seem to be 'taking things slowly'. I really needed my friend to be there for moral support, and I certainly didn't feel it from Dragon.

The one saving grace was my new friend and confidant Agaratte. It seemed with the absence of Klaur and the anaemic friendship of Dragon, Agaratte filled my heart with a blooming rose of friendship. We would write to each other, talk on the phone and spend time together either before or after every Coven meeting. He understood my traditional convictions to the Craft, he was a passionate person with the same appetite for the future that I had, and he genuinely wanted to know what my dreams and aspirations were.

I don't know when I began to realize that I was beginning to have feelings for Agaratte that went far deeper than friendship. But I knew that I had to keep them in check to ensure that I didn't ruin a wonderful friendship. Part of me wished that Klaur possessed Agaratte's beautifully rich intellect.

At home, my father, a man who deeply believes in family and keeping peace and harmony between mother and me was beginning to show signs of extreme stress from volleying constantly betwixt us. I was growing concerned for him, but the more I pictured the return of Klaur, the more I realized there would be no future with him if I stayed here with my mother.

Moving to Penticton was the decision I made. It was a natural choice as we knew people there and it is beautiful and a magically empowered place. Dragon knew little of this land, and I was concerned that she might betray me to my mother if I stayed in Vancouver. I decided to let my father in on some of the things I was thinking and planning, and, to be safe, begged him to not tell mother. Father initially had sounded a great deal like Dragon. However, I was able to persuade him by insisting that regardless of whether he came with me or not that I was going. That if he didn't come with me, there would be a good chance that he would not hear from me for protracted periods because he would be with mother and that I specifically didn't want to have anything more to do with her. He was a man of few words and even fewer thoughts. His wife had successfully turned him obedient so I suppose it wasn't too surprising that I managed to convince him.

During this time I noticed Dragon's friendship with Lactavia growing and it hurt to the quick. I was being thrown to the curb and I was sure

I knew why: I simply knew too much. I felt abandoned like an old toy. She politely returned phone calls but never came to see me or invited me out with her, although she couldn't avoid me in matters of the Coven.

Another Samhaen festival was in the works and we had agreed to celebrate it in the forests near the University of British Columbia. I missed Klaur, but at least Agaratte would be there.

Samhaen may have traditionally been a celebration to mark the beginning of winter. It more accurately is the time when the veil between the world of the living and the spirit world are at their thinnest. It is for this reason that it is such an important time for practitioners of the Craft.

Tyra and I met with Dragon and Lactavia at Doll and Penny's prior to joining Agaratte and Margon at Wreck Beach; this is the name of the beach by the forest. Dragon was early, as usual, sitting with Lactavia and enjoying her coffee. They were smiling at each other and talking trivially when Tyra and I entered the restaurant. I don't know why Dragon always had to meet at this weird restaurant with fag waiters. The food was bad and the service was even worse; it had to be the coffee. Dragon looked up and smiled upon seeing me. I was happy to see that she was excited to see me. Lactavia turned and, as usual, didn't look very happy to see her spotlight taken away.

"Kat, Tyra. Hey guys, come on over and grab a seat." Dragon said in her loud and resonating voice, with the usual level of exuberance that made most of the restaurant clientele stop and turn to watch us. Dragon either had no idea how her voice carried or she simply didn't care – being discrete was not her strong point. Tyra turned to me, smiling as if reading my mind and agreeing with me. We smiled at each other and walked to the table. We exchanged hellos and Dragon wasted no time taking our coats and walking over to the coat rack to hang them like a gentleman.

"So Tyra, what have you been up to lately?" Dragon asked, sitting down again and waving to a waiter for more coffee.

"The usual: school, studying my craft and did I mention studying my craft? My brother moved out so I have the entire upstairs of the house to myself." She said, smiling, her golden eyes shining.

"Wow! We'll have to remember that for the next time we have a group study or maybe even for Samhaen." Dragon said. I then stopped the waiter Dragon had summoned by raising my arm and as politely as I knew how, asked him to get me a cup of Earl Grey tea.

"Kat, what evil have you been up to lately?" Dragon asked, grinning as if at a joke, but I knew she meant it seriously. I sneered back at her.

"I have been far too busy with exams at school and planning for Klaur's return to be of any true evil, Dragon." I said, pausing for a moment before I continued as the waiter had returned surprisingly promptly with my tea.

"What have you been up to lately? Hmmm? Spending much time in Canada these days, for the sake of Lactavia?" I knew this exposure would piss her off enough to leave me alone. Instantly Dragon's face became flushed with what I was certain was withheld rage. Her eyes squinted towards me, but she didn't say a damn thing. She had a hard time containing her anger and at least she had learned it is better to hold your tongue than to open your mouth and expose everything.

"You travel, Aileen?" Lactavia said, ignorant as I expected her to be. Obviously, Dragon had kept her even more in the dark then she kept me. This made me feel better. At least Dragon trusted me more than her. I would be quite annoyed if she confided all to that bloody neophyte. Dragon looked at Lactavia smiling with her big lying face.

"Kat's full of shit as usual. I don't go anywhere." Dragon said, waiting for Lactavia to look away before she shot me a dirty or threatening look. I just smirked back at her. What great fun it was to have conversations going on two levels. Dragon seemed to read my humour in it.

"No. I haven't traveled much, but I haven't had much sleep lately—how about you Kat?" She beamed.

"Well, I, for one, have been sleeping altogether too much." I said.

"Shitty...Some of the best times I have is when I am not sleeping." Dragon replied smiling very broadly.

"Truly Dragon? Are they indeed best times? I would wager they are anything but. You should get more sleep. If I had it my way, you would be sleeping more than me."

"There is nothing you can do." She had a smile that hinted at the fact that she felt secure that I was less powerful than her spectral lover.

"Soon the plane from Australia will land and then I will have the last laugh. I will finally have everything you do not." I returned the broad smile and watched her smile dissolve into deep thought.

"Only Kat and Dragon could argue about who sleeps more than the other, eh Tyra?" Lactavia said to Tyra reaching for Dragon's cigarette and stealing it away. I noticed the cigarettes. Dragon wasn't supposed to be smoking – I knew that her warlock friend disliked it intensely. Poisons like tobacco and drugs impeded magic. Besides, the famous rock star was well known to be part of the anti-smoking, anti-drug campaigns.

"Dragon, you are smoking? Who is the naughty, disobedient girl?" I said, grabbing a cigarette for myself. Again, Dragon only looked at me with a sneer and said nothing.

Tyra and Lactavia were having a side conversation about music and what new music they were buying and to what new movies they had been. Dragon took the opportunity to push her thoughts into my head. I was very surprised at how good she had become at this. I could very clearly hear her say, "You have been very busy with magic, my sister. You look like shit!" I tried to return the favour but her mind was utterly blocked, thanks to that ring from her fucking warlock master. I was reduced to using my voice.

"Obviously, we have both been very busy; you don't look that much better. At least my magic is from my own doing. I don't rely on anyone else." I whispered almost inaudibly.

"Why do you hate him so much?" She asked me again by pushing the thought into my head. I didn't like the idea that she could so easily now do this and I immediately put more energy into blocking my thoughts lest she find something I didn't want her to know. It worked; I could feel her dissolve.

"I trust you, Dragon; I don't trust him. I trust Margon. It is another Samhaen– you should bond with Margon, it is your place." Dragon rolled her eyes up to the back of her head.

"You know what, Kat? She doesn't want Margon. Can't you understand that?" Lactavia had obviously overheard me and wasn't about to let us continue this conversation without her five cents' worth. When Lactavia realized she had everyone's attention she continued.

"Maybe she has already found someone. It's her business, not yours. Besides, why does it have to be one of the guys in the coven?"

"Why indeed would it have to be a guy for that matter eh, Lactavia?" I said looking at her, because I could read her thoughts like an open book. She was completely in love with Dragon. Dragon could even ensnare females. Did Dragon also foolishly ensnare Bryn merely by her beauty?

"Well, I think it is time we got our coats and went to meet up with the guys at Wreck Beach." Tyra said, attempting to diffuse another Kat and Lactavia confrontation.

"I'm outta here." Dragon said, walking to the till to pay for all the drinks while Lactavia and I continued to eye each other coldly.

More is the pity, for as we joined in our Samhaen, I could tell that Margon had developed a real affinity for Dragon but she was too stubborn and blind to see genuine affection from a truly warm-hearted, wonderful young man.

Chapter 14

Combining work and school left me with very little time to practice any Wicca. It's not that school was hard, and I wasn't working huge hours, but my time for practicing the Craft was taken up by Bryn, and I was becoming somewhat sleep deprived. Reading break was a welcome two week pause from having to attend school. I worked more hours, but I could also get more time in my bedroom, and I needed that time. I kept having flashbacks to the Cathexisphere in England. That was an experience for the books! There was huge significance to this event for Bryn; I just didn't really understand what the whole thing was about. I didn't really care either. If he needed that, I was okay with it. I looked down at the ring on my finger and smiled. I cannot imagine two people closer than Bryn and I – and we lived on opposite sides of the Earth!

While I worked on getting through another school year in Vancouver, Bryn informed me that for various reasons he was going to be living in the United States of America for one year. That meant that all of the next year was going to be in either Los Angeles or New York City. I begged him to move to Vancouver for that year, but he insisted that he had specific work to do in the United States, ugly work, and that he had to go there. He disliked the U.S. even more than I did, so I knew that this had to be some business indeed! Besides, what would he do, drive me to school? So I focused on ECAW, my classes, and the hope that future 'links' with Bryn would mean that we at least would finally both be in the same time zone.

An older friend of mine moved back to the big city from Edmonton and we wasted no time resuming our friendship. I didn't have a great deal of time but when I did, Jasmine and I went out dancing. Dancing is Jasmine's life, shopping and dancing that is.

"So it's Friday night Aileen, wanna come out and dance yourself to death?" Jasmine called me at the salon. The salon shuts down at 6:30 pm and I was just closing up the shop when she called.

"I'm pretty beat but, what the hell; lots of time for sleep in the grave eh?" Jasmine laughed on the other end of the phone.

"Wanna come to my place to get ready? I know you love to shop in my closet." Jasmine was an expert seamstress and one hell of a designer. Why she waitressed I had no idea; she could have made millions as a designer. I, however, enjoyed trying on all of her concept clothes. She had the largest collection of dresses, skirts, shoes, and tops of any woman, I was sure. I never went out with Jasmine without feeling we were the best dressed women in the club.

"Yeah, I'll call mom and tell her I am crashing at your place tonight."

"See you in about an hour then. I'll make us some Rice a Roni." Jasmine said laughing.

"Another excellent example of your fine home cooking…see ya." I put down the phone and called my mom

"Helloooo?" My mother said, with her heavy German accent

"Hey mom…I want to go dancing with Jasmine tonight. Is it okay if I crash at her place?"

"Aileen, you know your father wants you to come home. Why don't you go out for a bit and come home. I am sure you don't need to stay the night at Jasmine's. You should sleep in your own bed." There were other reasons that I didn't want to come home. If I stayed at Jas' apartment I wouldn't run the risk of being disturbed by Bryn. I preferred to be left alone to sleep on my nights out. But I could tell that my mother was hinting that my Dad was getting choked with me constantly going out with Jasmine.

"Okay, fine, I'll come home. But don't wait up for me. The dancing doesn't really get hopping until midnight."

"Be a good girl, Aileen." Wasn't I always?

I loved getting dressed up, I loved dancing. I didn't enjoy the men, in various states of drunkenness that would attempt to clumsily ensnare me with a yet more ridiculous line on why we were to go with them to their car, a restaurant, or their house. They disgusted me; it seemed upon entering a club we were besieged by young men. I smiled and even danced with them but we wouldn't let them sit with us and we wouldn't allow them to buy us drinks. In fact, Jasmine and I had a "one drink a night" rule. The sole goal for the evening for me was to dance till the wee hours of the morning. Jasmine was more interested in fraternizing with the men. The legal age for these clubs was 19 so I was under age, a condition I was very accustomed to. Fortunately, I was rarely asked to provide proof of my age. I had a strictly "Get Lost" policy on men at the clubs, remarkably similar to my non-club personae. Jasmine however, occasionally gave out her phone number or would agree to meet some of these guys. After all, she was 23 and that was perfectly normal.

"I can't believe how you have grown since I left Vancouver and moved back. It's only been about four years and in that time you have blossomed."

"Well, I was twelve when you left, Jazz."

"Yeah but you have like grown a foot in height and not to mention everywhere else. When I left I was still taller than you. Now look at you, you're a giant." I just laughed. It had been a long time and I had changed a lot. My life had changed in ways I hoped she would never know.

"That DJ really seems to be interested in you, Aileen. Why don't you go talk to him, see if he wants to give you his number?"

"No thanks."

"Come on, he's cute."

"Not my type."

"Well then what the hell is your type?" I was beginning to realize that this was a recurring theme with my friends. I had to come up with some kind of rationale, so, since my friends were joking that I must be gay. I thought that the illusion of me being a dyke seemed to work well; if it stopped them from introducing me to guys I had no desire for.

"Well he's a guy, and that is not my type."

"So what, you really are a dyke?"

"Don't worry you're not my type either…"

"Lactavia is though isn't she?"

"Yeah, I'm taken; so get off my back." I laughed to let her know I wasn't meaning it in a cruel way. I motioned that we should go on the dance floor and dance, which we did.

As soon as I got home that night Bryn dragged me over to his place in Los Angeles for a quick round of sex and small conversation. I was dead tired. Once he was in the U.S. we'd hook up two to three nights a week fairly regularly. Whether I was awake or not, I was procured to satisfy Bryn's prodigious needs. At times, it was too much for me, I was still a kid. I was tired and sore. I never let Bryn know my pain and I never let on that the intensity of our relationship was wearing me out. I just kept seeing him in my head, a couple of years ago, with tears in his eyes, saying I wasn't ready. I had to prove to him I was. I never told a soul about us. Instead, I just tried to find ways to cope.

Chapter 15

Kat reunites with Klaur

The interminable ticking of days finally ended as Klaurs' planned arrival came: June 27 I had planned it all with Klaur by phone and letters, planning ever more elaborately how we would live and be together. I thought about Agaratte, about how close we had become in Klaurs' absence. I had to make sure Klaur never found out about our closeness. I just needed the bond of a man while he was gone. Unlike Dragon, I rather enjoy, and perhaps require, the company of a man in my life. My father came with us, I told him that my mother's dominion over our lives, and constant verbal abuse, were no longer tolerable. I also said that I had no intentions of returning. I figured that if the anger against his wife wouldn't win him over, the threat of loosing me would probably do the trick. As predicted, he was ready fly the coop with me.

Bringing my father with me was important for two key reasons: he possessed an automobile and a diver's license, of which I had neither; and he had money, again which I had none. We picked up Klaur at the airport and drove directly to Penticton.

This rendezvous was done discretely, without any members of ECAW knowing save one, Agaratte, because, for one, we were in a rush, and, secondly, Dragon despised Klaur and made no secret of it, so I couldn't see that she would want to meet him at the airport. I knew Dragon would not approve of my moving to Penticton. I was so excited, even thrilled, that for once I would have a life which my mother denied me. I would wear what I wanted, do what I wanted, without worrying that the 'God-Squad' was watching me. I waited, barely containing my excitement, as Klaur's plane landed and issued it's occupants. I saw him exiting the customs office and WOW, had he grown! It had only been one year but the transformation was staggering. He was well on his way to becoming a man: some facial hair, a tan, and much taller than I last recalled. The photos he sent me did him no justice. On our four-hour drive to Penticton, we eagerly talked about our plans, holding hands and kissing all the while.

Barely a week after my requisition of accommodation and installation of the phone, mother contacted me. I was surprised that she would be resourceful enough to find out my whereabouts and unlisted phone number so quickly. I immediately suspected Dragon, of course -- that rat! Wasn't she my sister? A friend? How could she betray me? I resolved to not tell Dragon too much of my goings on, as I was convinced she would tell my mother. I was fairly terse with my mother on the phone, as I wanted her to understand that I was not a baby, subject to her will any longer. I wanted her to know that she no longer had control over my father or me anymore. She threatened to freeze the bank account so that Father and I would no longer have access to money, but I managed to convince her that this small manoeuvre would not amount to anything.

Solving that problem and putting my fathers' nerves at ease, I turned my attention to the boy for whom I had deserted Vancouver. I wanted Klaur to know that he was the king of my world and was happy to see how much change one year in Australia had affected him. After the first month of our being together here in Penticton, Klaur took on the role of man of the house.

"Kat, wake up!" Klaur commanded.

"Yes master." I replied with a smirk on my face.

"Pleasure me." He returned the impish smirk and turned it into a huge boyish grin.

"Yes master!" I said, and dove under the blankets, kissing down his body as I worked my way to his loins. I was pleased at how good I was getting at satisfying him. I liked this game; it helped me forget Agaratte because it was about giving the power and control over to Klaur. Now that I lived in the same town as Agarrate and he was a great friend of Klaur's, he was around a great deal and I found myself from time to time wanting him, missing our intimacy.

I heard Klaur groan and soon he was shaking from the size of his orgasm.

"You are a good slave." With that he rolled over and went back to sleep. Realizing that he would not sleep for much longer I quickly went into the kitchen to make breakfast. When I was done I quietly walked into the bedroom and whispered into Klaurs' ear that breakfast was ready. He smiled and mumbled,

"Yeah okay. Thanks babe."

I then proceeded to the rest of the daily grind: cleaning the apartment, vacuuming, and doing the laundry. Of course, when Klaur awoke to eat his meal, I stopped doing the housework and knelt down beside him just in case he required anything during his meal. He ate his breakfast and then smiled down at me.

"You're a dirty little slave, aren't you?" he said playfully.

"Yes master"

"You want a spanking don't you?"

"Yes master, I beg it."

"You don't have the right to beg for anything!" We both laughed at what great fun this game was. I just loved playing slave girl. Klaur enjoyed playing games too and that made me happy.

I had a shower and Klaur got dressed and headed for the door and his shoes. I didn't want to appear like a parent that needs to know everything, but I wanted to know where he was going and when he would be back.

"Give me some of your dad's money" He commanded while tying his shoelaces.

I decided that this time I would just trust him and didn't ask him a damn thing. I ran into my fathers' room and grabbed his wallet, I then returned to Klaur with the wallet he opened and withdrew the entire contents of the monies. He then left the house. He came back at 5 pm with his friend Agaratte. They were smoking pot in the livingroom, waiting for dinner, which I was preparing. I was almost finished making dinner when I heard my Klaur call me:

"Kat, come into the livingroom for a moment"

"Sure, what's up?"

"You are a good slave girl aren't you? " I was stunned that he was playing our little game in front of Agaratte. I was embarrassed, but I didn't want to show any sign that I cared what Agaratte thought. I just had to think quickly so I decided to play along.

"Yes, master I try to be a good slave." It was hard not to have a certain degree of hesitation in my voice.

"Tonight you will be pleasuring my good friend Agaratte". He smiled broadly at me and put his hand on Agaratte's shoulder roughly. I couldn't believe my ears! I didn't know whether to be happy, scared at possibly that this was a bad joke to test and see whether or not I had any feelings for Agaratte, or what?

"I'm afraid your slave girl is a bit hard of thinking. Surely you jest?"

"I command it."

"Well, if you command it," I said, hiding the sudden welling of joy that filled my heart.

"Dinner is ready." I said quietly. I kept watching the two guys to see if either was about to erupt into laughter because the joke was up, but neither party did. Instead they headed into the kitchen and filled up their plates with food. Then they ate, talking and laughing all the while. When they were done I could hear Klaur and Agaratte talking about the ongoings of the day, and plans they had to go to Vancouver to do some business. It sounded as though Klaur had no intentions of my coming along, and this spiked my anger at this game perhaps getting a little carried away. I pushed the thought from my mind and instead focussed on the rest of the kitchen conversation. Klaur was planning to meet up with Margon tonight and told Agaratte to fully enjoy this night with Kat as he might not feel so generous again. When the guys rejoined me in the living room, Klaur reached for his jacket and headed out the door without a word. I was furious and I wondered how much of this hostility to direct towards Agaratte. He sat on the couch and I decided to play along to see just how far he thought he could play this game.

"What is your wish?" I said quietly as I knelt beside him on the floor trying with all my skill not to sound like I wanted to knock his red head off his shoulders..

"Kat, we are alone for the evening. You can get up and sit beside me. As you can see, the village idiot has departed." He said calmly. I looked up and smiled, thankful that at least Agaratte was still my good friend.

"I think Klaur is pushing this a little too far. You don't have to do anything tonight that you don't want to." He took one of my hands into his hands.

"I will always be your friend Kat." He said soothingly.

Tears began to well up in my eyes uncontrollably, and I fell into his arms. He hugged me back. I kissed him and he returned the kiss.

"So, it appears that Klaur has settled in quite comfortably. How is your father? Where is your father?"

"You know I don't know what he does half the time. He comes and goes. Sometimes he goes for walks, sometimes to church or to functions that the veterans here have. But most of the time, I honestly don't know.

"I don't wish to alarm you Kat, but the betrayer is your father, not Dragon. He frequently sneaks off to have long phone conversations with your mother."

"He what?"

"Don't become upset. It really is of little consequence."

"How do you know this? Have you been spying on him?" I was stunned that Agaratte would know more about my father's day to day goings on than me, his own daughter. It was also unsettling that he knew I suspected Dragon. I never confided this to anyone.

"Let's just say I like to be a person in the 'know'." He smiled and got up to go towards the door.

"Let's enjoy a walk shall we?"

"Wait a minute. Why would you think that I would blame Dragon for betraying me to my mom?" I got up and walked towards him, not letting my eyes off him. I wanted to make sure he wouldn't lie to me. You always have to watch a person's body language especially someone as mysterious as Agaratte.

"Dear Kat, you have made no secret of your more recent resentment of Dragon." He smiled and motioned towards the door.

"Agaratte." I paused and reached for his shoulder and waited for him to turn to face me.

"Do you find Dragon more beautiful than me? Would you be swayed by her if she came wooing?" This caused him to furrow his eyebrows at me and then smile in what looked like humour or incredulity.

"Kat. I can honestly assure you that I consider the two of you to be completely different creatures altogether. I personally prefer mammals over reptiles." This of course caused me to erupt into laughter. It was the sweetest thing he could have ever said. We walked out the door and went down the stairs of our three story walk-up apartment building and headed for the streets of Penticton for some sun and pleasant company. I instinctively put my hand in his and he didn't object.

"Why then would Klaur not want me to go to Vancouver with you guys? I know there is to be an ECAW ritual and meeting and I can't imagine why he would want to be anywhere near the Dragon's lair?

"Well, I told you that I personally do not like reptiles. Klaur is a snake however, and I hate to be the bearer of bad news but I would be lying to you if I told you that he wasn't just a bit smitten by your golden haired colleague. I don't think he really lusts after her or anything. I think he sees her as a power rival and is bent on toppling her. You and I both know how successful he will ultimately be."

I understood Agaratte's words. I knew that the bad guy was Klaur. But my jealousy and growing resentment, or was it hatred? Whatever it was, it was driving me to distraction towards Dragon. I found myself wishing she were dead. I thought about Rodan, Lactavia, Bryn and now my own Klaur. What if she ever conquered Agaratte? I would indeed kill her with my bare hands if that event happened. Then the most wonderfully evil thought entered my head. This idea was almost as wonderful as my plan to sever Dragon from Bryn. Why not try and get Lactavia to move to Penticton? Lactavia is far more easily swayed, and wouldn't Dragon just fall to pieces without her precious Lactavia, the only person Bryn would allow her to be intimate with?

"Agaratte. Can you do me a favour?"

"I will try."

"Why don't you offer the welcome to Lactavia first? I am sure that if she were to come, then perhaps Dragon would be persuaded. I do so miss my friends." I tried to not look upset about Klaur's licentious ways. He stopped walking and turned to face me.

"You truly have a wicked mind. I like it. But I would caution you: consider the consequences if you got what you wanted. Imagine Klaur's ego if he were to have all four of you girls here? I daresay he would become quite intolerable. "He smiled and continued walking. I could handle Klaur, and it would be worth it to see Dragon with no Bryn and no Lactavia. The thought cheered me up to the point of floating on a cloud.

We returned to the apartment after our brief walk and spent the remainder of the evening touching casually and talking. There was a beautiful honesty to our relationship, and it was so simple. At 11 pm Klaur came back home and grinned at his friend,

"So Agaratte, I trust she pleased you satisfactorily?"

"Of course, but now I must make my way home." Agaratte lied putting his jacket on.

"Remember, we leave for Vancouver next Saturday." Klaur patted his friend on the shoulder before he left the apartment.

"Got it! Good night Kat." He said smiling and winking at me.

Chapter 16

I knew that Kat had bided her time at school appeasing her mother prior to Klaurs' arrival from Australia where she then put her plan into motion. I was a little shocked and deeply concerned, but believed that Kat must know what she was doing. I didn't like Klaur and I was convinced that pitting one parent against another was unhealthy. It showed me another cold, cruel side to Kat.

This numbed our relationship. Not surprisingly that my contact thereafter with Kat became less frequent. In its place, my relationship with Lactavia grew. Lactavia and I spent a great deal of time together. Soon the time had come, Kat was off to what she was certain was freedom, and I suppose if it was truly freedom that she was destined to find, I could not hold it against her. I knew what she went through living at home, and while I found her tactics Machiavellian and utterly ruthless, I couldn't begrudge her an opportunity to attempt a move to independence. After all, what would I give to be with the man of my dreams?

The following weeks I was overwhelmed by phone calls from a first sad, frightened Mother Smith and then angry, hostile Mother Smith. In fact, my parents began to get quite irritated at the disruption that Mrs. Smith was causing me and the household. I think that my parents were also surprised by her candid conversations with us in our livingroom when she recounted the story leading up to them 'running away.' Mrs. Smith told me in front of my parents how this is all happened because Kat was adopted and her real mother was an Arab woman who conceived her through an unsavoury alliance with a married military man. That because both parents were Godless sinners, that they could only conceive a sinful daughter like Kat. My father absolutely loved Kat and thought her the most polite and friendly amongst my friends and did not take well to this ridiculous accusation of Kat's moral character. He actually kicked Mrs. Smith out of our house telling her that her familial woes are not his problem and certainly not his daughter's. I was very proud of my Dad for sticking up for Kat. Frankly, I was glad he got her off my ass. It did the trick too, and she never bothered us again.

About a week later my mother caught me alone in the kitchen and decided that she wanted to instil a bit of her insights on me.

"Aileen. I want you to think about your friend Kat. She is living with a teenaged boy and her father is not really mentally responsible. I believe Mrs. Smith mentioned that he has Alzheimer's disease. It could be possible that these kids are getting into some real trouble because for the most part they are unsupervised and to the best of my knowledge they are neither working nor attending school. You should at least call occasionally and make sure they are safe." My dad had a 'hands off' approach, but it was clear that my mom felt that duty to your friends meant helping them, even if they didn't want your help, if you felt they were potentially in trouble. I knew my mother was right.

"I promise I will stay in touch, and at the first sign of trouble, I'll do something proactive, Mom."

"That's my girl. Just come to me if you have any problems." She reassured me and ran off to her kitchen cupboard by the coffee maker where she stashed her chocolate.

I admit that it was only a half-hearted promise, as I firmly believed that fate would be her best teacher and that she would come home on her own accord after some terrible, yet life learning, event. This is the kind of tough love theory that I learned from my father, who used it on my older brother and me, so I naturally assumed it would work for Kat. I remembered a moment from my past. The summer before I went to Royal Oak, before I was introduced formally to my ghost, I was fourteen... well I was in my Dad's recreation room downstairs with a friend. We bought some pop and got into my Dad's imported Rum. Like a couple of girls it was 95% pop with a tablespoon or so of rum in it. Well, until Dad came in and saw us having our illicit drinks. He walked over to his bottle of 80% Stroh Austrian rum, proceeded to fill our almost empty glasses with rum again – straight rum, and forced us to drink it, all of it! I never wanted to drink alcohol again. My father missed his calling; he should have been a military trainer. He was a master at aversion therapy. I laugh now reflecting upon it. Kat was about to get a premature crash course in life, love and adult responsibility – welcome to my world.

It was Thursday night, and the summer was at its peak as July spread hot, sunny weather in the waterlogged city of Vancouver. Jasmine was going out tonight on a date. I phoned Lactavia to tell her that tonight was a bad night for me to go out. I made some lame excuse about going out with my mother. Tonight Bryn had arranged to see me, and I wouldn't let him down.

"This place is kind of grodey." I remarked looking at the small hotel room and then finally sitting at the edge of the bed. Bryn was in the bed, under the beige blankets with a white T-shirt still on.

"Come here." He said, sounding almost like a polite command, patting the portion of bed immediately next to him. I humoured him and crawled over to him. He opened his arms and we hugged for a while. While we hugged I couldn't help but notice how even in this modest hotel room, with nothing more than a plain T-shirt on, he was so singular in beauty and charisma; dark, brooding, and fiendishly sensual. It wasn't that big of a surprise he was a star.

"I can't stand the media; everyone is getting on my case. I feel like I can't do anything right." Bryn sounded tired and very depressed. He looked at the blanket, his eyes darting down, shadowed by his long lashes. I stared for a bit at his white profile before speaking – admiring how every feature added to the other contributed to his stunning visage.

"You need a break Bryn. What magic are you doing that is draining you so? You said the money didn't mean that much to you. Take a break and get a fresh perspective." Reflexively, I took his cold hand into mine.

"I don't belong here. I long to go home, to be in England." He said stroking my head with his free hand. I was aware of his annoying habit of not answering my questions.

"Bryn…" I paused, speaking as gently as I knew how. "What are you up to here in Los Angeles that is wearing you out? I can tell that when you use a lot of magic your emotional and physical state declines, you should stop for awhile." I coaxed him to look into my eyes to read his expression. I wasn't about to let him avoid answering my question. There was a pregnant pause, his gaze never wavering.

"No, I can't stop. But I really do need you Aileen. I simply can't do anything without you, especially now. He stopped, grabbed both of my hands and kissed them. I was enjoying it all well and fine but he was stubbornly refusing to talk.

"What are you up to Bryn? Just tell me." I took my hands away from his face and glared at him.

"I can't tell you."

"You can't or you won't?"

"Both." He returned my glare, daring me to push him further. I hesitated, I was familiar with his temper, and I was in no mood for a fight. But was I in the mood for a stand-off? Well mom and dad didn't give birth to a fool.

"Can you at least tell me why you have to make everything so complicated?"

"My primary purpose in everything I do is to protect you, my love. By the way, life is complicated."

"I don't need protecting, it looks more like you do." I was beginning to accept the fact that I was never going to get any answers and just to sit back and enjoy the ride as Rodan put it to me once.

"Well, keep your secrets. But you look like shit. Turn over onto your stomach and take your shirt off." That made him grin deviously and quickly his shirt was off and he was chest down with his face turned to the left. I straddled his hips and gave him a back massage.

"You know you are my only light…" He said quietly. I just kept rubbing his back and working my way down to his lower lumbar. He really did look tired, and I was growing increasingly concerned that his health was in jeopardy. He had lost a great deal of hair and already had surgery to replace it. I worked silently until he lost consciousness.

RRRRRrrrrringgg….RRRRinnggggg…RRingg……

"Hello?" I inquired to an irritating phone, it being nine pm or so.

"Hi Aileen? It's Lactavia. Would you like to meet up with me downtown after work to do some shopping tomorrow?" She showed no concern that I was at home, when I told her I had to go out with my mother.

"Sure, how about 5pm?" I figured if she didn't question, I wouldn't try and justify why I was at home.

"Sounds good. Meet you at Doll and Penny's then?"

"See ya there, Ciao." I said in a tired voice before hanging up. I laid back on my bed, put my hands behind my head and looking at the ceiling and thought about 'him'. Well, at least Bryn would get some sleep tonight, poor guy.

Doll and Penny's was my favourite restaurant. The place to be seen if you are a member of the Gay scene. Maybe we didn't belong there on Davie St. but that didn't matter. I enjoyed the wild people, scenery and, most of all; the gay men left me alone.

The dark interior hallmarked with all manner of glitzy pictures of golden Hollywood stars like Marilyn Monroe and Jean Harlow. The décor was eclectic with Gothic tables and chairs, black and purple paint and velvet curtains for accent. Twinkling lights on the high ceiling afforded little light to this heavy atmosphere and, as a final touch, the waiters would occasionally dress up as their favourite Hollywood women.

It was entertaining just to go to this restaurant for the ambiance of the setting, the waiters in drag and, of course, the colourful people who called this place home away from home. Certainly not a restaurant for those who had problems accepting that such bizarre people populated this city. But this is Vancouver, home to the bizarre – wet and wild, a city I call home. The subject of discussion tonight was not of a Wiccan nature, nor of Kat and Klaur. Today Lactavia need only know what we were to do for entertainment, my favourite subject. I wasn't keen on a movie or walking by the seawall, so we agreed to do some shopping on Granville St. We promptly left the restaurant and headed down Davie street.

"Why don't you stay overnight at my place? That way you and I can get up early and go to Stanley Park before we meet up with the rest of the gang in North Vancouver." Lactavia invited, pulling on one of her small, red-laced gloves as she marched beside me.

"Yeah, just that I won't have a change of clothes."

"You can borrow something of mine."

"Man! You and I have very different taste babe. I'm allergic to pink." I laughed and jabbed her.

"Very funny Dragon, I am sure I have something you'd be willing to wear."

It was great having that friendship that was normal; we talked about music, movies, books, clothes and food. Lactavia made me laugh hard and this was a time in my life when I needed a few good laughs. I found it hard to say good-night to her; consequently I spent the odd sleep-over at her place. A night away from my room was a welcome departure for me. My parents didn't seem to mind me spending the night at Lactavia's parent's place as opposed to Jasmine's apartment. Lactavia had moved from her mother's house and was living with her Dad in Downtown Vancouver. It was convenient to crash at her place as she lived on Davie and Bidwell.

After a short shopping romp on Granville St we walked back to her Dad's flat at sunset, got into the building and into the elevator heading for the 21st floor. The elevator had that funny smell; it was a slightly sweet almost almond-like smell of cockroach pesticide. Lactavia would insert the key into the lock, open the door and you could hear the sound of hundreds of roach feet pounding the hardwood floor, scattering to find a hiding spot before we turned on the light. I still have an intense cockroach phobia to this day because of that damn apartment. The apartment was about 700 square feet with a small balcony overlooking English Bay. The furnishings were modern, consisting of teak and leather. Like Bryn's house, another bachelor, the rooms were bare and Lactavia's dad, being European wore heavy cologne too –So the house smelled of Aramis. All the food was tightly sealed in plastic containers and it was obvious that the roaches had little if anything to feed on.

We had to share her bed in her room, which was a small waterbed I hardly found comfortable.

"Nat, do you mind not crowding me? I'm like, dying of heat."

"I can open the window a little more…"

"No, cause then I will freeze my ass off in the middle of the night. My body just doesn't produce any heat –I'm not a furnace like you…"

"Too hot, too cold, you really are a lizard." Lactavia laughed and then grabbed my hand,

"Well then at least let me snuggle schmedley." She said smiling hugging my hand.

"Schmedley? Who the fuck is Schmedley?"

"That is the name I gave this hand." She laughed and then kissed my hand.

"Grow up." I turned and tried to get to sleep. I didn't like hurting her feelings.

"What do you want to do tomorrow after the ECAW meeting in North Vancouver?"

"My mother got me an interview with a restaurant friend of hers, so I am going to see if I can get a job there. It's a Greek style restaurant. Want to come with me?"

"Don't you think that would look bad? I mean you shouldn't have friends join you at an interview for a job."

"I wouldn't worry about it Aileen. I will get the job because the owner owes my mother money and therefore a favour." I thought to myself, Geez, must be hard when your mother either gives you money or gets you a job. But I didn't say anything. My parents always left me to fend for myself. I had to go over the job opportunities, fill out applications and do interviews – real interviews. My dad took responsibility very seriously. I lived in the city and he made sure that by the time I was fourteen that I had plucked chickens, gone fishing, hunting, cooked and cleaned the whole house and I didn't get an allowance for it either. It was my responsibility to provide for our household too. I suppose he thought that it would give me pride or a sense of contribution. More often though, it made me want to get a job where I would actually get compensated for the work.

"Well, that settles it then, I will just go home. I have a pile of homework to do anyways."

The next day came and Lactavia and I had a meeting with the other Coven members first thing in the morning. I wasn't expecting too many people there as half of the crew was in Penticton. I arrived at the appointed place with the books and we sat in the woods and waited for whoever would show up. There was a rattling of the bushes and then Margon, Klaur, and Agaratte appeared. No Kat. When Klaur saw me he grinned,

"Dragon, the answer to your frigid prayers has just arrived. There is plenty of me to go around." I was rather stunned and appalled at what I had just heard and I saw the look of pain in Agaratte's face, I think he actually winced at the comment of his compatriot.

"Fuck off Klaur!" I spat back at him.

"Oh come on, you know you love it." I was thinking about heaving one of the books at him when Agaratte seemed to read my body language.

"Let's just get to the meat of the deal instead of fighting shall we?" Agaratte interjected with a smile at me and pushed Klaur's chest to sit down.

"Where's Kat?" Asked Lactavia

"Not here this trip, she is waiting for you all to move to Penticton. Sorry Dragon." Klaur sneered as he sat down next to Agaratte. I decided to take Agaratte's advice and just ignore Klaur and I opened the book to the ceremony of the circle and began preparing the ground. Ashes from the previous ceremony were collected and distributed to the cardinal points. This ceremony required only one small fire in the middle or a candle – I opted for the candle. I recited the words of invocation so that everyone could repeat them. We joined hands and began the ceremony.

"Goddess we invoke the wind of the west and the element of Air, the rain of the east and the element of water , the snow of the north and the element of Earth and the sun of the south and the element of fire. In the words of Armaros we ask for guidance to develop our craft in magick. "

Slowly, but with increasing strength the power flowed through all of us, more powerfully than ever before. The grip we had on each other became harder and harder, as if we were all afraid of letting go and becoming sucked up into an invisible vortex.

"Empowered by the will of the Goddess, in her Service to our realm we humbly thank her for her gifts."

With my last words the huge feeling lifted. I sighed a bit of relief, similar probably to when a parachuter pulls his chord and the parachute fills with air and his free fall is broken. There was no doubt to the immediate inference I was getting from this circle; we had an excellent mix of positive and negative spiritual flow. Agaratte was unquestionably powerfully poled in opposition of Margon and Lactavia. I was certain that I could feel Agaratte's mind noticing the same thing I was – Klaur and I were like energy sinks compared to Agaratte and the others. How is it possible that with all my experience, enchantments and obvious spiritual link I always have that I feel like Margon and Lactavia have more innate magical power than I do? I was more than a little disappointed in myself.

For about a solid five minutes, nobody spoke. The ceremony was a great success and we were all rather surprised at the level of power generated within the circle. When I saw Lactavia settle near a tree by herself I could see an expression of surprise. She probably was unsure what she had just experienced. That expression was undoubtedly what I looked like two years ago. I was wondering what the next time would be like, would it be even stronger? The positive side effect of these group ceremonies was an increase in our own abilities. It is not uncommon for groups to quickly disperse afterwardwards to work on developing independently our skills. It seemed that this was going to happen today, we couldn't wait to get away from each other.

I knelt down to collected the remains of the candle and my book. I was putting them into my bag when I noticed a visitor perched on a low branch. A small black crow sat, occasionally ruffling his feathers as if to convince someone he was going to fly somewhere. This crow and I watched as Klaur and Agaratte left the forest where the ceremony was.

"I don't think you had to worry about Dragon. She wouldn't have gotten in the way if Kat was here. Besides Kat wouldn't let Dragon take her away. We should have brought her. She'll be pissed." Agaratte said as he exited the last of the bush to the road. I could still overhear them.

"Honestly Agaratte, it has nothing to do with Dragon. I am going to tell Kat that I don't want her practicing Wicca anymore. I really felt something bizarre in that circle. I know that she must have an incredible amount of skill in this occult stuff and it bothers me that she is probably way better at it than me. No, she will no longer be allowed to practice." He punched Agaratte in the shoulder expecting him to understand and agree with him. It was clear however that Agaratte was surprised by Klaur's indefensible insecurity. I walked a little closer to listen in better.

"Do you really think she will stop just to please you?" Agaratte politely probed with the same bewildered look. Klaur just smiled and said,

"Of course she will; she loves me." Agaratte smiled back politely and unconsciously shook his head.

With those final words emanating from Klaur's lips I saw that crow open up his wings and take flight. Well, I may be a poorly powered witch, but I was an observant one. That was Thromm and I knew Kat had her servant follow Klaur. I also knew that Kat probably heard and saw everything that went on. I watched the crow disappear and grinned to myself. Kat made considerable efforts to know what was going on in her life. I should take a tip from Kat and get some real answers from Bryn as to why I seemed to be such a featherweight in the realm of magic. I made a mental note to pursue this the next time I was with him.

The rest of the month of July seemed to peel away without much eventfulness, with one noted exception, Lactavia. What to do about Lactavia? It was clear she had a crush on me. She wanted to hug and touch and probably more. I wasn't really into it, but I was increasingly becoming more convinced that if I wanted to get my friends off my back in terms of why I never dated, I pretty much had no other option. Lactavia as my girlfriend was a pretty easy fix. With Lactavia as my girlfriend, I would be branded a dyke and presto, no one bothers you anymore. It was so perfect; I couldn't believe that I didn't come up with it myself. Lactavia had to do the thinking for me.

Holding hands, hugging and the odd kiss were strange at first but after awhile it became pretty normal. I was beginning to think I had both Lactavia and myself fooled.

On some subconscious level however I was becoming aware of the fact that my romantic overtures with Lactavia weren't just to compensate for friends thinking I was a freak for not being with a guy. I was also compensating for my life with Bryn. I felt in control with Lactavia, something I never felt with Bryn.

Lactavia and I would often walk on the seawall together. We would go to restaurants, in our endless pursuit of the ultimate ethnic food experience. Biking, swimming, and of course shopping which was standard for teenagers. I don't know, but I suppose I enjoy contradictions and Lactavia was a walking contradiction. She was short, cute, and her pink sweaters and mini-skirts seemed to jar against her witchboots and cutting sarcasm. She was irresistible and I enjoyed the distraction.

"Sure you have to go? It's only 7 pm." Lactavia was standing at the electronic entryway to her father's apartment building looking at me disappointedly. We had walked most of the afternoon around Davie and Denman Streets.

"Yeah, I gotta work in the morning. Besides, It's a new moon tonight and I shouldn't be walking the streets at night, you know, it gets dark." I grinned at my inside joke, but I was also kind of choked that I was parting good company because I could just hear Bryn turning on the fatherly vibe, so not sexy.

"Well then I will wait at the bus stop with you."

"Sure." So we about faced and headed for the Davie Bus stop. Of course while we were there, Lactavia had some ideas of holding hands and giving me a kiss, which I was thoughtlessly dismissing. She misread my distraction for rejection.

"Why do you care so much about what other people think?" She sounded very annoyed and while I did turn to her, I was still in a bit of a fog. I was thinking about well, other things.

"What?"

"Why do give a shit what other people think?"

"Why don't you give a damn at all?"

"I care what you think and maybe anyone I care about, but really Dragon, you're never going to have the approval of the whole world so why even bother trying."

"Come on, I'm not that anal. I'm just not the type to show affection publicly, that's all." I was pretty sure this was an outright lie, but it sure sounded plausible.

"I would give anything if you could just summon up enough balls to kiss me just as the loaded bus came to pick you up!" She said stirring my competitive nature.

"That sounds like a dare. Do you really want the world to look at you and say, 'Hey, that chick is a dyke! " I countered her challenge.

"Better that than, 'hey, there goes frigid freak Aileen!" That hurt, it made me just want to say, 'well actually I am seeing someone so get off my back.' I have wanted to say something to someone for so long it made me furious. But what do you say? You'd just be laughed at. Even this was better than launching a confession that would lead to ridicule. The bus came, and it was loaded. I turned to Lactavia and gave her one big deep kiss and boarded the bus. I put on my Walkman's and didn't look at a single person – fuck 'em! I have to admit, it felt pretty good to do something a little out of character.

The drudgery of senior years at school paced on while Kat was in Penticton. Lactavia and I were working and completing grade 11. Bryn was getting great musical experience working and learning from some blues musicians in California and New Orleans. I knew he was up to other stuff too, I just didn't know what. Also, lately again he had been out of contact. He warned me this time that he was up to his ugly business and so at least I wasn't surprised. No matter, Lactavia and Jasmine kept me busy enough. What was left of the summer was quickly drying up and I made as much use of my weekends as I could. The very next Saturday after my bus stop kiss with Lactavia we were dining at, where else? Doll and Penny's.

"When is the last time I saw the fucking sun 'Tavi?" I said to Lactavia while stirring my coffee.

"What the hell is a 'sun'?" She grinned looking up at me and twizzling her straw through the ice in her cola.

"Ha ha, very funny. Why do we live in this fucking city when all the weather does is churn out homicidal maniacs?" I took a big sip, caffeine was my addiction. I put the heavy cup down on its saucer in my usual too rough manner and it clunked heavily as I looked at Lactavia's eyes in a sincere yet humorous way. She of course grinned back at me and immediately ensured I neither delved into weather nor politics.

"Beltane, another coming together of the circle will soon be here."

"Well then, how are things with our coven then? Any new revelations from Margon, Agaratte, or dare I ask word from Kat or Klaur?" I asked her, taking in another deep sip of my coffee. God's drink you know.

"Margon did submit a paper he researched regarding the …" She paused to look at the title before continuing, "Electro magnetic poles and relative ratios of neutral matter/energy to polar matter/energy. I read it and I couldn't make heads or tails out of it, maybe you can." She then handed the document to me. It was fairly thick, maybe 20 pages, it included photocopies of the original manuscript he had found and used as reference.

"Aileen?"

I looked at my friend all clad in pink and black as if to say yes.

"What the heck is he talking about? This doesn't look like magic, it looks like physics." She asked quietly, as if the question itself was embarrassing.

"Well, everything is made up of matter and energy, and in the microsphere we call the forces positive as what you have for Protons, negative as in what you have for Electrons, and neutral as in what you have with neutrons. Everything living and dead is made of these forces; this energy makes up matter that in turn makes you and I. ECAW has been working on the body of knowledge for quite some time that the macrosphere or the world we live in, the world of billions of assembled energies/matter are easier to manipulate than the microsphere, which scientists do when they split atoms or play with particle accelerators. We employ a totally different technique to what they do." I explained convinced that my description was very understandable.

"Is that what ECAW does? How is that Wicca?" She pushed.

"I suppose it is what all Wiccans do, whether they realize it or not. Everything in history was thought to be magic until science caught up." I said, not looking at her as I was attempting to get a drag queen's attention for more coffee.

"So when are you going to teach me something?" She was thumbing through the menu for something palatable.

"First you have to learn to channel your own energy. You have been to a few ceremonies to know what the energy feels like, now you must create it on your own." I said to her as a drag queen finally finished flirting with an attractive gay man by the window and grudging came to serve the 'fish' at the high table. 'Fish' is the stylish and complimentary term they use to refer to naturally born women – flattering eh?

He/she came, took our orders, topped up my coffee and we plunged back into our conversation.

"So when I can do that you will teach me something useful?" she asked

"Depends on what you call useful?"

"How about a love spell?"

"Gods! You have got to be kidding. Why?" I laughed at her, not intending to hurt her feelings. Everyone initially thinks of a love spell probably because it is a reasonably harmless spell that you can gauge the results on quickly. However, it is not nearly as useful as others. I saw the expression on her face, and thought I better explain my rudeness.

"What then?" she insisted.

"How about channelling energy so you can read thoughts?" I suggested.

"So… you can read my thoughts right now?"

"Yeah, I am totally in a state where I can channel energy to read your unimportant thoughts at this moment –NO! But if I sat here for awhile and focused something in your head would jump out at me, or maybe I could even suck it out!" I laughed ripping open a creamo to tip into my newly refreshed cup.

"Go for it!" She challenged. So I looked down on the floor and focused my energy and pushed my spiritual energies into her mind, something I was noticing I was getting better and better at. Of course, she couldn't block out energy as well as Bryn or Kat. I know she had the power, but no training on how to do it.

I saw a young blonde man, tall and slim dressed in leather and looking every bit the rebel. Like a stolen peep-show, I could see her surrendering herself to this young man. They were at work and he was running into the back of the restaurant, grabbing some pizza boxes, and then walking over to Lactavia to grab her breast and give her a kiss before he shot out the back door. Another intense thought of her was of her fornicating with this guy on a mattress on the floor in a small apartment with little furniture – his fine digs, no doubt.

"You are in love with some blonde, punk asshole that drives a motorcycle and you have been keeping it a secret all this time." I said, still looking down at the ground but I was pretty surprised.

"Who freaken told you?" she said stunned.

"You just told me!"

"Ya right, someone at the restaurant I work at must have squealed." She retorted

"Whatever…You lying little cow!" I was mad and I wasn't even entirely sure why. I mean, she didn't tell me because she thinks that I am only seeing her and that this would be a betrayal of our relationship. I could see that. How could I be upset or surprised? I suppose Lactavia and Kat were both now of the age where it was time to have boyfriends their age. This would totally blow my cover if Lactavia divulged her relationships with boys to other ECAW members.

About one week after my 'lovely revelation' with Lactavia I got a call to go haunt my love. This time I was going to ask him some questions and I wasn't going to let him weasel out. When I materialized, Bryn was lying on the floor, the lights were off, and there were five lit candles all around him. I was near his feet, he seemed uncertain that I was there. That was so unlike him, it immediately put me on edge. Something was wrong…

"Bryn? Are you all right?" The next thing I noticed was his face, how very drawn it looked; he appeared half dead. He opened his eyes slowly and held out his stone signalling with it for me to come into the circle of candles. I dropped to my knees and crawled up the length of his legs to his pelvis.

"How about a hug?" He whispered. His eyes were barely open and he looked pale, like all the blood in his body was missing.

"You look spent. You look magically spent. What have you done to yourself?" I put my arms around him and descended for a hug. He didn't answer me for about two minutes just slowly moved his arms around me. Then he slowly tracked his lips along my jaw line to meet my lips. Then he twisted his hips so that I was lying on the floor beside him. We must have laid there for a good half an hour just kissing and touching. Then he surprised me by jumping up and turning the lights on. When the lights came on, I saw that in fact he looked great. He wasn't pale, gaunt or drawn. He actually kind of glowed.

"Do you want to take a drive? I rented a Corvette." He smiled adjusting his pants, there was a noticeable lump.

"Wait just a minute, what the hell just happened? You looked like shit just a second ago."

"Well, I'm fine now. I just needed time to recuperate from some heavy handed magic, that's all. Come on, let's go for a drive.

"Will it be ok? I worry that I will look like an apparition in your car and the press hound you enough." I said being as sensitive to his situation as I knew how he hated the press, and just minutes ago he looked so dead.

"My windows are tinted and only mirrors and cameras will reveal your Ka, all people looking at you will see what I see." When he said Ka he meant spirit. After all that is all that I ever brought to England. The rest was magic, black or white I didn't know and I suppose I didn't care.

"Wait! I will go with you, as you wish, but first answer a question for me." I walked over to his bed and sat on the end of it.

"Yes, my inquisitive accomplice, what is it?"

"At the last circle in my Coven, I couldn't help but notice that the sheer power of that circle had little or nothing to do with my spiritual energy…Others in the group have far more power than me" I was rocking my leg, shifting my weight, and looking at him and I knew that I looked uncomfortable about this confession but I was. I mean we had done the binding ritual so there was no way he could push me away now. I guess it just made me feel inadequate in some way. But instead he looked at me very sincerely and sat on the edge of the bed next to me.

"It really troubles you?"

"You have so much power in magic. I try. I study; practice and I don't think I will ever match Kat. What possible benefit do I offer *us*?" I became aware that I was ready to cry. I could see that my pain at this confession got an instant reaction from Bryn. He put his arms around me and laid his head on my shoulder. He stroked my back for a minute.

"Aileen, you will have to just trust me that when the right time comes you will learn the true awesome nature of your gifts. I know you have big questions, and they deserve well thought out answers – I promise to answer them very soon, but my love, not tonight. Tonight I want to drive by where my brother and mother are. They will see I am well and will not trouble me anymore." He said smiling as he opened the hotel door.

He sprang up like a little schoolboy filled with giddy energy and jumped to the door.

"Apres vous, Mademoiselle." He said as he opened the door and jingled his keys out of his back pocket.

We drove out of the crowded roads that connect Los Angeles to outlying areas. The amount of traffic was tense. He pulled onto the interstate 10 heading for Santa Monica on the coast and explained that his mother was staying at the Holiday Inn and would soon be returning to England. He pulled up to the hotel and reached into the glove compartment for some documents.

"I just have to run these up to Mum. Won't be a minute, luv." With that he got out of the car and locked the door behind him. I saw him walk into the building. I was too scared to look around much, certain that a camera would be flashing. After about ten minutes I started getting bored and went looking through his glove compartment, tapes, maps, and a piece of paper I found on the floor. Nothing of any interest turned up. After about twenty minutes I noticed the lobby door opened and Bryn's mother came out, I began to panic. As she walked towards the car it seemed as though she saw me, she walked up to Bryn's car door and attempted to open it and then smiled at me and signalled to open the car door. Slowly, I reached over to his door and opened it. She opened the door and stunned me by not seeming the slightest bit disturbed by my appearance.

"So my son is keeping secrets from me I see. 'Allo! I'm Bryn's mum, Rose. Come inside and 'ave some tea wont you?" She put out her hand to shake, and I was immediately nervous that maybe I would not be solid enough. But at that moment Bryn came running up to the car, saving me.

"Mum, I told you I have to drive her to the airport right away. I just had to drop off those documents for the accountant."

"Well, I am just so happy to see you doing well. Who is your lady friend? Why didn't you tell me? When will you let me see her again Mr. Busy?" Her son looked at her with a flustered and embarrassed expression typical of any guy when his mother was mothering him in public.

"I'm coming home for Christmas, Mum. I have a lot of work to do on this upcoming album until then." He kissed her on the cheek and then jumped into the car, and we roared off towards the hotel room again.

"See? She didn't have a clue, that's how powerful the Talisman and we are." He said looking at me for a split second and grinning. All I thought of was yeah, you mean you and the Talisman – I contribute nothing.

Chapter 17

Vancouver's English Bay faces west, towards the setting sun. Walking in the evening along the sea wall is particularly soothing to a tortured soul…

There is a fire and intensity when you are young; full of dreams, anxious to explore new places and new faces. Long before the drudgery of adult responsibilities and the regrets of maturity immobilize the heart and mind, we are perfect creatures walking along the scenic path brimming with ideas and passions. Well that is how I was feeling while I walked silently enjoying the view with Lactavia. The ocean spilling against the seawall in waves ever higher as the tide rises as if attempting to reach the walkway. The setting sun reflects off of the multifaceted skin of the ocean, a sky blue pink jewel; the water appeared to be on fire.

On one side the burning ocean and on the other the hulking mass of ancient Cedars and Fir trees reaching towards us as if to hug us like a mother. I had never walked along New York's Central Park, nor indeed London's Hyde Park. But I was willing to bet that Vancouver's Stanley Park was an entirely different creature altogether. When you are in this Park, it is hard to believe you are still in the city. Something lives in this air; it stirs the soul. It is wet, ancient, and mystical. The Coastal Natives who first shared this shoreline with the bears and eagles must have realized how incredibly blessed they were. Even now, when you stand upon this sacred promenade you know you are among the luckiest, richest mortals walking the earth today.

"Quite the sunset eh?" I said, turning towards Lactavia with a smile breaking across my face.

"Yeah, nice to get a break from the rain…" She returned the smile.

"So how is life, living with dear old dad?" I inquired.

"Well, he found out that I was using his car."

"You mean stealing his car and then stealthily returning it before he comes home from work"

"Whatever Aileen, anyways I got in serious shit and he told me that if he catches me again, he will kick me out and I do not want to move back in with my psycho mom."

"Why do you feel the need to take your dad's car all the time anyways? You are walking distance from everything except your job."

"Gotta drive, love to drive, it's like a drug." She said jabbing me in the side jokingly.

"How is hanging out with the superslut doing?" She didn't like Jasmine. I didn't know if it was jealousy, but I didn't really care –Lactavia was one part of my life and Jasmine was another. I smiled inwardly realizing that my personal life was highly compartmentalized.

"Great, she leaves me alone." I answered, smiling and putting my arm around her and we strode along the walk.

"So teach me some magic – It's about fucking time." She said keeping up with my stride, the red steaks in her hair flying in the wind.

"Well, remember when I was telling you about tuning into people to read their thoughts? Or if you'd prefer, I could teach you the basic technique of Tyrrean Trance. Both of these are things that you would have to practice in order to get any good at it."

"I think I would rather learn to read thoughts, I want to know what you are thinking sometimes. You pretty much shocked the shit out of me when you told me that you knew about Bill." She said grinning. I could have told her that she would be wasting her time; the ring rendered reading my thoughts impossible. But I wasn't about to crush her desire to learn nor was I in any mood to explain why reading me was futile. I smiled at her and began to tell her the whole technique with great detail. Lactavia listened carefully; I could tell she was actually taking this information in and would probably go home and try it. I was surprised by all accounts as she seemed, initially at least, more sceptical than I was.

"Aileen? How old are you now?" Lactavia looked up at me thoughtfully.

"Seventeen. Why?" I raised my eyebrow, anticipating what she was going to say next.

"Why aren't you dating?"

"I can't believe that, of all people, I have to discuss this with you." I shook my head in disbelief. But I knew this falseness in my life would eventually be challenged by her.

"I am just wondering when you are going to start dating you know, guys. I mean, it's like you are hanging on to your virtue as if it makes you better than any of us." She said.

"Do I walk around acting like I am better than you?" I snapped.

"No, but I have been closer to you than anyone and I know you are not really gay, so what are you waiting for?" She turned again to face the ocean and watch the wave's crash against the seawall.

"No, you're right. I am pretty sure I am straight. But you wont tell anyone right?"

"Who are you waiting for?" She asked.

"I am not waiting for anyone. Would you get off my back if I just went out and did it with any guy? Shit!" I took my arm away from her and put it back in my jacket.

"You're a weird one Aileen, you know that eh?" Lactavia began laughing.

"Come on, I am not that uptight."

"No? Let's see, you don't drink, you would never dream of touching any drugs, not even pot. You hold on to your virginity like a nun. I have never known you to lie, cheat, or steal. You don't even cheat on tests – I mean you're pathetic." I had never had anyone describe me that way before. So my 'goody two shoes' image bothered her. Well, frankly it bothered me.

"Maybe I am saving up for when I am fifty or sixty years old. Then I will be sitting in a hot tub with a bottle of tequila, an eight ball of cocaine, smoking a Cuban cigar with three or four of my favourite cabana boys, and a dildo stuck up my ass." I said laughing back. That caused Lactavia to reel in a fit of laughter.

"Well, if you ever change your mind. I know a couple of guys that think you are pretty hot and I could always introduce you to them."

"Thanks but no thanks. I can find my own dates. For now I would prefer to spend my time with you, even if you think that makes me lame."

I just kept walking along the seawall for a while not talking. Lactavia was probably talking but I wasn't listening. I was looking out at the bay and the barges, thinking about how unbelievable the last three years had been. I was changing, growing up, and in some ways too fast and in others not fast enough. Bryn told me that after the ritual we could no longer have the luxury of 'fun and games', or be entirely carefree. It was all serious from now on. Its not that I minded being responsible and focussed. It was the adult nature of our relationship; it was often overwhelming. After all, he was a man and I was still a teenager and let's face it his 'needs' were intense, regular, and well, regular.

Being an obsessive warlock had other drawbacks. He had specific rules regarding my body and me. I didn't always feel I had complete control over my own body for instance, he would lovingly refer to it as my 'vessel'. He acted as if he owned me like chattel. He would get very upset if I polluted my 'vessel': chemicals like alcohol, cigarettes, and drugs were off the list. From time to time he had requested that I fast and a host of other common Wiccan practices to appease him. He would tell me that the magic works best when I was clean. Sometimes I just wanted to rebel against the rules. The rules felt 'imposed' upon me; I wondered why I hadn't impugned any rules on Bryn? Why the hell not? I felt increasingly rebellious to these imposed rules.

"Let's turn around, pass Lost Lagoon and head back towards Denman St. I have a craving." I said stopping and turning towards Lactavia.

"Well, you could only be craving one of two things: me or a fucking coffee." She said tilting her head with a big smile.

"How about both?" We turned and marched back to civilization. Maybe this time I would find a decent cup of coffee.

Lactavia told me that she dumped the blonde guy she worked with, and was on to other young men. Dating and boyfriends kept her and Jasmine both very busy which was a good thing as school was back in order and I was quite busy with school, work, and Bryn.

Another ceremony was coming up on the weekend and I couldn't get over the feeling that it was yet another opportunity to demonstrate my spiritual weakness to the group. Nothing like a moment like this when you are supposedly the leader to join into a circle and essentially advertise how much you suck. I planned to work that Friday afternoon and the whole Saturday at the salon so that I could arrange to be free on Sunday for the ceremony. I knew that would make time with Bryn non-existent and fortunately he relented and gave me leave. Of course, he had no problems with distracting me during the week and that was exhausting enough. Sleep deprived, and as always, my preoccupation with other matters, usually meant that I was slow oh so painfully slow in fully appreciating other more important on goings in my life.

"You're late!" I said as I sunk my creamo into the hot cup of black coffee. We were at a restaurant on Kingsway street. I was thinking about how she was dating all kinds of guys like some kind of serial monogamist. She had stood me up on a few occasions. Today as she walked into the restaurant, I read her thoughts and knew that she paid a visit to a male friend who was in the hospital. I was tired and in a bad mood so it just seemed it wasn't a good enough excuse – I was still mad. I had sat in that restaurant alone with my coffee and unopened menu waiting for her to show up fuming at the fact that she was always late.

"I'm always late, Dragon. Why should that surprise you?" She had sauntered in eyeing me as she walked towards me, daring me to raise my voice and temper.

"Where were you last night?" I inquired

"Oh, I'm sorry; I didn't realize you were my mother!" She spat back.

"You know Lactavia, I have put up with so much shit from you, and I am tired of it. Why don't you go find someone else to annoy?" It seemed no amount of creamo would turn this coffee to a nice beige color. I was convinced it was impossible to get a decent cup of coffee in this city! I was deep inside her brain too; I was reading her unguarded thoughts. Vaguely, very vaguely I suppose the thought had entered my head that I sounded and behaved like someone else I know. The thought upset me so much; I pushed it out of my head.

"You are drinking and smoking pot. Good idea! Any other great aspirations Tavi? You know, those co-workers may not be the best influence on you." I said not about to look up from my coffee. I could see she was now hanging out with some real troublemakers. One in particular, the one she was enamoured with, was an alcoholic and had already been abusive towards her.

"Well Dragon, I don't need to explain myself to you. If you don't like having friends without getting your nose into all of their personal details and preaching to them about it, you just shouldn't have any." Lactavia's dark eyes narrowed and I could tell she was ready for a fight. She wasn't about to listen to anything I would say. There was an anger and hostility to her I had never before seen. I knew things that I was sure even her parents didn't and I wasn't about to let her get off. She was in over her head and I wanted to make sure she knew, that I knew.

"Don't be coy with me. Your new group of friends are losers and you are going to get into a whole pile of shit. In fact, I worry that the one guy you are so hot for is going to seriously hurt you before you smarten up and move on. I also know that your dad is mad at you as well and is threatening to have you move back with your mother."

"Don't you ask permission before you invade people's brains? You are such a bitch! I'm moving out on my own anyways."

"Where the hell will you go?" I motioned to the waitress for a refill and glared back at her.

"Oh maybe the Okanagan, I was invited there by Klaur at our last Samhaen…"

"Are you nuts? You want to live with that asshole?" I threw my fist down on the table and screamed the words aloud enough to attract the attention of the restaurant manager who threatened to kick me out if I didn't settle down.

"Dragon, will you just relax! I just said it is an option open to me, I'm not saying that I am going to Penticton. What the hell is happening to you? You used to be fun, now everything is so serious. I can handle my new friend's just fine. I don't need you to judge people you don't even know. The person you should be worried about is yourself! Nobody wants to be around you anymore because you are becoming the biggest pain in the ass. You will have all kinds of time to be a stuffy boring adult when you are out of high school or college – Geez! I don't know what the fuck is biting your ass so bad these days, but you better deal with it." She didn't look at the menu; she knew it off by heart and was motioning to the waiter for her order.

I was angry and hurt with Lactavia. I felt a kind of ownership of her, something I didn't feel towards my other friends, let's face it, we were close. She didn't get on my case about my life aside from her, so why was I getting so uppity about hers? I knew she was getting into some stupid stuff that is typical for a teenager. Part of me thought that fellow Coven members were immune to, but why was I so worked up about it? So she was like any other kid? Big deal. We ordered food and although for a while we did not talk to each other I had to agree with her. I was loosing my temper with everyone. Was I mad at them or myself? Probably what was really biting my ass was that they could engage in reckless abandon in terms of sex and drugs while I had to keep completely clean. Words of Bryn haunted me, 'Powerful magic requires a clean body.' And of course, 'I have to be able to trust you...' I wanted to be a stupid kid too. I resented the edicts, I resented that Bryn wouldn't answer my questions. .

Bryn was overwhelming, in every sense. Was I just fed up with the conspiracy of silence? Was it my rage at not being able to improve our situation for now? I was impatiently waiting for normalcy? While he was here in North America, he did indeed seem to be nefariously preoccupied. I was aware of my rage at being excluded, on purpose, from knowing what he was up to. There would be periods of two to four weeks when I would not see or hear from him and I was noticing that my temper was difficult to control during those times. I didn't know what was going on and Lactavia was right, I seemed to take it out on everyone around me. Kat and the guys were in the Okanagan, Lactavia was pushing me away, and I was becoming keenly aware of missing Bryn. It made me think about his past indiscretions and now it made me hot with fury. Does he still have other women on the side? I was beginning to wonder about many things when my growing rage was interrupted.

"I've completely lost you haven't I? You haven't heard a word I've said. Whatever is making you this miserable you need to deal with it. What the hell is going on with you Aileen?"

"Tavi, just finish your coke and your damn Greek salad. I need to go home and study for my exams." I cut her off. A decision that probably wasn't the best choice all things considered. Well, that was a short visit with Lactavia. She probably hated me. I was miserable and as usual no burgeoning cup of forthcomingness. I remember Bryn once saying, 'one day I would hate him', I was beginning to see why, and in a strange parallel twist , I was seeing why Tavi would get to hate me too. I was somewhat aware of ruining my relationship with her...but I needed to see someone and get some answers.

"The tabloids are just filled with garbage about me...they think me random." Bryn took the handful of magazines and issues of The Mirror and threw them on the table beside me. I had been stewing over Lactavia all day and now to have to come to Los Angeles and deal with the emotional baggage of Mr. Bryn was beginning to get to be a bit much. I mean I wanted to talk to him, but considering my mood, it probably wasn't the best strategy.

"Someone has hired detectives to watch my every move. It makes doing my work that much more annoying. It's not that a few thick headed blokes would be any real challenge, it's just that there is so much work to do here and I fear I won't have it all done in the timeline I was hoping. I really want to leave this country. My mum is quite worried about me. It is becoming harder to hide everything from her. She just doesn't understand the enormous responsibilities I have. Photographers, press, and fans, continually hound me and yet I still need to do so much more work that has nothing to do with this music business. I'm just so tired and frustrated." He knelt down into the chair in front of him that was next to me and looked into my eyes with that piercing, intoxicating gaze until I felt that sharp pain in my heart. Normally, this would have caused me to melt for him emotionally, but not today, I was probably just as pissed off as he was.

I wish I could be of more comfort to you. I can't relate to any of your problems with the exception of friends thinking that I have lost my jocularity. I want to help; I would do anything to ease your pain. You are my soul mate. But you stubbornly refuse to divulge anything to me."

I tore my eyes away from his hurt expression and flipped through the magazines he had tossed in front of me. I was noticing how most of the pictures of him had women around him and, of course, there were headers to the pictures that were accusatory. He noticed me looking at the covers of the magazines and reached over and pulled each one out singly towards me saying:

"This is my doctor who is helping me with my hair transplant. We were at the clinic when they snapped it. This is me with my cousin, Denise. This is another singer I hired to do back up vocals on the upcoming album." His voice became increasingly louder. He then slammed the magazines down on the table again. He looked at me for a moment.

"I'm not shagging anyone Aileen!" He drove one hand into his jeans pocket and pulled out his rock and pointed it out towards me,

"No! That rite with you and the Talisman has taken care of that – I CAN'T shag anyone else!" It's bad enough the rest of the world believes this crap. For the sake of the Gods, don't you start worrying about this shit or I am really going to loose it!" He got up out of the chair, and stormed into the livingroom, punching the wall as he walked by. Bryn's temper fully engaged. At some level, I had to smile at how well I knew this apparition in my life. I watched him walk away from me, hot with a flood of anger that was so familiar. It made me wonder, do all men run off, smash something and then quietly pout alone or is it purely an Englishman's thing? I didn't know, it was definitely a Bryn thing. Aside from my father and brothers, he was the only man I ever knew. I had learned the politics of talking with Bryn was simply carefully considering what I wanted to say and how I said it. I never was in the habit of diplomacy with anyone else. He was my only exception. His sudden and rather abrupt confession shocked me. While I knew he was still probably hot I thought that if I controlled the inflexion in my voice and remained calm he would reciprocate.

"Bryn? What do you mean? What exactly did that ritual do?" I couldn't see him so I thought he must be in the next room. For a moment I wondered if he had heard me and I was about to get up to look for him when I heard him loud and clear in my head,

"Come to L.A. Visit me while I am stuck in this accursed prison."

"Come to Vancouver, come to me." I said out loud.

"I have obligations here for another two months and I can't get away. But I could just send a nondescript letter to you with tickets to L.A. and arrange to have someone pick you up at L A.X. and take you here to the Hotel." He walked around the corner, leaned against the wall, and stared down at me. He then opened his mouth and used his vocal chords,

"Please say you will come. I want to hide you here for just one week…I need you Aileen – please?"

"But what about my classes? What about my –" I stopped in midsentence. I looked into the hurt look in those incredible eyes. I just changed the subject,

"Let's get back to what we were discussing before you divisively changed the subject. What do you mean about that ritual? Tell me!"

"I told you it was a binding ritual." He said impatiently.

"What did it do to you?"

"I didn't know for sure, but apparently the side effect is that I am impotent when I have the Talisman." He seemed incredibly embarrassed, even his ears were flushing.

"You don't have that problem with me…how did you find this out?" I asked out of pure innocent curiosity.

"Exactly the question I knew you would eventually drive at. What is of more importance is if I'm in working order when you are with me in the flesh – It is way overdue!" His anger was taking over again; in fact, his eyes were beginning to glow. A weird side affect I was beginning to notice increasingly and I attributed it directly to him using the Talisman. When he first met me I would have been too embarrassed to pry, but not anymore.

"Well, Bryn since I have kept my vow to you, I think I deserve to know what happened." I stood there with my arms folded in front of me, I wanted an honest answer, and I wasn't going to let it go without the truth. His eyes went heavenward and then he looked at the floor. He took in a deep breath before relaying the story.

"I was in the studio with an American blues guitarist. There was a woman who worked for the studio that was there. When we were done and the guitarist left, I was alone. I was packing up my things when she came into the sound room and told me her name, asked for my autograph and the next thing I knew while I was writing something for her she was all over me. So there I was trying to write on a record, while her head was by my trousers. I was about to kick her away from me when I realized that even though she had liberated what she wanted, my body wasn't responding at all. You have to understand that while I wanted to get rid of her the discovery kind of shocked me. It shocked her too I think."

I listened intently and then began to laugh. Bryn must have thought I was mad. But my grin seemed to soften him a bit.

"Please come to me?"

"Of course I will." I said feeling that fear welling within me. He smiled his boyish smile and kissed me hard, pulling holding me down to the blue-carpeted floor.

He paused after awhile and pulled his face away from mine. He didn't say anything he was just looking at me. He then smiled again and kissed my eyes for whatever reason.

"I can't wait to see you. I bet you are even more beautiful in person." This caused me to squirm in uncomfortable shyness.

"I just hope you aren't disappointed." I paused and kept looking at him. We must have been staring at each other like a couple of idiots for minutes."Why am I so crazy about you Bryn?"

"You are a sucker for abuse?"

Three weeks later, that letter came. There it was, American Airlines. I opened the ticket to see what the flight dates were, Dec. 2 departing Vancouver and Arrival of Dec. 9 back to home. So now I had to come up with an excuse as to why I was going to be gone for a week: from home, school, work, and ECAW. I just couldn't think of any good excuses just off hand so I hid the tickets in the bottom of my undergarment drawer.

Well, the flight day was fast approaching and I was so busy with work, getting through math and chemistry, and appeasing my parents, I couldn't think of leaving for L.A. I knew that wasn't the main reason. I was filled with dread, a real tangible fear. I wasn't too keen on going to the United States. I really didn't like the idea of being alone with Bryn. I was worried about the press; I was worried about Bryn. What if I was a disappointment in the flesh? What if I really looked too young? What if we got into a fight? What if he used that magic while I was there? What could he do? Why was I so fucking scared? Part of me wanted to be with him so badly. I packed. I unpacked. I thought of excuses to tell my dad for leaving for a week. I just couldn't think of anything my dad would believe. I just couldn't get away – I just didn't want to go. It didn't feel right.

Bryn wanted to see me the night before I flew; I knew I had to tell him that I couldn't make it. I was dreading it; I didn't want to tell him that I was afraid. how angry he would be if he sent a driver to collect me at LAX and I wasn't there. That prospect scared me even more.

Sitting in the faded light of numerous candles on the dining table, I could barely make out Bryn, he was pouting over a plate of food. He had a fork in his hand. He glanced up at me, those green-grey eyes and I instantly sensed there was no joy at seeing me.

"Why?" He spoke almost inaudibly with his strong English accent, jabbing his fork into some peas he had no desire to ingest. I backed towards the wall behind me, the gig was up – he knew.

"Now is a really bad time. I am very busy preparing for exams and my parents would freak if I left this close to Christmas." I tried to reassure him, trying my best to sound brave. Bryn threw down his fork, looked at his watch and got out of his chair. My eyes followed him as he paced to the window and dared to look out.

"After all we have been through, after all this time, after all the self imposed control and patience I have proven to you that I have, how can you still be so scared of me? Of us?" He continued looking out the window, as if sensing that I would be more likely to talk if he didn't look at me.

"How can you not trust me? How can you not know me? What can I do to disarm you?" he said throwing up his arms with his back still facing me.

"I am so fucking sorry…" I choked, my knees buckled and I fell to the floor crying. He turned around and faced me,

"Look at me Aileen, What is there to fear? I'm just a man!" He said a little loudly and irritated. I wiped the tears from my eyes and kept my head looking at the navy carpet.

"Like fucking hell! No, Bryn, I don't know what you are but you are no man." This whole thing was a perversion of nature, and I suppose the truth of it finally hit me and it was a stark confession coming out now. He could never hide under so mundane a concept as 'just a man'. This was a perfect example. I couldn't even set the tone for my conversation – he read my thoughts as easily as I read the paper. I looked up. He walked over to where I was, grabbed both of my hands and looked into my eyes. His mind was deep inside mine I could feel him. Was I supposed to get used to feeling violated?

"Aileen, you have this damnable ability to make me so angry. You alone can drive me beyond any comprehension of coping. Look at me." He paused and made sure I was looking at him but I really didn't want to. My eyes were wet and red.

"I want you to feel part of something larger – part of me. Open yourself up to this…to what we are. Don't fear me or you destroy us. We have yet so much work to do and I have a promise to fulfill."

There was a white light and then just like a flash of a camera, we were on my bed in Vancouver! There he was almost completely solid.

"Aileen, I know you are ready now…What do I have to do to ease you? You have but to ask." His hand stroked up and down my real non-ghostly body.

"I don't know. don't know why I am so scared all the time. I sometimes think that you are lying to me."

"I never have, nor ever will lie to you. When you come to see me perhaps the knowledge will eliminate your fear." He moved his thumb across my eyes to wipe away my tears.

"Bryn, I am a little tired of your secrets and your Talisman."

"Aileen. You need time to understand what your heart and body already know. I will not battle your stubborn mind. I will dismiss you from this night and from the visit to Los Angeles. However, I will deny you for a measurement of months. Understand this, you have no choice so you might as well get used to this whole thing. Your inability to accept your reality because it is so unique is wearing my patience thin. I can do this the pleasant way or the painful way – it doesn't matter to me in the end." With that, he evaporated and I was alone again.

I couldn't believe how cold he could be. I cried myself to sleep. I cried the next day, until there were no tears left in me.

Time wore on; Kat persisted in staying in Penticton with her merry band of followers. They had endured almost half a year and I was beginning to suspect that perhaps she would actually stay there after all. I received occasional letters and they increasingly became more bizarre. The letters began initially with the predictable: 'Let's tell the Vancouverite how sunny it is here in the Okanagan.' Followed by, "I am soooo in love. Why don't you move here and be with Margon?' She had capped all that and instead was eagerly telling me about her little 'games' her and Klaur were playing. How she enjoyed pretending to be his little slave-girl. She even told me that she liked calling him 'Master'. Why did this make me so violent? It was her life, if she is happy why the hell should I care? I became so incredibly distracted and upset I couldn't read the rest of the letter. I grabbed my mountain bike and biked for six hours. I biked to Deep Cove in North Vancouver and back again. I was trying to figure out why my fury was barely containable. The hard physical workout helped. Soon my mind was clearing and I was able to focus on my own internal anger. I realized that my life was about taking back control at this point. If my life were as simple as Kat's or Lactavia's it would be such an easy thing. Perhaps they were reckless because reining in control was an easy matter. However, for me, there was no hope of getting control. His words were clear; 'I can do this the pleasant was or the painful way, it doesn't matter to me in the end!' He kept me in the dark, kept me stupid until I did that ritual, and now that he 'owned' me I was powerless to stop him. The question was what was it he intended to do? I had to stop taking my rage out on everyone else. There was only one person who had earned that privilege. Part of me wanted to be conciliatory and kind and still hold out for his explanation and part of me was ready to go to war!

January, another year came around and I was busy with high school. I was ticked off about Bryn, but I missed the intimacy that he had gotten me used to. I was enjoying the normalcy of my months away from him. My parents were happy with my rededication to school and I was actually becoming motivated about my future.

I hadn't seen Lactavia for a month and I was worried and thought perhaps I should apologize for being so judgmental towards her. I put on my favourite leather outfit and boots, and got a bouquet of flowers and a card to give her. I took the bus all the way downtown to see her. I knocked on her apartment door and eventually her father answered. There I was, T-shirt with a dragon on it, black leather pants, boots, trench coat and feathers in my ears, with a bouquet:

"Is Tavi here?"

"No."

"Well, can you give her these when she gets in?"

"...Yeah, sure..." He took the flowers and quickly closed the door in my face and I had a moment to reflect on how the whole thing must look like from his perspective... I had to laugh.

I waited for a couple of days, and when I still hadn't heard from Lactavia. I called her place and left a message on the answering machine. It wasn't until about a month later that I found out what had happened to her. Apparently, she had packed up her stuff and had moved to the Okanagan with Kat after our argument at the restaurant. When I found out this little tidbit of information, I did two things: first, I rolled my eyes up and put my head into my hands and blamed myself for the whole thing, realizing that I inadvertently gave flowers to her father. Secondly, Lactavia was so mad at me that she never called to tell me where she was. Then I remembered my rage at the idea of her going there and realized I got exactly what I deserved. Way to go Kovacs!

So now Klaur had both Kat and Lactavia and was probably floating in a self-righteous cloud of contemptible egoism. I received a letter from Kat and, considering the date on the letter and the day I received it, it was clear that Klaur was ensuring that I received little intelligence regarding his world in Penticton. I was sure that Kat beseeched her love, Agaratte to send this letter to me. Mind you, he took his time getting it to me. It was January and the letter was dated mid-November.

My Dear Sister Dragon, November 15

I hope this letter finds you well. I hear you are doing well in school. Congratulations. I am currently very busy tending to my love. I can't describe the satisfaction I enjoy by submitting myself to him. I wonder if you have any male companions yet. Are you not tired of your relationship with Lactavia? Surely, she cannot please you the way a man can. I experienced the ultimate pleasure with Agaratte. Klaur was kind and perhaps foolish enough to command me to be with Agaratte. I think the reason for the high degree of electricity between us is the fact he is so powerful a warlock and, as you know, myself not lacking either. You could experience this too; you should come and take the hand of Margon. You know he is the best match for you. You are my sister and I tell you this as a person who cares: you are only half a woman until you find your match. Are you still wasting your time with that foolish warlock Bryn? The press says he's Gay, and I question his motives. I worry about you Dragon. I want to see you happy and I know Margon could make you happy.

Winter is descending upon this arid land.

Your sister,

Kat.

I remembered how close Agaratte and her had become while Klaur was away and I wondered what would happen to her if Klaur found out how she enjoyed being shared. From that point on, I received no more letters from Kat, nor did I receive any answer from the phone when I called. I was concerned for her but I was just upsetting myself too much by worrying impotently. After all, she had made her bed; she should lie in it for a while. She was in no position to question my affiliation with Bryn. What she knew was speculative and hearsay at best. Nevertheless, her comment about warlocks and the electricity struck a chord. Perhaps my feelings when I was with Bryn were more a condition of his magic influencing the environment than a defect in my mental coping of our relationship. It was possible that Bryn was unaware of how that would affect a person.

Without any doubt, I was now aware that my life is a perversion from the norm. My drive towards having some modicum of control over the supernatural aspects of my life was slipping and I found that it brought out my anger and fierceness. My subordinate status with Bryn was a growing thorn in my side. The letter was a reminder that I had lost Kat and now Lactavia to that jackass Klaur. The girls were supposed to be here in Vancouver with me. The guys were supposed to be obedient to me, not defiant. It was as if they were having an adolescent rebellion against me and I wasn't even a parent.

I continued with my work. I really participated at school. I joined the school choir, drama, and was actually even making friends in my new school. I was going out lots with Jasmine, and the dancing made me happy. I would occasionally think about how much had transpired since I was five. I had been keeping myself busy in the most normal of ways and it was joyful. December was the last time I saw Bryn. It was now mid January and no sign of him. I hated admitting that I really missed him. I wondered how long he would make me wait. As much as I missed him and I mean physically. When I did go out dancing with Jasmine I was surprised how little interest I had in any man. I would dance with a guy; go out on a date, some of these guys were real hunks too, I even let the odd one kiss me and nothing! – I mean absolutely nothing! Obviously, the ritual had the same effect on me as Bryn said it had on him.

Chapter 18

Kat masquerades as Dragon

Klaur spent a great deal of his time with Agaratte, which for me was decidedly fortunate as it afforded me more time to figure out just what manner of artefact Bryn was hiding in his drawer and how I could devise a strategy to liberate it from him. It was going to be a challenge and I was ready for a challenge. The further aggravation was having to hide every piece of Wiccan paraphernalia I had from Klaur. Today was another such day. I waited for Klaur to leave the house and I set up my candles, book, and closed my eyes to focus on Thromm. I focussed on seeing what Thromm saw. I had done this before, it was not the easiest trick, but I could follow him anywhere and see through his eyes. Thromm had a clever plan concocted for the visit to Bryn. From the closest vantage point that Thromm could afford, we could see a plain hotel room with two people who seemed highly engaged in a conversation. It took a while for the faces to become discernable. I had hardly realized that the blonde female was in fact Dragon when the man who I instantly recognized as Bryn held up a blindingly glowing object that was approximately fist sized. Instantly, Dragon disappeared. Then Bryn laid down on the floor and went into a deep enough trance that

I could see he looked dead or barely conscious. A sudden rush of joy welled up within me. If he was in a regular habit of foolishly 'trancing' out and going to his precious Aileen, I had a good chance of liberating his prize. This artefact shone so brightly it was virtually impossible to tell what it was. But I could feel Thromm's excitement at a plan. We would wait and watch till Bryn pulled out the amulet or whatever it was and while he was in trance, we would make our move. It was risky; as this would require Thromm take on a more solid, powerful form in our world. This would require a sacrifice and huge cost to me. But I could hardly care when I thought about owning that glowing treasure.

"Knock Knock" The apartment door was being struck heavily.

"Hey Kat, It's me Lactavia, got room for a fellow sister for a couple of days?" I could hear Lactavia's voice on the other side of the door; she must have known I was home.

"Shit! Thromm, don't go far we have much to discuss!" I opened my eyes, I could feel the drain immediately on my body from my 'link' with Thromm. I felt dizzy getting up.

"I'll be right there, I'm in the washroom." I yelled as I ran into to kitchen and hid my stuff. I raced to the door and opened it.

"Welcome Lactavia. Always a pleasure to see you."

She came in and looked at the livingroom floor where I noticed I had forgotten to put away my book of shadows which was still open.

"What are you up to?" She asked putting down her luggage and moving her eyes from the book on the livingroom floor to me.

"Oh, just meditating, you know there is nothing more relaxing." I said as I strode over to the book and quickly closed it.

"Kat, I was wondering if I could stay with you for a while? I should be able to get a job fairly quickly and then I can move out on my own. I moved out of my dad's house and I am so mad at Dragon…"

"Lactavia, you can stay here indefinitely I am sure. We will ask Klaur when he and Agaratte get back. There are three bedrooms and

Klaur and I use one, Dad is in the other one and he is considering going back to mother which means we could use a roommate."

"I would really appreciate it Kat." Lactavia appeared relieved and made her way to a couch where she collapsed and curled up.

"I couldn't get any sleep on the bus. I think I will take a nap. Hopefully Klaur will be back soon."

"Great, I will go for a little walk and be back within the hour, okay?" I said sitting delicately at the edge of the couch and stroking her leg in an almost empathetic, motherly way. I smiled at her, got up and reached for my keys and locked her in. I then headed for the nearby bush.

"Thromm. Come out and have a word with me, we have some serious planning to do." I said to the vacant air, focusing my energy to find him.

"Hheeee mussssst have great artefact ..." hissed Thromm in the shadow of a bush. I was unsure if Thromm actually had ever had a form or had experienced a life as a human. But for this meeting it seemed he had decided not to take on a form at all.

"Are you sure that kind of magic cannot be done by any other means?" I asked out loud, not worried that I may be overheard.

"Yessss it can be done, but not without ussssing the black artssss ..." came Thromm's reply.

"Maybe he is lying to Dragon, and he is using the black arts then?" I didn't even believe this myself but was playing devil's advocate, trying to fish some information out of Thromm and in an attempt to control the excitement welling up inside me.

"No, if he were ussssing the black artsssss to ssssuch a degree he would be near dead unless he can use other soul's energy." He rattled the bush and seemed to come closer to where I was kneeling.

"Are you telling me that the myth of taking the life force of a person in substitution to your own can actually be done? I didn't think that it was actually possible.

"Of courssse..."

"I tried to wrap my head around everything; Bryn of all people, a warlock?, Dragon, a mere child, his consort?, Bryn's power sourced from black magic fed through a powerful artefact that he happens to possess? It seemed beyond my ability to believe it. Yet I couldn't despute what I saw with Thromm's own eyes, and mine the summer previous. Could I become the most powerful witch the world has ever known? The thought caused an involuntary grin to spread across my face. I couldn't even fathom the limits I could achieve with this power.

"I shall take this artefact and punish Bryn. I will do what I want, when and how I want – who will stop me? " I said laughing, thinking again about my dear adopted mother's comment, "You're not even white!" No Mrs. Smith, I am not white. But I will see you suffer.

"Me too, Thromm too!"

"What do you want Thromm, what is your price?" I asked annoyed that he would have such ambitions when he was nothing more than a familiar.

"I want what Dragon and Bryn already sssshare, I want to live in both worldssss thisss ssspiritual dreamworld and your prime material world. I want to flicker between both worldssss." He hissed knowing that this would redirect my anger back to Bryn.

"My dear familiar you shall have your turn. First I wish to try one trick I have yet not performed." I got up and headed for the back of the apartment complex. Klaur showed up at the house at around dinnertime, stoned as usual.

"Klaur, I have wonderful news!" I said coming to the door and smiling brightly.

"What?" he said waving his friend Agaratte off.

"Our sister Lactavia has come to stay with us."

"Can she cook?" he asked grinning as he looked at the couch where Lactavia was waking up.

"Yes, and more." I responded a little annoyed that all he seemed to think about was himself.

"Okay then. Hey Lactavia how are you? Why did you leave your girlfriend?" Klaur said laughing.

"She is not my girlfriend and I just needed to get away from Vancouver for awhile."

"Did Kat explain that we have an extra room?" He asked.

"Yes."

"Well, rent will be based on how good of a cook you are."

"I suppose I had better find a job soon then." She was clearly pissed off at his precocious statement. I knew that she would have to slowly but surely accept our lifestyle if she were to be accepted into this household. She resisted at first but soon found her own way of getting along with Klaur and Agaratte.

It was some weeks before I got a break from Klaur, but finally he decided to yet again go to Vancouver and leave me in Penticton. This was no problem as I had much to do. Since Bryn is such a famous musician his whereabouts were common knowledge. He was spending a calendar year in the United States and was calling Los Angeles home.

That meant that his time zone was similar to mine and that any great Wiccan tricks I had I could play tonight. I went to the back of my drawer and fished out my book of incantations and my jewellery box containing my amulet. I ran to the kitchen and ensured that I had enough beeswax candles to complete my task for the evening. I spoke briefly with Margon prior to him leaving with the guys for Vancouver about my plan to acquire a great magical artefact. I also informed him of Lactavia moving to Penticton. However, it seemed clear he was more interested in seeing Dragon again. In fact, it was getting irritating trying to tell him about my plans. I had to tell someone, because having seen some of the magic that warlock Bryn could do made me nervous that any blunders could result in dire circumstances for me. Margon was to be my rescuer, as he always was for all of us. He would not ask probing questions and instead would just keep an eye out for me. He was truly wonderful that way. I knew however that his feelings for Dragon and that stopped me from divulging anything about details of my plans. He expressed concerns for Klaur's behaviour but seemed happy that I was happy. I assured him that I was happy and that Klaur and I were getting along well.

This may be easy for Bryn but Tyrrean Trance is no small trick. I always prefer to have some music quietly playing in the background to help me defocus. Lying very still on the bed in my room I pushed out my Ka and focused on its appearance. I concentrated on the appearance of my dear friend Dragon, noting every feature and detail. As I noted each detail, I changed everything about the appearance of my Ka. I have shifted my Ka before; I took the time to ensure that I looked just like her; after all, I wanted to look my best for Bryn. Knowing what a magically enfeebled Wiccan Dragon was I made sure I didn't just show at Bryn's room. No, I called him in her voice, knowing that she would rely on him to do all the work. I hovered, seemingly helpless in the spiritual sea between him and I for what seemed a very long time probably around 10-20 minutes. I was surprised that I wasn't being snapped up, so I thought I would call him.

"Bryn, take me to you." I said, thinking Dragon would not have cute pet names for Bryn. True to estimation, soon I felt the most powerful 'pull' I have ever experienced. I nearly forgot to stay in her physical form I was so scared and shaken by that 'pull'. As if a fog was lifting, I could see clearly Bryn lying on his bed, candles surrounding him and a surprised expression on his face.

"Aileen, how happy you make me with this visit." He smiled and patting a space on the bed next to him.

"I missed you so I thought I would come by and give you a kiss." I was hoping that whatever I said sounded like Dragon, but hey, who cares? I looked like her.

"Come kiss me then." I slithered over to where he was patting and put my arm around him. He gingerly kissed me on the cheek.

"What brings you to Los Angeles?"

"I was wondering if you could teach me some magic. I want to be as good as you." I knew that he had been teaching Dragon some things so I thought that this might be a good way to get him to show me his artefact, I wanted to see it up close.

"Oh, I will teach you some magic my luv. But first, I want you now." He said pushing my mostly solid body onto the bed and kissing me. He then removed my panties and put his fingers to work.

"I said I came for a kiss, whatever happened to our conversations?" I asked him trying to pry him off me, while trying to push my energy into that impenetrable wall he calls his head. He then grabbed both of my wrists in one hand and looked straight at me.

"Once again you grossly underestimated me Kat. Why do you continually find yourself in these bad situations? Could it be because you are too foolish to leave well enough alone?" He then grinned evilly.

"Let me go you fucking devil!"

"Not yet." I tried to force my Ka back into the spirit world but somehow this bastard warlock had blocked off my access. I figured that if I distracted his mind he would stop.

"Why do you waste your time with Dragon when I am a much stronger witch and obviously better suited to you?" I asked praying that he would stop hurting me. How solid this body felt stunned me. He stopped what he was doing for a moment.

"Kat, is that an offer? You are indeed a clever and cunning young woman. I admire your tenacity. However, you are in way over your head here and stubbornly refuse to leave well enough alone. This is where you run into problems with me Kat. You risk your precious life by frustrating me."

"What do you see in my retarded fledgling witch beyond good looks?"

"You truly don't know do you Kat? You have so much arcane knowledge, yet there are holes in your skills. Surely you must know that you can't have this much power and be long for this world unless you have a powerful healer to save you from death's door." He grinned and then he released my hands when he grabbed my shoulders suddenly the world blurred. When I could see clearly again, I saw him standing on the rocky edge and he was holding me over a cliff. I was suddenly frozen, stunned by two realizations, first that I was dangling precariously over a cliff being held on only by his will and the drop down was not less than 100 meters and secondly, the sudden realization that Aileen being a powerful healer would explain why this devil protected, coveted and secured her.

"So you are using her?" I yelled baring my teeth; I was just praying he would not drop me. He brought his head up to my face again and then bit my neck.

"No. Your Dragon is mine, she has always been. You see, you have nothing to offer me as you cannot regenerate me –almost no mortal can." He said removing one of his life-line arms from holding me up and waved it over my face, which caused my own physical appearance to materialize – somehow I was powerless to interfere with his magic. I looked down and I was terrified that maybe, if he did let me go, that I actually would die.

"You may have Dragon in the spiritual world, but she is mine in the physical world. If I do not get what I want, I could make your life very difficult!" I snapped. It was utterly impossible to read his thoughts – I was, for the first time in my life, completely outclassed in magic.

"I know what you want, and you will never possess it or me. If you do anything to hurt my Aileen, I will kill you! Think heavily on it Kat!" With that he pushed one hand outwards towards me and I felt myself falling uncontrollably down, I was sure that I was about to plunge to jagged rocks below. But I had the most unpleasant decent back into my body.

I had never read anywhere in any book that kind of power. Obviously, he could control just about any energy source—he was very knowledgeable. I had no doubt that he could assassinate anyone, anywhere on earth with little or no effort, and then run to Dragon for more life. Well, I definitely knew what I was dealing with now. I don't know what purpose he had but he was definitely no holy cleric. There was only one way to get it. I knew the costs and the consequences – I was actually considering giving up.

Chapter 19

The following month, Klaur came to Vancouver accompanied by Agaratte and Margon. Klaur decided he wanted to gloat in person about having both Lactavia and Kat in Penticton. Wiccan circles and studies aside, I really hated these guys and told them so over the phone. I had no intention of meeting them anywhere. But Klaur was not to be put off from his purpose, so he came directly to my home. He then proceeded to tell me how happy Kat and Lactavia were and that if I had any brains I would join them in the Okanagan.

"Seriously, Dragon, I want you to come to Penticton and join the rest of us. I keep the girls very happy. We could make you happy too. I could please you in ways no woman can."

"I am certain if I wanted the pleasure of a man, I could find one better than you!"

"What man would want you? Face it, it's us or nothing."

"Then I suppose I will have nothing, now get lost!"

"Dyke!"

"Go Fuck yourself, Klaur" I stormed into my house. I was glad that Lactavia hadn't told Klaur that our 'relationship' was kind of a sham, but I still couldn't stand being called a dyke. I was eighteen next month and I suppose everyone who knew me knew I wasn't seriously dating, and was wondering why. I was feeling physically sick over my long absence from Bryn.

Bryn made me wait until after his birthday, but on March 10 I was once again in Bryn's enchanted embrace and he blotted out all of our painful memories to this sublime moment. I had taken time during his absence to try to come to terms with my reality. I was in it now and there was no turning back. I might as well enjoy the ride, right? I wasn't really going to start a war between us, was I? Besides, my recent dating fiasco made it painfully real that I had to accept that I had to give up my dreams of a normal life – this was my destiny. My fear was a major problem. He had never seriously hurt me; I had to believe that he never would.

I knew that magic drained him, but he seemed in surprisingly good shape. Obviously, the last three months he had used little magic, not like last time. He was back in England and was very happy to be out of America. We were in his livingroom. I had just released my hug from him when he stepped back looking at me.

"You have been smoking since we have been apart. Why?" Bryn was dressed in a suit, looking as if he had just come from some formal public affair –his cologne was all over him. I missed the smell of him and for a moment I didn't hear what he said or catch the incensed tone in his voice as I was utterly intoxicated by being in his presence again. He walked up to where I was, put his hand on my chin and moved my face up to look him in the eyes and readdressed me.

"I leave you for a while, and you are smoking and kissing strange men, why?" I didn't know how to respond. I was so happy to be with him again. I didn't want to get into a fight right away. Besides, I didn't know why either other than I just needed to piss him off, cause sometimes he pissed me off. I was wondering why I should even answer, I mean, if he was digging around my brain to find this stuff out, he should know the reasons why too.

"You have come to me your vessel impure and now I must contend with either postponing our next ritual or risking its effectiveness." He then let go of my chin, turned from me shaking his head and sat on his overstuffed chair putting his fingers on either side of his forehead and messaging his temples.

"I'm sorry…" There was tiredness, a calmness in him that put an edge on things. I suddenly realized I wanted him to get angrier. I was suddenly struck with a sense of him feeling fed up.

"I can't be surprised; I know what I have put you through. I suppose I deserve this. Please just promise from now on to be a good girl – my good little girl." I walked over to the chair and sat on his lap to give him a hug. A smile crept across his face.

"I promise…" I whispered before he pushed his lips to mine. I closed my eyes; surrendering to the sense of his soul amalgamating with mine. My heart felt like a volcano exploding and the earth beneath me shook uncontrollably –insane passion. I would have never known that I missed him that much. There are no words in English to describe that feeling; it just seemed too much for it to be anything normal. It was weird because when I was alone, I was doing okay. But at this moment I felt that being away from him was agonizing, as if deprived of oxygen and yet living. We eventually parted space and I retreated to the couch while Bryn dug out a deck of cards.

"Bryn, is it possible to resonate in the neutral pole in Wicca?" I asked as he was shuffling the cards.

"Aileen, you are poled to resonate in the positive –you know that. Right?" He said without moving his eyes from the cards.

"Well, not for sure but okay. But is it possible for someone to be resonating on the neutral polarity?"

"Of course. It makes up the majority of the human race. However, that is precisely why most people are ineffective in spell casting and Wicca in general." He glanced up at me smiling, having finished shuffling the deck and dealing out five cards each.

"Those resonating on the neutral pole would have to be trained and trained hard. I resonate neutrally Aileen. The game is three draw poker. Strip poker." He arched an eyebrow waiting for me to pick up my cards.

"How can you have so much power and control if you operate on the neutral realm?" I said, stunned that he was not poled negative or positive.

"Easy. I was trained by No, I possess the Talisman, and I found you." He saw me put down three cards and he replaced them with three new ones.

"How is finding me of any benefit?" I said abjectly looking at the three cards he gave me noticing none of them did anything to improve my hand.

"More ways than even I possibly know my luv." We continued to play a few rounds with me loosing consistently. I considered the chance that he was cheating.

"Well, not only do I suck at spell casting, I suck at cards."

"Hah! I have a full house – Tight! I win again!" He shrieked, throwing down his hand and glowering at me as I turn red and decided what other article of my remaining clothes to remove.

"Well you know what they say Bryn, Lucky in cards…"

"You think me unlucky in love? Would that be you thinking yourself more of liability than a benefit again?" As per usual, the reaction I got was not what I was expecting. I realized that perhaps his unexpected reactions were due mostly to the fact that he spent as much time listening to me as he did reading my thoughts. I hated that.

"I have promised you well thought out answers to the many questions plaguing you. I sense your growing tension because I have not adequately answered many of them. There is one more favour I have to ask, and then I promise I will bring you to England and answer everything." That was the most forward and frank concession he had made since we began together. It caught me off guard and in fact, I was dumbstruck.

"What's the favour?"

"One more ritual at the Cathexisphere before you come to England." The hairs on the back of my neck instantly began to rise, as a cold chill ran through me. Oh no! No fucking way I was going back in there and doing something else. His magic was so powerful, I was already noticing the myriad of 'after effects' the last ritual did. I was in no mood to have a bunch more. My eyes probably instantly gave away my absolute refusal.

"Anything but that!" I finally said, putting my cards down and looking to put my clothes back on as obviously playtime was over. I was expecting him to get angry, yell and try to convince me, but there he sat like stone staring at me without evincing any emotion. Then at length he closed his eyes, shook his head and put one of his hands to the bridge of his nose rubbed it for about a couple of seconds before he opened his eyes again and looked at me. I was completely re-attired.

"I expected as much. I have always known that not everything in this life was going to be pleasant. Can you do something else for me then?"

"Christ! What? Why don't you do something for me?" I wrapped my arms around my legs and glared at him.

"Fine I will make you a deal. You fast for twenty four hours, and I will do whatever you ask."

"You want me to fast? Why the fuck for?"

"Just humour me."

"Do you just get off on being a freak? Fine, I will fast, you will do me a favour and come visit me in Canada, within two weeks of me fasting."

"Deal." I couldn't believe he said deal! Did I hear him right? He promised to come and all I had to do was fast for a day. What the heck the two had in common I had no idea. If that was all it took, I would've fasted every week for a couple of day's years ago!

"Buddy you gotta deal!" I put out my hand for a shake to make the deal official. He paused, smiled at me then reached his hand down for a shake.

"I will tell you the day I want you to fast, but most likely March 16."

"That means you have to be here by the first week of April."

"Fair enough."

"Seriously though, why do you want me to fast?"

"Maybe I just want to see if you have the discipline to do it. A serious witch would do it regularly. You really don't practice very hard in developing your craft. Besides, while we have been apart you have polluted your vessel, you should purify."

"I suppose it is shallow for me to complain about my skill when I do little or nothing to develop it."

"Bryn?"

"Yes, Luv."

"It's been almost three months, isn't there something we are forgetting?" He cocked his head to one side for a moment and then smiled at me when he realized what I was driving at.

"No. I will not reward your conduct of the last three months. Fast and purify and I will be in Vancouver soon." He got up, knelt down, kissed me on the forehead and I was in my bedroom again. All I could think about was that I only had to fast for one day and he would be here in Vancouver and I couldn't wait to have him all to myself. I wondered if everything would feel the same flesh and blood.

Monday came and I was floating on a cloud. I decided to be a good girl and I threw away my cigarettes. I kept reflecting to our moments when we made love. Bryn had a habit of looking into my eyes while we made love. It was so intense, I wondered if he would do that when he came to Vancouver. The rabble of the school drifted by me from class to class, people milled about me at bus stops and on the bus, I was completely absorbed in my own world. Tuesday came, and in the morning I heard

Bryn's voice clear as a bell, "The deal is on for March 16th". I was so excited because that meant he would be here sooner rather than later. Wednesday after school I received a phone call from Jasmine,

"Hey girl what happened to you last weekend? I had a blast out at the clubs; I was hoping you would join me."

"Sorry, I had a paper due and I had to get the work done, it was due Monday." I lied.

"Well tonight is Ladies night at Clementine's, let's go! You've earned it." I really wanted to go out, but then I thought about Bryn. He wasn't going out and partying, and with him promising to come here, I refused to do anything to jeopardize that.

"You know what Jas? I have a mid-term in math and some other scary exams that I need to study and prepare for. I just can't get away. Maybe after all the exams and stuff I can go out with you. I'm really sorry, but you know how it goes."

"Well, I am really impressed that you are finally taking your education so seriously. That's awesome. I'm going tonight anyways, I'll ask some of the girls at work. See ya." So I was off the hook for Jasmine.

The rest of the week peeled away quickly, I went back to my book of shadows, and re read the section on purification of the body. It was actually much more detailed than just a fast. First I had to first bathe in a specified scented water. Then I had to 'anoint' my body in peppermint oil. Which I didn't have so I had to go buy it at the health food store as you can't just buy any kind of crap. It has to be REAL oil extract of peppermint. Then the fast itself begins at midnight to midnight and only water for the first twelve hours and than absolutely nothing for the last twelve. But that is not all. Then you have to light candles and sit and meditate and purge the mind and spirit of all thoughts, both calming and stressing. What a hassle, but I just kept focussing on the final objective. Bryn was going to be so proud of me. So at about 11 pm on the 16th of March I was crashed out for the night. I was hoping that on the 17th Bryn would tell me when he would be here and where.

I woke up at seven in the morning to the sound of the phone ringing. I got up and went to answer it.

"Good morning luv. Will you come join me at the Geogia Hotel? I'm in room #214. But be a good girl and just get dressed and come to my room, don't eat, we'll breakfast together."

"Great. I am so there." I hung up the phone. I ran to my room trying to think of what to wear. I decided on my leather pants, a black blouse and my boots. I brushed my hair, my teeth, and decided to forgo makeup. I ran out of the house and caught the next bus to downtown. I went into the venerable old Hotel, took the elevator to the second floor, and found the room labelled #214. I knocked on it nervously. Slowly it opened and there he was. He was wearing sunglasses, on a grey day, indoors, which seemed odd, but I just thought rock stars probably want to be incognito all the time. He probably didn't want to be recognized in case it wasn't me.

"Come in." I walked in and took off my boots while he closed and locked the door. The room was very posh and dimly lit and the curtains were all drawn. I put my coat on the hanger and was about to turn to him when he seemed to wander off to the next room. I followed him; I was so excited that we were finally together. When I got to the bedroom where he had led me, I noticed that he still had the stupid glasses on. I was about to tell him to take them off, along with all of his clothes when he seemed to read my thoughts and took them off. The glasses landed on the floor and I felt a sudden stab of panic. The glasses made no discernable noise when they hit the floor, and his eyes were glowing. I almost couldn't believe what my gut was telling me, I could feel the adrenaline building in me – why would he lie to me? He wasn't really here at all, but it was all too late. He walked right up to me, held me in some kind of paralytic hold. He held me and his face was expressionless.

"I'm sorry. Pleasant or painful, it has to be done." Then he took some damp cloth that was sitting on top of a dresser and pushed it into my face. The smell was sickening. I tried to fight him and get away; I tried to swing my body violently to get a momentary break in his grip. It was obvious that his grip on me was magically enhanced. We had wrestled over the years, and this was nothing like those times. I desperately attempted to scream, but the cloth was wedged over my face tightly. My flailing caused me to require an immediate breath and that required that I breathe through the cloth, which made me dizzy. I remember completely loosing consciousness in his arms. I knew the instant I saw those glowing eyes that he wasn't really here at all. I couldn't believe that my ghost who I had trusted my whole life could do this to me. After our last time apart I had told myself to trust him. He had finally won my trust for what? To do this to me?

When I awoke, I was naked on the bed. I felt wave after wave of nausea and of course, every time I threw up nothing but bile came up. My back felt burned, my legs, thighs and glutes hurt, and I felt very weak and sick. More than anything else, I felt rage and betrayal. I wanted vengeance. I looked around for the remote control for the TV. The first thing I needed to know was what day it was. The TV said it was March 18th and six in the morning. The next thing I thought about was finding out who had rented this room, in case it wasn't Bryn at all.

"Yeah, room service? This is room 214. Could you do me a favour? I forgot who the signing authority is for meals in this room. I want to order and I want to make sure who is paying."

"Your room is covered by the credit card you left at the front desk. I am speaking with Aileen Kovacs, yes?"

"Yeah, I'm Aileen. I have a credit card at your front desk?"

"We left a message on your phone about your Visa card you left here." I didn't own a credit card.

Thanks. Could you send me up a jug of water, some coffee and toast?"

"Right away Ms. Kovacs. We'll bring up your card with breakfast." I hung up the phone. When my coffee came, I grabbed the Visa card and called the number on the back.

"Hi, Visa. Yeah I am a card holder, here is my card number. I am not supposed to have a credit card; can you tell me who authorized this card?"

"Just a moment the voice on the other end said. Yes, Ms. Kovacs you have been issued a secondary credit card with your own credit limit by a family member. This is a new card; you just received it under a month ago.

"Yeah, what family member issued it please?"

"Well it says here Bryn Walker, relation, uncle. Did he not tell you?"

"No. Uncle Bryn is always full of surprises." I said trying to hide my anger and irritation.

"What's my credit limit?"

"$5000.00 Canadian dollars. It seems it was issued in the U.K." I hung up the phone. That fucking cocksucker! Did he think he could just buy me off? I chewed on my toast and thought about how much I would like to kill the bastard. But part of me was thinking about how nice it would be to go to Holt Renfrew and buy a bunch of clothes and make that bastard pay for it all! Right now though I felt way too sick to be shopping. I stayed in the hotel until about 2 pm and headed home. I was going to max out that credit card and I was damned if I was going to spend one more fucking minute with that asshole. That was it, I was done.

The next couple of nights I had weird dreams. I was standing by a building. But the building was older architecture the kind you see in Europe, not here in Vancouver. I seemed to be waiting for someone. Then I feel someone put their hand on my shoulder, I turn to see who it is and I see the face of Bryn. I panic and run up the road, while I am running it turns darker and darker until it seems to be the middle of the night I think that I have gotten away from him and I turn to look behind me and suddenly I am in Bryn's backyard, the Cathexisphere. Bryn is standing over me and I can't move.

"Purificare, Sanctificare, Sacrificium" He says and then I wake up screaming. Both times, I awoke and my heart was racing. He really had succeeded in scaring the shit out of me. Both times my mother ran to my room to see what was wrong. I just told her I was having nightmares – the truth really. It took me about a week to recover and heal. But there are things one doesn't recover from, scars that would never heal. Days turned into weeks and I never heard from him and I was actually glad. I eventually did go to Holt Renfrew and spent about $1000.00 on clothes, but it didn't make me feel any better. My eighteenth birthday came and went and I still heard nothing from Bryn. I still didn't care. I wanted to do something for the first time that was purely for me. I wanted to violate every covenant I had with Bryn. I began dating. This time I went out not with the intention of experimentation but with the intention of consummating it.

I finally settled on a guy my own age. Tall, blonde and nothing about him reminded me of my past. He became my steady and I decided to let him have me. The whole experience was mechanical and emotionless. I derived absolutely nothing from it. I knew this was due to the rituals I had endured at the hands of Bryn. I didn't care; I had to learn to fake my interest. I suppose I wasn't very convincing as he eventually dumped me. So I had a boyfriend for April to the end of May when he decided that it was impossible to please me. That is exactly what he said when he dumped me, "You're too hard to please..." I cried. Not because I was in love and he broke up with me. I cried because I had begun to realize the extent of what my life was going to look like in the aftermath of Bryn. It made me curse him even more. I took the golden heart necklace with a diamond on it and the lengthy poem that this boy had wrote for me and put it in my jewellery box. I began to wonder how many more mementoes from men who would foolishly fall for me I would acquire over the period of my life. But I was not to be deterred. I kept going out with Jasmine, out to the clubs to meet people and date.

I also went to the library and took out a number of books on rape, and abuse. They did nothing to comfort me. In many ways, I could see that I was a victim of an adult male with perverse sexual needs. The books described pedophiles and violent sexual offenders in detail. These men are mentally sick; with obsessions of sexual abuse, control and that they often tell lies to their victims to scare them into maintaining the conspiracy of silence. The only thing that didn't make sense, was how I met him and what I knew he could do. I hadn't imagined that, and that was definitely not normal. But that didn't mean that he couldn't be a warlock with sick perversions.

On June 5th, I received an unexpected letter and phone call. The letter, I was stunned to see by the stamps came from the U.K., I ran into my bedroom and ripped it open

My love,

I take great risk by writing this letter. But I want you to have something real in your hand to think about. Right now you hate my guts. I know that and I don't think you can ever forgive me unless you come to England and let me explain. You said you trust me and I told you I would tell you everything. Please call me.

Bryn.

The letter had no senders address, so how much risk could it really be? The letter began a huge flood of emotions. The words felt like every wound on me re-igniting in pain. My heart just wanted to break. I ripped it up and burned it right on my mirror dresser over a glass dish I usually kept change in. Something about burning that note relieved some pain. Before I could drown deeper into my sorrow, the phone rang.

Chapter 20

Kat calls a Dragon

Perhaps it was guilt over my feelings for Agaratte, or more likely my desire to try a new game in my relationship. I propositioned Lactavia to join Klaur and myself in a little ménage trios. At first she seemed offended by the request and politely declined but I persistently invited her for over a week and to my surprise she finally relented. The following Friday night when Lactavia knew she was coming home early from work and Klaur was on the couch finishing a can of Pepsi. I finished preparing dinner for all of us, and Lactavia and I had decided to drop the bomb on Klaur after dinner.

"Klaur, dinner is ready; after dinner I have a special gift for you." I said as I kneeled down.

"Whatever it is you made, it smells great!" He put his empty can on the end table and strode to the kitchen table. After a relatively quiet dinner we retreated back into the livingroom. I took Lactavia's hand and offered it towards Klaur.

"Klaur, I offer you Lactavia as a gift this evening." I couldn't help but smile a little bit. He smiled back

"Are you two serious?" He asked, not taking his eyes from Lactavia's very large chest.

"Yes, master." I said.

"Go for it Sean." Dared Lactavia.

"Let's go then..." He then reached out, took Lactavia's hand, and escaped into her room. Soon I could hear the tell tale sounds of something going on in the bedroom. The agreement was to join them, but at that particular moment I suddenly felt it would be better that I go for a walk in the fading sun, rather than attempt to interfere with them getting acquainted. My mind and my heart had another in mind: Agaratte. I knew that on a night like tonight he would be at his usual haunts and I enjoyed the opportunity to hunt him down. True to form he was heading towards one of his favourite meditating spots by the Lake.

"Agaratte, where are you going?" I asked catching my breath. He looked at me and pulled his blood red hair out of his eyes.

"What else? I am going to the Lake, care to join me?"

"I was hoping you would ask.." I said sliding my hand into his. He brushed his lips against my hair and we pressed on down the main street. Soon we were at a secluded part of Okanagan Lake and we found a place to sit.

"Where is that idiot you live with?" He smiled.

"He is back at the apartment with Lactavia." I said quietly but perhaps with some degree of bitterness.

"So is Klaur finally getting a piece of Lactavia?" He quipped.

"I suppose..." I shrugged wanting to change the subject. He put a hand on my hands that were on my lap and smiled at me.

"Dragon will kill him when she finds out. I can hardly wait to see the fireworks." We both laughed. But part of me wasn't amused about Dragon at all. Dragon had that asshole warlock on her side and I wondered if she were to get mad enough at Klaur would she sic her warlock on him? I crossed my legs and closed my eyes and tried to push the thoughts of Klaur, Lactavia, and Bryn out of my head.

"Hey, Kat I can tell that something's bothering you. Any chance I can help?" "Sometimes I wonder if anything in this world makes sense. I offered Lactavia to Klaur tonight and I am hoping that is not a courtesy that I regret."

"Why did you do that?"

"Probably guilt over you."

"Well don't worry Kat, I have it on good authority that no good deed goes unpunished. You will rue this night. That, I can guarantee."

"Thanks for the reassuring words."

"Well, be reassured by this then. I will always be there for you –always."

"Thanks, that really does mean a lot. I don't know what I would do without you." He smiled and then closed his eyes.

Agaratte and I meditated for awhile. Its amazing how rejuvenated one feels after meditation. I started to feel better all over. Whenever I was with Agaratte I felt content with the world. When I was done I reached up and stole a kiss from him, which caused him to reciprocate. We lay under the stars kissing and holding each other until the witching hour.

"It's midnight Kat. You should go home." He said stroking my long hair.

"I would rather spend the night with you." I said, somewhat surprised by my own boldness.

"Not tonight, maybe another night." He got up and held out his hands to help me up.

"You are a little tease aren't you?"

"If I just put out, I wouldn't be much of a mystery or a challenge to you, would I?" He said.

"How well you know me. Goodnight."

The following week, Klaur was kept quite busy keeping two women satisfied. Occasionally I would sneak out to be with Agaratte. We would kiss and touch but he would never make love to me. I didn't know why but I decided it was because he had traditional sense of loyalty to his friends and therefore would never touch his buddy's girlfriend. Although it may have seemed odd considering at one point Klaur did offer me to him. However, I decided that Agaratte operated at a higher level of morality than did Klaur.

After the first week, Klaur began buckling under the pressure of two women. This eventually led to him spending more time with one than the other. I don't suppose I should be surprised that he would spend it with the new woman.

At first this was not a problem as I was so busy with Thromm and Agaratte, but soon I was getting jealous. I could solve my Lactavia problem so easily if I had that artefact! I had to get it.

Maybe Thromm would have an idea as to how I could get that stone without doing the pact. The pact required a fair amount of human blood.

One night, as if reading my thoughts, Thromm appeared in my dream. In my dream he appeared as a small dark man, all in shadows. He whispered in a way that only I could hear and understand.

"Brynnn in grave dangerrr when no Dragonnn. You get Dragonnn mad at Brynnn, sheeee never seeee him againnn, Then warlock getsss sick. Then weee have chance get rock when he weak." Then he vanished in the fog of my dream as easily as he came.

I knew exactly what would get Dragon angry enough to never see Bryn again. But how could I tell her so that she would believe me? I couldn't probe her mind as Bryn had given her a powerful protection spell on her damn ring. Thromm had found that much out for me, you could see the magic in his realm as bright light. I also couldn't get to her while she slept as Bryn had warded her room. I had to give him credit; he secured his life insurance plan well. I was stuck with the more vulgar means of either writing her a letter, or calling her. I decided to call her. So the next Saturday morning I called Aileen from Margon's house.

"Dragon?" I asked

"Kat? It's about time you called, how the hell are you?" Said a friendly voice that I missed a lot.

"I need to talk to you sister to sister."

"What is it?"

"Well, I don't want you to get mad. I am going to talk to you about someone you spend a lot of time denying and lying to me about. But here it is. Bryn has come to me on a few occasions. He has assaulted me, threatened me and told me that if I were to tell you what I am about to, that he would kill me. Nevertheless, you are my sister and I love you, so I have to tell you that you are in mortal peril. He is using you to heal him from all the magic he is wielding. You are some powerful healer and he is siphoning off your life to save his. I also wanted you to know that when I was trying to Trance several months ago he found my astral projection, took it to him with the most amazing pull I have ever known, then I became almost completely solid whereby he then proceeded to violate me." There was a long pause on the other end of the phone. For a moment, I thought that maybe she had hung up the phone as soon as she heard the name Bryn. Finally, I heard her inhale deeply and exhale slowly and loudly.

"Kat. I truly apologize for any suffering you endured at the hands of that asshole. I haven't seen or spoken to him in about three months and I have no intention of doing so in the future. The next time you see him, remind him that if he ever tries to harm you or any member of ECAW that we will ensure he suffers equitably. But now can you at least wish me a belated birthday?"

"Yes, happy birthday sister. I hope otherwise things are going well for you."

"When will you come visit me in Vancouver?"

"Well, I hope you reconsider and join us here. Margon is still unattached." I said in the warmest voice I knew, trying hard not to sound too happy about hearing Bryn had lost his precious elixir of life.

"Well tell Margon he is always welcome to come visit me here in the big city. In fact, tell him I would enjoy taking him to dinner." She said.

"Dragon, you must come visit me in Penticton?"

"Well, school is almost over."

"I can't wait to set an extra place at the dinning table for you."

"I should go now. Take care Kat, great hearing from you." She hung up the phone and I could tell by the resignation in her voice that she wasn't lying. She was no longer fighting to defend him. She sounded truly done with Bryn! I couldn't believe my luck. What did she say? She hadn't seen him for three months? By now, he would be hurting. He may not even be able to wield a lot of magic –my advantage.

I walked out of the room and went to where Margon was waiting patiently in the kitchen of his parents' house.

"I spoke with Dragon and she has agreed to come visit you and me here in Penticton after school. However, she has officially invited you to Vancouver whenever you come to visit. Trust me, Margon that is the closest thing to being asked out on a date with her a man could ever ask for." Margon's expression seemed to brighten.

"Did she really say that?"

"I would never lie."

"Well, the next time Klaur and Agaratte go to Vancouver, perhaps I should go with them. "

"I think that is a wonderful idea Margon. This is your moment – go get her, Tiger!" We walked out the door and he and I walked excitedly all the way back to my apartment. I knew that the minute we got in the apartment Margon would distract Klaur with a plan to visit Vancouver. This would allow me an opportunity to have a frank discussion with Lactavia.

As I predicted, they were engaged on the couch but the rare enthusiasm of Klaur's long time chum soon had him pulled away from Lactavia.

"Tavi, may I have a word with you outside for a moment?"

"Sure what is it?" She asked in a wary tone. She knew I didn't appreciate her 'hogging' my man.

"I was wondering when you were going to go out and find a man of your own? I recall offering you one or two nights, I didn't think that you would turn around and betray my trust by stealing my man?"

"If he was really yours, I wouldn't be able to steal him would I? Besides, I think it's pretty clear now whose man he is now." Her words were so hurtful, so cruel I hardly could believe that this was the friend I invited into my house to begin with. I remembered Agaratte's words, 'no good deed goes unpunished.' At least Dragon never wanted to have anything to do with my men, even when they threw themselves at her.

"We shall see who has the last laugh Lactavia." It seemed with each passing day I needed that artefact more and more.

Chapter 21

I put the phone down. I had this letter from Bryn in one hand and this bizarre conversation with Kat on the other. I didn't want to believe a word she said. It seemed too bizarre. But I had seen some pretty amazing things since I had Bryn in my life. I thought about her description of how she felt solid on the other side. The way she described what she went through made me believe that she had actually experienced what I had. As much as I didn't want to believe it, it was hard to dismiss. What she said about me being a healer also touched a nerve. I had seen Bryn go from pale and half-dead to lively as a trapped wildcat upon one of my visits. It was indeed plausible, even though it sounded insane. But there was one nagging question? What the hell was he doing with Kat? Was he trying to get me upset enough to confront him? None of this made sense. I knew if he really wanted to be a bastard, he could come and get me and I couldn't do a damn thing about it. He could appear on the streets, in my room and in a hotel. If he really wanted me he could. He was giving me space to come to him of my free will. I also couldn't figure out why he would violate her? Did she mean sex? He told me he couldn't do that. These questions bothered me, but I wasn't about to go running back to Bryn for the answers. He made me wait once, it was time to return the favour if nothing else.

I went to my room and grabbed my purse. You know what, Aileen? It's time you got your driver's license and got a car. I bet that if I crank up this credit card, it will magically be paid off by my dear uncle. I laughed to myself and called up Visa to find out how I could pull cash out of my Visa credit. The following week I had paid for driving lessons and was shopping around for a cheap car. The driving lessons were great and when I finally bought a small used Chevy Chevette I wasted no time getting practice in it. I waited until the first of the month and sure enough, the credit card got all paid off. My mother was so proud of my ability to save money from my hairdressing job. I just lied and told her I was making really good tips.

Within the month I wrote and did my driving test and was issued my temporary license. I could drive to school now – Yippee! No more depressing bus and soggy bus stops. I came home and ran up the stairs on a Tuesday after school, to find my mother waiting for me at the top with an angry expression. She held a rag in one hand and an all-purpose spray cleaner in the other,

"I want to remind you that when you move into your own home, you can keep your rooms any way you like, but while you live under our roof –you clean your mess up!" I just looked at her, stunned.

"Follow me." She took me down the hall to my room.

"I suppose you don't remember making this mess? You know if you have something you need to write down use a damn notepad." She then threw the cleaner and rag onto my bed and stormed out of my room. I was amazed when I looked around my room.

The felt pens on my desk were all open and my walls were covered in writing.

'Absolution' must have been scrawled about ten times. Then on my mirror there was a note saying. 'Please give me one more chance.' I didn't know what absolution meant, but I was pretty sure I knew who my vandal was. I closed the door and attempted to scrub off the writing. It didn't work. My mom struggled with English and she had the most comprehensive Webster's dictionary in the livingroom, so I looked up the word. It was some biblical word meaning total forgiveness or something like that. Yeah. I don't think so, Bryn.

"Mom? I am really sorry. I will repaint this room and I promise it won't happen again."

"Well, just don't do it again. It's kind of creepy to walk into your daughter's room and see something like that. You aren't doing drugs are you?" I just laughed.

"No, I saw this punk rock designer room and I thought that the style might look good in my room. But you are right it looks lame." We parted company and I contemplated going into Trance to give Bryn shit. But I knew that is exactly what he wanted – he was finding ways to provoke me. Instead my mind drifted back to someone I had almost forgotten about, someone who seemed to know a lot of stuff that I sure didn't. Maybe it was the use of the word 'Absolution', I don't know. But I got in my car and headed for Langely, BC. I had to try and remember where Rodan lived.

It took me a couple of dead end cul-de-sacs but I finally found the house. The lights were on and I hoped that he was home. I hadn't even made it up the driveway and he came out the door to meet me.

"Dragon, what brings you here?"

"I need a favour from you. I know you are no longer involved with the Coven, but I fear you are the only one with the answers I seek." He looked around for a moment as if the trees were hiding something, as if someone would overhear us.

"Come inside then. But you can't stay for long; I have a prior engagement I can't avoid." He motioned for me to get into the house quickly. He seemed unusually cagey.

"What is it you want to know?"

"Where is the, 'Hey, how's it going? I missed you', conversation?" He looked at me and shook his head.

"I'm sorry I don't mean to seem ungrateful for the visit. You just seemed rather urgent to have some questions answered and I didn't want to delay you with pleasantries."

"Well, Rodan, I miss you and wish that you were back in the group. Kat and her new group of guys are all in Penticton and only Tyra and I are left here in Vancouver."

"Well, there are advantages to solitary Craft I suppose."

"Remember way back when I asked you about Enoch?"

"Yes."

"Well do you know much about Shemhazai?" He looked at me for a long time before answering and I had never seen him behave so oddly before. He got up and ran down the hall without answering me at all. I was about to just get up and leave when he came back with a small leather bound book in his hand. He walked up to me with a weird, grave expression on his face.

"I want you to have this. Read it. Read it all." He grabbed my hand and placed the book in it.

"Okay, you are really freaking me out now. What the hell is this?" He looked around a little more and put his face close to mine. He then put his lips to my ear and whispered,

"This is the Book of Enoch. Everything you need to know about him and Shemhazai is in here." He then kissed my ear and moved his head away.

"I'm afraid I am going to have to ask you to leave."

"You know something don't you? Why won't you tell me?"

"Please go, you know to whom you must direct all your questions." At that moment, I froze as I looked at him. He knew! Somehow, he knew. I took the book and my purse and stormed off to my car. I went home to my room with all the insane scribbling on the walls and read the whole damn book. I didn't sleep a wink. Well now I knew the characters and what went down, but it didn't help answer any fucking questions I had. Shemhazai was an angel that left heaven and taught men magic. He was punished. Enoch was some holy man that was shown many things about the earth and heaven by angels. So what? It was a crazy book that had no bearing on why Bryn was such a freak. The book didn't talk about healers, warlocks, astral projections or the Talisman. Rodan was no help at all. Suddenly my astounding ignorance bothered me to distraction, I couldn't sleep at all. I kept thinking about Rodan's words, 'you know whom you must direct all your questions…' Yeah, there was only one person who was begging to tell me everything, and the thought of that made me physically ill.

I hadn't done Tyrrean Trance for months, which was something like March, It was August now, and, believe it or not, you really can loose your skill at this with that long of a gap. I made my way home early from my job and was in my room and in Trance by 4pm, midnight in England. I was angry and ready for a fight.

In the sea of the spirit world, I called out for Bryn. It is very difficult to judge the passage of time when you are in that state. I was floating and in that state for a very long time, it felt like hours. I was wondering why I was waiting for so long, and was contemplating just giving up, when suddenly I felt that pull grabbing me out of the nothingness and into a room.

I was expecting to find him at home, so I was surprised to find myself in a hotel room. I was noting a fear beginning to well up in me as I now suddenly realized I had an intense fear of hotel rooms. This hotel room was average and non-descript, however, it was a hotel room and I didn't equate it with great memories even though it was an entirely different one. The lights were off and only candles were lit. Did Bryn have a problem with using electricity? He was as obsessed with candles as I was with coffee.

I was standing in the foyer of the hotel room, which spread out into a living room /bedroom; Bryn was on the bed with candles all around him. He turned his head towards me and I couldn't believe my eyes. He was lying on top of the bedding naked; his skin was sheet white and looked papery, like a 90 year old. His eyes seemed sunken and he looked like he had two black eyes, withered and old. In fact, the only thing I recognized was his eyes and that instant surge of energy whenever he was near me. My fear and my anger immediately turned to dire concern.

"Bryn? What the hell? Are you okay?" I said racing to his side.

"Do you dial 911 for doctors in this country?" I said looking for the phone.

"Aileen – I am so sorry..." His voice was raspy and he sounded a little delirious.

"No doctor can heal me...Touch me. I used most of my remaining strength to bring you across." I could see he was actually beginning to shake. His shaking reminded me of what happens to accident victims when they come out of shock.

"What? You need a doctor!" I said loudly looking for the phone book.

"Just please touch me!" He sounded so earnest and his shaking was getting worse. I had to put the phone book down and humour him. I walked over and took his hand into mine. I looked down at him and tried to put on a brave smile, but I was shaking my head.

"What the fuck have you been up to now, Warlock?" I felt him tug on my hand and I knelt down to give him a hug. After a couple of minutes he put his wrinkled lips to mine and we kissed. My brain wanted to push this shrivelled up man away from me, but I fought the urge. As he kissed me, his grip got stronger and his kiss wetter, if there was any doubt before, it certainly disappeared now: just by kissing me, just by holding me, he was getting stronger. That surge of energy between us, that intoxicating feeling was washing over me, I could see that energy moving from me to him. It was like watching someone being snatched from the clutches of Death himself. To my utter astonishment he found the strength to roll me over and fitfully removed my pants. It was like an out of body experience. In complete conflict with my brain, this corpse was touching me, I wanted to stop it, but my body was aching so badly for him, that the pain was tangible. My body was responding so instantaneously that I couldn't believe the difference between this moment with a hideous carcass when only a couple of months ago, my body would do nothing for the gorgeous young man I was dating. I watched in horror as I realized that my body was under the control of other forces. I looked up at Bryn while he was stared down into my eyes, expressionless, his body moving rhythmically. Everything that Kat said was true, his skin smoothed, his hair appeared fuller and his body seemed more virile and substantial. I could see the blood infuse his body as he plumped out and took colour. In the flickering light I could see the fire in his eyes returning…Bryn was being resurrected. The man I saw just half an hour ago was gone, before me was the powerful Bryn I knew and loved. He rolled off of me and ran to the bathroom mirror.

"Dragon, you must come to England and stay with me for a week. Please say yes." He ran back into the livingroom and held my face gently in his hands.

"Look at you… just as beautiful. Channelling doesn't change you. You are so powerful."

"What are you talking about?" I asked putting my hands on his arms as if to make him stop touching my face.

"The power to restore me is not from me, it's your power." He said smiling.

"But I have no control over it. How can it be my power?" I asked. He stopped smiling and looked at me very seriously. "Promise me you will come to England and I will tell you all I know."

"Will you tell me what you were really doing in the United States that was draining your energy like you were today?" I wanted to let him know that I knew he was up to something – something dire. He sat at the edge of the bed and looked at me seriously,

"I will confide in you everything. Honestly, I was not keeping secrets from you because I don't care. I was worried that if you knew, other forces would find you; you would be in great danger. I did it to protect you."

"How come you didn't tell me before that I was a healer? I have always wanted to know what it was that you saw in me."

"You don't actually think that the only reason I have you around is for healing do you?"

"Well, the thought had entered my mind, especially after the last time we were together."

"To be honest, initially I wasn't convinced you could heal me. By the time I realized that the prophecy was bang on, I worried that you would draw such a conclusion. I had hardly realized your power when I had to address other things before you came to England. Please come, let me finally tell you all I know. I think we are ready –the timing is now finally on our side."

"You buy the ticket, and I will go to England. But I get to keep the credit card." I rolled off the bed and went hunting for my pants.

"Deal" he returned.

"I plan to go to college so you better get me those tickets like now." I paused from putting my pants on when I felt him in my head again, rooting around for whatever.

"Why are you still afraid Aileen?"

"I hate it when you go digging in my head – it's rude!"

"I'm sorry. It just jumped out at me, honest."

"Look, I just am. You think your jackass stunt at the Georgia Hotel isn't good enough reason to be afraid? I should hate you! Why don't I hate you? Why didn't I just leave you here to die?"

"Wow! No risk of subtlety there. I'll stay out of your mind unless invited." He said looking hurt.

"What exactly was that last ritual you did with me Bryn?" I asked.

"A protection spell. The binding ritual in my Cathexisphere bound us and set the level of mortal priority to me, the caster. I had to do a very nasty form of protection on you to ensure that casting priority doesn't lead to your Ka aborting its coil."

"Do you think it worked?"

"I think the ritual may have solved most of our problems. I would not ask you over if I was not confident that I could do it with minimum risk to you, my love." He scooped up my hands in his and kissed them lavishly. I believed him.

One week in England alone with Bryn made me think of the books on abuse I had read, and some of the painful things he had subjected me to. I needed answers and this was the only way I was going to get them. I was determined to go, and I was determined to protect myself, just in case. I packed my Finnish hunting knife, it was sharp and Warlock or not, 5 inches of steel would slow him down if need be.

I took the time off work and made an excuse to my parents about going to the Okanagan. Bryn had tickets waiting for me at the airport for British Airways purchased under his brother's name. Because of my dual citizenship, my father always made sure I had an updated passport, so it was not a big deal. I didn't want to be escorted or planned. He protested at first because he is so damn overprotective or as I like to think, controlling. However, he eventually relented. I was going to take the train and find his place on my own. I had decided that much. He came calling on me the night before my flight and was probably relieved that I didn't try and get out of it this time. I was still very scared, after everything we had been through. An older, eccentric, wealthy man and I was going straight into his lair – I mean, he could do anything to me and no one would even know where I was. But I was excited too.

Deep down inside I thought that if he actually saw me, he wouldn't recognize me or that I would be not what he expected. That constant nagging fear that maybe I *was* crazy after all.

But the time of reckoning was here and I had to put this behind me. So here it was, August 18, I went to the International departures at Vancouver's International Airport in Richmond with my passport and duffel bag in hand. Off to England alone. The flight was long, as I had a layover in Toronto. But I was so filled with anxiety it went surprisingly fast. I kept playing scenarios over and over in my head. What will I say? How will he react? What if his mom is there? Once off the plane, I had to retrieve my bags and find out how and where to get on the tube heading for Surrey.

There are trains that go all over England; it is amazing. They don't fool around when it comes to moving people around that small rock of a country. I suppose I could have tried a little harder to figure out what bus to take. But I had already had one hell of a trip. I got out at Horely station and called a cab that I found in a phone book.

The street he lived on was full of larger homes. Bryn's front yard was actually somewhat ugly, comprised solely of vehicles, his American Corvette and Lotus both being there. I crawled out of the cab and gave the driver his money, a collection of pound notes I got from a bank in Vancouver, and he drove off.

I just stood there on the sidewalk, a little too scared to enter the property. As I was standing there contemplating my next move, a figure came to the downstairs window and looked at me, then the curtain flashed and a tall, very thin figure opened the door a tiny crack. As my eyes adjusted to the shadows, the telltale pale skin and sharp angular features immediately let me know I was here and that was definitely him. I gasped. My stomach was filling up with acid and my heart began racing. Shakily I reached down to the ground for my duffel bag and looked back at the shadowy figure at the door. I walked towards him, each step feeling like I was walking closer and closer to the edge of a great cliff, and that the next step was more and more assured to be my last. I started to breathe heavily and sweat, but I kept walking, his features becoming horrifyingly more real! When I was about 3 meters from the entryway, I stopped. His face had taken up so much of my field of view that my legs seized. My hand went instinctively into my pocket with the sheathed knife. The thought hit my head, what the hell am I doing?

"You…" said the voice at the door in a hush.

"Me…" I replied, my voice rasping. Instantly he bounced forward, grabbed my duffel bag in one hand, and jumped back to his door.

"Come inside." He said looking at me before turning and directing me to the entryway and closing the door behind me quickly. Instantly he spun me around to face him and hugged me. He then pulled away looked me into the eyes and gave me a lingering kiss on the lips.

"Wow!" I said when he slowly drew away.

"Thanks for coming." He took my hand that was still in my pocket holding the knife. He ignored my duffel bag and brought me into the house. The house was instantly familiar. We walked up the stairs, he sat on a familiar chair, and I took the couch. He sat down, staring at me, in fact, not taking his eyes off me for a long while which made me feel uneasy. Finally, he broke off his stare.

"Young, you are so very young. Tyrrean trance definitely hides your age. I feel old." He said. He was looking kind of old. His skin and hair was definitely showing signs of aging and the stress of his career and, of course, the drain from his link to that fucking piece of rock.

"Bryn…"

"So here we are flesh and blood – we have waited far too long. You are so fucking beautiful." He smiled and nervously pulled back his scant bangs from his eyes. But those eyes, how they glowed, how they burned. What makes this man what he is could not be commented on tersely or flatly stated. What made Bryn such an enigma was probably never directly told to him. This was a man who left an indelible mark on every life he touched, his charisma is huge.

I was pissed off at him and I wanted answers but for whatever stupid reason I couldn't stay on that couch. I didn't cross the earth and train my way to him from Heathrow Airport to sit on his couch. I crawled off the couch as if hypnotized and wrapped my arms around him, my lips on a quest for his. I pulled him off his chair, we were on the floor, I didn't know where I ended, and he began. My whole body was on fire; my entire mind clouded up and became unable to focus on anything except this moment.

I awoke in Bryn's bed instead of my own for the first time in my life and it was the best thing in the whole damn world. It was still dark outside; I turned to see him sleeping blissfully. His arms and legs still entwined in mine, I felt more joy and happiness than I ever thought possible.

"Bryn? Baby, are you up? I only have like a million questions." I sure needed a good nights sleep and he was sweet enough to give me just that. That would be Bryn. Thoughtful enough not to make me sore the day I came off the flight.

"No. More sleep." He rolled over. There was one thing that was still nagging in the back of my head about what Kat told me. I was determined to find out who was lying to me. No time like the present I thought.

This was the perfect time to do a little hunting in his brain, as Bryn was blissfully unguarded. I focused my energy and tried to penetrate that heavy curtain which guards his mind. Slowly but surely I could find all kinds of random thoughts. I tried to focus on thoughts of Kat. Suddenly, I saw a visual picture of him assaulting me. I waited a little longer, and sure enough, his mind was calling her Kat, but it was definitely me!

"What is it you wish to know, my luv?" He was awake now and turned again to face me.

"Kat called me the day I received your letter. She told me some disturbing things, but she told me truthfully that I was a healer."

"hmmmph. I might have guessed. Your friend is impressive. She does not belong to any of the major sects of arcane knowledge yet she is unusually adept, resourceful and skilled. However, you should know she has her own objectives and they conflict with ours. I really should get rid of her. I frequently overlook her, but she could jeopardize everything."

"What the hell did you do to her?"

"Not what you are thinking. I can't do that, remember? I gave her a taste of trouble for sure. She is determined to tear us apart. You know that, don't you?"

"Did you have to make her look like me?"

"I didn't. She came to me shifted as you. She actually thought that I wouldn't know the difference. This friend of yours has been pursuing my Talisman and I am fed up." He reached into his drawer, pulled out his stone, whispered something unintelligible and immediately his hands glowed red. He then flicked his hands to the ceiling and the red streaked across the room, up into and through the walls. He then turned to me with annoyance.

"What did you do to her just now? You wouldn't dare hurt her would you?" I thought he just might be crazy enough to do that.

"In fact, I would dare. She has no idea what she is blundering into. Aileen, she would be dead by now if it weren't for you." He was serious and I was stunned by his coldness. I was angry with Kat for violating my private life, my secret life with Bryn. Somehow looking at his face I suddenly became aware of my own possessiveness, how dare she!

"By the way Aileen, was it not your request that we stay out of each others' minds unless given permission? If you had asked, I would have told you whatever you needed to know. Why can you not trust me?" He grabbed some blanket and turned over. I was suddenly aware of an old feeling. That feeling that I have done something rash and inconsiderate. Again, Kat's lies got me into hot water. Way to go on your first night in England, Aileen– dumb ass!

Eventually we got up and dressed and joyfully blamed it on my jet-lag. I had to eat, I was starving. This caused a dilemma as I refused to let Bryn leave the house until he spilt the beans about his stay in the U.S. that meant I had to eat whatever I could find in this house, which wouldn't feed a mouse. I walked away from the barren kitchen to the livingroom and sat down looking at Bryn who was already sitting on his chair waiting for me.

"Aileen, before I tell you my dark business you must vow to never take up a career, business or profession which will expose you to government, fame in such a manner as to risk exposure. You must remain hidden."

"What? What do you mean? Like what if I wanted to be a cop?"

"Gods! Why would you want to do that?"

"Cause it sounds like interesting work."

"Why can't you go to University and be a teacher?"

"Boring Bryn, and I don't like kids."

"Funny, coming from a kid."

"Bite me. If I am a kid then you are a pervert" he cocked up an eyebrow as the implication was an obvious sore point.

"I'm serious, Aileen. We are not the only ones that can read thoughts. This information is of a highly sensitive nature and I want you to assure me that you are committed to a career that will keep you safe and hidden in the rabble – teacher is perfect."

I got down on my knees and looked up at him kind of sincerely, kind of my usual goofy self when in an awkward situation – essentially immature.

"I vow on our bond that I will do this you ask, just please tell me what is draining you so." I could tell by his expression that he was willing to overlook my goofy overture and press on.

"Sometimes Aileen, a mortal with a little bit of knowledge and a tremendous amount of power can be the most dangerous combination. Such is the case in some parts of the world but most especially a few organized groups in the United States."

"What do you mean a little bit of knowledge? What knowledge?"

"Well I know part of what your ECAW group does is study different religions and look at similarities, yes?"

"Yeah. So?"

"Well, you are aware of the global flood story?

"Yes, of course. It occurs in most cultures. It is one of the most common stories throughout all known civilizations."

"Well, there are many other similarities. Another common thread amongst all mortals is the belief in spiritual immortality. The concept is a simple one, that man is limited in his duration of time upon this Earth. That he will graduate to an eternal spirit world if judged worthy. Now over time a few powerful groups became convinced that they could stop this transition or, if you prefer, ascension of man's race from the earth to the ethereal. To accommodate the established faith systems adapted their faith to a belief system of a perfect existence on a perfected Earth. However, the organized groups I am primarily concerned with know that the most ancient texts refer to man's immortal ascension to the spirit realm at the end of days. Greed, avarice, power, and fear are the main reasons that these people want to stop this change for their kind. They don't want to ascend; they want to continue to dwell as mortals upon the Earth generation after generation. Why wouldn't they? They make up some of the wealthiest, most powerful people who are utterly incapable of ascetic living. There was an antecedent race of beings that had their own lands and culture. They know I'm due to return prior to the end of days, but they have not yet figured out who I am. They are ever closer to learning my identity this life. They are convinced that by killing you and I they will stop the end of days and the ascension of the Edenites."

"Your identity this life? Who do they think you are? Why would anyone want to hurt me?"

"Well, Aileen, before I answer those questions. Let me give you a little more history. For instance, you are familiar with the Aztec's and their reference to ages or 'gates'?"

"Not really..." That won me a disappointed expression before he pushed on.

"Like the biblical references in Western civilization, there is to be no sixth gate for the children of Eden in Aztec faith. The closing of the 5th gate is supposed to be foreshadowed by a specific set of circumstances, astrological alignments included. These powerful sects have experts who have read the signs. Armed with this knowledge, these organized groups for the past fifty or so years, have infiltrated parts of the United States government at various levels to engage in covert operations around the globe. What I mean is simply that they are currently covertly controlling and sabotaging independent countries for their own agendas. While currently focussed on Central America, Afghanistan, Libya, and Iran, these operations are not limited to supporting terrorists and coups they are also heavily involved with large-scale plans of global control. The advantage of this to them is that their target people could infiltrate any government and attempt to eliminate a sign or you and I. There are things brewing about globally you wouldn't believe and I will not trouble you more with the details. As to why I was in the United States I need you to understand the gravity of the situation you and I find ourselves in. My business was to establish Sentinels to protect us. They are located globally. But most importantly I have programmed some American citizens to ensure that the gate stays closed until I am given the word. Currently, there are some 20,000 American citizens that have been programmed to respond at a specific time to sabotage parts of their own corrupt government. They are composed of doctors, lawyers, politicians, military men and a large population of teenagers who are growing up fast. It's like taking down a very large animal with nothing more than ticks. The 5th gate has to remain closed and you protected as ever until the return of the child."

"What happens when the gate opens?"

"It is foretold that the earth will shake and all will be engulfed in fire. All Edenites will perish. Their ascension shall take place." He said.

"Then why are you also postponing the Gate opening, sounds like your doing exactly what these Sects want."

"I am postponing it not to try to alter the course of Edenite destiny –I have a promise to keep which is absolution for the Ancients."

"So what does a returning child have to do with you?"

"This child is the reintegration of the ancient bloodlines and soul-lines. It has been happening around the world. The Nephili bloodline is coming together again, in preparation for the 6th gate. But the child I am referring to is the avatar whose blood can actually consecrate the Earth for all Nephilim and the Ancients."

"You've used that expression before. If all the Edenites die, what is left? I mean Wiccans are Edenites aren't we?"

"Most Wiccans, yes. You are right. But not you."

"Here we go again, what are you trying to tell me?"

"Sit down."

"What?" I realized that in my bewilderment in all this that I was standing.

"Just do me a favour and sit down; this may upset you at first." I sat back down on the couch, hanging impatiently on the rest of his tutorial.

"You are what has been not so lovingly referred to as the ancient race, Viracocha, or Nephilim." I suddenly recalled the Book of Enoch that Rodan gave me.

"The Nephilim were the children of Angels fornicating with mortals. They were all destroyed in the flood Bryn; I have read that much in the various Bibles we have at ECAW."

"In fact many were. However, some survived."

"How would you know this? Did the Talisman tell you?"

"Well, let's say my association with the Talisman has broken all of my 'veils' and I remember with great clarity all of my previous lives."

"So you were there?"

"As were you." That earned him a dirty look of disbelief from me.

"Did we know each other?"

"You were my first wife."

"First?" The very idea got my blood boiling. He could see my expression and of course, it brought an instant grin to his angular face.

"I had three wives. I had many children with two and none with you. I swore to honour and protect you and also I vowed to leave you barren, against incredible objection from you."

"Why did you marry me then in the first place?"

"You were the only love I ever knew. I was informed of your, shall we say, unique lineage and that I should shun you. When we met, I found you to be not only beautiful but good, and not using your power for ill to anyone. Forces were at work to ensure your safety, all things considered, no other mortal or Nephili could have protected you as I could. I took you and hid you with me. Your ancestor, Uriel, then made a deal with me."

"Isn't that the name of an Arch Angel? Tell me your not referring to an angel."

"Look, think of the Angels as a spirit form for a race of beings you have never seen. You may have seen half angels, or even more than half angels. Just look into a mirror. For my part, I am not Nephilim. There was an antecedent race of being that had their own lands and culture. They have been variously called Watchers, Fallen, Angels, Atlantians, and Viracocha to name a few. The ones that survived the flood fled to the lands of the Edenites and some merged their bloodlines."

"So you are telling me Angels are actually an ancient race?"

"Yes, I am."

"So if I am Nephilim, what were you?"

"You chose a lowly Edenite for your groom."

"Did I have a name?"

"I would imagine you had two names, the name from your father which I wouldn't be able to pronounce and the other from your mother which I called you, Daizabael."

"Who was my father? What was my husband's name?"

"Your father Aileen was none other than Shemhazai himself, as to your husband, Enoch." I was aware of goose bumps beginning to appear all over my body.

"Enoch, the prophet?" I asked in an almost whisper.

"Enoch, Elijah the Tishbite, John the Baptist. These have been my mortal names."

"You are fucking kidding me!"

"You are the daughter of Shemhazai. The Talisman he created from the magical wood only found in the realm of his people. But the leader of his race took him and his followers and sacked them for meddling in Edenite affairs and he has been in chains ever since. I have been shown more than any the ways of your ancestors and the spirit world. I have worked through these 10,000 years to find absolution for your people. The 6th gate is for the fallen and their Nephilim. We will do this, they have suffered long enough. I promised you I would, but the payment you promised me in return is that you will come in the end and join me, with the children of Eden. You will never be with your father…" I knew he was driving at something. But I was still trying to comprehend his incredible story. If he was going to stop at nothing to end the mortal days of the Edenites he needed some child didn't he say?

"So, if the 5th gate closes before this avatar child returns, the fallen and their Nephilim are doomed. Whose child are we going to be protecting?"

"Why don't you contemplate that for awhile and tell me?" I was overwhelmed. I was confused. I sat there staring at him wondering what the hell he meant, then it hit me! I didn't need to think about it for too much longer, I was pretty sure I knew the answer and my exasperated look transformed to shock.

"You must have the wrong person. I can't be Nephilim. I am magically weak, and Nephilim were supposed to be powerful giants."

"Well, consider that you have no one from your race to tell you how your kind is supposed to do magic. Then when you consider how much you can do when you are doing it all probably wrong. You're doing quite well. Besides, don't think for one moment that I wouldn't know my own Daizabael." The sound of him calling me that sent a kind of shock through me.

"So if my father made that Talisman, if I touched it, would it talk to me?"

"I suspect far more than that. I imagine it could be potentially very dangerous. I was over 360 years old when I was taken up. You made me promise you a world for your people. I told you that I would forgo children with you and instead bring them all out of eternal darkness. I swore that I could prove that even the purest of Shemhazai's race could not resist the temptations of this mortal world. They sent the leader's son and I came to him while he toiled and through him I was given this final task. But you are mine; I will not lose you to the 6th gate. You must promise to never touch this Talisman. I will be honest with you and tell you that through it, Shemhazai might try and undo all that we have done, in his haste to be free. Can I trust you?" His expression was very serious, so serious I had to acknowledge that I would never in my life touch that Talisman.

"Bryn, you know you can trust me always. But why would you go to all this trouble for a people, a race that you do not belong to?"

"Because of you. I love you. I saw how you suffered. Because as Enoch I bore the burden of learning your kinds secrets, I was instrumental in the demise of many of your ancestors. I can remember so many times coming home from the front lines, even on the coldest days; you would be outside waiting for me. I strictly forbade you to use your Nephilim magic but you would always do something crazy to welcome me home. One time you had the tall grasses wave wildly in no wind and the sound was like music. Another time you knew I was coming home in the night and lit the path with magical light right to your feet. But my Edenite wives shunned you and I knew how they mistreated you while I was away. Yet you never raised a hand to harm either of them. I felt honour bound to do the right thing. But make no mistake, many of your kind were monsters." He got out of his chair and walked over to me, knelt down and took up my hands, kissing them. I had to hand it to him; he was romantic, passionate and sincere. I didn't know how to respond. So as usual, when in an awkward situation, Aileen to the rescue with another poorly appointed moment to bring up a sore point.

"So what exactly did you do when you trapped me in that hotel room in Vancouver? " He looked up from my hands into my eyes, making me aware that the timing of my question was a painful one. But he didn't get getting angry, he continued to be sincere.

"The binding ritual between us has had more far ranging consequences than I had ever anticipated. We are not just bound together, your spirit would exhaust itself to feed mine. Above all, we cannot afford to loose you so I did a ritual, which No thought would stop you from channelling your very life. My concern was again that if it came to that, if your soul was near me – you would let me die." The sudden thought of me being alone on this forsaken planet without him was the most horrifying thought I had never before this moment contemplated.

"What makes you think I want to live without you?" I said reeling from the thought.

"What makes you think I want to?" He shot back. He paused, got up and walked back to his chair,

"If I fail Aileen, I loose you, my Daizabael, forever...Do you now see how deep we are into this mess? I knew that ritual would be a painful one and I knew that in this form you would still suffer so I arranged to have you unconscious here and blocked your passage back to your body. I completed the ritual in the Cathexisphere. Remember, you have the control. When we are together, you unconsciously heal. You must train yourself to stop the flow of energy. You have to focus on breaking the connection. I suspect you feed on that flow like a drug addict – no offence."

His comment offended me, but there was a vein of truth in it. I knew now what flow of energy he was referring to. I know how much like a drug that feeling was. How could I not get off on it? Why would I try to stop it? It was the most inexpressible pleasure I had ever experienced in my life – how do you control it?

"So, let me see if I understand this. If I don't control this flow of energy, I could kill myself?"

"In a nutshell, yes. For instance, right now you are still draining yourself. Turn it off, because, as you can see, I am fine."

I tried to turn off the energy flow but I just didn't know how. I spent the next hour having Bryn teach me how to do it, but I occasionally let it go and enjoyed the ride. It wasn't killing me.

"What would happen if we lived together and spent entire days, or months together?" I pushed, not wanting to get off subject. He lost his smile and rubbed the back of his neck.

"As I said before you need to learn to control it." He turned his face from me and walked towards the edge of the livingroom.

"Bryn, how did you know where I was and that I was a healer?"

"I didn't. No found you. Only those in the spiritual realm can see the colors and species of spirits. Healers are all green. All I know is that we tried to find you at regular and frequent intervals. But in the mortal realm, you are basically invisible, that is why when we were kids the connection was so fragile. When you attempted the Tyrrean trance No instantly returned to me declaring, "I found your Daizabael. She lights up the realm like nothing else from Earth." We had to instantly grab you before anyone saw whence you came."

"Oh? What would happen if someone knew who I was?" I pushed.

"There are probably hundreds of people, some more skilled than your friend Kat, looking for you. They have orders to kill you. If not with magic, they will locate you and pay a professional to kill you." The Avatar that you could conceive would seal their fate."

"Why?"

"Have you not heard a word I told you?"

"Okay, Okay I get it. I think." The truth was that I sort of understood, but had such a hard time believing that there would actually be people out there that seriously believe that I somehow controlled their destiny enough to justify killing me.

"I have spent the last four years installing Sentinels all over the world. You are as protected as I could ever make you without keeping you in a cage." He grinned at me and I returned the smile but I was still taking in the massive download of information.

"I still can't believe I'm dating Elijah."

"You're not, I was Elijah. Bryn is another life in another age altogether. My words are disseminated differently, and my mission is for a different people." He seemed tired of talking, headed for the kitchen, and rustled around putting some of his scant rations together. I was still sitting, absolutely stunned, digesting impossible to believe concepts. I was trying to imagine the two kinds of people in the world right now, Edenite, the vast majority, and Nephilim. I just didn't think that I was that different looking than any Edenite.

"Bryn?" I raised my voice as he was now in the kitchen mucking about.

"What now woman, I am hoarse." He snapped a cupboard closed and turned to face me across the house.

"Doesn't this whole child avatar sound a little messianic to you?"

"For the Fallen, yes. For the Edenite Sects more like their Anti-Christ, I hate these constructs. The Roman Catholic Church created these bizarre notions, they are childish and inaccurate, please rise above them luv. In this global game all have suffered and sacrificed. In the end, we all get something that we want, but not everything. Shemhazai will have his world for his kind. He will not have you but he will have his grandchild. The Edenites will have their heaven, but not a heaven on earth. You my love pay the heaviest toll and receive the least compensation, except that you alone have redeemed a race. Myself, who has done nothing but served, hope to ascend to perfection with you by my side, as I am a tired soldier. But enough of this, I have kept my promise to you, now please save your remaining questions for another time, we should eat."

That seemed difficult to do after what he said. But he was insistent that all the dirty legwork had been done and all that was left was to wait and watch the years unfold carefully and eventually have a child.

I was a little perturbed that he was so blithe about having a child. It may be just another thing on his to do list, but to me, since I was the only woman under creation he could procreate with, it was an entirely larger and significant issue. We spent this second day at home.

All this talk about Gates and calendars, Aztec references to the Viracocha was stuff that was not my expertise. I made a conscious effort to not ask questions for at least an hour, but then my patience wore out. I asked him a bit about his past lives and of course my thoughts wandered to whether he would tell me about my past lives. He smiled at me and then patted my shoulder.

"This is your second life. You have only been Daizabael and Aileen. Your Nephilim soul cannot take into a pure Edenite body. You had to wait till the Nephilim flesh from your ancestors reintegrated to house your soul, which is so like your father's."

"Kat told me I was burned at the stake as a witch in 1472."

"Well, she obviously mistook you for someone else."

"So you have lived in this world without me and I have never lived without you."

"You will recall that my two lives without you were void of wives. I lived very short lives. I did what I needed to do and I left."

He had me there. I read most of the Christian/Hebrew texts, John the Baptist was beheaded young, and Elijah was taken away from the earth very young. In both cases he was widely known to have lived piously and celibately. Bryn the prophet? I couldn't picture it.

I was wondering what insights Tyra would supply in terms of calendars, numerology, and astrology – this branch of history and Wicca were her realm. I refused to go outside. My mind was reeling, so I reeled and he went to his downstairs room and vibrated the whole house with his synthesizers. That night Bryn decided to make sure that all of our plumbing was working properly in the flesh. As he predicted, everything was a go and he seemed greatly relieved.

The next day I was a little more relaxed from his non-stop stunneramma of information. I realized that I hadn't had a coffee in forever and was about to needle him into getting me a coffee machine and some coffee, when he sauntered into the kitchen.

"Tonight, luv, we are going out for dinner, someplace posh!" He walked up to me and gave me a hug. He looked at my face, cocking his head to one side,

"I 'ave coffee, want me to make you some?"

"Are you in my head again?"

"No. I just know that expression."

"Where is it?"

"I bought some instant."

"Yeck! You can't be serious. I refuse to drink it."

"Fine we'll do some shopping." His idea of shopping was creating a list of things he needed. Ring up his mother and ask her to get the groceries for us. I couldn't believe his nerve. But she dutifully showed up and delivered the goods. Said her hello's, had some tea with us and was off again to her own affairs.

The evening came and I showed Bryn all the nice stuff I was buying with his money. He seemed to enjoy the fact that I was an idiot with my new credit card. I let him pick out what I was going to wear for dinner. He picked a black dress I got from Holt Renfrew.

We got to some main street in the heart of London. We pulled up to the valet and got out of the car. FLASH – FLASH went the cameras as predicted. Followed by three people circling Bryn with questions.

"How was your time in the U.S? When are you planning another Album? When will you do another tour of North America? Who is your friend there? She looks young."

Bryn said nothing to anyone, took my hand into his, and raced up the stairs towards the entrance. Soon the door was closed behind us, we were in a large, open room with chandeliers, quiet music, white with burgundy clothed tables and servants in black and white walking in every direction. The man near the entrance greeted us and took us to a corner, where a small table was reserved for us. He then opened the chair for me and handed us menus. I could feel a hundred pairs of eyes burning holes into me. They didn't know who I was and of course, they weren't going to let Bryn leave until they found out. Bryn sat down and looked around quickly surveying the crowd. He then looked across the table at me and smiled widely.

"Take a breath, my luv, everything is just fine. You look beautiful; this lot is just not accustomed to seeing me with such a looker." He opened his menu and I opened mine. There were a lot of French sounding foods, with no prices on it. Soon a waiter was at Bryn's side asking him about wine. Bryn didn't even ask my opinion, he just ordered something that sounded Italian.

"I hope you are hungry, luv." He reached over and took one of my hands. Everyone in the restaurant watched everything he did. Whenever I looked beyond Bryn or my menu, I could see the faces of people staring at me – I hated it. I don't know how Bryn could put up with this, I just felt like getting up and telling everyone to go gawk at something else. When the wine came and the waiter was having Bryn test the wine, a gentleman from another table walked over to Bryn,

"Bryn, are you going to introduce me to your friend?" He asked smiling a toothy grin and winking towards me. Bryn smiled at the man, put down his wine glass and nodding to the waiter that was still there.

"I'm sorry, where are my manners? This bloke here is Ed Fry from the band, ClawStruck. Ed this is my friend." He said and smiled at me mischievously.

"Well does she have a name Bryn?" Ed pushed, not in the least bit amused by Bryn's rudeness.

"Why yes, I suppose she does." He said taking a sip of his wine and looking straight at him.

"Madam, if this lout should bore you, feel free to join our table. Good day." He nodded towards me and sneered at Bryn and returned to his seat after which everyone at that table hovered around him with questions."

I felt Bryn push his thoughts into my head,

"How are you? Today is day 3 and I was wondering how we are doing? Are you drained?" His words were so clear in my head it startled me. I thought I would impress him and reciprocate the spell.

"I am tired. I wouldn't mind turning in early tonight if it is alright with you." He obviously was expecting my response as his mind was receptive – which for him is rare if not impossible. He nodded in comprehension. Dinner continued between Bryn and I quietly, most of what we said was channelled into our heads; we didn't care what people thought. At one point, Bryn cracked a joke about one of the customers that caused me to erupt into a fit of laughter, which would have seemed crazy. To anyone watching we seemed to be laughing at nothing and not talking at all during the meal. It was also clear that Bryn was elated to be able to just talk to someone without using his voice, or more precisely, to eat in public and to have the conversation utterly private. I spent my time amazed that this is what his daily life outside the house was like – I hated it, and now I knew why he hated it too.

"They make a wonderful chocolate/frangelico ganache cheesecake here that I know you would love. I want you to order it." Bryn pushed his words into my head. When the waiter came by to ask us if we were done and to take our dishes away,

"Sir, may I have a slice of your Frangelico ganache cheesecake?" I asked quietly, being that I hadn't really spoken all dinner.

"Madam, I was about to recommend it. Yes, right away." As the waiter left, Bryn took my hand and said out loud,

"You are amazing."

"Why do you say that?" I said smiling and putting both of my hands into his.

"Do you know what Frangelico or ganache is?"

"No."

"That's what I mean; I could create new words in your mind. That is usually very difficult to do in telepathy, and you said it perfectly!" He reached over and kissed one of my hands. Then he backed away as he saw the waiter come to the table with some kind of cake with chocolate sauce all over it. It tasted incredible and I learned that Frangelico is a liqueur. Bryn took care of the bill and we were out of the restaurant without so much as one soul learning who I was. I could see the press release, 'who is Bryn's date?' I asked him to take me on a drive into the country, which he agreed to do as he truly does love driving. I enjoyed watching the small hamlets melt away along the highway, and Bryn enjoyed driving fast. We eventually made our way back to his place and his mother was there waiting for him.

"'Allo Aileen, you having a nice time with my boy?" She said smiling.

"Absolutely, he just took me out for dinner."

"How did you two meet anyways?" The question was an obvious one; she wanted to know if I was another star-struck fan trying to get to know her son so I could sell a story to the press. I looked at Bryn who tried to hide a mischievous grin.

"I met him in my home town of Vancouver. He was lost and I gave him directions." She looked at me and continued to smile.

"Well dear, you shouldn't keep secrets from your mum. The good news I wanted to tell you is that everything has been handled with the paperwork from the U.S. It seems our Solicitor has finalized the paperwork and those men who questioned you can no longer hold you as a suspect as they have no evidence. Bryn's face instantly transformed to almost tears, he seemed overjoyed. Wordlessly, he hugged his mother and kissed her.

"If you want to marry my son, you will have to move to England. My boy doesn't care much for America." She said as she handed Bryn some papers and smiled at me.

I was about to protest, I wanted to tell her that Vancouver is nothing like Los Angeles. But the world became black and I lost consciousness. When I awoke, I was on a hospital bed in a small room. I looked around and saw Rose, Bryn's mom, sitting next to me.

"You gave us quite a scare, dear." She said soothingly.

"Where…Where is Bryn?" I asked.

"He is at home, I rang but my son insisted that I stay here with you and not him. I can't believe my own flesh and blood would behave so cowardly – I am so sorry my dear. He did tell me to call him the minute you awoke. Is there anything I can get you?"

"Water, I am thirsty." I said weakly. Then I noticed the I.V. in my arm and followed it up a metal pole that had a pack filled with a unit of blood. My heart was beating fast and I looked at Rose who quickly saw the concern on my face.

"They said you were down almost 3.5 pints of blood dear. You have been sleeping for about three hours. I'll tell the nurse you are okay, get you that water and ring up Bryn." She got up and headed for the door. Shortly after, two nurses and a doctor entered the room and began asking questions.

"What have you been eating for the last week?"

"Is there any history of anaemia or cancer in your family?"

"Do you know how you may have lost the blood?"

"Have you ever experienced this kind of thing before?"

They took my temperature, blood pressure, poked me everywhere and asked me if it hurt. They said that they wanted to keep me overnight and tomorrow they would take more blood, and urine samples. I barely spoke to them and just closed my eyes to get some rest. I had barely closed my eyes when a police officer came into the room. He sat on a chair, looked at the medical record board and then wrote for about ten minutes in his own pad of paper before he spoke to me.

"Ma'am? Could you answer some questions now?" I could barely keep my eyes open, but I think I may have nodded.

"Did Bryn do anything to cause this condition to you? Remember you are safe here and we can arrange safe accommodations if you require them."

I was shocked at the accusation at first. But then I realized, it was true, I was with Bryn too much and it was draining me too fast. I forgot to shut off the energy drain.

"Ms. Kovacs? If Bryn hurt you just nod your head yes, and I will take care of everything else." I shook my head to say no and don't remember him leaving the room. I fell asleep. I woke up to the sound of arguing outside of my room. I could tell by the voice that it was Bryn. He was swearing and threatening the staff. He came into the room and knelt by my bed.

"Aileen? Do you think you can walk?" I could tell he was frantic.

"Yes." I murmured. His expression changed, he turned around, got up and looked out the door to the doctor. 'We are taking her home.' Bryn pulled his housecoat out of a bag he was carrying and laid it on the bed while he gathered up all my stuff and put it into the bag. He then smiled at me and motioned to a nurse to remove the I.V. The nurse bandaged my arm, cursing at Bryn while she did it.

"Do you need help getting out of the bed luv?" Bryn asked me. I lifted my head and shoulder and Bryn slid his hand under my back to hoist me into a sitting position. He then put the housecoat over me, put one of my arms around his shoulder, and helped me out of the room. We went down the elevator and when we got to the lobby there were a couple of photographers clicking and flashing away. Bryn lifted me up and ran to a rather non-descript van. It was dark and I knew it must have been the wee hours of the morning. He strapped me into the passenger seat and in a flash we were on our way.

"I am so sorry, Aileen. You are going to stay at my place tonight and I will stay with mum. I will set you up at home and if you are not better by morning you will have to leave England a little early." He was trying very hard not to speed.

"I understand." I said and just fell asleep in the seat.

I woke up in Bryn's room, on his bed, candles were lit around me. After about an hour, I felt a little better and thought that I should try to get to the kitchen. I stumbled to the door to find it locked. Well, he doesn't trust me entirely, I suppose. He obviously didn't want me sneaking away. I walked back to the bed discouraged. I spied a glass of water so I drank it all and went looking for the remote control. I was flipping through the channels when I hit the morning news and just as luck would have it, there was filmed footage of Bryn running to a van carrying me in his arms.

'In other news today the police are busy investigating a possible assault charge for England's very famous rock star, Bryn. No charges have been laid at this time but our cameras picked up this footage of Bryn carrying the alleged victim to his dad's van. Police won't say who the woman is, but the doctors at the hospital insist the woman left with her own consent.'

Great, I thought to myself, more bad press! But after the shock of the media problems a more serious and overwhelming thought entered my mind, how can I be with Bryn if being with him drains my blood, and ultimately kills me? I was an idiot for relying on Bryn's ritual too much. I hadn't even been trying to curb the energy flow. Maybe all the telepathy at the restaurant wore me out.

I thought about this whole crazy business. I instantly hated our situation. The Talisman brought us together, yes. But it had this huge, ugly purpose that I felt ruined any possibility of Bryn and I having anything resembling a normal relationship. This was a perfect example. After everything Bryn had told me about the 5th gate, how could I expect him to throw away the Talisman? How could I ask him to forget about any hope for a 6th sun for the Viracocha or Nephili or whatever? How on earth could Bryn and I raise a child together? I was sad, I was mad, I felt ripped off, and most of all – I was hungry. I went back to sleep due to lack of things to eat. It must have been close to noon when I heard heavy, fast footfalls up the stairs and the bedroom door unlock.

Chapter 22

Kat concocts a plan

I was beginning to get a little tired of Lactavia and Klaur always being together. Talking to Lactavia was no help so I thought I would sit down and have a heart to heart with Klaur in the evening after dinner. Tonight would be excellent timing as Lactavia worked at the restaurant till 1 am.

"Master, if you don't mind may we discuss something of great importance to me?" I said respectfully knealing at his feet in the livingroom while he watched TV.

"You may speak." He said.

"I would like very much if you would join me a little more in our bed, rather than always being in Lactavia's." I said as politely as I could considering how insanely mad and jealous I had become.

"You may not ask for any such thing. I bed whomever I choose. However, I am bedding with you tonight."

I was filled with rage, mostly at myself for getting myself into this position in the first place.

That evening I changed into my prettiest cotton and lace nighty and joined Klaur in our bed. It was late and I was only two feet from the foot of the bed when I distinctly heard a voice calling my name in anger and felt my insides ripping apart.

I screamed and dropped to the floor clutching my belly. There was no blood but I felt as if I was being cut in half. I instantly recognized the voice; it was Bryn. He was screaming something about deceitfulness to Aileen and the grip on my insides would not relent. Klaur jumped off of our bed and tried to lift me up, but I just shrieked in agony.

"Who the fuck said that?" Klaur said looking at me helplessly. When I didn't respond to him, he ran to the living room,

"I am calling 911." He called back to me. I could hear him frantically talking to some person about my condition and where we live.

I curled up into a foetal position on the floor, clutching my belly with tears streaming down my face. I tried to remain calm and to not scream as it would just cause Klaur to become more aggressive and I could hear his voice in the next room talking to the call center person; he was becoming angrier because the woman would not let him off the phone till the Ambulance people arrived. Fortunately, they arrived promptly; the attendance came to the apartment, lifted me to a stretcher, and whisked me away to Penticton Hospital. The doctors ran a series of tests, but the x-ray was clear -- I was bleeding internally.

Apparently when I was a child, stricken with cancer and seriously considered a low likelihood of surviving, the doctors had convinced my parents to use experimental staples internally. It seemed that these staples, which had never caused me a moment's concern, all ripped open simultaneously. If it weren't for the staples showing up on the X-ray, I have no doubt I would have died. Of course the doctors thought that I was perhaps working too much or had been doing some extremely strenuous work to cause this to happen, but I knew exactly what had transpired. That bastard had done it! He could kill me with a word, and not even be in the country at the time. I needed to do something drastic if I was ever going to match him. I realized the pact with Thromm was the only answer. I was prepped for the operating room and was quickly operated on; all staples were removed and painstakingly sutured up. I awoke with yet more scars on my abdomen and Lactavia at the side of my bed. There were bandages running like a roadway across my abdomen and obviously I was bleeding nicely as the bandages were partially soaked with blood. I thought back to my conversation with Dragon. There must have been something that I said to her that she, in turn, ratted to Bryn. I probably shouldn't have told her that Bryn assaulted me. That would have been enough to make him homicidal. But the extent of his magic bothered me. He wasn't just some silly warlock. Who was he? Who the hell was he, really?

"Kat? Are you okay? The doctor says I can take you home in two more days." Said the kind voice sitting at the side of my bed, I lifted my eyes to Lactavia's face.

"Lactavia, how good to see you. Where is Klaur?"

"He was here all night, I sent him home because he didn't really sleep at all – he's worried sick." Lactavia said standing up and drawing the curtain around us for privacy.

"Good, I hate hospitals. The sooner I am out of here, the better." I groaned. But I was angry about far more than the fact that I was in a hospital. I wanted Dragon here and I wanted her with Margon. I wanted Lactavia out of my relationship with Klaur. I wanted to be healthy and more than anything else right at this moment, I wanted Bryn dead. I did indeed spend another two days in hospital and Klaur was a continual fixture by my side. When I returned home, Klaur all but forgot about Lactavia. He bathed me, fed me, dressed me and kept me company all day long. I felt so much love from him I thought I would cry. Lactavia was a little upset but she seemed to accept the circumstances as they were. Agaratte also came by to spend time with me and ensure I was recuperating well. After about four days after the 'incident' I thought I might get Lactavia to call Aileen to see what she knew about this.

"Lactavia, do you think you could call Dragon and see how she is doing and what she has been up to lately?" I asked her.

"Why would I call her, she would just lecture me about being here. Besides I don't give a shit what she's doing, it's probably boring whatever it is." Lactavia said without lifting her eyes from the novel she was reading.

"Please Lactavia. Just humour me." I persisted.

"Fine. One call coming up." Lactavia put down her book and picked up the phone. She knew Aileen's number off by heart and pushed it into the phone.

"Hello, is Aileen there?" Lactavia asked.

"Well, do you know when she'll be back?"

"No, don't bother leaving a message; I'll call her again when she returns."

"Yeah, yeah…uh huh…ok, yup… Ciao!." She then hung up the phone and turned to me with a smile.

"Aileen is not home. She is visiting Kat in the Okanagan. I guess she didn't tell her mother that I am living here too." Lactavia said with a smile.

"You mean she is on her way here?"

"No, Aileen's mother says she is back tomorrow. Says she has finished her week there." Lactavia laughed and I began wondering where Aileen could be? Where is she if she isn't here? Where indeed! I had a sneaking suspicion she was with Bryn! Maybe she decided to see him for real. That would figure! That warlock now had his magical artefact and his healer. I began to feel numb. I was so absorbed in trying to come up with a plan to send that warlock back to whatever daemon made him.

"Where do suppose Dragon is?" Lactavia looked concerned.

"Who knows…" I was consumed in my hate for that warlock.

"Is something wrong Kat? You look upset."

"Oh, no. Just thinking about stuff."

"What kind of 'stuff'?" She asked.

"Like when can I run around again?" I smiled.

"Soon enough Kat, soon enough."

"Actually Lactavia, we have a moment to ourselves, and I have a question for you."

"And that question would be?"

"Do you think that there would ever be a day when Dragon and Margon would get together?"

"No."

"Why do you say that so confidently?"

"Because she never shows him, or any other man, the slightest interest."

"Is she really that deeply in love with you that being with a man is unattractive to her?"

"I really doubt it. She usually gets quite annoyed when I bring up the idea of her dating so I try hard not to. She just has no interest in any man in her life right now and we have to accept it and move on.

"You and her aren't really a couple are you? You never were really, were you?" I looked at Lactavia who seemed to be thinking hard and squirming. She was clearly contemplating how to answer the question.

"Look, Kat. Between you and me, I am straight. I don't really know what Dragon is. At this point, I am willing to guess she is a plant. I think she is straight, but I also think she has some serious issues. We have fooled around, but she almost never carries it out, it's like she is scared of me or scared of something."

Lactavia broke off and purposefully put her novel to her nose again. Obviously, she noticed that something was going on with Dragon behind the scenes. She didn't know what it was, but she knew it was something. I knew what it was and for a moment, I seriously considered spilling the beans to Lactavia in an effort to have an ally. But looking at Lactavia and how she talked about Dragon, I was still convinced she was a true and deep ally of Dragon's and would never do a thing against her. Dragon was almost as resourceful as Bryn at securing their path. Aside from Thromm, my only true accomplice was Agaratte. I knew that those two would never betray me, and Agaratte had skills beyond his already accomplished magical talents. Maybe getting that artefact was possible after all.

As soon as I was able to walk around freely and go about my business unsupervised, I was looking for my good friend Thromm. I needed to make the pact as soon as I had enough strength. The pact would ensure that any wards I cast would be strong enough to keep Bryn out of my sanctuary. The only thing I didn't know was how to steal life force like Bryn does? I don't think it would work to have Dragon as my healer; Bryn would probably sense instantly if anyone tampered with his precious energy source. Thromm would have to be consulted, as perhaps he could find me a tap. Thromm arrived in his usual fashion during the day, possessing an unsuspecting crow.

"When would be the optimum time for the pact Thromm?" I asked him totally dispensing with formalities like hello etc.

"Any month when the moonnn isss almost gone, sssoonest isss Sssseptember 25th. Mee mosst sstrong for your material plane. Sun ssshine on moon decreassse the sssspellsss power." This was more than two weeks away, but if I continued to heal at the current rate, it would be ample enough time for me to perform the pact. But there was a nagging problem of what it would do to me. I needed a healer, like the one that Bryn used. If the pact turned out to be more than my compromised health could tolerate, a healer could save my mortal coil.

"I want to use a great deal of power right away. I will require a healer, find one!" Thromm took to the skies and was gone for hours before returning.

"Healersss are rare, one in a million or sssso. The nearesst one isss in Kelowna, but he bad candidate asss hisss powerss are minimal."

"Isn't there anyone nearby with Dragon's power to heal?" I asked.

"No. I think only two other mortals on earth now with sssuch an aura..." He said.

"Where are these others?" I asked stunned by this revelation that would make Dragon one in about two billion.

"You call thissss land China, both are there. One isss an old man and a sssmall girl." He whispered.

"You mean there are only three people on the whole Earth that are half decent healers?" My voice grew quite loud, my shock was obvious and I had to control my dismay. Considering I was still healing from surgery, this was more bad news. How do you get healed from a mortal that you have a language barrier with? I thought for a moment at how I could survive this pact without a healer – I didn't like it.

"Is there was any way of getting the energy from Dragon without her warlock finding out?" The question caused Thromm of laugh in a creepy kind of way.

"Sssoon I think Dragon diesss, lovess Bryn ssshe does. He is very powerful right now. I think sssoon he will look for another." I was stunned I was sure I misunderstood him.

"Did you say that Dragon is almost dead?"

"Yess, sssshe go to him and he take much life from her. I go and watch him at sssafe dissstance, I ssssaw her aura asss he carried her to car – aura almost gone."

"Benevolent Gods! Can she get any of it back?" I always thought of Dragon as invincible, if Bryn killed her – I swear I would make him pay!

"Me don't know...Bryn powerful, maybe he got ssssome sssspell bring energy back into her...don't know, doubt though."

"Can you check on her tomorrow?" I asked. I knew Thromm could watch her as she came and went from the house.

"Thromm, One more thing, could we do this pact without a healer?" I asked dubiously.

"Dark pact with blood. Bind mortal ssspirit with mine and we can do powerful magic. Yessss! It messssy but you live, Talissssman easy worth it." He ruffled his feathers and slanted his head at me in a very crow-like way and said,

"I go..."

Thromm spread the crows' wings and flew up into the sky. I was really worried about Dragon; I am not a heartless person after all. Obviously if she was due home soon, that meant that she has been in England for a while anyways. Obviously she was in England when Bryn decided to cast that last spell on me. I couldn't overcome my bitterness at Dragon for letting him do that to me if she was right there watching him. I had to come to realize that Dragon was not a friend anymore. I couldn't trust her. She would do anything for her Warlock and that made her a liability. ECAW didn't need a liability and neither did I. The only other trump I could think of was to get Dragon, and use her as a bartering chip against Bryn. If I could trap Dragon here in Penticton, took away her ability to be with him. Wouldn't he just kill me from anywhere? If Dragon survived, and I had Bryn's power source Dragon and I would be safe. There was no way around it, I had to get the artefact and render him powerless I just hoped I could do this before he did away with our ECAW sister. It was only as I wandered back to the apartment that I remembered that Thromm referred to Bryn's artefact as the Talisman. I had completely forgotten to ask him if he knew anything about it. I had to remember to ask him the next time I saw him.

One thing I was confident of, was just how powerful Bryn was becoming. If Dragon really had that much healing energy and he almost killed her...

I thought about the blood pact that Thromm mentioned. I knew what he was driving at. I had read it often in the darkest annals of Black magic there are the blood pacts. They are the heavy duty black magic spells that require large amounts of fresh blood – mortal sacrifice, fine, as long as it isn't mine. They were reputed to be very risky, very dangerous, and rife with the potential of not being able to abort the pact after you initiate it. Let's face it, no mortal wants to share their coil indefinitely with a spirit. But desperate times call for desperate measures and the fresh sutures in my abdomen were enough of an inducement for my decision. Once I had that artefact, I think I would be able to handle my Thromm issues if I find I had any.

Chapter 23.

“Turn it off right this minute girl!” a familiar voice commanded.

“Good morning to you too.” I said sitting up and taking him in.

“I’m serious!” He then strode into his bedroom and turned to me. I was closing off my connection like Bryn had showed me – I hated doing it.

“How are you today? Do you feel any better than yesterday? If you don’t then the last ritual didn’t work.” He knelt down and looked at me pulling my hair away from my face.

“Honestly Bryn, I am feeling much better.” I said to him grabbing his hand putting it to my face and smiling at him.

“I want to take you out for breakfast. We will have to be more careful for the rest of your visit if you decide to stay. Keep your floodgates closed off and I will ensure that the Talisman and I are not present together when you are around.” He returned my smile and bent forward to kiss me.

“I want to stay but does that mean as long as I am here you will spend the nights at your parents?” I sounded a little, well maybe a lot disappointed. He shrugged and winced at the look on my face, shook his head and walked over to his closet.

"No, I suppose you would hate me if I did that… Would you be a happy girl if we packed up and I took you to Stonehenge, we still have two and a half days."

"Ya hoooo!" I yelled in excitement crawling out of the bed to give him a hug from behind.

"Gather your things; let us not dawdle. I will leave the Talisman here where it is warded and we will leave together." He said like a father.

I won't lie; I wasn't completely back to normal. I was much lower in energy than my usual hyperactive self was. He probably knew it. However, I was not as bad as Bryn was afraid I would have been. Maybe that last ritual wasn't a complete success. Part of me wanted to delve deep into more questions and start the old argument of, 'how can we be a normal couple if we can't be together?' But I wanted to enjoy my last few days with him and I didn't want to open the wound that drove him crazy. I watched him help me gather my stuff into my suitcase and I think it was right then that I realized for the first time since he told me everything that he and I were never meant to be a 'couple'. There would never be any hope for a normal relationship between us, not in this world anyways. There never was and their probably never would be. I thought about him and his conviction that I follow him to wherever the 'children of Eden' go. Would I not be a total alien there? Could we finally be together the way I dreamed? I was deep in thought and actually wasn't helping pack at all. He closed up my duffel bag and handed it to me.

"Earth to Aileen? You going to get your toothbrush and makeup from the loo or do you want me to do all of your packing?"

"Sorry, I was thinking about something."

"I can tell. Let me just pack a few things for myself."

I got to choose which car we went in and I opted for the Chevy Corvette complete with the driver's seat in the wrong place, the right place if you live in North America. We drove on 'motorways' called M3 and M4 and in around an hour we were there.

We got out, took in the sights and stopped in one of the local restaurants. The stones were huge, and we weren't allowed to go too close to them. I was reading the information brochure that I nabbed about how they were the some of the oldest Neolithic things ever uncovered. Stonehenge was thought to be built 5,000 years ago, with an inner circle being less somewhere around 2,000 years old. I was enraptured with the stones regardless of the surrounding urbanized and commercialized spills all around this incredible ancient and mystic site. Bryn appeared to enjoy my enthusiasm; we paused by a particular angle showing the central stones.

"So does this place remind you of anything?" I looked up from my brochure confused.

"No. I can honestly say I have never seen anything like this."

"Seriously, think smaller scale. Think stone circle and pillars…" I still didn't know what he meant. I just stood there staring at the central stone; it looked like an altar, like an Aztec altar for sacrifices.

"Think of my back yard." He pressed. Then it hit me, of course, this is like a large scale of the Cathexisphere, right down to the central dais. I turned and looked at him hoping he would enlighten me.

"This was created by your ancestors. It is far older than your brochure pontificates. It was created by the Ancient race and by the time the Druids found it, they had no idea what it was for. But you do now don't you?"

"Did they build others?"

"Of course they did. There were whole cities. Most are under water now."

I looked at this mind bogglingly ancient structure and thought about its real purpose. I thought about how their souls were referred to as Angels in so much of the historical literature. There must have been an age when this world was entirely theirs. I knew what the Cathexisphere could do; it opened the door between the mortal and spirit world. Talk about a lost technology.

"How did you know how to build your own?"

"I had help. No, and the Talisman."

We didn't waste much time and we were back on the road. He said we were heading to Lands' End and would be spending the night in Cornwall. I watched as the towns peeled away and the land surrendered more and more to lush green lawns, fabulous gardens, rivers and smaller hamlets. There was the occasional castle and cathedral. After about three hours on our journey, I began to think about many of my burning questions and I thought I would try some of them and hope that it didn't spoil the mood.

"Bryn? If you and I were at your place sleeping and you have the Talisman, would I unconsciously drain myself?"

"Well for this visit I would not risk investigating it. However it appears so as I believe that is what happened to you in the first place."

"So while you have the Talisman, we couldn't live together." He kept driving, quietly, his eyes never straying from the highway. After awhile I pretty much understood that he didn't want to answer the question because it was a 'mood killer'. I suppose it was a rhetorical question, but his silence made me a little choked. I relented and changed the subject a bit.

"So, since I am, well, young; what kind of timeline did you have in mind for fatherhood?" I asked looking away from him and out the window.

"You don't think I would pressure you now do you?"

"Well, I was hoping this would be something that we negotiated."

"Negotiate? Interesting term. My work in the U.S. was pressing, this is true, but my work there is done, things will take care of themselves – I was very, very thorough…Don't expect me to negotiate with you for some time on our last and most important ritual of all." He reached over to my shoulder and rubbed it, no doubt sensing my intense level of stress.

"Thank heavens!"

"Why would you do that?"

"Do what?"

"Thank the heavens?"

"Figure of speech."

"Aileen, we will postpone until we are both very well prepared. If you need a timeframe, I definitely assure you that the next five years are out, possibly even ten. Have we not been together in one form or another for the last thirteen years or so? Don't be so hung up on time and age…Enjoy the sights, hey, look over there, at that ruin on that hill, what a gorgeous day." Bryn was pointing at some hill, which appeared unnaturally attained or manmade, and then the building built on it – crazy.

We traveled southwest from Stonehenge approaching my favourite thing on earth besides him, the ocean. We went for a walk near the steep rocky cliffs at the southwestern edge of England at Land's End. Then we drove to a place called Lizard peninsula and stayed at a Bed and Breakfast called Tregaddra Farm or something like that. It was beautiful and here, away from the bustle of London and its immediate areas, this place was a welcome respite.

"I need to know honest answers to a couple more questions before I go back to Canada." My back was to him as I was looking at the waves crashing on rocks. The wind and the waves were loud.

"So where exactly do the Edenites, you and I go after the 5th gate closes?"

"End of mortal days. You join the rest of us in the spirit plane, which isn't quite what people think when they go to Christian church to learn about 'heaven'."

"But I thought that my spirit is different than your spirit? Can we exist in the same plane?"

"Of course. There will be some of the pure line of your ancestors there too."

"But I will be the only mixed blood?"

"Yes. However, I recall you were least Nephilim of all that I saw as Enoch."

"Will we be finally like a happily married old couple? You know, holding hands and being together like we are now? Wake up in the mornings together?" He laughed and then turned away from me and walked back up the path. I was not in good shape but I wasn't going to have him avoid answering a question again. I repeated the question to his mind because I was in no shape to run up to him and I didn't feel like screaming up the path. He stopped and turned to face me.

"Daizabael. In the spirit realm you have no gender. That is a mortal construct. You and I will be together but not like anything you would be familiar with. It is more a sense of universal love than two souls alone. I'm sorry but that is the best explanation I can think of in mortal language."

"What future have you planned for my race then Enoch, betrayer of the Edenites. Messiah to the Nephilim." The strangest look came over him. Hearing me call him Enoch and referring to him as the betrayer of the Edenites and messiah to the Nephilim won me an immediate reaction.

"I am not a Messiah, I have betrayed no one. I am a general. The fallen and their bloodlines will in turn live as we have, inheriting a poisoned, raped and desecrated garden bequeathed to them by the Edenites. They shall multiply, toil, live and die in mortal blessing and suffering. As for their souls, they will wait for the next gate after death."

"Why can't we have that? That is what I want!"

"You have forgotten the deal is already struck. The Gods' will not allow it, besides, I have fathered a race already as Enoch I don't wish to do it again. I long for an eternity of peace with you."

"Why does sweat, blood and tears sound so much better to me, even if it is for a short period of time?"

"Because you are the daughter of Shemhazai most likely, and in dire need of spiritual mending." He laughed as he said it, but I was certain that he was half-serious. I dropped the subject and decided to not talk about it again. My life with Bryn wasn't going to be much of a life and I had an eternity of bullshit to not look forward to. Well, I better go to school and find a career I really like, cause I am quite sure I am not going to get any fulfillment otherwise. That nagging issue aside, the last two days with Bryn without the Talisman were fabulous. He drove me to Heathrow Airport on my flight day and there were tears in my eyes when I left him for security check in.

As the plane lifted off England's green and pleasant land, I immediately began to feel pangs of pain and remorse. The trip was draining while I was anywhere near that Talisman. I was quite certain that we wouldn't be doing that again for quite a while. It seemed forever to get to Vancouver, but it sure felt great to be back in my hometown.

When I got through customs, I dragged my sorry bones out of the Richmond Airport and flagged the first cab. Yellow cab of course, guaranteed to have an immigrant driver with no comprehension of the English language. I always love giving these guys directions through town and watching them drive. He told me about how he has been in Canada for one year that he came from Pakistan and is still getting used to the black ice. I assured him that one could be born and raised here and still not handle black ice on the roads any better than a foreigner. Soon we pulled into 26th Ave., off Rupert St. and I was home. I reached into my coat pocket and found a wad of bills a certain Mr. Bryn must have placed there. They were all British Pounds.

"Do you mind if I pay in Pounds?" I asked wondering if he even knew what the exchange rate was.

"For you lady, ok. $15.00 Canadian, you give me ℑ10.00 UK." He said. I handed him a10 P note and went out of the car while he exited and grabbed my luggage from the back of the car.

I walked towards the house and my mom came out of the front door all worried and offering to help me with the luggage.

"You look awful Aileen, you should have some soup. I made vegetable soup…" She talked on and on about how vegetable soup is so good for me. But I just wanted to crawl into my bed and sleep, maybe when I wake up eat a 40-ounce steak.

"I just want to sleep mom, it was a long bus ride. That's why I took a cab from the station." I was drained, miserable that this relationship had no real future and frankly, high on my list of things to do was to get over to Tyra's place and ask her to do some research for me. I asked her to reference any information regarding an ancient race that predates the flood myths. I asked her to tell me what she knew about 5th and 6th gates or ages for mankind. I asked her to look into Angel cults. I don't know if it was the fact that I knew that she was a wiz at astrological charting or maybe I was thinking about my bizarre relationship with Bryn but I gave her my birthday and his and asked her to do a compatibility chart. She was excited because she thought that I was potentially dating. She told me to wait approximately two to three days for her to gather the completed information. So we arranged to meet again at her place the following weekend.

I made my way to her place in North Vancouver on a Saturday morning.

"What have you found out for me, Tyra? And, by the way, I really appreciate your efforts." I said sincerely as I stood on the other side of her dinning room table admiring the copious amounts of paper in front of her. Their entire house was a clutter of records, books and magazines of two people obsessed with collecting.

"No, I was in the mood for a challenge. I dug deep for this stuff and I am quite proud of myself. But let's get down to business. The Aztecs believed that mankind lived on the earth in ages. They believed that these 'ages' were measurable periods in which we could live and thrive before an upcoming disaster. So the last age they thought was ended by inundation or flood. You know the flood myth with Noah?"

"Yeah, I follow you Tyra. Go on…"

"Well the next age is said to end in fire and earthquakes. They believed that this last cataclysm would be the last age for man. In fact they even put a date to it."

"Do we know the date?"

"You bet we do. Archaeologists converted their calendar date to our calendar and the date is Dec. 23, 2012."

"Wow!"

"Next you wanted to know what is out there for Angel Cults, and I have to say there is a bewildering amount of crazy cults. I don't want to get into everything I found. However, I did review material that seemed to coincide with your interest in the Aztec doomsday clock. What I found was a universal belief among just about every established religion of a race of divine beings or Angels that descended to Earth. Whether they were teachers, conquerors, or prisoners depends on the philosophical text you are reading. What I can tell you is that they are universally accepted as being far advanced technologically, and physically than us. Even in the obscure pantheon of ancient Egypt there were thought to be nine or so core Gods and Goddesses. They in turn sent their deities to Earth, much like the fallen Angels. Osiris and Isis presided over the matters of Earth. Their child Horus was the soul that was continually sent to earth as the living Pharaoh of the people. Which isn't bad considering Isis had to resurrect her husband in order to have the child…"

"Isis… Yeah, I remember reading that. Wasn't Osiris killed by his brother and Isis brought life back to him. Through her magic they were able to conceive a son." I paused for a moment thinking about the parallel.

"Now that is what I call a healer."

"Well, I have never heard anyone refer to Isis as a healer. For the rest of the religions, Aztecs aside, the fallen angels are vilified. They are thought to have become evil and are either in chains awaiting judgement or are dead with the last age or gate. Which brings me to the last request you have and that is the birthdates you gave me."

"Well, what is the compatibility score?"

"Well, I worked very hard on it and I must say that you have chosen some interesting dates. In fact, I would go so far as to say that I am pretty sure you are playing games or testing me."

"I am?"

I would never have found the correlations otherwise, but as you mentioned all this Aztec calendar and last gate stuff my mind was thinking of numerological correlations. As you know, in astrology we refer to astrological ages much like the Aztecs do. We are currently in the age of Pisces. The first birthday that you gave me is this time period, which is also the time when the end of this sun is supposed to happen according to the Aztecs we will not have an Age of Aquarius. However, it is interesting to note that it is thought to have been in the age of Taurus that the last Aztec Gate occurred, that would be the other birthday you gave me. I also found it interesting that one birthday had mostly masculine signs and the other mostly feminine signs. One was born on the Full moon (masculine) the other New moon (feminine). The Pisces also had mostly hard aspects and are mostly inharmonious. The Taurean on the other hand had almost no hard aspects and they were mostly all harmonious. I could never envision these two as a couple but I can picture these two people. The Piscean is a very hard man, cold and calculating probably works for military intelligence. I know this Taurean birthday is yours Dragon, I just can't believe that it describes you. I know you don't believe all this astrological mumbo-jumbo but you have a weird chart, it is oozing soft, feminine Venusian overtones which is hard to picture. The bottom line though is that these two birthdays are in complete opposition of each other, it works out to the worst compatibility chart I have ever done."

"Well, it is interesting. But I wouldn't put a lot of stock into what you say about these charts."

"Whose birthday did you give me?" She lifted an eyebrow to me.

"I don't know, I was just doing some digging around and found it." I attempted to sound casual, but I was struck with a look of incredulity on my face that I am sure she noticed.

"Well, an astrologer gets so used to looking for compatibility in charts; at first the lack of compatibility is what first grabbed me. I had never seen so little overlap. I really wish you would tell me who this antithesis of you is."

I just wanted to get out of her house and deal with what I already knew. As I walked down Lonsdale road towards the Seabus, I became aware of the crux of my situation. I was never meant to be, 'happily ever after' with Bryn. Our destinies were about duty, they had nothing to do with sharing our lives together. If we couldn't be together, our destinies lay apart. How could I even think about having a child? I was only eighteen. In five or ten years would Bryn just magically appear and impregnate me? Why would I want that?

You can only agonize about the future for so long. You can only mope around and feel powerless for so long before you begin to get on your own nerves. That was me, walking the seawall alone. Thinking about how I was doomed to walk this wall alone. What is it about Stanley Park's sea wall that caused me to become so deeply reflective? Kat was gone, Lactavia had followed her. I watched that giant orange and pink sun sink into the ocean. I watched couples, hand in hand and without any ability to control myself the tears just ran down my cheeks. I would never be them; he would never walk down this seawall with me. I had to admit I had no idea when I would see him for real again. The next morning my depression was already disgusting me. By the end of the week, I committed to changing my attitude. Wallowing in self pity was a game for losers and my daddy raised no loser. You have to take the joys life gives you and remember that life doesn't owe you 'happily ever after'. I studied witchcraft, Cabbala, and Hermetic magic –I understood that all in this realm is rendered at the cost of something somewhere else. But knowing these things and accepting them are mutually exclusive. I needed to go to the bars with a friend and just enjoy being young. Whenever I had that feeling there was my dear friend Jasmine. I could forget about everything and just have a great time. Saturday night came and I was itching to party.

I plunged myself into the 'normal world'. I didn't read or cast any spells, although I routinely kept up my meditations. Slowly I was beginning to feel better, more like my old self. The only evidence of my insane life was that ring on my finger and when I looked in the mirror. Since my visit to England, I could see wrinkles that weren't there before. My vision had deteriorated further and I was diagnosed with Bursitis in my hips. I knew it was the left over payment for spending all that time near Bryn and that Talisman.

I kept working at the salon, my money laundering scheme. I was enjoying work as it was definitely interesting enough. The odd guy in the salon was queer and that suited me fine. We would eye up and critique young guys that came into the salon. When I went out with Jasmine I found myself looking at every man I met and endlessly comparing them to Bryn, one that looked and perhaps had his mannerisms, maybe some of his iciness and none of his ability to drain me. Part of me was trying to run away from what seemed my destiny. I was hoping that just around the corner there would be some simple, loveable guy with no draining strings attached that I could feel something for. I wanted to get out from under that long, overwhelming shadow of him.

Chapter 24

Kat goes on a quest

The day was fast approaching for the pact. I decided to make it one day before the new moon so that I could do the pact on one day and acquire the artefact the next day. I was healthy and gathered all of the things I would require to complete the pact. I discussed the time and the place with Thromm and we were well on our way to taking the last step to my becoming as powerful as one can get and remain mortal. I thought day after day about the consequences. I discussed them with Thromm who assured me there would be no change from the deal we have currently. I was relieved. But I was aware that deep down I didn't trust Thromm. What if he was lying? What if this pact was irreversible and gave all the benefits to him and nothing to me? I didn't want to be a victim like Dragon. I had very little information about this spell in any of our books and I was hesitant to talk to Agaratte or Margon about it because I thought they would try and stop me. But nothing ventured, nothing gained and I wanted that artefact. Hopefully if anything untoward happened, Margon and Agaratte would be able to help me. It was more important to keep my mind on the prize.

Cotton bandages, a sharp knife, earthenware bowl, a large bag of salt, a pestle with a collection of herbs, spice, candles in glass bowls, matches, a bottle of Okanagan water, and of course my book. I was ready to head out for the arid hills between Naramata and Penticton. When I got there, I found a dark secluded place far from the lights of any home. I made a large circle on the ground by pouring out the salt. Then I lit the candles and put them in the cardinal points. Everything else went into the circle along with me. I opened the book and spoke the warding spell; I'm not an idiot like Dragon. I won't do this pact unwarded so that just any spirit could participate. I opened my book of shadows to the newest spell I had put into it. The spell is just an offering of a mortal coil to the spirit world and referred to as a dark pact offering. Water to prepare the bowl to receive the sacrifice, herbs and spices to anoint the offering, I was ready for the main event. I looked up towards the sky and took in a deep breath of the sweet smelling air, held up my athame and carved my forearm open and watched the blood flow into the bowl. It was very hard to not pass out, the process made me a little sick.

I then called out to Thromm to approach the circle.

I needed to use a lot of blood and I was worried that I didn't have enough in the bowl. I was about to carve my other arm when I felt the tingling sensation of the spirit world around me. I could feel enormous power waiting just outside the circle waiting for the offering, waiting for me to step out of the circle. I closed my eyes and focussed on my trance to make sure that I recognized it as Thromm, which it was.

White as a sheet and almost unable to stand, I got to my feet and stepped out of the circle with my bowl of blood in hand, "Spirit bond, bind mortal cause to spiritual power; take hold now."

Then I felt a stinging sensation as something was penetrating my mortal coil. As I fell to my knees I could sense that only one spirit was inside me: Thromm. The rest was the power from the spell and the energy that is my due payment. As the power climaxed within my body I became increasingly aware that Thromm was taking control of my body and I was being pushed far back. Soon I became no more than a quiet observer as he grabbed the cotton bandages and tightly wrapped my wound. He quickly put all the material into the backpack and then we prowled back towards the Penticton city limits, back to the apartment complex. On the way back we passed a barking dog. I felt a sickness come over me. It was like a burning thirst. We reached out for the dog and slashed open its throat with the knife, and then we did something I still can't believe – we drank its living blood. Each draught eased the burning in my body; I could sense an ecstasy throughout me. It was quite disgusting. When we had drained the animal, we tossed the body of the dog aside. I could see blood all over my jeans and cotton shirt. I was very concerned as we had to get into the house unnoticed; hopefully everyone was asleep. We opened the door, slid in and looked for a bag to stuff the knife and bloodied clothes into. We then stuffed the bag into a corner of the closet. When we closed the closet door we heard footfalls coming towards us. We knew it was Klaur; instinctively we raised my hand and motioned towards him. "Thud" I heard him fall to the floor. As we came around the corner, we saw him sleeping on the floor. Apparently, the magic we had was powerful enough to evoke sleep spells on mortals. I was giddy at this new power, but fearful of how my life would be sharing my body with a spirit. Thromm didn't control my mind or consciousness rather he controlled the motor functions of my body. I was unable to control where I went or what I did. We went to the bedroom and fell instantly asleep.

I awoke in the morning feeling as though I was once again my normal self, totally in control, but with one major complication: the light streaming from the window horrified me and burned my eyes – I had to get out of there. I pulled myself out of the bed and carefully walked to the closet. I opened the door, walked in and shut myself in. Instantly my anxiety subsided. There was one overwhelming thought which entered my mind as I enjoyed the fact that Thromm seemed to not be in control of my body…Am I a living Vampire? The thought chilled me to the bone. I curled up with the shoes and spiders and slept for many more hours. I crawled out of the closet at about 4 pm, and carefully snaked my way to the kitchen where the curtains and the stick and rope for the blinds were. I pulled on the blinds and twisted the stick to close them up tight. Still light shone in between the cracks but I felt it was worth taking the risk. I stood up and drew the curtains. The blinds turned the light into horizontal blades, which felt like knives on my stomach. I yanked the curtains and then fell to the floor like a wounded animal.

The pain subsided as I sat there. I thought about the fresh surgical wound that was struggling to heal, none of this was going to help me. This Talisman had better be worth it. Fortunately, the kitchen was partially obscured from the light. Great I could make it to the fridge and chow down. I crawled to the fridge, hoping not to accidentally hit any light and opened the fridge door. There was pop, milk, bread, and cold pizza – but the thought of eating any of it instantly repulsed me. I laughed a little, thinking about how Vampires don't eat. But I knew that it was most likely due to the fact that I was sick and very anaemic. Instead I crawled to the living room, which was much darker and cooler and I turned on the TV and waited for sunset. While I was sitting on the couch Klaur walked in from a visit to his good friend Agaratte.

"You look like shit! Are you okay?" Klaur asked stuffing some potato chips into his mouth. I knew I hadn't eaten for a long time and that I should be famished, but in fact thinking about eating anything made me sick.

"I don't know. I think I am okay. Let me just lay here for a little while and see if I can make some dinner." I said to him pulling myself into a sitting position.

"Maybe we should take you to Emergency, something could be wrong with you since that surgery. What is that bandage on your wrist?" He said coming to sit next to me.

"No, I'm fine, really. Besides the hospital requires those beds for people who have real problems like all the serious car accidents caused by geriatrics with driver's licenses in this town." As he came towards me to look at my wrist more closely, I moved away retracting my arm.

"Well, at least you haven't lost your sense of humour." He smiled at me, oblivious to my annoyance and patted my back. I strained to force a smile back at him, as I was suddenly aware of the fact that I was getting hungry just looking at him and at the same time I felt my old friend 'awaking' and slowly taking over my motor functions again. I became desperately afraid that he would kill Klaur to get to his blood and I would not be able to stop him. The thought crept back into my mind, 'am I a vampire?' I could feel a deep surge of power, spiritual power in me as I sat there in frozen contemplation. I felt the power, I felt Thromm waking up and taking over, but most of all I felt a horrible fear as I realized that I would be in this state quite possibly for the rest of my life, unless I could get rid of Thromm. My body slowly began shaking and I quickly got up and walked to the kitchen before Klaur would notice. As I walked into the kitchen, I felt the last ounce of control evaporate and again I was merely a spectator in my own mortal coil. I felt myself turn around and head back into the living room. I was terrified that Klaur was about to become dinner.

"I am going out for a moment to give something to Agaratte." I heard myself say in a steady voice. I then proceeded to the door; I didn't wait for permission.

"What? I thought you were making me dinner?" Klaur spat. I put on my shoes and opened the door.

"Cook your own damn food!" With that I waved my hand and Klaur appeared to be forced to sit back on the couch. I then headed out the door and down the street seemingly looking for anything that moved. Eventually something crossed our path, a cat. I quickly scooped up the grey and black cat and bit hard into its neck and sucked out every last drop of blood in it. I instantly felt better, and my shaking stopped. The thoughts of my intruder mingled with mine,

"We ssshould try and get to Bryn and hisss artefact tonight." Thromm said out loud unnecessarily.

"Do we have enough power to move our body through the veil and push the artefact with us back to here?" I asked.

"It cannot pass through my realm, it would be inssstantly desssstroyed. We must pusssh through the veil take it and mail it to ussss… Diabolic no?" He said and then snickered. "I know where Bryn keepsss hisss ssstationary and hasss sstamps in the sssame drawer." He continued. I was impressed by how simple this sounded. The most valuable thing on earth and I need only wait for the postman to bring it to me.

"Where shall we cast this spell? We need a safe spot." I asked while thinking. " I know why don't we try over by Margon's house?" I said.

"Let's go..." he responded.

"Thromm?" I asked as he turned my body towards the quiet road heading for Naramata.

"What?"

"Am I a vampire?"

"What's a vampire?" he asked sounding confused.

"An immortal monster that drinks blood to live." I said, surprised that he didn't know this. Surprised that someone from the spirit world wouldn't know what a Vampire was, weren't they supposed to be from his realm.

"I don't think so, you are definitely mortal. The blood isn't for you, I need it to stay in you – it's for me." He said attempting to sound sympathetic.

"Please do not eat Klaur."

"I ssshould eat him, I would be doing both of usss a favour." He snickered some more and then held out my hand as if to hitch-hike. Soon we attracted a pale coloured sedan and were off for Naramata. Of course Thromm, being an opportunist, decided that the charitable driver would make a nice hors de overes. I heard him whisper in my head to buckle up the seatbelt nice and tight. As soon as I did, I could feel the power surging inside me and no sooner had I felt it than I felt the car spin out of control and roll over at the opposite side of the highway. The driver was not wearing a seatbelt and launched himself right into the windshield and was only semi-conscious when the car stopped moving. I unbuckled my seatbelt and walked over to his side of the car. I gently put his bleeding head into my hands and I could feel myself smiling at him reassuringly. I then cut his neck with my ritual knife and wrapped my mouth around the wound gulping down the hot fluid his heart was beating to eliminate. The amount of blood in a human being is a lot when you have to drink it. It was the most exciting feeling I ever experienced. I closed my eyes as I felt every draught fill the horrible emptiness inside me. If I thought about what I was doing I would certainly loose my mind. I had to focus on that prize, I was so close, just another couple of kilometres on foot and I would be in a safe and magical point to get that artefact. It will be mine! Thinking about the unlimited power in my grasp quickly made me forget the blood drying on my chin and all over my shirt. I snaked across the dimly lit road and followed the darkened orchard to my destination. Finding my way in the gathering darkness was no problem. I knew I needed to conduct my ritual in a spot where my magical power would be heightened. Finally, I reached my destination, a knoll by the old stone mansion. I was ready and so was Thromm, soon that artefact would be in my hands and Bryn would be powerless to do anything.

Chapter 25

Grade 12 was drawing to a close and I was worried about my girlfriends in Penticton, I wanted to know how they were doing. So as it happened, I couldn't care less about the upcoming prom, about what dress I was going to wear or what teenage idiot was going to be showing me off at prom night. I felt like a drone, pulsing through life; going to school, doing homework, going to work and dancing at the clubs with Jasmine whenever my schedule allowed. I was surprised at how easily I had fallen back into my old routine of keeping myself busy as a way of avoiding the usual painful 'realities' of Bryn. I avoided him, and he was busy too. For awhile I knew he would not be suspicious of my absence. I needed an emotional and psychological break, and I am sure he sensed it. I never received a statement in the mail regarding my credit card. I never really knew what my balance was, but I never thought too much about it. It was always clear for me to use. I tried to be careful not to purchase too much stuff and alert my parents – however, one Friday night when I was off work and looking forward to a good time with Jasmine, my dad called me into the livingroom.

"Aileen, come out here. We want to talk with you." I was in the process of putting my makeup and a couple of pairs of new shoes into my bag. I preferred to change at Jasmine's as I didn't want my parents to see some of my more expensive clothes.

"Yeah, dad. What's up?"

"Mom and me were wondering who the hell is buying you stuff? Mom noticed the ghetto blaster in your room."

"I bought it."

"Aileen, your mother and I have been doing the math and the stuff she has been finding in your room and the small amount of hours you work don't add up." Coming up with a good lie on the spur of a moment requires a professional bullshitter, which I am not, my ears were getting warm and I shifted my weight. I didn't want him to know I had a credit card, so I couldn't tell him I bought stuff on credit.

"I told mom before, I make tips."

"So what I am asking you is what you are doing for those kinds of tips?"

"Honest dad, I am not doing anything and I don't have a sugar daddy if that is what you are implying."

"Aileen, if I find out that you are letting someone buy your affections you are going to be in deep trouble and I am going to kill that guy. I am going to drive you to Jasmines to make sure that you are actually going to her apartment and not some old man's, and then I want you home tonight."

"Come on dad this is stupid, I have my own wheels."

"Aileen I saw one of your dresses in your closet in the window of Holt Renfrew. I asked inside what the price was, they told me $739.00! Who got you that dress?" My mother looked at me evenly. She didn't look angry like my dad, but she looked like she had done some research and that if I told her that I bought it somewhere else for cheap that she wasn't going to buy it. I was pretty sure I knew what dress she meant, I can't say I bought a designer dress at Mariposa. I was busted.

"Okay, I wasn't going to tell you but I applied for a student credit card and they actually gave me one. But I have been really good and I have been making regular payments." I pulled my card out of my purse and showed it to them. The best part was that my dad seemed instantly relieved. My mom didn't look so convinced.

"So you were approved for a credit card as a minor with no co-signer?" Think Aileen, think…

"No mom, I told you it is a student credit card it has a low credit limit." It sounded believable to me and I was hoping that it would to her too.

"Where did you get this sudden taste for designer Haute Couture? I don't think I have ever seen any of your friends wearing such things?"

"It was just one impulse buy mom, sorry." I used my whiny voice hoping to get her off my back. She gave me a look that I recognized as disbelief and both of them proceeded to give me a lecture on how to be financially responsible with credit. I tried to look interested, and then finally my dad drove me to Jasmine's. When my dad got to Jasmines door, he walked in, looked around and then interrogated her. She confirmed that I had no boyfriends at all.

"What the hell was that all about Aileen?"

"My dad thinks I have a sugar daddy…" This caused Jasmine to burst out in laughter. You have got to be kidding, you? Boy is he ever barking up the wrong tree. So we both laughed. I never spent much money when I was with Jasmine and so consequently she had no idea that I had a credit card or that I was possessed of an unusual prosperity.

The following week, while I was restraining myself financially, I received a letter from the Okanagan. It was from Margon.

I quickly tore it open and hungrily read the contents. He explained to me that he was taking a great risk by writing the letter, for if Klaur were to find out, there would be grave consequences for all involved. He insisted that the on goings were of such an imperative nature that he felt compelled to write me. He then went on to tell me that Kat was being treated no better than an alley cat. Apparently, she had fought pneumonia and had surgery for internal staples which had come undone, yet Klaur still expected her to do all the cooking, and cleaning. He went on to say that Klaur would frequently smack, verbally, and emotionally abuse Kat. He had found out through Agaratte that they were stealing money from Kat's father to purchase marijuana and that Klaur was seducing Lactavia into this 'lifestyle'.

Margon also eloquently described incidents where Klaur had given Kat to Agaratte for a night, and that Klaur was sleeping with Lactavia as well. He described incidents where Klaur would publicly humiliate Kat and provided an example where Klaur chained her to a pole outside a restaurant, while he went inside to meet friends. I had to read the letter twice just to make sure that I wasn't imagining the contents. But by the end of the second read the feelings of rage were manifesting into every muscle and fibre of my being. Of all people, why would Kat allow herself to be degraded so? Was she that in love?

"Playtime is over; you're going down, Klaur!" I said aloud in my bedroom after reading the letter. I was going to get those girls home, and I didn't care if I had to take them kicking and screaming! The smell of the fresh paint in my room still lingered, a reminder that my personal affairs were also less than normal, less than healthy. But I resolved that even if my life was a huge mess, there was no reason that theirs had to be.

Well, I had a car and a credit card so I had the means and the money to go to Penticton and get them. I couldn't believe that Kat was allowing herself to be so polluted and defiled. Wasn't she a witch? She was supposed to be above foolish teenage shit like drinking, drugs, and Master/Slave headgames. I went to work and completed my shift and put the money into the bank slot by 8:30 pm. I got into my car and drove all night to the Okanagan, my anger not waning for one moment, which was a good thing as I drove all night without a wink of sleep. At one in the morning I pulled into the driveway of Margon's house and sat below his bedroom window thinking of how I could rouse him. Well, I was supposed to be a witch, might as well use some Wicca. So I focussed and pushed my words into his unconscious head – which is very difficult to do. It didn't take too long and he was peering out of his window and staring down at me knowing full well who I was.

"Come to the back door, I'll open it." I walked over to the back door and waited for him to quietly open the door. He smiled at me and led me to his basement den.

"When did you get my letter?"

"This morning."

"Didn't waste your time eh?"

"No, it's about time this gong show was ended. I would have eventually come and grabbed those girls. Don't feel guilty or responsible because you wrote me that letter."

"Well, Kat has been very strange since the accident."

"Yeah, you mentioned that in your letter. You said she had emergency surgery because all of her staples in her abdomen ruptured. How long ago did that happen?" "Well let me get my journal and I can tell you the exact date." He left the room and I was glad I stopped here first as I was finally comfortable and just finally beginning to relax. He returned with a small brown leather daytimer and was sifting through pages.

"Ahha! August 20 she was rushed into emergency with Klaur in tow." Something about that date made me stop and think. That wasn't too long ago, just before school started. Then I remembered clearly jetting off to England and my first morning in Bryn's house. I instantly flashed back and I remembered his anger, his glowing hands. That he had done something. Kat may be annoying but Bryn could have killed her and that scared me. Margon saw me lost in thought.

"Hey, I'm sorry to bum you out. Kat is fine now, all healed up. It's just that she is behaving a little odd. She seems depressed about Lactavia and Klaur, and it is hard to get her to smile like she used to. So you want some tea?"

"Tea?" I looked up at him in utter confusion. As if I had said that word for the first time in my life and even now wasn't too certain what it meant.

"I'm sorry, who am I talking to? Would you like some coffee?"

"I need some, thanks." I had coffee and talked to Margon about his plans to get into Architecture and the hours peeled by. By five in the morning I told him that I was going to go to their apartment now and take them home. Margon was kind enough to give me their address and directions to the apartment complex where I drove to in haste. I parked and got out of my car. As I was walking up the stairs, thoughts of the letter were hotly pulsing through my skin; I was so angry, so ready to take out every bit of rage I had pent up inside me for the last year.

I knocked on the door and then opened it myself. The little apartment was sparsely furnished; the décor of the apartment building was reminiscent of the 1970s era of dark cupboards and mouldings coupled with homage to the colour olive. Clothing was strewn about for want of any hangers or dressers. I walked directly to the bedroom where I saw Lactavia already packing her things. Five in the morning and Lactavia had anticipated my coming and was packing. She never woke up at that hour of the morning, so I wondered what had transpired to have her up.

"Lactavia. I'm here to take you home to Vancouver. It's time to come home." She didn't turn to me. She didn't look excited to see me. She kept looking at her meager belongings and I heard;

"I know. Just give me a second to get it all organized." Just then, I heard a door close rather loudly, followed by Klaur appearing by the doorway where Lactavia and I were.

"Where is Kat?" I asked as calmly as I could. Klaur just shrugged his shoulders with that sneer I couldn't bear. Before I could control the left side of my body, I turned and watched my arm tighten up and explode in the direction of Klaurs' face. Boy did that feel good! I began to walk towards Lactavia, who was notably frightened by my sudden violence. While Klaur ran out the door holding his face, I asked her,

"When did you last see Kat?" Before she could say a thing, as if being in the room the whole time, Agaratte walked in the room, looking flustered as if he was trying to convey something to a dog or cat.

"Aileen, I think you should go to Naramata, Kat is there..." Something in his expression was very troubling. The sincerity of his words and graveness of his expression told me that something was very wrong. I didn't even stick around to ask him what he knew or how. I grabbed Lactavia and we drove to Naramata.

Chapter 26

Kat finds her path

Since Thromm and I had done the pact, the rest of this ritual was easy. Our spirits were not one, but intertwined. I sat on the cool earth, lit a candle, closed my eyes and began the chant. Words chained together which are so old that they are meaningless by today's measure, yet helped me pull my spirit out of my mortal coil. I could feel the massive tentacles of Thromm, which so easily moved into the spirit world also pulling me. My spirit seemed a small fragile thread intertwined with Thromm's huge dark expanse.

On his wings, we flew to England. We spiralled around Bryn's house. His house was dead easy to see, it was the only piece of prime material plane object lit up like a Christmas tree for all the magical wards surrounding it. Thromm and I both knew we would have to disarm it carefully and ensure we didn't alert the rather powerful occupant; this was going to be a stealth job. For the most part I found that these wards were easily removed. Thromm seemed to be able to utilize my spell skills along with his ability in the spiritual world quite adroitly.

In no time, we were in Bryn's bedroom, Thromms' massive ethereal spirit seeming to shrink to fit the tight space. We saw the box perched on top of his dresser, with no apparent magical glow to it at all. We were instantly suspicious – surely, Bryn would have a separate ward on this box? There was nothing more than a mortal lock. Then I noticed our error when I looked behind us, we were tricked, the room itself had not a barring ward, but clever Bryn had put a 'trip-ward' on the room and when we entered, we tripped it.

"Well Thromm, no point in being delicate, he must know we are here – let's get on with it and hurry..."

The intersection between spiritual world and material world is a delicate one. Unfortunately you can't just steal a material object and whisk it away in spirit form. Our plan was to spiritually transport into Bryn's house and manipulate his artefact into an envelope with a stamp and my address on it. The only risk would be that I have to stay sufficiently solid to put it in the nearby post box. Of course once I had the artefact that should be easy. Once it is in the post box, I don't care if I become less solid – I would be heading back to my body by then. The hardest part would be this part, opening this locked box; as I don't have the benefit of the artefact for that. All we need do is move the metal into the correct position to open the box.

Thromm and I worked for what seemed an hour attempting to move this metal, but finally we got it opened. Opening the box was much easier. Unfortunately, we also heard the sound of a roaring engine and breaks squealing as some vehicle screamed into the driveway, followed by the sound of rattling keys in locks downstairs! I flung open the box and there inside was the most non-descript wooden shard. It looked like something from a weapon, tool, maybe a staff. I couldn't tell. But I could tell that it was made of a kind of wood that I had never seen and it seemed stone-like. We reached for the shard that was glowing impossibly bright white in this spirit plane. I heard heavy, rushed footfalls climbing the steps soon to approach the door to this room. I knew it wouldn't matter, once we had the artefact, we had the magic not Bryn.

As Bryn ripped open the bedroom door I grabbed the shard, there was a blinding flash of light, and I was suddenly aware of two things; first, I could feel my body become solid and Bryn's enraged face; secondly, I felt Thromm tearing away from me, withering away to dust with the most horrific scream I had ever heard. I fell to the floor, with a noticeable thud. I could barely open up my eyes, but I could see Bryn hovering over me.

He took my hand with the stone shard in it, and held up his other hand towards my chest. He said something in a low tone, I could see a glowing aura around him, then I saw his face change completely. He then took my prize from my hand, shaking his head sombrely, and I felt myself 'snap' back to the lit candle in Naramata. I don't know how long I was lying on the cold earth, my eyes looking towards the sky. I didn't know if I was dying. I do know that while I held that rock, I could see that Bryn was surrounded in light and I knew that the artefact had saved me from a spirit of great darkness. But there was something else. When I saw Bryn, he wasn't just some stupid rock star. I couldn't escape the word in my head. I wanted to say the name aloud, but just as I felt I had the strength, I saw a shadow kneel beside me. Of course I should have realized that that bastard Bryn wouldn't let me just die in peace; no he would want to come to Canada to check up on me and make sure he had finished the job. There still was a glowing light around him.

"So we meet yet again in unfortunate circumstances, Kat." He whispered.

"I must admit I never thought that there would be a mortal on the earth who would go the extent you did to get my Talisman. I can't help but wonder how you know about ritualistic pacts with entities yet don't know that my Talisman is from a sacred and ancient artefact that nothing poled negative can touch?" He looked at me, perhaps surprised by how almost dead I was.

I couldn't believe my ears. It occurred to me that the reason why I was so drained was due to the fact that I not only sacrificed everything to give Thromm my mortal coil, but that he was fully intent on continuing to control my mortal flesh. If Thromm knew what this Talisman was and its properties it is possible that he hoped that my body touching it would only kill me and leave him unscathed – that bastard. While Thromm's mind was entirely bent on attaining the power, he had no idea that his spirit could not touch it. Bryn stayed with me while I seemed to float in and out of consciousness. He held me up and I could feel his magic in his hands. I could feel a real sense of who was holding me and the recognition was most unsettling.

"I know who you are now Bryn. Tell me what that artefact is? Suddenly, Bryn laid my upper body back down on the earth and stood up, looking around and then looked at me again.

"You are a lucky cat, Dragon is coming. They say that a cat has nine lives, how many do you have left?" With that, he faded into the darkness. Soon I heard a car pull up and the sound of footfalls coming in the direction of my candle.

"Oh, for fuck-sakes, Kat! What the fuck are you doing?" She blew out the candle and lifted me up off of the cold ground.

Dragon, wonderful Dragon the healer. I felt life in my bones the moment she touched me. I was going to live. There was something more, there was an image burned into my brain. I could sense in my heart a kind of fulfillment, a peace, and wholeness. Bryn hadn't cast some damaging spell on me; in fact whatever poisons my heart and soul had from my association or pact with Thromm, he had cured. There was wholeness, a deeper spiritual awakening, a love I had never before felt. While Aileen was talking to me, I looked up at the sky and smiled for I had felt my soul had been touched. Like rain drops, my spirit was cleansed.

"Elijah!" I gasped.

Chapter 27

Kat managed to find a hill in Naramata, light a candle, no doubt just to lie down and die. It didn't surprise me that she would sooner find a quiet hidden spot and welcome death rather than to come home to her mother, or to face me that contrived fun and games with Klaur was an utter failure.

I took her back to Vancouver and, between Kat's mother and me; she slowly got stronger and healthier. She registered in high school and I was relieved to see her back on track. Except for one very nagging concern I had, where was Kat? I mean, when you are someone's friend, you are generally well attuned to their habits and personality. Kat's whole demeanour and personality changed.

I watched everything that I knew and understood as Kat slowly disappear, piece by piece. First her habit of using proper English, then she cut her hair. I mean she completely hacked it off to just below her ears. She then followed up with an uncharacteristic disinterest in magic, and a predilection for the colour grey in her wardrobe. Her fire, that inner compulsion to take on the world, evaporated. Kat turned into an ordinary high school girl named Jennifer, a girl with shoulder length brown hair and a penchant for bland grey clothes. I was supposed to be supportive I tried to ignore the overt changes in her personality. I tried to tell myself that she must have had some catharsis on that hill in Naramata that finally made her give up her habit of being troublesome and intrusive with her witchcraft. Maybe she finally settled down and was prepared to do in life what I wished more than anything I could have – a normal life. I found it very difficult to be happy for her, the transformation was unsettling.

She found a nice young boy at school and began dating him. At least one thing about her didn't change: she always needed to have some guy pandering to her. But was she really happy? Was it possible that this was just another game or roll play? Where was Kat the devious plotter, hell-bent to get into trouble? The metamorphosis of Kat to Jennifer was utterly unanticipated and I didn't like it. She loved being Kat, didn't she? Unlike me, she loved standing out in the crowd. She wanted to be different, she thrived on being unique – so who was this?

She was pleasant enough, but as I was talking to this person I couldn't get over feeling that Kat was gone. I didn't know this person. Why had she exiled herself to this fate? I decided not to interfere in Kat's new image as her 'accident' was still quite fresh and she had enough inner healing to do. Instead I focused on my graduating year, on what I wanted to do for post secondary education, and when I didn't occasionally check in on Jennifer, I was engrossed in work and school.

That magical month, September, once again brought ceaseless rains to Vancouver successfully permeating every crevice of the streets, gardens and every person who called this city home. Glum expressions were as ubiquitous as the black leather, shinning from the morning's silver reflection cast down from the heavens. Today was another 'therapy' day: I was going to see if there was any chance I could help Lactavia get over Klaur. I thought about her whole disposition towards Klaur. She seemed to have an excuse for just about everything he did. She loved him even after all the truth about what went on was out there for all to judge. I knew she needed a friend to be there with her to comfort her.

I had to be careful not to slam Klaur too much as she was very protective and resented my criticism. She was in utter denial of many of the bad things he did. Of course it's not like I was anyone to talk. Not like I was in a position to give relationship advice. Bryn and I were not a condition of obsession in my mind. More like a tragic relationship.

The process of going to Lactavia's to discuss her emotional health made me think about mine. It never took much time for me to miss Bryn, his reflection in every puddle I walked through. The exquisite misery of our relationship, it was easier to push him out of my mind and resign myself to simply missing him always. Somehow the pain of long periods without him was easier to handle than confronting him on impossible ultimatums. I enjoyed the time we spent together in Trance, but my heart was sick for want of legitimacy. For now, I was comfortable being an emotionally tortured soul.

I got into my car and fought downtown traffic to Bidwell Street looking for parking.

'BZZZZZZZZzzzzzzz!' The apartment intercom made a lovely buzzing noise, I sure wouldn't want to be woken up by it.

"Hello?" called out an electronically enhanced voice

"Yo Tavi, it's me." I said into the face of the intercom.

'BEEEEeeeeeeeep – Kachunk!', The familiar noise of the electrical signal and the locking mechanism being disengaged. Lactavia was back to living with her dad, as Kat was back to living in the house in North Vancouver. So up to the 21st floor of these great Vaseline towers I went in the elevator. Lactavia loved living in the concrete and glass in the west end of Vancouver, as did her father. I opened the apartment door to find her across the apartment, on the balcony, smoking a cigarette looking out at the English Bay.

I walked in, took off my boots and jacket and walked towards her. She threw out her cigarette and slowly turned towards me.

"Klaur called and said that he loves me and that he wants to try a normal relationship with just me." I wanted to smack her in the face for wanting to continue with that idiot, but I controlled my anger,

"You live in a city with over a million people and you have to go back to that asshole. Why don't you just go for it? If you couldn't figure it out when you were in Penticton, maybe you'll never figure it out – Klaur and you -- Yipee!"

She shot me a disgusted look,

"You really can be a bitch Dragon, you know that?"

"I am sorry Tavi, but the guy is an utter scum bag. You can do way better than him."

"How's Bryn?" She inquired – completely out of the blue.

"Who? How the hell should I know?" I quipped back uncomfortably.

"Jennifer told me about some of the things you and she would do."

"And you believed her?"

"What? That you can move your spirit to anywhere on the earth and have a relationship with a musician? Of course I don't believe it. I just want to know if you are as crazy as she is." She turned again to face English Bay and the horizon on the ocean. She then became quite serious,

"If you had any weird powers you would tell me about them wouldn't you?"

"Oh no problem, did you know that I have the power to tell when a guy is wrong for you? – That's one of my powers. The other power I have, knows when a friend of mine needs to go out for Japanese food and a movie." I said reaching for her pack of cigarettes – I needed one.

She laughed for a moment, nodding her head, reached for her cigarettes, lit one and looked out towards the barges filling the harbour.

"But what about all that weird ECAW shit? I never did get any good at reading your thoughts, but you sure seemed to be able access information from somewhere. Then there is the ceremonies…I joined in the circles and I felt the energy flowing through me." She said taking in a deep puff from her cigarette.

"Maybe it is like they say in sociology books, you know, mass hysteria. People who belong to cults often claim bizarre things happened but it is usually the product of mass hallucination brought on by a charismatic leader, sleep deprivation, and poor diet." I said smiling. I decided to kill any belief she had, maybe it was because of everything I went through with Kat. I just didn't want to do it again with Lactavia. I wanted them all to embrace a normal life. Why should they suffer?

"Well, you and Kat aren't charismatic leaders, I don't have a dietary deficiency, nor suffer from insomnia – however, I suppose that I could have imagined it." She said smiling, and patting my shoulder. I know one thing for sure, I always feel better when you are around."

"Look Tavi, I can't stop you from going out with Klaur. Just promise me that your education and future will be your primary focus. Don't get distracted and get into bad shit. Margon told me about the Marijuana, alcohol, and other stuff and I am a little freaked out that you will slip back into it with him." I was suddenly aware that I sounded like Bryn, which irritated me.

"You don't think I learned a damn thing while I was in Penticton?" She said ensuring I realized that she was serious. The gravity and conviction of her voice was all the convincing I needed. I was relieved. We grabbed our coats and headed out the door.

Lactavia and I shared a lot; she was a dear friend. But Kat made my life difficult enough with the little she knew, and because of that,I had no desire to confess to anyone else, particularly when I thought about some of the grave things Bryn had done. He scared me enough that I genuinely feared for anyone involving themselves with him and me. Perhaps after everything that Lactavia saw, she just wanted an honest answer from me. She wanted to know what everyone wants to know, what is possible out there? But it wasn't my destiny to teach her or to tell her a damn thing. I knew that if one were willing to search through the massive amounts of literature out there, the answer would be found. For my part, my responsibilities were only to keep my big mouth shut and hold my vow to Bryn above all else. My life depended on it.

We went out that night and caught a movie, hit a dreaded record store or two and found a cool restaurant. I dreaded record stores these days as I was destined to see the face of the man I loved and yet needed to forget for gaps of time.

"So what? No magazines, no records? What's the matter with you Dragon?"

"Just don't feel like buying any music, more into dancing anyways."

"Still going to those bars under-aged, eh Dragon? Have you met any good looking men?"

"Sure, there are all kinds of good looking guys out there."

"Have you dated any of them?"

"Tavi, get off my back."

"So nothing has changed since I left."

"I have dated."

"Are you still a virgin?"

"No."

"What? You aren't going to tell your best friend the story of your pathetic life? Who was it?" Now I felt backed into a corner. I wanted to get her off my back so bad I just came out and said it and now I had no idea what story to tell her. I sure the hell wasn't going to tell her or anyone else the truth.

"Nothing really to tell. I was dating a guy from school and voila."

"Well, do I know him? What's his name?" I thought about the only other person I had been with.

"That guy you used to hang around with at school, John." I said, remembering how mad I was at Bryn. I remembered going out with John, just to piss him off. Yeah, that was a happy eighteenth birthday present to myself. Vera was nattering about John but I was reminiscing about my hollow experience with John and how awful and bittersweet my trip to England was. The whole stupid experience made my face turn red and uncontrollable tears began to stream down my face. I ran out of the store and sat on a bench that was just outside on Granville Street. Tavi came out, sat next to me, and was oozing sympathy. I wasn't about to tell her the real reason for my tears, so I made something up.

"Geez Dragon. Sorry. I didn't mean to upset you. Are you okay?"

"Yeah, I'm fine. I just thought about something upsetting and I am okay now."

"What the hell happened with John?"

"Well we dated for awhile. He really wanted me and he just helped himself."

"Did he rape you?"

"No, I just don't think I was ready, that's all."

"Shit, that sucks. Next time it will be better. But you know Dragon, you have to feel something for the guy. One day you will meet someone that you fall hopelessly in love with. I am sure of it." I couldn't believe that she had just said that. I stared at her, It made me just want to curl up in the foetal position and ball my ass off. I fought the urge and instead tried to focus on something, anything else.

"So when you graduate, what are you going to study?" The change of subject caught Lactavia off guard at first, but then she smiled, realizing that the change in subject was therapeutic.

"I think I want to join the Vancouver City Police. So I want to take Criminology."

I was thinking about how I had also wanted to go into police work. I was also thinking about how Bryn wanted me safe, and I had to be a good girl. I knew I was probably going to go for a degree in science. This would make my ghost happy and I did everything I could to make him happy. I was disgusted with myself.

Lactavia was more forthcoming about her misadventures while she was living in Penticton. She freely admitted to having an affair with Klaur, experimenting with drugs and alcohol and general adolescent tomfoolery. Kat, on the other hand, was not very forthcoming at all. She seemed agitated by the events that happened just before I showed up. She had been hospitalized. She insisted that Bryn did it. I knew that this was probably true. However, I let her know that I was aware of her objectives. I also took a bold leap and informed her that I was aware of her purposeful deceptions. I suppose that it was really water under the bridge, and that I need not know what actually all happened while Kat lived in Penticton. The bits I knew were damaging enough to her ego. Kat had great plans for her world away from Vancouver and her mother and in the end; it wound up being more of a nightmare than anything else.

Whatever had happened to Kat on that hill in Naramata, when we found her, she was bleeding and was later diagnosed with mononucleosis. She would not talk to me about what she was doing there. But I had seen similar damage before, on Bryn. I was confident that whatever she was doing, magic played a large part. Agaratte never explained how he knew where she was. There was one small thing stinging me in the back of my head. When I kneeled down to pick up her scrawny body, that night in Naramata, she looked up towards the sky and I could have sworn I heard her say in a gasping voice, "Elijah". That meant only one thing to me. Kat may not have been suicidal; she may have been up to more of her Talisman acquiring tricks, and I knew Bryn's patience was wearing thin.

Kat, or should I say Jennifer, had changed so much that I hesitated to visit her. But again, Samhaen would soon be upon us and I wanted to get a feeling from her if there was any chance that she would entertain the idea of helping me plan it again, like old times, this year. So up to Mahon Street in North Vancouver I charged, leaving my car at home and opting for the SeaBus to see her. I found her quaint little house and knocked on the door. It opened a small creak as if she was fearful of strangers and then opened the door and welcomed me. As I walked into her living room, I noticed that her new 'boyfriend' was over.

"Hello…" I said to the young large man seated on the couch.

"Hi, my name is Mark –Jennifer has told me about you, nice to meet you." He replied, standing up and I could see he was easily over six feet in height. He roughly grabbed my hand and shook it. He appeared to be your garden-variety young 17-year-old. However, as I have said before, she reformed. This made me more hesitant in asking her about Samhaen, but I figured –heck! What could it hurt? I mean, chances are, this guy wouldn't even know what a Samhaen was.

"Aileen, I am so glad you came over. There is something I need to talk to you about and it's important." Kat said in her new, less Oxford English.

"Sure Kat-er Jennifer…" I said correcting myself and looking at Mark.

"Well, I'm off Jennifer. See you tomorrow at school – I ain't hangin' around for chick-talk." Mark walked over to Kat, kissed her on the cheek, grabbed his knap-sack and headed out the door.

"He's not hoden, are you sure he's yer type?" I said grinning. That won me a dirty look from Kat.

"You should be so lucky Dragon…in fact that is what I wish to speak with you about."

I looked at her confused and sat on her couch after removing my coat and shoes.

Kat went into the kitchen and made some Japanese green tea and brought it out for us. She poured me a cup with the grace one usually only finds in aristocratic circles. She took a sip and turned to me.

"I want to talk to you about Bryn…"

"NO! We will not talk about him – ever!" I cut her off abruptly.

"Silence Dragon, let me finish." She took another sip of her tea. I put my cup down, folded my arms across my chest and glared at her. Did this girl have a deathwish?

"Stay there." She commanded. She then ran into the kitchen and came back with salt and a candle. I hadn't seen her do any magic in the longest time but there she was lighting the candle, evoking an incantation and pouring salt around us – she obviously was sealing the two of us on the couch—what was she scared of? Who would she be afraid would overhear us?

"Now, where was I? Oh yes. Bryn!" She looked at me again. Oh, so she was going to tell me something and she didn't want Bryn or any of his minions to overhear or oversee.

"I know the source of his power, Dragon. I also know about how he gets that much power without it killing his mortal coil. I worry that it may one day kill you. Do you know any of what I am talking about?" She broke off and just peered at me.

I felt naked and uncomfortable. I knew all of this but I still lived in denial that everything that was going on between Bryn and me was like a kind of adolescent nightmare, a very long and realistic nightmare. Hearing Kat talk was like pins poking me because I couldn't run away from her words; it made everything too ugly, too real.

"Kat, know now that I know more than I ever wished to know. I went to England and he told me everything…" I sounded exhausted almost defeated.

"Well, know this. If Bryn truly loves you, as he says he does – the solution is simple: get rid of the Talisman and you get rid of the problem between Bryn and you. You must mean more to him than his career. If he doesn't, isn't it obvious that he is just using you for his career and his magic?" She grinned and took another sip of her tea.

Of course it seemed so obvious to her. But Kat knew nothing of the 5th gate closing. Even if she did, there would be no way that she could have guessed Bryn's role in it – or mine. But she was right about one thing that had been nagging in the back of my head for some time. Until the time of the 5th gate opening, Bryn could technically put the Talisman away and we could have some semblance of a normal life. Why hadn't he?

I didn't want to talk about this anymore; I was desperate to change the subject.

"What about Samhaen? Are we doing Samhaen this year?"

She smiled politely and insincerely and got up to walk to the kitchen.

"Dragon, that magic I did just now is the last I shall ever do in my life. I am done with the Wiccan arts, the learning, and the Coven. If you had any sense at all you would be done with it too." She looked as if she was shaking, something was bothering her – I had never known her to look scared.

"What is the matter Kat?"

"Nothing, but you can just call me Jennifer from now on." She looked down at her sink, still shaking a bit, and then she looked up at me,

"I need you to do me one last favour."

"Sure, just name it." She paused took in a deep breath and I could see tears in her eyes.

"I don't want you to be in my life, while Bryn is in yours." With that she ran into the bathroom apparently to get some tissues. I was stunned! After everything we had been through, after the lengths I had gone to save her ass – she was out of ECAW and out of my life? I didn't know if it was jealousy, fear or both.

"You couldn't leave well enough alone. You had to meddle with us and the Talisman. Now because you finally have met your Wiccan match you will turn your back on me and the group and hide in your grey clothes." Tears were still streaming down her face and she looked up at me shaking her head.

"Please don't be angry at me. I have been shown how close I came to loosing everything. I have been given another chance and this time I won't mess up. I need to make amends in my life and I need time to heal, I have never known fear like this." She said, wiping her eyes. I don't know what possessed me to do this, but I was angry and without thinking about how it would feel for her, it just came out.

"Welcome to my world Kat. I tried to keep this all from you. I tried to protect you. Now you have had a taste of my reality and you run like the Napoleon you always were."

I stormed out of her house, my face hot because I was so mad! I couldn't believe that after everything we had gone through together, that she would kiss me off like this. I didn't even bother with the bus; I walked down Lonsdale drive all the way to the Seabus, hoping the chill in the air would cool me off. Somewhere down the hill towards the Seabus I did make a connection between Rodan and Kat. I recognized the fear. They didn't really think that Bryn would off them did they?

Days turned into weeks and I thought and thought about Kat. I dissected every moment that led up to this and couldn't think of what I had done to deserve being banished from her life. I went through what everyone goes through when they experience loss: Anger, denial, sadness, and, I suppose, some form of acceptance. Somewhere along the transition from denial to sadness, I thought about what Kat had said about Bryn. Couldn't he just put the Talisman away? Kat had obviously put closure to her life with ECAW and me – perhaps it was time to find closure with that apparition in my life. Closure sounded too close to coming to the end with Bryn, something I was not prepared to consider. I did not want to seek out the ultimatum from Bryn, in fact it appeared to fortify the opposite in me that was the reason I avoided him. But as the saying goes, "if Dragon will not come to the mountain, then the mountain will come to Dragon."

'Ring… rrrring…rrrrinng…' The phone was ringing and ringing and no one else was home on a Thursday evening accept me, studying for a mid-term. And since the caller was letting the phone ring sooo much, I assumed it must be Lactavia wanting to avoid studying and go for a drink instead. I strode to the little green phone, and grabbed it.

"Hello!" I said brightly.

"Well, you are home. Guess where I am right now luv?" said a slow easy masculine voice with an English accent that sent a chill down my spine till I nearly fell on the floor and dropped the phone. Instead there was a huge pause…

"Happy to hear from me aren't you luv? I'm in Vancouver, and I wanted to know if you could come out and play?"

"How did you get my number?" I asked nervously, breathlessly, almost whispering.

"Not a lot of Kovacs in the phonebook. I'm staying at the Sheriton Landmark downtown, room #2101. Come now – we need to catch up. I'll buy dinner." I was excited to see him again, but I was scared because of what happened in England. Why was he here? Surely it wasn't just to see me, that wouldn't be a good enough reason to leave England – he hated leaving England, he hated traveling. I had nothing to wear! He was so sensitive about my age; I knew I would have to show up looking older so he wouldn't be embarrassed. There was soo much to do what did he just say?

"Sheriton downtown? The revolving restaurant on the top?"

"Ah, you are listening. Yes, that's the one."

"What room?" I interrupted.

"Room 2101. Don't talk to the front desk man, or he won't let you up – I told him I want no interruptions or calls forwarded to my room tonight, just come up directly. How long will you take Aileen?" His voice was of course quite commanding at this point.

"You know me Bryn, I will be there sooner than you expect looking better than you imagine." I said assuringly.

"That's my girl! Cherio luv." He laughed and hung up.

I jumped into the shower, did my hair, got dressed, put on my makeup and ran out the door. I had a very fancy black organza dress that I thought was a bit of overkill. But I thought better too fancy than not fancy enough. My black leather coat was full length that I thought was elegant enough. I blew dry my hair and put it up and put on my black and gold stilettos that had gold metal heels – I looked mighty fine. I raced for my car, and in one hour and twenty minutes I was knocking on the room numbered 2101 and my heart was pounding so hard you would have thought that I ran up all twenty-one stories instead of taking the elevator.

The peek-hole shadowed for a moment and then I heard the door open. Before I could figure out for sure that it was indeed who I thought it was, he opened the door, grabbed me and pulled me into the room. I spun around to see the dimly lit but vastly huge hotel room when he put his hand on my chin and spun my head to face his wild eyes – my whole body froze at the sight and the smell of him. We stood there, staring at each other for what seemed quarter of an hour – wordlessly. His eyes searching mine in some Tartaric euphoria, then slowly he pushed his lips towards me and rewarded my aching body with a deep, slow kiss. He didn't stop till I could feel the room spinning, and my knees begin to buckle. Bryn sensed this, drew his face from mine and led me to the large couch by the door. He walked over to his bar and returned with a bottle of water.

"Here drink this. You look stunning." He said as he knelt down in front of me.

"Thanks" I said not taking my eyes from his.

"I hope you are hungry, let's go upstairs and eat."

Bryn grabbed his jacket and we exited his room and headed towards the elevator. It was plain to see that he was very happy to see me. He was full of smiles and very polite to all the serving staff. He let me choose the wine for dinner, knowing full well that everything I ever learned about wine was from him. He talked excitedly about some of his new projects in Europe including concert tours, advertisement promotional contracts, and charity work, essentially how he had finally seemed to conquer the entire Euro-media market. He looked at me, probably realizing that I had been sipping Chianti for the last 25 minutes just listening to him talk about himself.

"But enough about me and my good news, what is new in your life?" Bryn said finally putting his wine to his lips.

"Well, nothing as noteworthy as your news. I have midterms. I hate Economics. Lactavia is not a very reliable study partner. Kat has told me that she no longer wishes to be my friend while you are in my life…"

"Why would Kat say that?" Bryn interjected.

"I don't know Bryn. What I do know is that she was scared, of something. She kept talking about the Talisman, how you need to get rid of it in order for us to really be together. That if you didn't, it meant you love your career more than us…"

"Meddling Kat. Glad to be rid of her frankly." He said more to himself than anything.

"Bryn, did you bring the Talisman here?" I asked, bringing him back to the real world.

"That is enough of this talk for now. I will not discuss this here in the restaurant. For now you need not worry, you are safe with me tonight." He reached across the table and opened up his hand, begging for mine. I put my icy cold hand into his, and he brought it up to his lips for a kiss.

"You will stay the night?" He asked softly. I knew I had classes the next day. I knew I had a quiz in Economics. Hell, I knew that Lactavia had agreed to pick me up at 7:30 am to take me to school. But suddenly, it just didn't matter.

"If you answer all my questions later, I will stay." I said, taking another sip of my wine with the other hand.

"Always you negotiate." He said smiling.

Dinner came and I had lobster and prawns. Bryn had steak and potatoes. When he wasn't a pop and cheeseburger man he was a steak and potatoes man. Neither of us had room for dessert. Besides, it was obvious that now that his hunger had been satiated, there were other appetites that required sating. I debated whether to talk to him first or to wait until afterwards -- Bryn decided for both of us. Talk would have to wait.

There is a cold, controlled aspect to Bryn that could be erroneously construed as cruel perhaps even sadistic, something that over the years I had learned to fear and at the same time I suppose it comforted me – it was simply all I knew or understood. But tonight, it was gone. There was an almost softness to him, in his every movement, touch and his kiss – like it wasn't Bryn at all. This was the first time he had ever left England without the Talisman. I could 'feel' that he left it back in England. He looked great; I could tell he hadn't been doing much magic. I wanted this night to last forever, and while it lasted for what seemed hours, and we rested for a while – I knew my question would be a mood killer. But I was still basically a shit disturber.

"Bryn, I need to talk to you about something…" I said, my voice breaking the silence. Bryn was up moving around the hotel room looking for something to drink. My voice caused him to spin around and look at me.

"You are getting cum all over the bedsheets, go have a bath." He commanded with a sly grin on his face.

"Fuck the bed sheets." I returned with the same grin.

"No thanks but is that an invitation for another round?" He dove back on the bed and kissed my naked shoulder. We wrestled for a while then he pushed me into the bathroom, so I bathed and dressed.

"Bryn I want you to get rid of the Talisman." I blurted out after stealing a pair of his jeans and one of his T-shirts and putting them on.

"I know..." He was lying on the bed watching me pull on his clothes.

"Well, don't you think it is time to get rid of it? You don't need it anymore."

"Don't I? Look at my career, I just finally have it to the point that I want it – I am on top! I worked so hard to get there; I have had to put up with so much crap to get here. I need to know how far I can go with it. " He paused and walked over to me and put his hands on my shoulders and looked me straight into the eyes.

"Why can't we just have it the way we do for only another five years? I can put a pile of money away in another five years – I have to think about our future, what is so bad about the way we are?"

"Bryn, I am tired of seeing you physically drained by using that damn rock! I can't be near you when you have it. Trance drains both of us, and it isn't the real thing – I want this Bryn –I want tonight all the time. I want a normal life; I am tired of making excuses to people because I spend most of my time with a ghost!" Bryn removed his hands from my shoulders.

"You can never have a 'normal' life with me – ever!" He said, turning his back to me and walking away. why can you not get that through your stubborn head? Get comfortable with us not ever being normal." He then turned and faced me again.

"All of this is not due to my being power hungry Aileen; this path more heavily burdens me than you know. I try not to trouble you with this as I know it upsets you so. I spend evenings thwarting plans and manoeuvres by a C.I.A. man named Casey, who I will probably have to assassinate soon, then go do a concert that same night. You are my only solace in all of this. You gave yourself willingly in our first ritual; you vowed to share my burden –forever!" Bryn sat on the floor by the curtain, I could now see that this was the discussion, the confession, he was dreading from the moment we bonded.

"I thought you said that the U.S. stuff will now take care of itself? You don't seriously mean to commit murder? You cannot be capable of that could you?" In order to look as healthy as he does and still being as active as he says, he had to be 'using' his Sentinels.

"I haven't actually been that busy in the U.S. As I have said, my work there is done. However, I have noticed that it isn't enough and that I have had to cast my attention to the Middle East and South America. While there are currently lots of things going on in the Soviet Union, my issues are what the Talisman directs me as relating to the 5th gate and in that business, we need to postpone as long as possible that event."

"You wouldn't assassinate someone would you?"

"Oh, wouldn't I? Check your history; I have had to do it before. In my first life as Enoch, I did it to protect you and your kind. By leaving you barren I had to ensure some of your bloodline existed or you would never have been able to return to this realm. As Elijah, I annihilated two armies. Frankly, it's what I do best." He looked up at me; he really wanted to get a reaction out of me. I really wanted to disappoint him, but how could I? He was just sitting on the floor confessing to being a butcher. A chilling thought finally slipped into my rather thick skull. Whom was he serving? He had the Talisman but he admitted that he didn't serve the creator of it. Whom did he serve?

"Bryn, are you always this much fun on a date?" It was the last thing he expected me to say and it won a grin across his face.

"Baby, I want to just fly into your arms but I can't if you have that Talisman. Are you just going to hang on to it, casting me aside, until you are ready to procreate? I get the fact that you are some soldier on a divine mission. I don't know who we are exactly serving, but I will always stand by you – even when you scare the shit out of me which is pretty much all the time." I said shocked by my frankness.

"I never cast you aside Aileen. I have never complained about the fact that our relationship is this for now –I have committed to you even though it is in Trance most of the time." He put his elbows on his legs and his hands on his head.

"My heart aches so bad Bryn..."

"Aileen, how can you truly know the joys of a meal if you haven't gone for a prolonged period of hunger? How can you know the intensity of love and passion if you haven't experienced the pain of restraining it? Besides, it's not that easy, we have other problems as well: you don't want to relocate to England, nor do I wish to relocate to North America. I think we both need time, you are still so young, I know you are not ready to pack up and shack up –don't threaten me with ultimatums." He folded his arms across his chest and stared at me defiantly. I hadn't mentioned ultimatums but this isn't an ordinary conversation with an ordinary man. He knew what was in my heart; he read my thoughts as if I said them. This was the terminal state of our relationship, him staring at me so cocksure, with a heart so strong; and me trembling and weak.

"I can believe that you do indeed love me and that I am not just another healer in a long list of healers – here just to provide you with the energy to work your Craft. I can accept that I have made a vow to be there for you and that this dark burden is mine as much as yours. I suppose, in five or ten years we can talk about the child. But I do know this; I don't think my heart can take five to ten years of us being like this." I grabbed my coat, my mother's dress and other stuff that I put in a bag and headed towards the door. As I did, Bryn strode to the door as if to bar my exit.

"If you walk out this door, Aileen, and put me through another agonizing four months of ignoring me – I'll cut you off!" His hand was on the door, his face was menacing and angry.

"Give up the Talisman for a year then!" I said tears rolling down my face; I was so sick of him making me cry.

"Finish your schooling, get your degree, don't be so DAMNED impatient!" he snapped.

"Let me go Bryn. Come for me when you are ready to put down the Talisman. Until then, I need to find a partner I can hold." I bravely looked up at him.

"Who the hell are you going to find? Go ahead then, just fucking try! Watch yourself run from one to another searching for someone to fill your heart, you will never find it, because I own it –eternally." He kicked the door, and backed away from me. I opened the door and took one very brave step outside the threshold.

"Don't look back Dragon, I'll be long gone!" He slammed the door behind me. I crumbled on the floor in a horrid mess of tears utterly unconcerned that anyone would walk by and see me. I don't know why I was crying so badly, I knew this was going to happen. Shouldn't I be happy? I was finally free to have a normal life. I could date without having to feel guilty or have Bryn's ghost pushing me to go into Trance. There were times that my very life was in danger; there was a very real fear of the drain taking more than my vision. What kind of a life can you have with a person who can't even go out for fear of being mobbed by fans? I should be so relieved to be out of it! I got up and looked at the hotel room door, and then I looked down the hall to the elevator. I had to try to live without him; he had been in my life forever. I needed to find out who I was without him, but while I knew being with him like this hurt, what if being without him would hurt just as much, or worse.

There were two thoughts that immediately occurred to me: what would Bryn do if he drained himself hugely and, secondly, what about the child?

Chapter 28

The music was pounding in this packed nightclub. Vancouver's Luvafair, a landmark alternative nightclub, was a welcome change of pace for me. Although not the most favoured club of Jasmine's, I was able to convince her to join me at least for a while. The dance floor looked more like a mosh-pit these days, but I enjoyed watching the Halloween costumes and the people grinding and rubbing against each other in a primitive and carnal way. The bodies were all sweaty, the multicoloured lights dazzling against shimmering costumes, clarity of vision diminished by the dry ice machine spewing out smoke. Jasmine was in the dance pit grinding out to a favourite song of hers. She always danced feverishly when we went out. Lately I had become more of an observer. I would dance with her but mostly tonight I was nursing a few beer. Downtown Vancouver, this is where I was last with Bryn.

I had lost count on the beer I had drunk, must have been up to five or six. I was feeling fuzzy. It had been eight years since I walked out on Bryn. Immediately afterwards, something about Vancouver felt wrong, I couldn't stand her anymore. Something about London, Vancouver and Bryn all seemed to be the same to me. After I graduated from high school, I traveled Europe with my dad for a year. Every time I had a flight layover in London, I made sure I was completely hammered before the wheels of the plane touched ground.

I travelled to Sweden, Norway, Austria, Czechoslovakia, Germany, France, Italy, Denmark, and Hungary. It was a great time everywhere I went, except for the empty, lonely, miserable feeling in my heart that nothing seemed to fill. But I got to see the world and realize how lucky I was to live in Canada. It was probably on this trip when I was tired of running all over the world that I realized what career would truly make me happy. I had resolved to go into working in Canada's Parks and wilderness areas. The year being up and my father deciding he still wanted to be in Hungary; I left him and headed home. I arrived drunk for a layover at Heathrow airport, waiting for a flight bound for Toronto. While I sat waiting for my flight back to Canada, I found my Visa card Bryn had given me. It suddenly reminded me of his dominion over my life up until this point and in a bit of a drunken fit, I folded it back in forth until I could rip it apart and threw it in the trash. That stupid card came from the UK and that is where I left it. It felt cathartic releasing myself from that card and knowing that when I returned to Canada, that I was going to work in the parks and recreation industry. I was going to be Ms. Independent. That was seven and a half years ago, and in many ways I was proud of whom I had become.

Jasmine looked out of the dance floor to me swinging her head to coerce me to join on the floor. She hadn't changed at all in all these years. She still waitresses, still single; and still on the prowl. Jasmine, the party girl of my circle of friends, I love her. She had boyfriends and ensured they never hung around longer than about one to two years and her average was more like four months. Life was a party and she was the centre of it. I suppose deep down inside she wanted a family and to find true love, but that wasn't going to stop her from taking full advantage of her youth. For me, it meant that I had an accomplice and she rarely interfered with my anaemic love life.

When I came back from Europe, I left Vancouver, which haunted me everywhere I looked. I moved to Edmonton and took four years of Environmental Management at the University of Alberta. I studied, I partied, I flirted and true to Bryn's words, I was bereft of any desire for any man. I was dead inside and I spent the last eight years getting used to it – alcohol helped. I successfully gained employment with Parks Canada on the Queen Charlotte Islands, a job I eagerly took, as I wanted to be as far away from civilization and the world as I could. I didn't come back to civilization very often, but tonight was Halloween and I was on shore leave, in Vancouver, and as usual, Jasmine was on another vain crusade to breathe some joy into my life. There she was again wiggling her head, which is her sign language for, 'Get the hell off the chair and dance!'

I downed my sixth or so beer and nodded to Jazz. I decided I would go into one of the cages and show off. It was about midnight or one in the morning when Jasmine wanted to go outside for some fresh air and talk. I nodded my head and followed her out.

"Let's bug out of here and check out some of the more mainstream bars. I want to see some better looking guys – Luvafair is full of freaks." Jasmine was lifting her curly black locks off her shoulders in an attempt to cool off.

"Jazz if it all the same to you, I think I will call it a night, you go on without me." Actually, I just wanted to go to a hotel with an attached pub and drink myself into oblivion. That way I could crawl to my hotel room.

"You are never going to meet anyone by being this antisocial…"

"Jazz, this is not how I want to meet anyone anyways. Besides, there are all kinds of good-looking guys on the Charlottes. Everyone I work with is a tanned god."

"I wish I had your job. Next time, I am going up to where you live and I want you to take me out and introduce me to these guys you work with."

"It's a deal."

"Aileen? Whatever happened to your girlfriend Natalia? You still stay in touch with her don't you?"

"Yeah, of course. Remember how she wanted to be a cop? Well she got into counselling psychology instead. She works for the Vancouver

Police and Victim services doing some kind of counselling and referrals. She is making some serious cash."

"Is she still a bisexual?"

"No Jazz, I think she is straight now. She has this on again, off again relationship with Klaur. You remember me telling you about him?"

"Oh yeah. What is he doing?"

"Chemical technician."

"Wow! quite the couple."

"How about you, any great men you have conquered in the Queen Charlottes?"

"A few."

"A few? Why do I find that hard to believe?"

"Well Jasmine, no one can conquer as many as you do. You are way out of my league." I laughed and she laughed too.

"If you want to stay here and be boring that's fine, I want to mingle with men that aren't freaks. Do you want me to give you a ride to your mom's?"

"No, I think I will walk to the nearest hotel."

"You gonna rent a room for the night?"

"Yeah, no point trying to get to my mom's, she's across town from any of the clubs you would want to go to."

"You gonna be alright?"

"Did you actually say that? Please. I know I haven't lived in Vancouver for a while, but I think I still know my way around –get a grip!"

"Well, then I am going to get my coat out of coat check and head over to Daddylong legs or Richards on Richards. Call me tomorrow."

"Yeah, see ya then."

I went back inside and had a few more beers. It was a freak bar, but for the most part the men were gay and didn't bother you. That is why Jazz hated it so much. Personally, I hated the meat market clubs she went to. After eight years of trying to prove Bryn wrong, I had pretty much given up on relationships. Just give me a large bottle of wine and I was set. I danced a little more, but without Jazz to dance with, I was bored and was looking forward to a shower and a clean bed. I had just arrived from the Queen Charlottes via the airport and I had already had a long day.

I was feeling pretty buzzed by the time I staggered out of the club. The cool air helped my faculties somewhat. The club was on Seymour street and for whatever reason I decided to walk along Homer street. This street was mostly storage facilities, wherehouses, and other types of office spaces, I decided that I was going to have a peaceful walk along Homer and head up the usually populated Davie street and find a hotel there. I was sure I was sober enough to walk all the way to the Miramar I was enjoying the cold air against my damp skin, shaking my hair in the breeze to dry it out, so at first I didn't see the man standing by the corner of a warehouse parkade. As I approached, I noticed that there were at least three young men. One approached me smiling and asked,

"Do you know the time?"

"Sorry, I'm not wearing a watch." I said turning my head back to my intended direction. When the other two men grabbed both of my arms and dragged me towards the shadows of the warehouse building. The momentary shock of it was all it took and they had me. My arms were pinned behind me and the more I tried to wriggle the more they twisted my arms back, which caused an intense burning sensation in my shoulders. Once they had pinned me to the brick façade the first guy that approached me ripped at the top of my dress, rubbing my breasts through what was left of the fabric.

"Fucken nice titties…" he said as his friends laughed, he hiked up my dress and began rubbing my crotch.

I couldn't believe it! I was going to be raped just blocks from the club. I tried to scream, but one of the guys that was holding me against the wall put his hand over my mouth while the other guy pulled out some duct tape. When he covered my mouth with duct tape, I knew that this was premeditated and probably worse; they were all going to have a turn. The first guy, ripped off my underwear and was undoing his jeans. I could smell the alcohol on their breath. I couldn't tell if I was in shock or on an adrenaline rush, but I felt completely sober. The more I writhed the more these two guys twisted and held me in place. It was very difficult to move my arms because I was losing circulation in them and they were burning. They both each had a leg and didn't seem the least concerned about how they were grabbing my thighs. Pinned to a wall with my arms against the brick, my mouth taped shut and my thighs wretched open I was powerless to stop the asshole in front of me. I watched in horror, almost like slow motion while they laughed and the guy in front of me grabbed hold of his organ. In that instant I could only think of one thing to do. I hadn't done it for over eight years and I was probably too intoxicated to do it anywhere near as well as I needed to. I closed my eyes and tried as hard as I could, considering the alcohol in my veins, to call for Bryn like I used to almost a decade before. I just kept calling him repeatedly. I was calling him with my eyes closed tight but I could feel that asshole's cock poking at me. I was just waiting for him to force himself inside of me when suddenly all three men pulled away from me and completely let go. I fell to the asphalt floor and was so shocked it took about a second before I opened my eyes. When I did, I saw the men pinned to the wall, just like I was not a nano-second ago. Their hands were all at their throats and their eyes wide in panic, looking directly towards the street. I vainly pulled my dress down and looked up to see what these creeps were looking at. There, right in front of me, not more than 20 or 30 feet away, I saw a tall thin figure in a long, black leather coat like a black angel. I knew instantly, it was him.

"Aileen, are you okay?" said a familiar, but very anxious voice. I ripped off the duct tape pulling out some of my hair, which those idiots had stuck in the tape.

"I'm fine, they didn't get far." I was shocked to see him. Was he really here? Was he in shadow form? It was so hard to tell.

"You see this one Aileen?" Bryn said as he levitated one of the men, the one that was attempting to rape me not a moment ago. The man had a terrified look on his face, his jeans were still down to his knees and when Bryn levitated him, his nakedness was stark against streetlights.

"Do you see this one Aileen?" He repeated

"Yes, yes I see him."

"He has done this a few times before, I can read his thoughts. This is what happens when you touch my woman." Bryn then snapped back one hand, the man fell to the ground, crawling as if to get away and then laid completely still. Somehow, I knew he was dead. Bryn had killed him almost instantly with the wave of a hand. Shortly after I heard the other two men scream in pain, drop to the ground, and after what was no more than a few seconds they scattered as Bryn approached me. He quickly walked up to me and took off his coat to cover me. I wrapped it around my body while he held my face in his hands looking at me, his eyes glowing, glowing so bright I knew he wasn't really here. This was his rigid ghost form, my heart sank, he was in fucking England. Then Bryn did the least expected thing I could have ever imagined. He smacked me across the face, hard! The power of that smack sent my wobbly legs out from under me and I landed on my ass.

"You foolish woman! Look at you, you are sodding drunk, your spiritual powers rendered to almost nothing and look what you are wearing – it's an invitation to anyone!" He snarled, pausing before continuing. "Part of me wanted to let them do their deed as a lesson to you – but I couldn't bear to see it. Instead you have made me kill a man in my rage." I sat on that cold, concrete ground, staring at those burning eyes, barely comprehending the gravity of his words. His rage, I could feel that. The heat of his rage. My face stung! It hurt so badly. I felt blood running from my nose in a stream, I could tell that my face was going to swell, so much that I will not be able to explain it away very easily. But in that crazy, bloody, fucked up instant, all that mattered: wasn't my stinging face, not how I disappointed him, not what an idiot I was, what mattered was that I could feel again. His rage, his passion, his love washing over me and I couldn't feel anything else, I was alive again after eight years. He was glaring at me, no doubt becoming violent by my obliviousness to his ranting. I pulled myself off the ground and wrapped my arms around him, reaching up to kiss him. At first, he tried to push me away, but he quickly relented and wrapped himself around me, and kissed me back. His arms around me his face buried in mine, he was awesome, he was powerful, and I burned with the touch of him. He walked with me to the nearest hotel. I wore his magical coat and he did a little spell so that the hotel person didn't see my huge, swollen face. I got a room and he met me inside it. We didn't talk; we put cold compresses on my face. He apologized profusely; I told him I richly deserved it. Dirty, with a swollen face, and a ripped up dress, I begged him to give me what I so desperately needed. In spite of his better judgement I am sure, he provided me with the physical gratification my body had all but forgotten, until I could no longer remain conscious. When I awoke, it was noon and the housekeepers were asking me if I intended to stay another night. I looked around the hotel room and saw a pair of pants and a blouse, with a note attached to it:

My Angel,

These I borrowed from your favourite dress shop, Holt Renfrew, down the street –coat had to come back to England, as you know.

Exile me if you must my love, but you have to come to England next year.

Bryn.

I just laughed. I put on the clothes and left my torn costume in the hotel garbage can. I headed back to my mother's. I was really scared last night. That was the first time I had been in serious danger and thought that Bryn would not come; I was never so terrified. It was also the first time I ever really understood what other people lived like every day of their lives. How he could have heard me I had no idea. There was no way I had any power to reach him astrally –he had to have been following me that night. I was not mad at him for that, I suppose this time I was relieved. Next year I would be 28, I knew why Bryn was telling me to go to England – there was something we still had left undone. But if I was going to have a child, the child was going to have a dad. Bryn had to know how I felt. Was I ready to move to England? No one could ever hold me in contempt for being so in love with Canada. The mountains, the forests, the wilderness, the pristine beauty were beyond words. I needed to be able to escape to the forests every now and again for my sanity. What would I do just outside of London? Well one thing for sure, I was ready to negotiate. Maybe Bryn would agree that we could spend some time in the U.K. and some time in Canada.

I took a cab to my mother's, no way I was going to take public transit. I looked at it in my purse mirror, my face was a going black from bruising, my right cheekbone and eye were swollen. I knew that when I got back home to the Queen Charlottes, I would have to get an X-ray to ensure that I didn't have any fractured facial bones. He really hit me hard. I suppose Bryn didn't realize the strength in his astral form. My face was sore and although the bleeding had stopped, I knew that the healing would take some time, even for me. I wasn't mad at Bryn I would rather have been hit by him than gang-raped by those assholes. Maybe I needed that to knock some sense into me. Suddenly I was aware that over the last eight years I hadn't found love and comfort, I had found emptiness and my only joy I had found without Bryn was my solitude in the forest.

As I approached my mom's, I realized that I had to come up with a story. The only excuse I could think of was that someone at the bar was drunk and punched me. Knowing that my mother would insist that I go to the police, I'd have to tell her that I already did go to the police. So that is what I did. It worked like a charm and my mother baked me one of her famous apple pies. When Jazz called, my mother relayed the whole story. Bryn wasn't back in my life by more than 12 hours and already I was lying, deceiving and covering up, Oh well, small price to pay I suppose.

Chapter 29

I told the government that I was taking all my leave time, holiday time, and lieu days together. I packed precious few items. There was no ceremonious departure. I knew I might be leaving for a very long time and yet, no one knew and I was surprisingly calm about it. Its not that I didn't care about my friends and family, it's just that I didn't want people trying to convince me that this was a crazy idea. Of course, this would be a crazy idea to everyone, after all what could possibly be in London for me? No this was the way it was going to go down. I would just take a leave and go. I just thought that when I got there an excuse would manifest and I could move on from there. I flew from the Queen Charlottes to Vancouver. The Vancouver International Airport had a facelift, and the new building pleasantly surprised me. I was a little disappointed that there would not be anyone to wish me farewell, but I just tried to stay focussed on the welcome that was awaiting me instead. For a precious moment, the thought of the forests lingered in my mind, reminding me that where I was going would be bereft of the kind of thick, dark forest that was my cathedral. I pushed the thought out of my head and focussed on the joy of finally feeling whole. At Pearson's Airport in Toronto, I took my British Airways flight to Heathrow airport. It was a familiar and long flight with the usual turbulence upon arrival to Britain. We landed; I deplaned and headed for baggage and to clear passport security.

When I got through all of that and finally headed out of the arrivals section I saw a thin man, wearing a baseball cap and shades walking towards me and waving over his shoulder to an elderly woman. Bryn and his mother came to get me incognito. The minor fracture of my cheekbone healed nicely and the damage to my nose was minimal, So while I was back to looking more or less like I always do. I was suddenly aware that Bryn or his mother would notice the disfiguration. I didn't want him to worry about how bad he hit me; I knew he would never do it again. Bryn scooped me up into his arms and we kissed right there, and I stopped worrying about anything.

"How was the flight, luv?" He said grabbing my luggage and leading me out the gates.

"No problems, the usual." I said smiling at his mom.

"Happy to be back to England? Bryn tells me this time you are here to stay." She said smiling.

"Oh, he did, did he?" I said smiling at Bryn.

"Oh, we will make her love it 'ere won't we mum?" we were out the door and Bryn had a van waiting for us.

"Mum I think I will be dropping you off today, we will visit tomorrow okay?" He said winking at his mother who seemed to blush in comprehension.

"Oh Bryn, really. I don't need to know your private life. You just give us a call and we'll have the whole family over for a barbeque at our house. Just like the Americans do." At the sound of the word 'Americans', Bryn looked at me with a joking wounded look implying that he knew I didn't like the term, 'American'. I rolled my eyes upward but said nothing. Like most Canadians, I silenced my deep patriotism, as I didn't want to appear rude or worse, obnoxious. After all, the first time she saw me was in Los Angeles.

"Mum, you know we wouldn't miss your bar-b-que." Bryn said.

"I love outdoor barbeques Rose." I said to her smiling and putting my hand on Bryn's. He glanced over and I could tell he was very happy to have me here in England again. When he got off of the M3 to the road that he wanted he looked at me and said into my mind very clearly and loudly, so loudly in fact that my whole body shook as if I was standing next to his concert speakers,

Aileen, you are draining yourself again like last time. I can feel it, shut it off!' He saw me shake with his words. It had been a long time since I had to do it so I was very out of practice and by the time we dropped off his mom I was still struggling to do it. Bryn just grabbed both of my hands and talked me through it again. We didn't leave the driveway until Bryn was satisfied I was blocked.

"Bryn this is exhausting, I can't possibly be expected to do this forever. What are we going to do?" I said looking out the window without looking at him.

"I have already figured that out. I have secured a place at my parent's home that I can safely put the Talisman for as long as we want." He then turned and smiled at me grabbing my chin and gently prodding it towards him to initiate a kiss.

"Your nose, there is a scar, a faint scar – I didn't…"

"Don't worry about it, it hardly shows and I hardly care."

"I am so sorry, it's inexcusable." He then took my hand and kissed it instead.

"So now all of a sudden we are both so conciliatory, all it took was almost a decade." I said smiling back at him.

"Of course, you had to grow up."

"I had to grow up? You mean you had to stop power-tripping."

"What makes you think I have stopped power-tripping? I'm stronger than ever, it sometimes scares even me."

"You know, Bryn, that man you killed? I followed the news. The doctor's said that he had a massive heart failure and they never suspected murder. I never dreamed that you could have that kind of power. You did that while you were here in London."

"Aileen, you wouldn't believe what I can do with that Talisman now. I have enough power that I could have killed every person in that club."

"As if! How would you survive it?"

"Dragon, you were right there. I could have taken the healing from you even if you didn't want to give it. I know now that I have set everything in place, the future of this world and its leaders are all set up. I am ready to complete my obligations with the Talisman. You must carry the hope of the first tribe into the next gate. I can protect you easily now."

Something about the way he said, 'you must carry the hope of the first tribe' bothered me.

"You should have seen how your eyes glowed that night; you looked like you were on fire inside." I said looking at the side of his face very intent on gauging his reaction.

"I think what you saw was the remaining energy as it dissipates. It feels like an explosion of energy erupting out of me. When you are not around, I fry badly. I can barely walk – I've had to do it. It took me a month to recover. When you are around I could probably go on for some time."

"Remember how scared of you I used to be?"

"You still are, Aileen."

"Smart ass! The last eight years without you have been so empty, I had my career and I do love working with Parks Canada. I had crawled inside the bottle because I thought you had given up on me. After that night when you rescued me that is when I realized how empty I had become without you. That is my greatest fear. If I have to endure the Talisman, if I have to join you with the Children of Eden after the 6th gate opens for my kind, I will do it happily. Just promise me we will be together."

"Quite an experience to live in fear isn't it?" He said smiling at me and his eyes were just beginning to glow.

"Don't be like that Bryn." I said shaking my head. He just smiled at me like a wolf about to feed on its prey.

"We will be together, I promise. You know I would move heaven and earth for you, you cannot be fearful of that. Look Aileen, you are home." I had to struggle to pull my eyes from those glowing eyes and looked out the window to see his house – our house. I jumped out of the van and ran to the door waiting for Bryn to open it. He opened the door and handed me the keys.

"This is your set luv; it has keys for the Corvette. You will have to drive it for awhile before I ever trust you with my new Lotus." I looked back and sure enough, the Lotus was a newer model.

"Groovy."

I ran upstairs to his bedroom; I knew he would have some surprises for me. He didn't disappoint me either. The bedroom had all kinds of boxes and right on the bed there was a brand new golden baby doll, just like any man to buy his woman sexy lingerie in her favourite colour. I ran into the bathroom and there was a vanity with lights and a chair with some smaller boxes on the top – yippee! more presents.

I ran over to the kitchen and there was mocha java coffee by the coffee maker and a huge set of Japanese dishes and a book on sushi. I couldn't believe how hard Bryn worked to make this place my home here. I ran down the stairs, where he was half way up with the luggage and nearly knocked him over with a hug.

"I love you Bryn!"

"Yeah, just let me get these to the bedroom luv." He heaved the luggage, himself, and me up the stairs and manoeuvred to the bedroom to drop the luggage by what was obviously my side – away from the window. He then fell back onto the bed. I casually crawled over to him and began unbuttoning his Levis.

"You in a rush luv?" His eyes were glowing; and that is when I realized that he had used magic to stop me from pushing him, the luggage and myself backwards down the stairs.

"Like you wouldn't believe." I said smiling. Continuing to undo his jeans I was in the mood to spoil him rotten, for his pleasure alone, no man deserved it more. It wasn't long and I had that big powerful man moaning like a wretched whore. When he was done he grabbed me and embraced me for a while.

"Don't ever leave me again Aileen. I don't think my heart could take it." He sounded like he was crying – tears of happiness. I had never known him to cry, it instantly made me cry. So we cried, I didn't care; no one had been through what we had. I wiped my mouth on my sleeve and kissed him and hugged him back. I must have fallen asleep; I awoke to the sound of synthesizers and keyboards blaring from downstairs.

I got up and began opening the gifts that were strewn about my side of the bed. He had my size perfect on everything including shoes, a trench coat, and an expensive Armani dress, black of course, and because he knows me, a pair of hiking boots. I spent that hour putting my stuff away including my packed clothes. I wandered into the kitchen and opened the fridge hoping to find some yoghurt or sandwich meat or something to snack on. There was pop, which I didn't drink, and little else. I grinned; same old Bryn, the guy never eats. I went downstairs and asked my man what he expected me to cook for us when we have no groceries?

"Did you have a good nap then?" Bryn looked up at me as I opened the door to his music room.

"Yes. Are we gonna get groceries so we can cook or are we going to starve?"

"You had a snack not three hours ago."

"Very funny..." I grinned at his sick attempt at humour.

"How about we go out for dinner tonight."

"Remember what happened last time?" I said to him more as a joke than anything.

"Whose fault was that? Just remember to shut off your energy flow and we will be just fine."

"Yes, daddy. When do you want to go? What time is it anyways?"

"It's 3 pm our time Aileen, you have plenty of time to get ready."

"Will you shower with me?" I asked. Bryn looked at me as if he had forgotten that I liked that.

"Sure." He shut down all of his computers and electronic equipment and then followed me upstairs. Naturally, showering led to other things but eventually we were cleaned and dried. It's a sad reality that after close to fourteen years of knowing each other I could count on two hands the amount of times Bryn and I had made love flesh and blood together. I had a burning desire to make up for lost time, Bryn was going to be the most satisfied man for the rest of his life if I had anything to say about it.

I put on a simple dress and handed him a small box.

"I have something for you. Something to remind you of the world I came from." He smiled at me and opened the box.

"It is a carving of an eagle in gold. The eagle is a symbol of strength and determination. You have the spirit of the eagle in you. I have a Haida friend who is an excellent carver, I got him to make this ring for you – even though I know you hate jewellery."

"It's beautiful. I'll tell you what, I will wear it tonight." Same eerie restaurant something like nine years later, we were left alone and I was glad that Bryn was no longer a top ten chart buster anymore. After we ordered I decided to interrogate my man a bit, I had no idea what he had been up to the last eight years.

"Bryn? I know that you have been very distracted from the music business since we parted company all those years ago, what have you been up to?"

"This and that..."

"Seriously, you know what I have been up to, what about you?" I pressed.

"I don't know Aileen. You know, my usual poor excuse for a life. I got sloppy with my music because I was so busy trying to normalize life without you. Every time I had to use some heavy handed Craft I paid for it heavily without you. I came to you a couple of times without you knowing it – I was in that bad shape."

"Are you serious?"

"Yes, are you mad at me?"

"No, why didn't you talk to me?"

"You wanted a normal life, I wanted you happy. There were no more than three or four times. I came to you when you were sleeping. I held you, and it hurt like you wouldn't know to just leave you." Tears were beginning to well up in my eyes and I fought hard not to make a scene in the restaurant.

"There wasn't anything 'normal' about it. Are all normal people that miserable?"

"I don't know. I have never been afforded normal either." He paused as he saw the waiter coming with our food. When the waiter left he continued,

"I didn't even know that I could just take the power from you like that. I was busy working some magic in Geneva, Switzerland; I realized my only way out was to take out some key individuals at this meeting. I succeeded but was left in my bedroom in pretty bad shape. I thought I was done for, when No showed up and told me to go to you. He said I could just hold you and be healed; that you never blocked healing from me and it would work even if you were unconscious. I laid there next to you, surrendered myself to your healing and then had to leave you there. I hated it."

With that he focused his attention to the steak he had in front of him. I pushed a thought into his head,

"So how many people have you had to take out since our binding ritual?" He just shot a look up at me, his heavy lashes concealing to all but me the glow in his eyes and I could feel his thoughts burst into my head so powerfully it almost knocked me over,

'I have had to eliminate about 40 souls by now.'

"We can't do that anymore Aileen; I can't do it without hurting you. I'm sorry. We can talk more of this when we get home."

The force of his words in my head stunned me, but I nodded in comprehension and focused on my meal that was cooling in front of me. We ate, and went directly to the car.

"There is a radical sect of Zionists that are on to me." Bryn said as he fired up the Lotus and took to the main road.

"What do you mean, they are on to you?"

"What I mean is they currently are trying to control various parts of the world. They have an inner group of powerful mages that have determined that we are alive and well on our way to fulfilling the prophecy and they are the one Zionist faction that realizes they are not the first blood. They want to destroy the first blood, that would be you and of course any children. They believe that if they do that they will secure their future, as they want it to be fashioned. However, because they do not possess all of the ancient knowledge, they do not realize that they cannot do it regardless. They don't fully understand the 5th gate. What they do understand is that they want to retain their earthly existence. Whether propelled by greed or a driving need for power it is immaterial to me."

"Are we in danger?"

"No, I don't expect so. While their mages are powerful and there are at least six of them now, they dare not expose themselves again. I have already killed one of them. They don't know who I am, but they know I mean business."

"So the last 10 years has been a war for you. Some life."

"I'm an old General – I'm used to it. As the time approaches, as these dangers increase, I believe that the Talisman has increased my ability to handle it all. It just has a few side effects that remove my ability to enjoy the things I used to do, like telepathy with you."

He turned and smiled,

"Watch this..." He removed his hands from the steering wheel and gearshift and put his hands behind his back. I was scared at first but quickly noticed that the car was driving itself, or rather Bryn didn't need to drive his car.

"I don't even have to watch the road..." He reached over and grabbed my head in his hands and proceeded to kiss me with no intention of returning his attention to the road. His skills were amazing, but I preferred to have him drive. Eventually my apprehension in the form of pushing him away and squealing won him over and he returned to controlling the car manually.

"Aren't Zionists really an extremist Jewish sect? Are you fighting Jews?" I asked. He looked at me for a moment and shook his head.

"I could tell you things that you would never believe. I will spare you the truths of the past. Just trust me when I tell you that the Zionist sect I am referring to portrays itself as Jewish, however they are anything but Jewish. The single common theme amongst them is global control."

"Why would they pretend to be Jewish?"

"It protects them more powerfully then any paramilitary service, or magic. They have instant media and public sympathy and there isn't a courtroom or lawyer that wouldn't rise to the opportunity to protect them. However, make no mistake; they are not followers of Hebrew doctrine. This group has been directly responsible for the deaths of many Jews and other ethnic and racial groups."

"How large is this group?"

"It's not how large the group is, it's how powerful they are. They are currently well on their way to controlling most of the major governments on earth. The mages that they have as I have said don't understand what is going to happen at the end of this gate. They are operating out of fear. They want to begin ethnic cleansing; they think they know what you and your child might look like."

"How could they know when he hasn't been born yet?"

"Well, that is why I get nervous taking you to hospitals. There are trademark differences between someone with your high Nephilim genetics. The blood-type, bizarrely low blood pressure, tall, pale, brain wave activity won't be normal, really low heart rate, primarily Caucasian with anomalous Asiatic traits, they probably know right down to the mitochondrial DNA. They have people everywhere that give them access to just such data."

Well, one thing for sure, he identified me to a tee. I had an EEG and IQ test done when I was twelve. They showed my mom my brain wave activity and explained what they saw as abnormal. They then comforted her with my IQ results; something like 168 which they thought was quite high. I also had very low blood pressure and an athlete's heart rate.

"How is it that by mixing our bloodlines with the other races that we were able to retain a pure bloodline today?"

"The surviving Nephilim created many of the bloodlines. Ulmecs, Indus, Egyptians, Sumerians and even long forgotten older races, It's not that they are in you; you are in them. Through some innate biomechanism the Nephilim bloodline is reassembling. The body I am in now possesses the last remains of the Nephilim genetics your coil is missing, a minor amount in order to house my soul. Our child will be Nephilim."

"Will this be the only child with the old blood on earth at the time of the 5th gate closing?"

"No. In fact there are many of them here already. But the mages want ours Aileen. The pact is specific: Only when a child of Shemhazai's bloodline has been born unto Enoch will the gate of redemption open for the Nephilim and the fallen. To the best of my knowledge it is a divine edict."

"So the edict specifically states you, but it is not specific that it be me? So you could have chosen another?" He shook his head and looked down on his lap for a moment.

"You are incorrigible. Do you really think I gave it a moment's thought?"

"I would bet you gave it a passing thought when we were apart for eight years…" I laughed infectiously and carried on picking his brain.

"What about this sect controlling governments and killing people. Do their mages have some of the ancient blood in them?"

"Remember what event took place on September 16, all those years ago?"

"That is the date of our binding. How could I forget that?"

"Some 3000 Palestinians were butchered on that night, as the Israeli army looked on."

"You're kidding…"

"I knew that this was going on, but I was powerless as that had to be our night. We lost some of our people in that. Since our binding no such huge losses were suffered. Soon our work will be done and the governments can overflow with the sects' paranoid vengeance, it will be too late – this age will fold and the next one will begin."

"Come on Bryn, out with it. Do those Zionist mages have ancient blood?"

"They would have neither the insight nor the skill if they hadn't. This is why I don't blindly go off killing indiscriminately."

"How long do we have?"

"Almost twenty years."

"Is your whole life on an itinerary?" I said shaking my head in disbelief.

"As is yours, my luv." He smiled. "Enough of this talk, you wear me out. What time do you want to go to mum and dad's for the bar-b-que tomorrow?"

"Well if it is a dinner thing how about around 4 or 5 pm?"

"Mum will want us to visit a little more than that I'm afraid. How about If we go there by 3 pm?"

"Fine by me, I will be just roaring around the neighbourhood in your 'Vette!" I said laughing.

"Well we should go for the dreaded grocery shop tomorrow too."

"I think I will go and get your mother some flowers. Can you take me to Buckingham Palace?" Bryn pulled into the driveway and shut the lights off of the car and tilted his head at me.

"I wanted to work on my compositions. If you help me work on it, I will take you to town on the weekend I promise."

"Deal." We exited the car and headed for the house. Over the years, we had been apart for various reasons. I always felt like I was fighting the fear that something was bound to destroy my perfect moments with him.

I was the first one out of bed, working out the puzzle of whose leg was where and how to manoeuvre my arms from his to make my way to the bathroom for a well-needed shower. After my shower I staggered over to the kitchen to make some coffee. The pot was making its last satisfying noises that it was finished when Bryn walked into bathroom after taking a quick look at me and smiling.

"Mornin' luv –got no milk." He said. Am I desperate enough to drink coffee with no milk? Damn right I am! Bryn didn't seem too disturbed by my partaking of caffeine, the only drug I suppose that is Wicca approved. I was sipping on my coffee at the table wondering why I ask Bryn questions when I know how much his answers disturb me when I heard a thud by the door. I went downstairs and peered through the peephole, no one was there. I then cracked the door open a bit and saw that someone had thrown a paper at that door. 'Hey, The London Times.' I closed the door and that caused my paranoid man to call for me from upstairs.

"Just getting the paper." I called back upstairs. I carried the paper with me upstairs and stared at it while sipping my coffee. There was babble about the Royals, stuff about the government, some ideas about where to go this Valentines Day, no major news. Bryn came out of the bathroom, the vapour sending the smell of shaving crème and cologne across the room.

"Get dressed, woman." He said, who, like me, had nothing more than a towel around himself. I drained my coffee and ran to the bedroom to get changed into a pair of jeans and a tight fitting lace shirt. I went to my bathroom vanity and brushed my hair, I couldn't help but smile. I could just let my hair dry naturally and the curls would be perfect, I only need comb my hair with my hands and my hair looked salon styled. In contrast, Bryn would fiddle with his hair for a solid ten or fifteen minutes, he had gels and mousses, and in the end his hair always looked the same.

"Shopping?" I asked smiling at him while he continued fiddling with his hair.

"Shopping." He replied rolling up his shoulders as if to say he had resigned himself to yet another bad hair day.

"Do you have a Marketplace or are we going to a grocery store?"

"Is there a difference?"

"Men…"

We went off to a huge supermarket called Sainsbury's in a place called Croydon. The store was not lacking for whatever we needed, so I filled up. Bryn provided little or no input into what was purchased. Bryn ate to keep his body going; he took almost no pleasure in eating. He seemed more interested in looking around, ducking into aisles hoping to be unnoticed. I had to see every section and by the time we got to the check out only three people approached him looking for autographs or to say hi.

"You gonna eat all this shit before it rots?" He said pushing his face into my hair and whispering to me.

"You gonna help me, or you plan on starving to death?" I said turning my face to his.

"I'm not much of a cook; in fact, I can't cook worth a sod." We paused for a moment face to face, grinning at each other. Any passing idiot could tell we were like newlyweds.

"Lucky for you I learned a few skills since I was a kid. I have a mission; I am going to find a type of food that you will get excited about. Be careful, I might make you fat!" I smiled.

"Isn't that my job?" he smiled back.

"Smart ass! Have you ever had smoked black cod?"

"What do you think?"

"Well I am going to find a specialty seafood shop and I am going to feed you smoked black cod poached in buttermilk served with cooked stinging nettles and you are going to know what the most divine food on earth is."

"Sounds repulsive."

"English men! Well, what do you like then? No, let me guess, fish and chips right?"

"I like the feeling that comes over you when you look at me. I like how your legs turn to butter when we kiss."

"That doesn't feed you." Just hearing him say that was making my legs weak.

"It sure does."

"You're impossible!" We put the prodigious amount of groceries in his poor excuse for a trunk. On the way home I continued to harass him by threatening to buy a station wagon or family minivan for all the groceries, pets and children. My endless threats to having him park a station wagon next to his Lotus made him laugh really hard. I had never had so much fun shopping.

Chapter 30

We went to the family bar-b-que and we stopped first at a florist so I could get Rose some flowers. Everyone was already there. I was introduced to the whole clan, which was actually surprisingly large. He had uncles, aunts, cousins, and everyone brought their kids. There was about thirty of us all together, which reminded me of how small my family was. His Uncle John's wife was particularly friendly and she wasted no time telling me where to go to get the best seafood in London. I took down notes while she warned me about all the foods Bryn would never eat. We laughed and she told me all the stories her husband told her about Bryn growing up. Eventually, with a beer in his hand, Uncle John came over to us and started telling us about the trouble Bryn would get into from dad and the schoolmaster. At some point in the hilarity Bryn shot me a look that very clearly indicated he was sufficiently tired of hearing everyone regale me with another bad boy Bryn story. I desperately attempted to change the subject but Rose beat me to it with a quick call.

"Okay, clan, food is served, Dish up yourselves. That means you boy! Put down that damn pop can." Rose said jabbing Bryn in the ribs. Everyone moved over to the table and filled their plates with all manner of salads, veggies, and bar-b-qued chicken and burgers. I took some of the potato salad and chicken while Bryn predictably just made himself a hamburger to go with his pop. The evening continued with talk, food, and humour. By about eight o'clock Bryn was looking anxious and was making excuses to go home. I was actually having a good time talking to everyone and hearing the family tales, so I reluctantly acquiesced to Bryn's repeated brow beating to put on my shoes. Rose just smiled at me and I wished her a good night and thanked her profusely for being such a fantastic host. Bryn definitely came from a great home with a very loving family; I realized that the sincerity and moodiness of Bryn was probably entirely a product of his work with the Talisman and nothing at all to do with any dysfunction in the home he grew up in. In fact, his family looked like they went out of their way to make him a happier soul. Occasionally, he obviously let them know that the effort was appreciated.

"Well that is certainly enough small talk for the next six months." Bryn said firing up his Lotus and pulling out of the street.

"Ya, you're definitely the extravert." I replied sarcastically.

"We are going to go home, shower, meditate, make love and go to sleep. All that talking is exhausting." He reached for my hand that was located on my lap. I didn't reply. Obviously, he was sick of talking.

We got home and did everything in the precise order that he had mentioned. We went downstairs and down the hall from his music room there was a locked door that I had only entered a couple of times in my life and never in the flesh, until now. He rifled through his keychain and found the two he was looking for and opened the two locks. Soon the door opened up to his back yard, the Cathexisphere. The house is built to give one the impression that the house is in the back portion of the property and the front yard is a large car park. The adjacent properties on either side were flanked with large trees that obscured the concrete wall. I wondered if even his family knew about this backyard.

He walked towards the center of the circle glancing back and motioning me to join him. He then straightened up and looked forward between two of the columns and raised his hands. Instantly a flame rose from one bowl, lighting the dais better. I looked around at the other columns and as I had suspected the other bowls contained the four elements attributed to the four cardinal directions, as I could see water dribbling down the side of one bowl. He then knelt down on the dais and I followed him, my back to his back. We sat there with our minds cleared and our spirits high above us. I hadn't meditated in a long time and I truly welcomed the opportunity to do it with Bryn. Once my mind was projecting, I could see from above the enormous light in the circle that was actually a sphere that reached within the earth and above the dais in a dome shape. Bryn was gone, no doubt to wherever the Talisman took him. I was content to drift above this place and enjoy the peace.

I can't describe the feeling of sitting in a meditative state in this place; I suppose the closest thing would be serotonin/endorphin rush of an athelete. You are so overwhelmed by the rush quelling the intense pain of pushing your body to such an extreme. This construct of Bryn's obviously amplified his power; I could see that from here he could feel the pulse of time. It felt like an amphitheatre. I felt like I could feel the gate, celestial movements like a galactic clock. I don't know how long we were there, but I was feeling exhausted when I felt Bryn back with me. When I opened up my eyes the flame was gone and he was already standing and heading for the door, which I noticed he had locked again on this side when we came in. He didn't bother with appearances and just waved a hand and the padlock flew from the latch and landed in a container on the side of the door. The door then opened and he reached one hand back without looking, waiting for me to take his hand into mine and follow him out. I missed the telepathy; it bothered me that he was beyond anything that I could handle. I took his hand and when I was on the other side of the door he took the time to padlock it with his hands and shook his keys back into his pockets.

"Aileen, you are doing it again. You are draining yourself. I can see it in your aura and now I can see it in your eyes." He had barely finished saying that when the world became dark.

The next thing I remember was waking up in a hotel room, I had no idea where. I was alone, and there was a note by the nightstand in Bryn's handwriting, the same writing that was once all over my bedroom walls.

Angel,

You fell into my arms last night. It was after midnight and I didn't want to alert my mother by dropping off the Talisman there so late, I will bring it there in the morning. For now, just get some rest and order up some food when you can and Aileen, for my sake, call me when you wake up and tell me when you feel good enough for me to come get you.

Love,

The asshole that caused you all this grief in the first place.

I am so sorry.

I picked up the phone and dialed his number, left a message and then called room service for some breakfast or lunch or whatever. I ate, Bryn called back and I told him I was fine and to get me the fuck out of this place. I tried not to let this piss me off, like it had the last time I was in London. I kept on trying to tell myself that I should make more of an effort to focus on severing the drain. But it was definitely annoying and I could actually feel the drain. He promptly came by and I was back home. The following two weeks went off without a hitch, because I was able to brow beat Bryn into abandoning the Talisman more frequently at his parents. Bryn clung to that rock like Frodo clung to his ring in, Lord of the Rings. I began a regiment of fasting, meditating and practicing Wicca again, so that I could control myself around the Talisman more. But I was sure happy that he would abandon it occasionally.

Bryn spent a great deal of time hanging around the house and me. I realized eventually that he was being paranoid and overprotective. I knew that he had work to do. The answering machine was jammed with messages Bryn didn't even look at. For some reason he seemed more worried about me being here in England with him than he ever was when I was without him in Canada. Once I figured out what he was up to, I immediately got on the defensive and told him to quit fathering me and go to work. Eventually my brow beating paid off and he went about his usual business. His business usually meant he spent a lot of time going into town and handling the ugly business of contracts for all the publicity and other public relations garbage one finds themselves immersed in when they decide to join the elite ranks of rock stars. I hated it, but it did pay the bills.

My job was to get fat, well, pregnant. But to me it just meant getting fat.

Rose was going to pick me up this afternoon and we were going to go to this seafood store after we went out for a late lunch. I was looking forward to seeing more of the city, as Rose loved milling about the press of people in London. So off we went, wallets in hand, ready to spend a great day in the city and I was looking forward to glimpsing Harrod's, hearing Big Ben chime, Trafalgar square, and the other overcrowded places a famous musician avoided. With any luck I would be bringing back some smoked black cod and poaching it for Bryn to try tonight.

Rose dropped me off at home by six pm or so and Bryn was not yet home so I was in some haste to get dinner on the table and surprise him. By eight pm he walked through the door and the smoked black cod was cold.

"Sorry luv, the photo shoot took forever and I had to stop off at mum's to get back my rock." He came upstairs to hand me some flowers, a token offering, and then looked at the table.

"What is that smell?"

"Cold dinner, are you still hungry?" I said trying hard not to appear angry. He smiled at me,

"I am starving; you didn't wait for me did you?" I grabbed the two plates and put them into the microwave successively.

"Of course I did. I had a big lunch with your mom in town so I wasn't totally starving." I reached for the bottle of red wine to open it. Bryn snatched the bottle from me and opened it for me and poured us both a glass. Finally, he put his arm around my waist and tilted his head down for a lingering kiss. No matter how much time would pass, however many years, Bryn would never be one of those men that would ever stop kissing his woman the way he did when he first met her. Was it him or the magic I don't know, but I had to fight to hang on to my wine glass while we kissed because he invoked a kind of cataplexy within me. We sat and ate in relative quiet and when we were done I brought the dishes to the sink.

"Well? What did you think?"

"What? The fish? It was different for sure. I suppose I liked it."

"Told ya. It's an acquired taste, but I love it – so get used to it." I said smiling.

"What do you want to do tonight?" I asked as he walked towards the bathroom.

"Knock you up. What else?" He closed the door and I could hear the shower turn on. Now I knew Bryn. There was significance to everything that he did and everything he said. I went to the calendar and looked up today's date, February 26, and sure enough the symbol plainly written on it, full moon. I had to smile to myself. I turned, did the dishes and waited for him to get out of the shower.

He walked out into the livingroom, a room with so many platonic memories, and we wiped them out over several hours. This business was not the ritualistic bonding I was used to with him. It's not that it was lacking its usual tantric tendencies; there were just no candles, no unintelligible words, or somatic gestures. He sure did have a thing about looking me in the eyes all the time though, I suppose I liked it. More likely though, it was simply all I knew. There should be a bumper sticker that reads, 'Warlocks make better lovers'. Somewhere around 11 pm or midnight while we were lying on the floor in each other's arms I felt a strange burning sensation in my abdomen. I was about to get up when I noticed Bryn's grip on me become painful. He reached his other arm to my other shoulder and brought his upper body over me. When he looked at me I could see that his eyes were on fire, glowing a golden red much like a deer's eyes when your headlights flash on them. His grip continued to pin me down hard to the floor and the pain in my abdomen spread further into my legs and guts. The pain began to get intense enough that I began to cry out for Bryn to let go of me. Soon my whole body was throbbing with a burning pain. Bryn finally released his hold on me and stood up, he was shaking. Then something really bizarre occurred. I could read his thoughts and I felt his fear. I had never felt fear from him before; I hadn't been able to read his thoughts for a very long time. I was also beginning to hear voices that were not speaking English but that I somehow understood. The voices were telling the tales of the travels of the ancient people – the ancient knowledge that Bryn had told me about. This was the endless stream of knowledge that he obviously had to listen to for as long as he had the Talisman, no wonder he hated too much socializing, what a racket! I don't know how long we were like that, it felt like an hour. Eventually the pain subsided and the voices stopped and Bryn slumped over to the side of me and closed his eyes.

I knew what happened, I was pretty sure now. What we had just experienced was conception. Somehow, this process sapped Bryn's power. I think Bryn anticipated the exchange of the ancient knowledge, but loss of his own formidable power was obviously something he was not prepared for. To me it made sense. Power is corrupting. Had he known, would he have done it? After about ten minutes, he opened his eyes and looked at me. I could see the confusion on his face, and more troubling, the fear. He was afraid of how much of his magic he had lost by serving the Talisman.

"You have lost nothing my love; the Talisman gave you this great power to prepare our people for the gate. Now you must share this power with your child, to protect it." I said quietly.

"How drained do you think you are?" I pushed.

"I just don't know…" He rolled over onto his back and then got up slowly and went to the bedroom. It was natural that this would take him a while to get used to. I was certain that as the child was not born yet, the Talisman would certainly not totally drain Bryn. But maybe Bryn was dreading the next step in the process; maybe he was suspicious that the next step would completely drain him. I think he feared loosing his magic entirely. I couldn't blame him; he had it almost all of his life.

It seemed cruel to take it away. I got up and noticed he had left the Talisman right there on the floor. I looked at it. I wanted to touch it, just once. I bent my knees and went to reach for it.

"Daizabael! Don't even think about it." I heard Bryn from the bedroom. So I left it there for him to deal with, and went to bed.

"Aileen, wake up. Look. Watch this…" I awoke to a smiling Bryn who was dangling a full glass of water over my head – using his magic of course." I think he saw the concern in my eyes as I was certain the next thing he was going to do was magically tilt the glass to pour water all over my head.

"I still have lots of my Craft left, hey old girl?" He said, finally grabbing the glass and drinking the watery contents to my relief. I looked at him and was even more relieved that he was happy and not resentful at me for what happened last night. It was the last thing I was expecting.

"What happened last night?" I asked noticing that I was still not feeling too great. Bryn turned to me,

"No told me that I would know when the moment of conception would happen. I never thought he meant that I would know because some of my magic would be imparted on the conceived."

"Last night you looked so upset, I thought you had lost all your magic."

"So did I."

"How much do you think you lost?" I pushed not wanting to make him grumpy, but to determine how vulnerable he thought himself to be. He just glared at me and I could feel him push a thought into my head.

"Enough that I can do this again without splitting your head." He was actually upset to be at the same spot he was when I left him eight or so years ago. Well, actually eight years, eight months and nine days since I walked out on him that night at the Sheraton Landmark Hotel on Robson Street in Vancouver – but who was counting.

"Well, you were getting just too powerful in my opinion anyways; I missed our ability to communicate non-verbally." He smiled got up and wandered over to the bathroom. My body had been through a lot in the last week and I was thinking that a doctor's appointment might be a good idea. I tried to get out of bed but I doubled over in abdominal pain. I felt like a train had hit me. Maybe I would just stay in bed today and go to the doctor tomorrow.

"Wake up sleepyhead, it's a nice day. We should go to town. I just have to drop something off and then we can spend the day touring around a bit." Bryn was shaking me gently, but it felt rougher than I knew it should have been. I must have opened my eyes and winced in pain, because he instantly knelt down beside my head.

"Are you okay?"

"Last night I felt like I was on fire. Today I just don't feel much better." I said quietly, surprised that I had fallen back to sleep and wondering what time it was.

"I think I will drop the Talisman off at mum's and come back. If you are not feeling better by tonight maybe we should call a doctor."

I nodded and he reached to the night table for the Talisman and was down the stairs to his car. I fell asleep and dreamed of a land that was surrounded by water. The city was reminiscent of iconic interpretations of ancient Greece, a huge stone city that took up an entire small island. The weather was hot and everyone was wearing gossamer-like fabrics and speaking this ancient tongue. The whole setting was like something out of Michelangelo's painting, 'The School of Athens'. Some people were sitting enjoying the afternoon sun on this massive marble staircase discussing various theories and interpretations of god knows what. I was standing on the bottom of the staircase looking up at them and trying to determine what they were talking about. Three elderly looking men with long greying hair looked away towards me and smiling beckoned me to go up the stair to join the conversation. I was about to begin up the stairs when I felt a hand clasp my wrist and pulled me back away from the staircase. I was annoyed and turned to see who the person detaining me was. That's when I awoke to see Bryn holding my hand and kissing it.

"Asleep again? I thought you would at least be dressed." I looked up at him a little annoyed that I had such a wonderful dream interrupted. But I knew I had to get out of bed.

"What time is it?"

"Two pm."

"What!" I said as I jumped out of bed to check the clock. The clock read 11:45 am. I turned to Bryn with an angry expression but he just laughed.

"Got ya outta bed, didn't it?"

I felt better and went to get dressed and we headed out the door.

As the week wore on I was feeling much better, although I did keep having that dream. But there was one dream that I had a few times that really seemed strange. There was a garden by a small house, with some similar houses up the hill. A woman was picking vegetables and putting them into a basket. She seemed young and beautiful. While she walked towards the house with her basket, two small, dark haired women who both seemed to be somewhat older as their hair was greying their faces wrinkled crossed her path with children in tow. They picked up their children and walked faster away from the woman as though she were a leper. The woman came to the door of what appeared to be her house and as she approached the threshold the other two women seemed to be talking to each other and glaring at her, finally one spat on the ground. The woman with the basket seemed unperturbed and opened the door. Just then a horse came squealing towards the house with a weathered, dark haired man carrying a long staff in one hand. He quickly dismounted and the children came running towards him. He hugged them all and then went to his pouch for small presents for the children in the form of small wooden type dolls. The women circled him and seemed to be angry and pleading and pointing to the house. Just then the one woman came out of the house again and the other two women instantly fell silent. The man walked to the woman by the door and carried her into the house, closing the door behind him, leaving the other two women and the children still outside. The dream would never go any further. But it was a tantalizing glimpse into what I might be able to know if I could just touch that Talisman. Conception alone was dissolving some of the veils to my past life.

I couldn't imagine having that life. As miserable as this one had been at times, to have been the shunned, hated wife, locked up and alone with no children to comfort me and yet surrounded by my own husband's children from other wives just seemed completely insane. Why did Enoch leave Diazabael barren? If this was some kind of agreement or treaty who did he negotiate this with? Did he not take the risk that she could never come back if there were not enough of our kind, surely, then as now, having children would have ensured my return? The more questions I asked the more questions and confusion I seemed to have – it drove me crazy.

Well my birthday was coming and I was going to be 28. I was almost 8 weeks pregnant and I had no problems aside from the vivid dreams. Bryn was planning another elaborate concert and still working on his new release CD. I was considering which room to annihilate and convert into a nursery. I was becoming fairly proficient at driving the Corvette in this backwards country through narrow streets, confusing motorways, and impossible roundabouts in a desperate effort to be independent. I had become fairly conversant with the expressions, slangs, and currency in order to purchase necessary items. Occasionally I had to ask people to repeat what they said, as I found some accents to be more difficult to comprehend than others. I had spent a day shopping and planning in town and was exhausted. I got home at 4 pm and made a b-line for the bedroom to lay down.

I reflected on this mighty and noble country. Their history spoke volumes of their tenacity, determination to be global leaders. This country was a living, breathing epitaph to ultimate sacrifice for freedom and dominion. They levelled their mighty forests, extinguished almost every resource to conquer all who had previously come to this island with the intent of usurping it. By the 1800's, the sun never set on Britannia's colonies. I was aware that my thoughts had strayed in this direction due to missing the forests and mountains of British Columbia. The irony of my home country and the name of my province were not lost on me. The indelible legacy of how Canada came to be. This Britannia, this United Kingdom after almost 400 years of industrialization, mechanization, and urbanization had a powerful impact on me; I had to get out and find some forest soon. I began wondering what it would take to drag Bryn away from everything for a quick visit to Canada when I heard the locks open and Bryn sweep upstairs.

"Aileen, you home?" Bryn, being a powerful warlock, surely would know where I am at all times, so why would he even ask?

"I'm in the bedroom." He came around the hallway and walked into the bedroom to find me lying on the bed relaxing, or, more accurately, bored.

"How 'bout we go out for supper and see a flick?" That made me sit up and think.

"What new movies are playing? I haven't seen a movie in ages." My expression brightened instantly and I could tell that Bryn was relieved.

"Well, let me think there is: Immortal Beloved, a story about Beethoven; Schindler's List, about Nazi prisoners; Ace Ventura, that goofy comedian; and a German flick called Faraway, so close about two angels."

"Ace Ventura, that goofy comedian is a Canadian you know. I love Jim Carrey, can we go please?" He rolled his eyes up into the back of his head, but I knew secretly he needed a ridiculous comedy as much or more than I did.

"I get to choose the restaurant then."

"So I suppose we are eating at McDonald's?" I said sarcastically.

"Just for that I should take you to McDonalds."

"Sure, I need a good junk out."

We went to an Italian restaurant in town called La Trattoo. The food tasted pretty bad to me, but the restaurant was elegant. We then went to the movie theatre and proceeded to laugh our asses off. It was dark when we got out but I managed to convince Bryn into a small walk along the Thames River. The walkway is basically a cemented promenade high up along the embanked river Thames upon which you can get an incredible view of the buildings and lights of London.

"I admit, it's a pretty cool city. But I would give anything to be standing on the sands of the wild, west coast staring off at the endless ocean."

"Aileen, I am inclined to believe that you are a soul that is never quite content. There is always greener grass somewhere and you aim to find it. There is something of a Gypsy in you I dare say." Bryn smiled and put an arm around my shoulder.

"Not fair Bryn and you know it. How long would you be in Canada before you would miss this? I think deep down inside you love London regardless of how frustrating the crowds and the fame are."

"Oh, I don't deny it. I hope that with enough time you will love London too."

"Well, so far you are the only thing I like about England. Well, you, Stonehenge, Big Ben, Peter Gabriel, Shakespeare, and Trifle with tons of Sherry in it. But I swear that is all I like about England." Bryn laughed,

"See, when you first came here. You said you didn't like a thing – improvement already."

"Yeah, don't get cocky!" I said laughing too and jabbing him in the ribs. He immediately stiffened as if I had stabbed him and froze where he was. I was wondering why a friendly jab would illicit such a reaction when he turned to me grabbed both of my shoulders, looked me in the eyes and without opening his mouth he said into my head,

"Fuck! I have a Sentinel down. The Sages found him, they have figured out that I have Sentinels and point people everywhere." He broke off his intense stare and was looking out towards the river across to the other side, but I knew he was connecting to his huge networked web across the globe. I stood there looking instinctively in the same direction in a vain hope that I could hear something too. We stood there for about another five or ten minutes.

'The bastards actually tortured him to get what they wanted. They know who I am now and they are notifying their people here, and you're right here with me. This is really bad!'

Then out loud he continued, "This is the most critical time, we are most vulnerable now! I have to get to the Cathexisphere. The war has come to me this soon." He looked calm but his words were anything but soothing. With an apologetic expression he turned, grabbed my hand, and ran for the car. Once there, he burned all the way to the driveway of our house.

"Shit, my Talisman is at mum's!" He looked at me quite upset and screamed out of his driveway towards his mom's house. When we got there he asked me to go to the house with him. He pulled out his keys and opened his parent's front door. When inside he ran upstairs to the room with the Talisman and ran back downstairs as his mother entered the livingroom to see what the commotion was.

"Mum, I need you to do something for me and you have to promise to do it right now and as quickly as you can." His mother was in her housecoat and seemed very upset at her son's expression.

"Bryn, what on earth do you need at this hour?"

"I will never bother you again for a favour like this, but I want you to take Aileen to Stonehenge. Don't spare a moment. Take my cell phone and don't let her leave until I phone you. Can you do this for me?"

"What on earth for?"

"Can you do this for me, or do I have to call someone else this minute?"

"Calm down son, I'll do it! Come on Aileen; let's hope that Bryn is in his sane mind. I suppose I would enjoy seeing the sunrise there."

"Bryn don't do this to me, don't leave me."

"You protect your future – our future, everything depends on it! I must go now." He handed his cell phone to his mother and was out like a shot. I pleaded that Rose drive me to Bryn and my home, but she would have none of it and soon we were on the motorway heading for Wiltshire. We had driven about half way there and Bryn was in my head again,

"Diazabael, my love, Stonehenge can still afford you some protection. In the astral realm your aura is obscured by the still existent aura of the Henge. Go and pray for all of us. I have to end this tonight." I didn't think that the death of six mages would be life threatening for him, but how many did he intend? I wasn't there to heal him and I know that he did that intentionally. Either that, or knowing that people were coming to get him hoping I am with him, it only made sense to separate us. His parent's house would have been the next obvious place the mages people would go. I knew that this was serious. I knew that Bryn's strategy was a sound, logical one. But I wanted to be with him, I was terrified that whatever he had to do tonight would cost him his life. I knew Bryn would have no qualms about sacrificing himself for our child. But I was mad that I would wind up a single mother with my only protector gone. I began to have a panic attack in the passenger seat. I was panting, and rocking myself back and forth looking crazy and Rose was getting mad at my behaviour.

"For goodness sakes Aileen, get a hold of yourself. Let's just get to Stonehenge and you can tell me why you and my son are behaving so crazily. We will be their in another ten or so minutes, there is no traffic at this hour."

We drove into a parkade and I shot out of the car to get to the henge. Rose tried to rush to keep up with me. I was almost there when I heard Rose behind me,

"Okay Aileen, you are family now. What the hell is going on with my son? I want to know!" All of her falseness and jocularity she showed her son evaporated. Her eyebrows were furrowed and she looked ready to tear me apart to get to the truth. Somehow, she knew I knew something. I turned while she continued to catch up to me.

"I think Bryn may be in over his head this time. I mean, I don't think he cares about consequences."

"What do you mean?"

"Rose, if I don't get back home, Bryn will get hurt. I know this sounds crazy, but Bryn is about to do something that may cost him his life." I was so upset I didn't even really hear what Rose was saying anymore. I turned and looked at the Henge. Somehow, in that crazy panic stricken moment, I was reminded of my first trip here. Years ago Bryn told me that that dilapidated Henge was once a fully operational cathexisphere built by my ancestors. It had to still have some power if Bryn thought it would hide me. In fact, remembering what he said about my spirit, it must have a fair bit of power. The thought hit me like a wave. Why couldn't I just get to Bryn from here? I was suddenly aware of Rose standing right next to me, shaking me back to her world.

"Aileen, are you listening to me? I told you I will not let you leave this Henge until my son calls me. I gave him my word." I turned to face her visibly upset expression.

"That's okay; I think I will just go meditate. I snuck into the henge, I had no idea where the security people were, no one tried to stop me. I knelt down and began to defocus. It was almost impossible because I was so terribly upset about Bryn. Something instinctively told me to remove my ring of protection and without knowing really what I was doing; I raised my arms up above my head and began singing something that was not really words but a harmony of sounds, like singing a melody to a song I had long forgotten. I was kneeling on the cold earth and my hands slowly descended to either side of my body. I kept singing this melody and it seemed to gather intensity. I felt pulled apart, but it wasn't painful. The energy from me began to move through me and out into the sphere, an intensity of energy that I never had when I did the ceremonies in ECAW. My eyes were closed tight but I could feel the pulling getting more and more intense until finally, I ignited. The sudden blast of energy shot through my mortal body out above me in a flash. There looking down through a veil at my body on the earth, I was huge, the brightness of which was so intense I felt like as far as I could see was blinding. This was my spirit form in its complete detachment from my body. My song became words then, I don't know what the language was, but I understood what I was saying,

"Wings, take me to Bryn." The sky then seemed to open like a massive funnel, I felt my illuminated spirit shoot through the air and

I was in Bryn's backyard, on the ground looking at his mortal body. I could see his comparatively small aura intensely red, when I looked more closely I could see many small openings in the space around him and threads of red aura flowing through them. But it was his mortal body, through the veil that made my heart go numb.

Bryn's feet were not touching the ground. He was levitated; his arms were raised shoulder height and spread out. He looked like a man being crucified. No sooner had I approached the circle than I noticed something dark dripping from Bryn's feet and onto the circle. His eyes suddenly opened and they were glowing red and his pale skin was cracking and bleeding. I instantly knew then what was forming a puddle below him – blood. He was bleeding, bleeding freely. Looking at the pool beneath him it was hard to imagine he had much left in him. For the first time in my life, I knew exactly what to do.

I instantly returned to the Henge, in my spirit form, which I had no doubt Rose could see, hovering over my meditating mortal body I looked at her and spoke,

"Rose, call for an ambulance immediately; tell them they will have to forcibly enter a double locked backyard door from Bryn's basement. He has suffered heavy blood loss and internal bleeding, he is not conscious. I will go to him now and try to save him." She dropped to her knees and circumflexed herself and then reached for the cell phone Bryn had given her.

I then returned to Bryn and came in time to watch him drop to the ground. I caught him and gently layed him down on the pool of his blood. Upon touching him I sensed that he had laid waste to thousands of souls. I didn't think I could save him. He truly was unconscious and moments from death. I took him into my arms and ascended into the chasm.

Like the sound of trumpets my song seemed to ring out across the sky

"Uriel! You will not take him. Have mercy on my wretched soul and return him to me."

I could feel the warmth of Bryn's body fading; I knew that if I healed him I may loose the baby and possibly myself. I was considering the possibility of healing him till we were all near death and possibly loosing the baby and having another one. But I knew that the ancient power was instilled in this one, this child had to live. I looked down at the lifeless body of Bryn wondering how the world could be so cruel as to have me do triage to my own family, when a song so pure, so beautiful almost made me cry,

"Diazabael: Angel of sacrifice, daughter to my beloved brother Shemhazai. This is your burden; you have the power to bring him back to you, and save the Avatar. Sacrifice your mortal bond for this gift and he will live. I looked up to see my uncle, who like me, was radiant light. I knew at that moment that my father's real name for me translated to Angel of sacrifice. I looked down at Bryn so bloodied, so cold.

"I break my mortal bond to you Bryn. I sacrifice my bond to you, Edenite, and I invest you back into your mortal coil." I proclaimed to the stars and descended back to his Cathexisphere. By the edge of his sphere nearest to his backyard door, I could feel my energy draining so fast into his lifeless body that he appeared lit in the darkness by a green glow. In moments I was shocked to feel a gasp for air which made me realize that he had not been breathing. I was still a massive glow around him when the paramedics arrived. The sight of us gave them pause as there were three of them and two men immediately dropped to their knees. The other wanted to touch me. I didn't leave Bryn to them until he opened his eyes and was squinting at the intense light. He was warm, breathing, and in terrible need of blood – on this I could not service him and so I touched his lips with my hand and said goodbye, and returned to my own body. I was cold, alone, and so drained that I could barely move, Rose had deserted me. I wasn't surprised, I suppose her fear for her son and my incoherence if she would have attempted to waken me would have left her little choice. I crawled to an area where there was less wind and laid there, quite prepared to die.

Chapter 31

Rose had contacted medics for me as well. The ambulance found me and drove me to the same hospital. I opened my eyes, relieved and annoyed at being yet again in a hospital. I always end up in a fucking hospital! I remembered what Bryn told me about hospitals and I knew I had to get out of there. My first and only thought was to get back to the Queen Charlotte Islands where the baby and I would be safe. I was about to push a button for a nurse when Rose walked in.

"Aileen, what happened to you? I saw you sleeping then there was this, this angel or something that told me Bryn was dying and I was so scared I had to go back. I tried to wake you up, but nothing worked. I called emergency and was off to Bryn's."

"Where is Bryn?" She looked at me darkly for a moment.

"He is stable and sleeping." She paused. I could tell she had so many questions. I could see that there was so much she wanted to know. She probably wanted to know why I was so injured. The poor woman was a mess of emotions and confusion. But she was an English woman to the core, she knew I needed to heal and she wasn't about to trouble me with questions just yet. I loved her; she was so much like her son.

I could see that his incredible self control and inner power came from this remarkable woman.

"How much blood did I loose this time Rose?"

"I don't know. But the doctors have been asking me over and over again what happened. I told them I don't know. You and Bryn were both admitted quite late at night and fortune has it that the media is thus far unaware of this event." I moved my hand over to her and held it for a moment.

"Thanks." I said and I could see a tear forming in the corner of her eye. She was as tough as her son too.

"I think I will go over to Bryn's room and check up on him. I will come back with a full report."

"Rose?"

"Yes?"

"Don't tell anyone what you saw." Rose shook her head, turned around and I could hear her saying to herself.

"I don't know what I saw. No one would believe me anyways."

It was late that same night when a nurse came to my room and asked me if I wanted to get into a wheeler and roll over to where Bryn was as he was awake. They had called Rose at home as she had not slept since the 'accident' and was getting some much-deserved rest.

I was overly excited to go. She brought a wheelchair for me to climb into and they took me to his wing. I just about jumped out of the wheelchair at the sight of him. They had all kinds of machines hooked up to him and one was measuring his heart rate. I got right beside him and reached a hand to his and put my cheek to it. We were alive. Last night as horrible as it was, was the first time I truly understood what Bryn had said about my 'untapped' power. I knew also that my foetus had survived the ordeal. We were all alive, and that is all that mattered to me. We had cheated death – together. I moved my cheek from his hand and gently kissed it. I saw his eyes open, those big blue, grey, green eyes that possess my heart so completely.

"Bryn, baby, I was so scared! Thank the Gods you are okay. How do you feel?" I said holding his hand. He kept staring at me without saying a word. I stared back at him wondering if they had him on any painkillers that would alter his state of mind.

"Are you okay Bryn? Should I call the nurse?" I saw him shake his head, which instantly put me at ease because I at least knew he comprehended what I was saying. But then he spoke and the words cut me like no knife could,

"Do I know you?" My eyes widened, the dizzying effect of those words reverberating inside my head and heart. I sacrificed my mortal bond with him, obviously that meant the spell removed his memory of me – of course. Cold mercy. I slowly closed my eyes and refocused on him while the impact of our circumstances completely coalesced.

"Bryn, you know me like no other." He furrowed his eyebrows as if trying hard to capture any memory of me. I could see him straining. I could also see it was futile; I had been erased from his memory banks. In the ten or so minutes that followed, Rose and Bryn's father strode into the room. I could see there was instant recognition. I rolled back on my wheelchair as Rose took Bryn's hand and asked him how he was doing and that everything was going to be fine. They were going to get him out as soon as the doctors said it was ok and that he would stay with her till he was strong enough to go back to his place. I had at this point begun to cry and didn't want to make a scene on so joyous a reunion. I wheeled myself back to my room and rolled onto my bed. The Gods are cruel, I thought to myself. When you think you have beaten the odds, you discover in the end they have won after all. There are no free rides, not even in Wicca. Had I been fully aware of this I would still have done the same thing. I knew that deep down inside, but somehow it didn't make it any easier. I thought about my dreams, I thought about all the questions I still wanted to ask Bryn, knowing that I would not ever get the answers now. I saved Bryn for everyone else. But Bryn died that night for me. My Bryn was gone; the funeral was in my heart.

I remained in the hospital for three days. In spite of numerous bandages I felt better than I looked. Rose was contacted and she came to get me. She knew that Bryn had completely forgotten about what had transpired that night and who I was. She insisted that I stay at Bryn's house and that he could go to therapy to get back his memory. I knew she was wrong. While I stayed a further three days in Bryn's house while he was still in the hospital, no memory of me returned to him. I realized that I wouldn't be able to bear to be with him, living in his house and having him feel that he had to share his privacy with a stranger. Even worse, I didn't want him to endure having to deal with a baby on the way from a woman he didn't remember; there was no way I wanted to add that to his despair. I was going home, to Canada. I was never going to return to this land. I had done what I was supposed to, and now I had discovered a pain, and emptiness worse than loss. I packed all my stuff, threw photos in the garbage, and called British Airways for the next flight to Vancouver.

"Let Bryn at least see you off." Rose implored as I hung up the phone.

"Why?"

"I know this is upsetting. You should at least give him a chance! We have all been through a lot, you especially. But you owe us and him at least that much." She was showing her irritation.

"Bryn needs to get his life back together. He doesn't need pressure from everyone around him to create a life that he no longer recognizes."

"Just give him a chance!" She repeated.

"Rose. He won't come back. The Bryn I knew is gone. I could see it in his eyes. Your son has returned to you. He was all I ever knew about love, and he died in our backyard." Just hearing myself say those words made me break down in a fit of tears. I was shaking and crying. There is nothing more horrendous to the ears than a woman crying. She held me for a while till I was able to control myself again. I called the Salvation Army and told them to come to the house and pick up some stuff. I obviously could not take everything with me to Canada. I had boxed up things that Bryn would not need. I took my keychain and handed them to Rose.

"So you are just going to run back to America. Will we ever hear from you? What if his memory did come back – how could he find you?"

"Rose, if Bryn's memories did return, he would find me without any problems. Don't worry about that."

She insisted on taking me to the airport. We didn't talk much, she was obviously upset with my decision, but I was certain that part of her knew that I had made a good decision for Bryn's immediate well being.

I was on the 9pm plane to Vancouver International Airport. I was home on the Queen Charlotte Islands on April 23. As soon as I felt some of my old strength back I put on my hiking gear, grabbed my compass and walked deep into the giant, ancient forest to feel better – to heal.

I drove down a logging road and began to climb some unnamed mountain. When I was close to the summit and breathing hard from the effort I stopped to sit down and view the world from up there through the trees. I was sitting on the damp moss, leaning up against a very large Yellow cypress, looking down the slope of the mountain that I had just climbed. The awesome proportions of these ancient forests can not be understated. These Cedars and Spruce trees were at least 70 meters tall, precious little grows in the darkness of the forest floor. But the air is thick with a cool, sweet smelling dampness that mosses and mushrooms love. There exists small cracks in the gigantic overstorey canopy that allow tiny slivers of sunlight, which glow in the mist to descend down like beams of magic onto the forest floor. In those infrequent pockets the gift of life is bestowed onto those seeds fortunate enough to have settled in that small part of the forest. In that sun drenched portion of the forest all types of herbs, shrubs and smaller trees were growing reaching for the sun. It made me think what a perfect metaphor for life nature was. I was one of those seeds. I was able to grow and thrive in that divine light. I should be grateful for wonders my life has bestowed upon me rather than bitter for its short season. I had climbed mountains before to wax philosophical and to comprehend the strange metaphysical world I knew was out there.

"Dark times are coming, but Bryn has ensured the transference of our kind."

Said a voice as if sitting next to me up the mountain. The voice was masculine and vaguely familiar. I was frightened and looked around – did Bryn miss a mage?

"You left the Talisman on Bryn's backyard flagstones and thus I cannot materialize." I recognized then that it was No.

"What exactly happened that night No?" I asked out to the vacant air around me.

"In an overly protective rage Bryn eliminated 12,079 people with strong magical abilities to ensure that the six remaining mages he told you about were dead. The mages had breeched one of his Sentinels in the United States Pentagon. They had learned that he had people at various levels of government, schools and other organizations that were trained to interfere or outright destroy specific plans interfering with our purpose. Also, the mage discovered that the perpetrator was Bryn. It would have been only a matter of hours before they connected you to him and come to butcher you. That is why Bryn was always very careful about hiding you from the media."

The thought of Bryn killing so many people just didn't seem to be plausible. I couldn't believe that he was capable of that even with the Talisman.

"Why are you here, No? Bryn is in England. He needs you more than I do." I said sounding bitter.

"Bryn was dead on those flagstones when you healed him. His magic spell to destroy all mages had its effect on his magic too. You revived the man, not the mage."

"I figured that out on my own, No."

"He made me promise to pass a message on to you during those last moments. While I find it pointless, a promise is a promise."

"Well, I am all ears."

"Bryn was well aware of the exact moment when you came into the Cathexisphere. However, he was quite infused with his work and his body was already in its death throes. Forgive my frankness, but I need to tell you this in context. He realized as he was dying that you would risk the child to save him. He also knew that if you revived him, he would have none of his magic and survive as an open target to betray you. So here is what he wanted me to convey..." He paused while I gripped to what my loves final words were.

"You risked everything by coming to me. You disobeyed. I pray that you did not risk our only hope. Hide our child. I'm sorry I couldn't be there for you and our child. I have been nothing but a disappointment to you and my only hope is an eternity to make it up."

It did indeed sound like something he would say. I wasn't crying, but I could feel tears burning down my cheeks.

"Where is the Talisman now?"

"After you left, Rose began the rather gruesome job of cleaning her son's blood off the flagstones in the back of the house. She found the stone and recognized it as some long since childhood keepsake of Bryn's. She put it in her pocket and has not yet decided to give it to Bryn. He has come to his mother's house and is recuperating well while his mother and father ensure all traces of you are removed from his house. You forgot to remove some nursery room items. This, by the way, certainly raised an eyebrow for Rose."

"Can't you watch over him and protect him?"

"Yes, I could watch him. However, any sense of me now would ultimately terrify him. Secondly, I cannot effect any protection for him if he cannot create any magic to will it."

"So he is a sitting duck."

"You were the one who wouldn't let him die with dignity."

"There is dignity in indiscriminate killing?"

"I'm sorry your life has been so complicated. I hope you find new happiness in your child."

"Do you have any idea what my life will be? Knowing that a man sacrificed his life for me and my child and I cannot even thank him? Do you know what it feels like to have his last dying words to say, I can't forgive you for saving me? I will never love again. I pray I can even love this child. Tell me this: is there any hope of Bryn being happy? I mean at least he will not be eternally haunted like I."

"We don't know how Bryn's mortal mind will handle the trauma of such large channelling of magic to where he is now. Time will tell."

"No, you are one of the ancients; right?"

"yes…"

"Bryn told me that my father was Shemhazai. Who was my mother?"

"He never told you?"

"Should he have?" There was a rattling that took me awhile to remember that is what No sounded like when he laughed.

"It is not my place to tell you this. However, as I was instructed to be your messenger one last time, I will tell you this as it may give you closure. Indeed your father is Shemhazai, great was his power. But he fell quite in love with a mortal woman on earth whose beauty was quite singular. He took this woman and claimed her as his own. That woman was Jared's wife, Enoch's mother, Azilal.

"Enoch and Daizabael had the same mother?"

"Yes."

"Enoch married his sister?"

"Enoch was instructed to take care of the young Nephilim child by his mother, a task he eagerly accepted as he did love her. He married Daizabael as that was the legal contract for care and protection of any woman, much less the hated race of half-breeds. Your familial affiliation was kept secret. Thereafter, the ancients, including Shemhazai, educated Enoch in all their magic, and technology. It was during this time that Enoch developed his strategy. Daizabael and he were brother and sister, albeit only half. He pledged a vow of celibacy, not to consummate his marriage to her. However he took on other wives and he protected other Nephilim to ensure that their bloodline survived the inundation 4th gate. Enoch is not a stupid warlock. He knew his power came from his righteous path; his purity is what makes him so powerful. Because of this, he couldn't allow himself to have that which he most desired. So he went about to ensure that he could in his next transformations. By ensuring that Daizabael had no children, the only way her soul could come back into the mortal realm would be when a mortal coil with significant Nephilim characteristics was born. He knew that wouldn't happen until the end of the 5th gate. By then the other Nephilim he protected would have spread throughout the realms and reintegrated when he knew he was to return. If he could not have Daizabael, then he would make damn sure no one else did. All this power and knowledge was given to Enoch by the Ancients under the condition that he secure the 5th gate for the Ancients and their Nephilim. So you see, the terrible suffering Daizabael has endured for the sake of Enoch and the Ancients. I am not surprised he did not trouble you with it.

I didn't know what to say. There was a kind of closure for the first time in my life. Finally, something was explained to me that just put all the pieces in place.

"That fucking greedy, selfish bastard!" I heard myself whisper. Everything made sense. That first night in his cathexisphere. The way he watched me as a child. How he protected and followed me relentlessly. He never anticipated that I would learn Tyrrean Trance. He became a rock star to help me find him. He had everything planned lifetimes before he was ever Bryn. Now I had come full circle and I knew the truth.

"No? Did Daizabael love Enoch?"

"I suppose she did. He was the only Edenite, besides her mother that showed her any kindness at all. Without him, she would not have survived a day. In fact she was murdered the day after Enoch was commuted. By the way, you need to eventually send your child up to retrieve the Talisman from Rose."

"Ya. When the kid is old enough to travel without me. I'll call her."

I got up and checked my compass bearing and headed down the mountain. I wasn't any happier, but I suppose I was mentally and emotionally more stable than when I went up. Before I reached my truck I suddenly remembered my good friend Lactavia. She had completed her graduate degree in clinical psychology and counselling. I might be able to get her to give me some grief counselling, of course, she would not know why.

Chapter 32

My daughter, Kasha, was a month away from her tenth birthday. In ten years I had my daughter and she was a joy in my life I never thought that I would have. She was a dead ringer for her father, complete with the extraordinary eyes, but she had her mother's blonde hair. When my daughter was five, I was persuaded to live common-law with a very wonderful and sweet man to whom my entire past was unknown. He was great with Kasha and very helpful for me. I suppose in some ways I had come to love him over the last five years. He wasn't happy about Kasha and me travelling to Europe, but Kasha wanted to see whom her real father was. Kasha and I never told anyone whom her father really was, I just told people with the amount of fun I had in Europe, I had no idea who the father was nor did I care. I explained to my man that we were going to be traveling and touring the buildings of London. David, having a real love of the wilderness and no interest in crowded cities, had no desire to join us. This was going to be a painful trip for me, but I needed to know that Bryn was okay, and Kasha needed her Talisman. We had planned to go to his concert and had even purchased concert tickets over the Internet. I planned to have my daughter get his autograph and leave. I also planned to contact Rose at some clandestine time when my daughter was preoccupied and inquire as to the Talisman. The concert was at a place called Brixton Academy.

"Kasha, do you have your CD?" I asked while we were locating our seats.

"Yeah mom."

"Well, I hope you like this concert. He puts on great shows even if the music doesn't remind you of rap."

"Mom, I don't just like rap. I like some of Bryn's music."

"I wish you wouldn't go into my stuff."

"I think you are psycho to hide stuff from dad, but why hide it from me? I mean what's the big deal, my real dad is some old rocker from the UK—so what?"

"When you are older, I will explain more to you. Meanwhile, I am keeping my promise aren't I? Soon you will get to see your real dad in concert, get his autograph and then we can have fun right?"

"Mom? Why didn't you tell him that he was a dad?"

"Kasha, not now. You have a dad isn't that enough?"

"Whatever..." She snapped her tongue in anger and turned to focus on the stage. The past two to three years she had been increasingly interested in her biological father and I just didn't know what to do. Because I was so bereaved for the first three years, Kasha had every realization that she was fatherless. I tolerated a minor amount of dating to bring male influence into the house for Kasha's sake and I suppose that is how I met Dave. He was so great with Kasha and never wanted to know about my past and that made tolerating him very easy. Now five years later, I had come close to what I could call a normal life. Kasha's interest in her roots scared me. I knew the moment Bryn appeared on the stage, a knife would stab me in the heart and emotions, long suppressed, memories long buried would flood to the surface and I would have to reach for the flask in my purse, loaded with whiskey, to dull the pain.

The music began, the lights went dim and like waiting for a cougar to pounce I waited for the spotlight to find him.

The concert lasted two hours. The special effects were quite excellent and the acoustics were very good. My flask was empty. My daughter shook my shoulder to wake me from my lost thoughts and indicated that she wanted that autograph before the musician left the building.

I found myself having to walk rather briskly to keep up with Kasha as she carved her way through the people heading for the stage looking for a way to gain access to the backstage. She spoke to two men, who looked like stage maintenance people. She pointed back to me, I felt like I was the sixty year old granny following a teen. The men pointed Kasha towards a back door. Kasha got to the door and waved at me frantically as if in a heated rush. As soon as I was ten feet away she opened the door and disappeared. I followed her down a hall and arrived in an open room loaded with all kinds of equipment and a few band people. She walked up to one of them and asked for Bryn. The one man smiled at her and nodded his head. As I walked up to my daughter I heard the man say very clearly,

"Hey Rose, where is Bryn. We have a young fan from Canada looking for his autograph." I froze as I saw Rose come out of a room to look at Kasha and then look up at me.

"Dear God, Aileen is that you?" She said the color fading from her face.

"My daughter just wants an autograph, that's all." I said. She looked back at Kasha and I could tell she was doing some mental mathematics and admiring Kasha's looks.

"Hello sweety, I'm Bryn's mum. How old are you?"

"I turn 10 next month." Kasha said grabbing her CD out of her purse and showing it to Rose. Rose looked up at me again.

"You never left an address for me Aileen. I'll get him." She said, but I saw Bryn right behind her. He seemed to survey his mother and the little girl and seemed to not notice me.

"What's your name?"

"Kasha sir, I came all the way from Canada to see you in concert – it was wicked." She handed him the CD and he smiled at her.

"What do you want me to write?"

"To Kasha my favourite fan, love Bryn of course." She laughed. Rose walked towards me and got up close.

"Just tell me this Aileen. Is that Bryn's little girl? I saw the baby stuff in his house when you left."

I nodded. I watched the expression on her face turn from disbelief to shock to joy as she turned to Kasha and then back to me.

"I brought baby photos." I said. Smiling to her, I knew this was a bomb being dropped on her and I was glad to see that it was a joyous one.

"Can you come round my house tomorrow around tea time? Bryn will be off boating." At this point Bryn had noticed his mother talking to me.

"Mum, you know these people." He said looking at me. His mother just nodded.

"I know everyone Bryn, you know that." He walked over to me and held out his hand and I was absolutely terrified to shake it. I hadn't expected this but because of the magical experience in the past of our touch, I don't know, I was just terrified to feel it again, or even worse to not feel it. I hesitated till it seemed very uncomfortable to everyone and then finally took his hand into mine and shook it.

"You are?" He asked.

"Aileen."

"Welcome to England, Aileen." He said still holding my hand. He then let go and I realized that my fear caused me not to notice whether I sensed anything at all.

"Thanks. And thanks for not throwing the security guards on my bratty daughter."

"I think its great that there is a new generation enjoying my music. As for security, I will have to have a talk with them." He said with a grin. I returned the smile and then put my attention onto my daughter.

"Well Kasha, I think we should go. You have your autograph, and that was our deal." I gave her my best threatening look and she shrugged and indicated that she would willingly leave without incident. As Rose took my arm and led me out of the back doors she reminded me to not forget about tomorrow at 4 pm. I assured her, I would be there.

We left and made it to our hotel and I told Kasha we were going to go to John's and Rose's house and visit for awhile, she seemed excited at the idea of meeting her real grandparents, I was not so comfortable. I was devastated when I left ten years ago and I wanted to protect Bryn as well as my daughter. Had I continued to come around, anyone who knew Bryn was the perpetrator would immediately recognize my daughter and if I had been stupid and continued to show up in London, looking for him and his kin. I had to keep completely out of his life. It was just as No said, Bryn was a sitting duck. Rose didn't know all this and probably thought I was a coward for abandoning her entire family after that most bizarre night. It was still probably a stupid idea, I was thinking that this may not have been the best idea…but Kasha was getting really impatient – what I wouldn't do for my daughter.

The following day, I dutifully arrived at Rose's house. I still remembered how to get there. The door opened and Rose looked at Kasha smiling. Kasha had a bouquet of flowers that she handed to Rose.

"Wow, thanks Kasha, they are beautiful. Come in, come in." She shuffled us into the familiar house and we sat in the livingroom while she went off to get the tea. When she came back she looked at me pointing into my bag.

"I hope you brought lots of photos." I was relieved that she was not in a mood to interrogate me in front of my daughter. I pulled out the photos and she motioned that I could help myself to tea while she poured over the photos. She rifled through about the first pile then smiled at one in particular. She put the rest down and looked up to me.

"You have got to see this." She then went to her wall unit that had photo albums on the bottom and opened up an old one to expose a yellowed page with a picture of a baby sitting on the floor, holding a bottle and smiling at the camera. She laid it open on the coffee table and put the picture of Kasha next to it. My picture of Kasha showed her in the exact same position with the same smile looking at the camera. She then grabbed the rest of the photos and rifled through the rest of them smiling to herself quietly. Kasha was looking at the yellowed picture.

"Is that Bryn?" She said looking up at me.

"No. That is your father, Bryn." Rose said looking up from the photos.

"Rose, why doesn't my dad know about me?" Kasha asked very plainly and I could feel a lump in my stomach as I assumed she was about to launch into a, 'it's all your mother's fault' story.

"First of all dear, you can call me Nan. Secondly, your father had a very bad accident when you were still in your mum's tum. He lost a lot of his memory. The following two or so years he was plagued with headaches, nightmares, and other medical problems. Your mother didn't want to further burden him and so she chose to go back to Canada. I really wanted her to stay; we could have worked it all out. But it doesn't matter, you are here now and finally I know that I am a grandmother."

"So I have no brothers or sisters?" Kasha persisted.

"No dear, I wish you did. Bryn married three years ago to a wonderful woman. She left him because he could not give her the children she so desperately wanted. Your dad is forty-eight now and I think any hope for children is gone. That is why you are such a blessing. Papa will be home in the next half hour and I told him about you last night and he is very excited to see you." I sipped at my tea, relieved that everything was going as well as it was. I watched as Kasha asked her all kinds of questions about her dad. Soon Kasha was sitting on the floor next to Rose looking at magazine articles, photos, and paraphernalia that belonged to Bryn.

The front door opened and I braced myself for John, who I knew was going to be far less forgiving for my sudden departure ten years ago. My back was to the entryway but the sudden loss of colour on Rose's face was a clear indication that she was not in fact staring at her husband, which meant only one thing. Bryn walked in wordlessly, surprised by his mother's expression. He then walked over to the coffee table and looked at the photo album that was still open and still had the two photos side by side. He stared at them for a while, we all sat in silence, and then he looked at Kasha and up to his mother.

"Christine didn't want to go boating today so I was going to ask you if you wanted to come." Bryn said looking at his mother with a raised eyebrow; just then John entered the house right behind his son.

"Bryn what are doing here?" John said equally surprised by his presence. Bryn paused to look at his father standing at the entryway. He then grabbed the other photos of Kasha on the table. He looked at them successively and then periodically looked directly at me. I began to turn red certain I was blushing. The silence in the room was as clear an indication as any that Bryn had stumbled onto something. He put the photos on the coffee table again and turned to Kasha.

"I forgot your name, what is it?" Bryn asked looking at Kasha who was looking at Rose for an indication of what to do or say.

"K-Kasha."

"Oh, yeah right. Kasha, would you like to go for a boat ride? We would only be gone for two hours or so." Bryn looked at me for approval, Kasha looked at Rose. I stared at John hoping that this mess wouldn't get me deeper into his bad books. We all sat there staring at each other awkwardly for what seemed too many minutes.

"John, why don't you join Kasha and Bryn on the boat ride? Then Aileen and I can catch up. Is that okay with you Aileen?" Rose said very calmly and smoothly.

"I don't see why not. Would you like that Kash?" I asked trying to sound as calm as Rose.

"Boy, would I!" She gave Rose a hug and jumped up. She ran over to Bryn and put her hand into his.

"Lead the way Captain." She said and we all erupted into nervous laughter, including Bryn. John grabbed a few things and they were out the door in ten minutes.

"You don't think he clued in do you?" I asked Rose looking at her after everyone filed out the door.

"What? Bryn? About you not telling him he is a father, even now? No, I suppose he will think you strange Americans enjoy coming to an old woman's house to compare your seven year old photos with forty year old ones. Of course he suspects."

"Ahhh…Yeah. Why send off John to join them? Bryn lost his memory, I still trust him. Besides, maybe it would be better if they were alone."

"Well, Aileen you haven't been around to know what's been going on."

"What do you mean?"

"For the last few years he has been fine but after you left for about three solid years, Bryn was heavily medicated to control his nightmares and hallucinations."

"What kind of nightmares?"

"It was pretty awful. He was terrified of everything for about three years. He was in and out of hospitals and saw shrinks. I thought his life was going to be like this forever. But slowly he began to get control and his mind settled and he began to behave more normally. I can't remember exactly when, but it was sometime about four years ago he began to ask me questions. He was having deja vous and remembering fragments of moments. He would ask me questions and I would just play dumb. I even found a magazine picture of a model that looked at great deal like you stuffed into his musical paperwork. I don't actually know what he remembers. He married a very nice lady, Christine, in the fall three years ago, and she has just recently left him mostly because of his inability to have a child with her. But also because for the last three years with him he has become increasingly emotionally unavailable to her and she felt her life with him was empty. It has been a real roller coaster for all of us, I can tell you."

"Rose, when isn't Bryn a roller coaster?" We both laughed bitterly.

"Look Rose, I know I should have done something to tell you about Kasha. I suppose I was healing in my own way too. I could never seem to find the right time or reason to call or write and tell you. But I would be lying if I told you that the biggest reason was I just couldn't handle seeing him again. I had heard Bryn got married. I put this off until my daughter began driving me nuts about meeting her dad. I hope you can forgive me."

"Aileen, please tell me what was going on that night. You were fine, then you were unconscious, then when you came to the hospital you looked almost as bad as Bryn." I paused and looked at her. I wasn't supposed to tell her a damn thing, but I just couldn't sit in her house knowing what she had been through and just walk away with no explanation.

"Rose if I told you, you wouldn't believe me."

"I am prepared to believe anything after what I saw. Aileen, I saw an angel, and it talked to me." She had raised her voice and was upset which she caught and filled her cup with more tea.

"Rose, basically this is what happened. Your son wasn't just a musician, he had some powerful skills in magic. He also had many tasks he had to complete. That last one almost cost him his life. He knew I was carrying his child and he also knew that there were other forces out there that wanted his child dead. Bryn saved his daughter's and my life that night." Well that won me an exaggerated look of disbelief.

"I told you, you wouldn't believe me."

"I remember all the strange things about him when he was a child growing up. I thought a great many things. I thought my boy was psychic, I thought he was a little crazy, but I never even guessed something like this." Rose sat there rather deep in thought obviously rummaging through forty plus years of history of her son to see if there was any possible way she could dispute my allegation. I put down my tea cup and picked up her photo album of him again and flipped through the pages.

"Aileen."

"Yeah?"

"There was one thing that Bryn said to me after you left that I think you should know." I looked up from the photo album.

"What?"

"He said, 'Mum? I know I did something really bad years ago, I just don't know what. The part that really eats me is why?' He then went on to tell me that two men came to his house claiming to be with MI 5 and questioned him on why a man found dead in the Pentagon would write down his name just moments before he died."

"Damn! When did that happen?"

"That must have been about seven or eight years ago now."

"Has he told you about any other people approaching him for information?"

"No."

"Thank Heavens!"

"What? What is it?" She asked obviously reacting to my sudden flush of fear.

"Rose, that I am going to my grave with. "

"Well, obviously Bryn did do something bad and he can't remember what."

"He did what he had to, Rose, that is all you and he need ever know."

Rose put down her teacup and looked at me like she wanted me to follow her upstairs. I followed; she was heading to the room Bryn had protected for his Talisman. We walked in and she went to the top of the dresser and opened the jewellery box inside was a leather pouch which she pulled out and handed to me.

"I want you to have these. They meant a lot to the Bryn you knew. He clung to these it had huge significance to him." I looked at her curiously and opened the pouch. Inside were my gold and emerald ring of protection and Bryn's Talisman. I paused for a moment contemplating whether or not to touch it. I could still hear my old Bryn in my head, 'Diazabael, don't even think about it.' I closed the pouch grinning to myself. I suppose I have caused enough trouble for one lifetime.

"I would like to take this frigging thing and throw it into the ocean! But Bryn would want Kasha to have it." Then I looked at the ring,

"So Rose, why didn't you give this beautiful ring to Christine?" She smiled and shook her head.

"Because Bryn never lit up around her the way he did when he was with you. From the time I saw you in Los Angeles with him, I had never seen him so on fire. Christine was right; he was emotionally unavailable to her. I think he loves her, but that fire was never there. He was never as happy. I don't know whether to love you for being in my son's life, or to hate you, Aileen."

"I could never have predicted all this Rose."

"You brought me a granddaughter. I suppose I can forgive you." I took the ring and the Talisman and brought it downstairs to put in my purse. I didn't know when I would give the Talisman to Kasha. Bryn had his when he was five. I saw what it did to his life and I wasn't too anxious to hand it over to my daughter, whatever her destiny may be.

It was around seven pm when Kasha returned with the guys from boating. I was starving and although Rose and John insisted that I stay for dinner and stay at their house I politely declined and we were back at our hotel room. Kasha was aglow with all of the day's events with her dad. She told me how he could drive boats, flies planes and had a really fast car. I knew all this and I suppose it warmed my heart to know that some things about Bryn were exactly the same.

"You know what my dad said to me on the boat?"

"I have no idea."

"He said you were the prettiest woman he has ever laid eyes on. Pretty wild eh?"

"I am sure he says that to every woman he meets." I said but I knew I was blushing.

"Mom, after I graduate from high school can I come back to England and live with Bryn till I get my degree?"

"No. Why the hell would you want to do that?"

"Bryn offered. He knows I'm his daughter you know; I didn't have to tell him a thing. He even apologized for not having any memory of you. He said he wished he remembered." I was thinking how lucky I was that he didn't remember, considering what No told me were Bryn's last words for me.

"Tell you what, why don't we discuss this when you are sixteen."

"Well, Bryn wants me to spend my summers here from now on."

"He what!?"

"Mom, he hasn't seen me for almost ten years. He has a right! I want to see my dad too." She ran to the corner of the room and began to cry. I, of course, felt like a selfish bitch but what was I going to do? What started as a simple 'see him and get an autograph' had blown up in my face into a visitation dispute. It's not that I wasn't sympathetic to Bryn's and Kasha's needs, it was that I was afraid that if it became known that Bryn had a child and if the wrong people knew who Bryn was, my daughter would be in danger. I consoled my daughter and told her that we could discuss this more another time and that I wouldn't deny her access to her real father, but we may have to modify the schedule she requested.

The next morning the phone rang; I rushed out of the shower and ran to the phone. Kasha already grabbed the phone and was talking warmly to whomever it was. She then smiled and said,

"It's for you, mom."

"Hello?"

"We need to talk." The hairs on the back of my neck were standing up and goosebumps were forming all over my body.

"Where are you, Bryn?"

"In your lobby." Now my heart was racing, I was going to pass out. I wasn't saying anything except breathing hard,

"Why don't you come downstairs, we'll all go for breakfast and then I can take Kasha to mum's and we can go someplace to talk briefly."

"Bryn, I never meant to… I just wanted…"

"Please Aileen, don't do this to me, don't take her away from me – For God's sake!" I could feel those old feelings again. My heart, what was left of it, could never refuse Bryn a damn thing, even the new Bryn.

"We'll be right down." I hung up and dried my wet body. We met him in the lobby, he smiled nervously as did I but his cologne…sweet angel of mercy, that cologne, opened the floodgates of my memory, sending me miles away to his house, to the genesis of my life, to moments of passion that I had long buried.

We had a very polite breakfast. Most of the time was spent with Kasha's endless questions about Bryn's music and life in England. Bryn was very interested in talking to her and telling her great stories of concerts in far away countries and risky adventures in places like India. Every now and again he would look at me, smile nervously and resume talking to Kasha. I had nothing to say. I was afraid of what I would say. I was even more afraid of what he would say once he got me alone. I was distracted the entire meal.

Soon Kasha was in the big arms of John as we pulled out of the driveway. Rose winked at me as we left. We drove to a nearby park and went for a walk. It was a cloudy day, raining off and on, but neither of us cared. We walked silently for the longest time. He wanted to ask me something but it was obvious he didn't know where to start.

"Pardon my crudeness, but we weren't just a one night fling were we?" He finally said.

"No, Bryn, we were certainly not that."

"Why then do I have such clear memories of everything in my life except you?"

"Because when the 'accident' happened, that is what you wanted."

"What do you mean, 'I wanted?"

"You wanted to forget me."

"Will you tell me what happened?"

"You wouldn't have wanted me to – for Kasha's safety."

"You are even more cryptic than my mother. This is enough to drive anyone crazy you know."

"I'm sorry. I had no intention of troubling you at all; I never expected to run into your mother at the concert."

"How much does my mother actually know?"

"Enough to recognize me, to remember us."

"She likes you, I can tell." He stopped and looked me in the eyes and for a moment I thought I saw a flicker of the old Bryn.

"I need to know something and I want an honest answer. Did I hurt you in any way?" I could tell that he was having a hard time even getting the words out. His eyebrows were furrowed and the expression of anticipated grief reminded me of my Old General.

"Bryn, please believe me when I tell you that you never hurt me. You have no idea to what lengths you would go to to protect your daughter and I."

"Then why did you stay away so long? How could you keep a child from me? You and my mum were going to keep Kasha from me forever, had I not walked in on you two. Why?"

"Bryn, you will never understand this, but you had your reasons at the time. You wanted me to keep our daughter away. I was doing what you asked."

"Was I crazier then, than I am now?"

"Not at all."

"What possible reason could I have had?"

"Bryn. You knew that Kasha's life was at risk if certain people knew she lived."

"Now that sounds crazy! But even so, I am not going to stand around idly while you and my mother decide whether I am allowed to be a father. Tell me this: my mother ransacked my house after the accident and she tried to remove all traces of you, I think. You lived with me?"

"For a time."

"Was I good to you? Did you feel loved at least? Was I emotionally unavailable?" I instantly recognized the use of those words. He wanted insights into who he was before the accident, really he wanted to know who he was even now.

"Do you remember seeing me in the hospital when you regained consciousness?" I inquired and saw him cast his head heavenward as if in deep thought,

"Honestly, no."

"Bryn, we were deeply in love. I think my memories serve as a greater distraction in my life than your amnesia, be assured of that." We walked a little quietly; no doubt he was digesting his revelations thus far.

"I am not so sure. I have these emotional and physical memories, but they are completely disjointed and don't belong anywhere. They are as intense as anyone could feel. The memories may be gone, but my emotions are like ghosts that haunt me. I see you and the emotions want to claim ownership to you. All I can think is, who are you?" I stopped walking; I stared at him, into his eyes like I did long ago. He stared back into mine. I put my hands on either side of his face, my eyes not wavering from his, and descended for a kiss. I was hoping for that old magic, that kiss that flooded everything and my heart felt like it would explode. Maybe even hoping that like sleeping beauty, my kiss would awaken our long life together. It was the same kiss but the magic wasn't there. This was the mortal Bryn, he wasn't a mind filled with the lives of Enoch the prophet, Elijah the Tishbite or John the Baptist. The veil had descended upon his memories and the 'Old General' I knew and loved was gone. I slowly pulled my face away from his.

"I'm sorry." I said.

"Don't be." I could feel my heart aching again, feeling the loss of him all over again. Tears just begging to well up in my eyes and I fought to stop them. I took in a deep breath and indicated that I want to keep walking.

"When will you let me see her again?" He said obviously noticing that I was on the verge of tears.

"If you stay here in England, where you are known and watched, it is more dangerous for your daughter. You sacrificed everything to protect her; I can't let you just flagrantly display her to the world now. If you came to Canada the media would not hound you and I think it would be much safer. The other problem is the emotional toll on me. I don't know how I would endure knowing you are right across town. I would never survive it – I can't believe I am telling you this!" I was shaking my head; this was getting out of hand. Just the thought of Bryn in my life again, this ghost of Bryn rattling at my cage that I had created to protect Kasha and me was being threatened again and I welcomed and cursed it simultaneously.

"Why can't we start over?" He said quietly, I almost thought I heard him wrong. The sound of those words sparked a feeling within me that was similar to drowning.

"I don't think my heart could take it. We have been through more than you could ever believe. You have been everything in my life since I was five. For the longest time I wished we both died on those flagstones together. The only thing that saved me was our daughter. She resurrected my life. If you had a house anywhere near me, I would run back to you in a heartbeat. I would break Dave's heart and he deserves better than that." I was shaking, panicking; I wasn't prepared for this at all. I could feel myself becoming unable to breathe.

"Stop it! Just stop it!" He stood in front of me, cutting me off from walking any further. He peered down at me with those steely eyes.

"Look Aileen. I am not asking you to radically change your life. I am asking to be a part of my daughter's. If you need to keep me as far away from you as possible, fine. I need my daughter as much or more than you do. I can buy a place somewhere in B.C. nowhere near you. Kasha and I can spend our time there. I could also bring her here on the odd occasion would that be covert enough for you –can't you tell me that I was at least in love with a reasonable woman?" He was clearly frustrated. I read the anger but I could see the control in his tone and his forceful yet non-threatening posture in front of me. It had been a long time since I had seen his beautiful angular features, his furrowed eyebrows, there was so much of the old Bryn in him still it was exciting. I just stood there looking at him, wanting him. I just stared at him, smouldering. Every part of me was ignited because in this moment he was so much like the Bryn I knew. He stared back at me.

He sharply levelled his head at me as if to indicate that he wanted to hear me say, 'You win.' But I was lost in those eyes. I don't know how long I stared at him smouldering, locking my body from doing what it was screaming at me to do.

"Why did you have to be so fucking beautiful?" He said, grabbing me roughly for another kiss. Well that did it. I lost every modicum of control completely. I grabbed him back and my hands worked their way down, I wanted him and I didn't give a shit about anything else, like the fact that we were in a public place, he was still technically married, I was common-law. So there in the park we were making out. People walked by and any idiot paparazzi photographer could have come along and snapped photos of Bryn making out with someone who was clearly not his wife. I was staring into his eyes lost like I had been when I was a young girl. His magic was gone, but his skill with me hadn't diminished.

"Would we always watch each other like this?" He said giving me a quick kiss.

"Intense and Tantric, you demanded nothing less."

"I've never felt an urge so overwhelming. I want to take you back to my place." I should have said no, but I couldn't.

"Let's go." We got back to his car and sped our way to his place and continued as if we hadn't broken off from the moment in the park.

"So where in BC were you thinking of buying?" I asked as I wandered around picking up my clothes off the floor.

"I don't know, I will go there for a visit and Kasha and I will choose someplace together."

I refused to assess the emotional damage this event in a familiar house was going to cost me. A great deal of his skill with me hadn't diminished. We cleaned up and headed back to his parents. Before we got out of the car he stopped me from opening the car door. The car had the familiar smells of leather and his cologne.

"What if I told you that I want to see you again?"

"Bryn. We met when I was fourteen years old. I grew up before your very eyes, I became the woman you wanted me to be. In all those years, life was never kind to us. Fate stood in the way of our happiness. The final blow was loosing you in the back of your house. I had grief counselling and raised a child alone. Part of you is indeed my one and only love, and part of you is a total stranger. Dave has given me five consecutive years of constant, steady partnership for my sanity and Kasha's I am inclined to jealously guard it."

"Well, Aileen, know this: Whether you regard this as a moment of weakness or recklessness is immaterial to me I've had a taste of us, expect to see me soliciting for more whenever our paths cross in the future." He said in an ominous way again, so much like the old him it gave me shivers. I knew that if I looked at him I would be reaching for his lips again, I opened the car door and without looking back I marched up to the front door. That man was pure poison, infecting my heart to its very core. I had to get the hell out of England before he cowed me into anything else.

"How did it go?" Rose whispered into my ear as I walked by her.

"Far too good, Rose." I said with frustration. She laughed and waved to her son, who didn't bother to get out of the car and instead drove away.

I bid Rose and John farewell as Kasha and I had some sightseeing to do.

"So did you and Dad discuss when I could see him next?"

"Yes, you will both be looking for a place in BC to buy that he and you can stay at and visit. I think it would be a great escape for you two on summers or maybe even Christmas."

"Thanks, mom! How did he convince you?"

"Your father has always been a very hard negotiator."

"There is a great place for sale just in Tlell, which is only twenty minutes from home."

"Kasha, why not choose a place off the island?"

"Why?"

"Well, how about Dave? It would break his heart to see you so excited about a father that hasn't been in your life for so long. Besides, I still don't want him to know exactly who Bryn is."

"What's the matter mom? Afraid to have Bryn so close?"

"Don't you dare talk to me like that young lady!" I snapped at her.

"I remember seeing you when I was growing up; opening up that box you keep under the bed. You would put on the music, read the letters, and look at pictures and cry for hours when you thought I was asleep or playing outside. I know how much he meant to you. I told him about the box. He was moved beyond words."

"You did what?"

"He was asking me questions about you. He wanted to know when I first found out about him."

"Kasha! That is my private business; you should never have told him that. Not only is it embarrassing, but it would make him feel even worse for not remembering me."

"He told me that the one memory he has always had since the accident was an overwhelming sense that someone who loved him deeply was missing. You see, in a way, he has never forgotten you -- It's really quite romantic."

"If we don't change the subject right this minute, I am taking you home on the next flight!"

"Ok, ok. Are we going to Stonehenge?"

"Right now, yes."

So our two-week holiday quickly ended. Kasha saw Bryn about every other day and usually spent the whole day with him. I decided I would be better off romping around England alone and not get in Kasha's way of getting acquainted with her father. On the day of our flight Kasha spent the night at Bryn's and he offered to pick me up at the hotel and drive us both to the airport. Because I am an idiot, I agreed. When I got to the Lobby I could see that Bryn was using his dad's vehicle; good thing, as he never seemed to own a car that afforded any trunk space.

Kasha was wearing brand new clothes and carrying about two or three electronic gizmo's that I knew Bryn must have been suckered into buying her. I looked at my punk of a kid, raised an eyebrow and then shot an accusatory gaze at Bryn.

"Great, now you're going to spoil her to bratdom!" Bryn's eyes opened widely in an innocent expression of 'who me?"

"Gotta make up for a 10 year absence, besides I will miss her birthday next month."

"Well, we better go, with all the airport security these days they need two hours to pump us through." I thought about how much the world had changed in the last ten years. I thought about how crazy it was to be standing next to a man who had so much to do with the changes that were happening around me, and yet he knew nothing about it. He had set up Sentinels, people in all parts of the world that were destined to do things that ultimately sabotaged any hope for this radical Zionistic sect of changing the destiny of the first peoples – my people. I looked at Kasha and Bryn as they walked in front of me towards the van.

Bryn had killed over twelve thousand people and had no memory of it. How many people would his Sentinels kill? How many people with real magical powers did he leave on the earth before he fell to those bloodied flagstones? Then a long forgotten thought popped into my head –Kat. Wait a minute, Kat? Was Kat alive? When she walked out of my life because of Bryn, I just wrote her off. I had no idea if she were alive or dead. I had to go back home and find out. Besides Bryn and I, Kat was the only other human I knew of that was alive and knew what Bryn could do – she was the only one that knew he had the Talisman. If she was alive, she was a huge risk to Bryn, Kasha, and to the world.

"Did you forget something?" Bryn said looking at my face as I sat in the front passenger seat. I looked up at him. I wished I could have just asked him. I wish he had the memories, to just tell me yes or no. Wouldn't it be great if he just let Kat live and wiped her memory too? I didn't think that Bryn would have had time to think about Kat though. He might have killed her –I was betting on it.

"I was just thinking about a friend of mine from back home. I was wondering how she was doing."

"Why is she sick?"

"Right now, I am hoping she is dead." I said absently, thinking about all the shit she pulled trying to get to Bryn's Talisman. Forgetting completely what I must have sounded like.

"Was she really a friend?" He said giving a dirty look before cranking over the engine. I just looked at him.

"She had an annoying habit of sticking her nose far too deeply into your business."

"Someone else I should know that I don't?"

"Her name was Kat. Ring any bells?"

"No. I prefer dogs."

"I am not surprised."

"Hey mom, what's this bag in your purse?" Kasha said, interrupting me from my interrogation of Bryn.

"Hey, wow! What a groovy ring. Where did you get it from?" I snapped my head to the back of the Van to see Kasha trying on my ring that Bryn gave me a lifetime ago.

"Mom, you have gotta try this ring on. It feels funny."

"Kasha put that ring back into my purse, right this instant." She just looked at me and then pulled out the Talisman.

"Hey, what the…" As soon as her hand touched the Talisman I could see her eyes were looking at me but they weren't seeing me, they were far off looking at something else.

"Bryn take that rock out of her hand this instant!" He looked at me and then looked into the rear-view mirror.

"Kasha, give your mother the ring and rock. Let's have a pleasant ride." Kasha reluctantly opened her hand and pushed the Talisman towards me.

"No! Just put it in my purse or give it to Bryn."

"Mom, why was it talking to me?"

"This is neither the time nor the place." I said to her motioning my head towards Bryn.

"Well, its mine. I know, it told me so. It used to belong to dad." She said also shaking her head towards Bryn. Bryn reached back and took the Talisman from Kasha.

"Let me see." Bryn asked. I was growing very nervous because I frankly didn't want either of them to have it. I wanted to throw it into the sea.

He looked at it, rolled it around in one hand and then looked at me.

"So why can't she have it? If it's mine and she wants it, let her have it." He said smiling. I exhaled loudly I was so relieved. I thought that somehow the Talisman would talk to him again, that somehow his magic would come back, but to him it was now just a stone.

"Kasha, you can have it another time. This is not the time."

"Promise?"

"I promise."

Back home. Back to Kasha's classes, homework, dance lessons, my vegetable garden, and back to Dave. Good old stable Dave, predictable Dave. No chaos. I tried to think of the last two weeks as an erotic dream. I didn't see Bryn, he didn't see me; no, Bryn was dead right? Yes, of course, Bryn was gone. This new Bryn was something else, a dream, a fantasy. I pushed the memory of us in the park and then at his place out of my mind. Well, I tried to. I was back to avoiding intimacy with Dave. God I hated myself. I just didn't want to destroy another good man over my pathetic inability to move on emotionally from what was after all really, a dead man – a memory, a ghost. But really wasn't that what Bryn always was, a ghost. Haunt my life; disappear only to return to haunt me again. I had to focus on something else. I had the perfect idea, locate where Kat was today.

The obvious solution was to locate her parents and ask them where Kat was. That was my first stumbling block. I hadn't seen them since high school and now twenty years later they were both dead. The only other option was to locate her via phone books or the Internet. Both options were not helpful she had no webpage and either had her number unlisted or didn't own a phone. I was strongly considering checking the obituaries for the event horizon when Bryn did his deed over ten years ago. I remembered Agaratte. Agaratte had a creepy ability to know where people were, if Agaratte was still alive maybe he would know. I had kept loosely in touch with everyone else besides Kat. I had an old phone number of his but I knew that he had moved to the United States and was probably flogging his skills in computer programming somewhere over there. There was only one way to find him, the Internet. I easily found him; no way would Agaratte forgo his own personal web page. I emailed him and gave him my phone number. He was quick to reply.

"Aileen, would love to talk with you. I am going to Penticton for a visit in two weeks, meet me there – we will talk."

Lance.

Aka, Agaratte.

I could tell by the brevity of the email he was in no mood to discuss Kat over the Internet. I told Dave that for Kasha's birthday we were going to visit grandmom and Auntie Natalia in Vancouver and go shopping. I dropped Kasha off with Lactavia, good old auntie Nat to Kasha, and headed for the Okanagan. I knew where I was going to meet Agaratte; he was going to be in Naramata, hanging out by the Lake and sure enough, he was.

He was still the flaming redhead, that hadn't changed. His sharp blue eyes squinted in the daylight and he waved to me calmly to join him on the picnic table. His hair was longer, just passed his shoulders, he was wearing a black suit and he was heavier than when I last saw him. He had a vermilion goatee that looked rather startling next to his luminous white skin. His looks still garnered attention, that's for sure – I thought for one crushing moment how much he and Bryn had in common, the bizarre color contrast. In Agaratte was even more dramatic.

"How was your trip here?" He asked without first saying hello or 'long time no see.'

"Tiring, to tell you the truth. But I am hopeful that you can help me locate Kat, I need to know if she is okay."

"Follow me." He got up and we walked away from the Lake towards the town of Naramata. There was a black Nissan 200zx parked by the road that Agaratte was heading towards.

"Where are we going?"

"You'll see, I think you will be surprised." I got into his car and we drove down the highway towards Penticton. Eventually we drove exactly where I didn't want him to be heading. He parked right inside the cemetery parking lot.

"Are we here for what I think we are here for?"

"I am afraid so."

"Take me to her." We walked towards the headstone and sure enough, it said

Jennifer Smith- Mathews

1967-1997

Beloved wife

May you light up heaven as you have my heart.

I don't know why I was surprised. Bryn knew she knew everything. Bryn knew she was a danger. But for some reason I just couldn't forgive him for killing her. I knelt down by the headstone and touched it.

"I am so sorry Kat. It is all my fault – it's all my fault."

"Actually Aileen, it is all my fault." Agaratte interrupted. I turned my head up towards him.

"What are you talking about?" He paused and looked at me and then put his head towards my ear,

"I am a Sentinel."

"You're a what?"

"Don't be stupid, Aileen. You know what I mean."

"Do you know how she died?" He sat down on the grass next to me, crossed his legs and spoke quietly as if he didn't want anyone to hear. Which was kind of silly as no one was anywhere near us.

"Remember a long time ago when you came to Naramata to find Kat on the grass in really bad shape?"

"Yes. I also remember that for some reason, you knew where she was and that she was in trouble – how did you know?" I asked this question, but now I obviously knew the answer. My life was full of crazy coincidences and unfathomable realities, this information should not have surprised me, and yet, it did. Somehow the thought that he was a Sentinel of Bryn's probably since the day I met him amazed me.

"Kat was actually in a blood pact with Thromm and she was trying to steal the Talisman from Bryn. Bryn should have let her die there, but he took pity on her because he knew you loved her. After that night, I was responsible for Kat's life. She became my problem. If there was the slightest chance of security breach; I had to dispose of her."

"Are you telling me that you murdered Kat? I thought you loved her?" I said towards him in a hushed whisper hardly believing what was coming out of my mouth.

"There was never enough time for me to figure out if Thromm was still alive and vengeful and pointed the Zionists to her, or if there were other agents at work that honed in on her. All I know for certain is that after Bryn killed the first mage, the other six redoubled their efforts to find him. Eight days before the remaining mages were killed, I found Kat telling her story about us, you know, ECAW, to an alleged writer for the Vancouver Sun. He was asking questions as to her experiences with the supernatural and the occult. When she got on the subject of Astral Travelling actually being called Tyrrean Trance, he was instantly alert and asked if he could interview her in greater detail. She agreed and they scheduled the following day at lunchtime to discuss it. As a Sentinel; I alerted Bryn immediately and asked Bryn to help me identify the man. That night, Bryn told me the man was not a mage but an informant to the mages. Kat had been targeted and identified. She passed away that night, in bed with her husband, of massive organ failure. Because of the amount of chemotherapy and radiation as a child, no doctor was surprised. Her husband buried her here because she always told him there was no place on earth she loved more than the Okanagan. I cared about her, Aileen, but she stuck her nose into something she wasn't supposed to. We all have our hands in this; my service is no more painful than yours."

"Agaratte?"

"You know, you can call me Lance now.?"

"Alright Lance, how many people have you killed so far?"

"Just Kat. I am not really the Sentinel that is supposed to be doing that kind of work. I work for the largest software development company in the world. I am the informant and saboteur, not the hired gun."

"Why are you telling me this?"

"Now that the Mages are gone, no one can invade your mind. In a way, we are safe. They have to resort to more vulgar means, and that is a whole lot more work."

"I'm serious, Lance. You wouldn't be telling me this unless you knew I was in on this. When did Bryn tell you about me?"

"Honestly, Aileen?"

"That would be helpful, yes."

"I had no idea until the day Bryn alerted us of the impending deaths of all the mages. He told me to keep an eye out for you. That you were with child. I won't lie, I was stunned."

"What was so surprising?"

"That our coven would wind up having two people in it that are so integrally involved in the business of the gate, because you are so much younger than him, and because even though it is obvious looking at you that you are Nephilim, I never saw it." He laughed.

"How many Sentinels are as skilled in the Craft as you are?"

"Almost none."

"How many people do you think are left on the earth that can actually do any magic?"

"Almost none."

"Then you are among the last ones left, eh Lance?"

"Actually, I probably am the strongest mage left. That is until you get off your ass and train that daughter of yours, lest she be like her mother."

"Lance?"

"What?"

"This is going to sound silly, but do you think you would be able to give Bryn back his memory?"

"Even if I could why would I? So he can appreciate completely how hopelessly impotent in Wicca he has to be for the rest of his mortal life? So he can remember everything and become a sitting target for torture by that asshole sect that dares to interfere with destiny? How would he feel looking at you when he knows that only reason that he is on earth now in impotent exile is because of you? There is just so much to choose from. Take my advice –let him die in peace since you removed his opportunity for dignity."

Well obviously there were no secrets between Bryn and Lance at the last dying moments of Bryn's memory. I felt like I had failed at everything except having my daughter. I thought about the Talisman. If Bryn were around today, the old Bryn, he would have given the Talisman to Kasha already. He would have begun teaching her already. I knew now that I had to do right by him and give her the Talisman and teach her what I knew. Looking at Kat's headstone was a chilling reminder of how much everyone has paid and sacrificed for me and my daughter.

"Lance?"

"What now, woman?" He got up, looking as if he had come to say what he had to and was anxious to go back to the U.S.

"Could you help me train my daughter?"

I would love to Aileen but I can't. I must be very careful now, as I have the armload of work that I was initially requested to do – I must do this as covertly as possible. Exposure to your child with me risks both of us." I suppose he could see the tears welling in my eyes and feel the fear in my heart.

"I know you are lonely, you feel like you have lost Bryn, Kat, me, and maybe yourself along the way. You have to be strong and do this – you were born to do this."

"I will miss you Lance. When will I be able to see you again?"

"2013 if they haven't found and killed me before then."

We then walked to his car, drove back to Penticton, to my car. He dropped me off and was gone in a flash, waved goodbye and drove out of the driveway. I waved back to him, turned and waved goodbye to Kat, sucked up my tears and headed out of the Okanagan. Enough looking back into the past, I had a future to make happen.

"Thanks for watching Kasha Lactavia." I pulled off my shoes and collapsed on her couch, tossing my keys to her coffee table. Kasha was in the computer room busily playing internet games, barely acknowledging my return from the Okanagan.

"How was the trip?" Lactavia sat next to me.

"Great, I met up with Agaratte. Kat did pass away. She is buried just outside of Penticton. We visited her grave. It was sad – such a short life."

"Well it was a miracle she lived as long as she did with all the surgeries she had the leukemia as a child and then all the shit that happened to her when we were living in Penticton."

"yeah, I suppose. I will never forget her. She taught me a lot of stuff. I don't think I will ever really know where she learned all the stuff she knew."

"hmmmph! Stuff you never taught me."

"Believe me; you are better off not knowing them."

"Well, it's late, but I bet you haven't had dinner yet. Why don't I drag Kasha from the computer and we go out to dinner? There are some good restaurants on Lonsdale road."

"Sounds good to me..." So we grabbed Kasha and headed up Lonsdale road. It was sunset and the streets had a beautiful amber tone to everything. The smells from the different restaurants was making me really hungry. I then realized that because of the excitement and depression earlier, I hadn't eaten all day. We were engaged in a negotiation of Japanese, western or Arabic style restaurant when two men in uniforms approached us. One was tall and average built with a thin brown moustache and sunglasses which was odd as the sun was setting. The other cop was considerably shorter with chubby cheeks and his uniform didn't seem to fit him well. The pants appeared to need hemming. They stopped short of us, blocking our ability to walk further and then they flashed their badges.

"Ma'am, Are you Aileen Kovacs?"

"Yes?" Something about the short, fat man put me on alert. Time for a Wiccan spell I thought to myself. I needed to read his thoughts. I easily focussed on reading this mans mind. He was excited about a pile of money he was going to be getting at Stanley Park when he delivered the goods. I was pretty sure I knew what the 'goods' were.

"Ma'am I'm afraid you are going to have to come with us. We had a warrant out for your arrest for abduction of a child from the biological father who resides in the U.K. Your daughter is to be deported to her father immediately and you are being arrested."

I saw Kasha's face light up when they spoke about her father in the U.K. She no doubt was actually getting excited about seeing Bryn again. I saw Lactavia argue at the flimsy legality of the warrant. I heard her making threats. But I was trying very hard to remain focussed on what I knew was 'really' happening. I turned to Kasha and for the first time in my ten years of having this child, I spoke to her telepathically.

'Kasha! We are in grave danger. These men aren't who they say they are. They are the men that want to kill you. I'm going to give you your Talisman rock, hold it and do whatever it tells you to do.'

Then I faced the men who were talking to an annoyed Lactavia. She was explaining how she saw the international request as something that needs to go to Canadian courts. They led us to two squad cars and the men directed us to them intending to separate me from my daughter.

"Look, I'll go peacefully, just let me give my daughter her purse." I then handed the pouch that Rose gave me that was still in my purse with the Talisman and the ring. The minute I handed it to Kasha, she opened it and took hold of the Talisman. The men then handcuffed me and put me into the back of the squad car. Before they pulled away I saw them put my daughter into the other car. I also saw Lactavia freaking out, yelling at them, threatening them that she was calling her lawyer while she pulled out her cell phone. As I suspected they didn't take me to the cop shop. We pulled into a deserted side road in Stanley Park. The driver got out and smoked a cigarette waiting for someone. Finally, a large black Cadillac pulled up and two men in business suits got out. They talked to the fake cop captor for a bit and then he came back and grabbed me out from the back seat, dragged me to about 5 meters from the men and threw me onto the ground.

"It's her, I checked her identification."

"Where is the child?" One of the men in the suits asked.

"She's safe, in a car parked nearby."

"Well, you won't get a penny until we see the child." There was a moment's hesitation from the man next to me. But then he pulled out a cell phone and made a call.

"Yeah, come join us, they want the kid too I guess."

"Yer gonna have ta pay us extra if ya want us to do away with both of them. I thought you just wanted her."

"We didn't realize she was going to be so young. She could still have children. It isn't worth risking; we need to get rid of both of them." I couldn't belive this was happening. For the first time in my life I had no one to protect me. Bryn was not Bryn anymore. Was this how it was going to go? My daughter and I both dead in Stanley Park? I had to think. I couldn't just get up and escape, I had to wait until my daughter was with me. Soon I heard another vehicle pull up and a man was walking up next to the cop beside me with his captive, my daughter, who was still holding the Talisman and her eyes were lost in thought. The men smiled when they saw Kasha.

"Yes! That is her. Put a bullet in her head and you can drive away with this bag of money." They then opened up a large bag that was next to them and exposed the contents which consisted of 100 dollar bills, a duffel bag full of them.

"You son of a bitch, don't you fucking touch my baby!" I heard myself scream in rage as I got up and ran towards my daughter and the cop. The second cop that was standing next to my daughter raised a long barrelled handgun that gleamed in the moonlight and then I heard a muffled thud or bang. The next thing I knew, I was on the ground and the most incredible shock wave hit my chest, I was shot! I fell back onto the cool ground and staring up, incapable of yelling or getting up again. The cop turned to my daughter and aimed his gun on her. Kasha raised her hand with the Talisman in it, said something I didn't understand and everyone around her dropped to the ground. There was a glow around her and the Talisman, and when she turned to me I could see she was no longer in a trance-like state. She moved her hand by me and I felt the handcuffs unlock. Just then a car came screaming into the road with its high beams on. I could hear heavy and fast moving foot falls and soon I could see Lactavia's face. Then I passed out.

I awoke in a hospital. I'd had surgery. The sutures were in my abdomen and I had to be thankful that handguns are notoriously horrible for accuracy in 'off the cuff' shots. Regardless, they obviously had to do a fair bit of clean up on me gauging from the twenty or so centimetres of butterfly bandages and tape I was sporting on my belly.

After admiring the skin mechanics work on me, I stared up at the pale, rigid expression on Lactavia's face.

"Kasha? Where the hell is she?"

"Calm down Dragon, she won't leave your side. She is sleeping on the floor next to you. She has been sleeping there all night after she found out that the surgery went fine."

"How did you know where we were?"

"Kasha told me"

"What?"

"It would appear that your daughter is telepathic. I was in my car, I had just got off the phone with my lawyer, making an appointment for tomorrow. I was heading for the Police station when she invaded my head and told me to come to the side road past Prospect Point. I didn't even know your daughter knew Stanley Park that well, you have kept her most of her life on that accursedly remote island. What the hell did those assholes want with you? I mean besides the obvious need to shoot you."

"You know 'Tavi, if I told you you wouldn't believe me."

"Try me, I just had your daughter send me a message directly into my brain. Then I dragged your shot up ass out of Stanley Park where four men were unconscious and only your daughter was left standing –what? You gonna tell me she is the daughter of Satan?"

"She's Bryn's daughter."

"Bryn? Fuck off Dragon, be serious."

"Told you."

"Okay fine. Let's say she is, why would someone want to kill you two?"

"Fanatical fans? Can't stand to see Bryn with a family?"

"Why do I have that overwhelming sense of Dragon bullshit wafting through the air again? Do you get off on being a secretive, lying bitch?"

"Look 'Tavi, no one can know Kasha's father is Bryn, okay? The rest I can't really explain and even if I could, I wouldn't."

"Fine. Just calm down or you are going to make your sutures bleed. Jesus, I didn't realize that Bryn had such fucked up fans. Good thing you live on the Queen Charlotte Islands which is almost as remote a location as being in Siberia or Antarctica. In fact, I bet that was on purpose from the very beginning wasn't it?"

"Actually, in a way, yes." That triggered a memory of Bryn. I told him I didn't want him buying property on the Queen Charlottes. I didn't want him close. Now, there was no way I'd allow him to buy anywhere else on this earth. Suddenly the reality of how safe we were in the Charlottes made me realize I had to call him and tell him the change of thought. The Queen Charlottes, being a remote group of islands to the north west of British Columbia they could only be accessed through one airport and air carrier and one gruelling 6.5 hour ferry ride. I knew everyone that worked in all ports of call. They knew I didn't like anyone eliciting information about me to anyone. They were all my friends, I was impossible to locate if you were an unrecognizable stranger.

"Kasha? Kasha baby wake up for a second." I called over my bed. I then saw my baby pop up by my bedside next to Lactavia.

"Kasha, are you okay?"

"Yeah, I'm fine. Just a little freaked out is all. Did you mean what you were just thinking?"

"What do you mean?"

"Can I tell dad to buy that place in Tlell?" Kasha was reading my thoughts. She had quickly developed some skills with that damned Talisman. She was a fast study, like her dad, but of course he told me she would be. I wanted to get mad at her. I wanted to 'normalize' things. But she had just saved my life and hers and was obviously born into her destiny, also so like her father.

"Yes Kasha, you can tell Bryn the happy news." I instantly thought about Dave. This was going to be very difficult for him. He wasn't going to like this at all. I worried that my lame excuses and lies were not going to be sufficient to settle him over my having Kasha's biological father in a nearby town and me going home after being shot.

"Kasha, I really need to tell you a lot of stuff that I haven't yet had a chance to tell you."

"Don't worry mom, grandpa told me everything. I know the whole story."

"Grandpa?"

"Shemhazai, grandpa Shem. I cant wait to meet him, and soon I will. We are gong to be together and do all kinds of things."

I had to shake my head. But of course the whole thing made sense. The Talisman can not channel Shemhazai unless the soul holding it was of Shemhazai's bloodline. That is why Bryn never let me touch it. It would instantly have channelled through Shemhazai and he could have attempted to alter Bryn's plans. By having me with him on earth after the 5th gate closes.

"Dragon who the hell is grandpa Shemhazai? It sounds Hebrew?"

"Just a family member everyone calls Shem or grandpa Shem."

"Is he telepathic too?"

"Yes."

Kasha smiled at me and I returned her contagious grin. Lactavia felt like she was purposely being kept out of the inside joke, and she was not happy about it.

"Fine keep your secrets. I know that you are the one on the gurney with stitches not me. I deal with people in all states of mental health and I never went through what you went through last night. Those men that were on the ground when I got to you were taken by police who said that they were in some form of sleep paralysis. One of them was an American. I found that out when I called the police after you came out of surgery. There was a bounty on your head. That is what the police think and that you are damn lucky to be alive. I know more than you think. I remember Kat telling me that you can heal really quickly and I don't doubt it. In fact, I am beginning to realize that maybe Kat wasn't crazy after all. Maybe everything she told me wasn't a lie or exaggeration at all. Frankly Dragon, that scares the shit out of me."

"Auntie Nat, it is far scarier than your worst fears. But mom doesn't have to worry anymore. I will always be here to protect her." Lactavia was an Edenite. Wherever she went after death, I would be joining her. My daughter had a different destiny. I had no doubt that her path was revealed to her last night. Kasha may have pure Nephilim but she was so much like her father. The blood of a warrior, an old general, were in her, at ten years old I could see it, and I felt safe.